FROM BACHELOR TO DADDY

BY
MEREDITH WEBBER

A SURGEON TO HEAL HER HEART

BY
JANICE LYNN

MILLS & BOON

Published in Great Britain 2018
by Mills & Boon, an imprint of HarperCollins*Publishers*
1 London Bridge Street, London, SE1 9GF

From Bachelor to Daddy © 2018 Meredith Webber

A Surgeon to Heal Her Heart © 2018 Janice Lynn

ISBN: 978-0-263-93338-3

Printed and bound in Spain
by CPI, Barcelona

FROM BACHELOR
TO DADDY

BY
MEREDITH WEBBER

MILLS & BOON

For the real Xavier and Hamish,
the two latest wee additions to our family.

CHAPTER ONE

EMMA CRAWFORD LOOKED anxiously out the kitchen window as she added milk to two small bowls of cereal. Above the tree-line she could see smoke growing thicker but the latest news broadcast had assured her that the bushfires raging through the national park on the outskirts of Braxton were still many miles away, and the town itself wasn't in danger.

Bushfires were the last thing she'd considered when she'd agreed with her father that a return to the town where he'd been born and grown up would be a good thing. Being able to bring up the boys in a country town had seemed like a wonderful idea, but it had been the thought of the spacious old home, recently left to her father by an aged aunt, that had held the most appeal.

Well, that and a kernel of an idea that had been germinating deep inside her…

Forget that for the moment! The move had been practical and that was what was most important.

City living was all very well, but the prices in Sydney had meant the four of them—her father, the two boys and herself—had been crammed into an apartment that had shrunk as the babies turned to toddlers—growing every day.

No, Braxton, with its district hospital willing to offer her a job in its emergency department, the surrounding national park, a beautiful beach an hour's drive away, and best of all the rambling old house in its magical, neglected gardens just perfect for two adventurous little boys, had been extremely appealing.

And they had bushfires in Sydney, too, she reminded herself, to shake off the feeling of foreboding the smoke had caused.

She deposited the bowls of cereal on the trays of the highchairs and smiled at the angelic faces of her three-year-old twins, Xavier and Hamish. *She* was off to work and it was her father who'd be cleaning up the mess that two little horrors could achieve with bowls of cereal.

A quick kiss to each of the still clean faces, a reminder to be good for Granddad, a kiss for her father, as ever standing by, and she was gone, her stomach churning slightly at the thought of the day ahead. Although she'd already spent a few days at the hospital, meeting staff and watching how their system operated, this was her first official work day.

'It's called plunging right in,' Sylvie Grant, the triage nurse on duty, told Emma when she arrived. 'The fire turned back out Endicott way and some of the firefighters were caught. It's mostly smoke inhalation—their suits keep them well protected these days. This one's in four.'

Emma took the chart and headed to the fourth curtained cubicle along the far wall, surprised to find the occupant was a woman.

'Your working hours must be worse than mine, especially at this time of the year,' she said, when she'd introduced herself.

The woman smiled then shook her head, pointing to her throat.

'Sore?' Emma asked as she checked the monitor by the side of the bed. Blood pressure and heart rate good, oxygen saturation normal, though the oxygen tubes in the woman's nose would be helping there…

'Let's look at your throat,' she said, using a wooden spatula to hold down the tongue so she could visually check what she could see of the pharynx.

'I can see why it's painful to speak,' she told her patient. 'You've had cold water?'

The patient nodded.

'No difficulty swallowing?'

Another nod.

'Okay, then I'll sort out a drink with a mild topical anaesthetic that should dull the pain, but don't try to talk. The hot air you breathed in obviously reached as far as your larynx so it's likely your vocal cords are swollen.'

She explained what she needed to the nurse, wrote it up on the chart with instructions for it to be given four-hourly and was talking to the patient via questions and nods when Sylvie came in.

And the day became just another day in an emergency department—a child with an ear infection, a woman with chest pains that turned out, after an ECG and blood tests, to be a torn pectoral muscle, a child from the school who'd fallen off a swing and gashed his forehead—stitches and possible concussion so she'd keep him in for observation—an elderly man with angina…

Until, at about two in the afternoon when, as often happened in an emergency department, the place emptied out and one of the nurses suggested they all take a break.

Well, all but Sylvie, and a nurse who'd come on duty for the swing shift.

Emma said goodbye to the firefighter, whose husband had arrived to take her home, and made her way to the small room they all used for breaks, coming in as Joss, one of the nurses she'd met the previous day and also on swing shift, bounced in through another door.

'Hot goss!' Joss announced, grabbing the attention of the three women already in the room, while Emma fixed herself a cup of tea and pulled a packet of sandwiches from the small fridge, pausing to listen to the tale.

'I had dinner last night at the top pub so had a front-row seat to the drama. You know that librarian from the school Marty's been seeing?'

All faces turned expectantly towards her, heads nodding.

'Well, they're sitting at the bar, obviously having words, and then she stood up, slapped his face, and stormed out.'

'Another one bites the dust,' Angie, the department secretary, said. 'Wonder who'll be next.'

They all turned to look at Emma, who had settled into one of the not-very-comfortable chairs and was enjoying her sandwich—especially as she wasn't expected to share it with two small boys.

Joss shook her head.

'No way! You know he stays away from hospital staff, besides which Emma's small and dark, and Marty's preference is for tall blondes.'

'I'm not a tall blonde and I went out with him for a while.' This from a complacently pregnant red-haired woman Emma hadn't seen before.

'That's Helen,' Angie told her. 'She's on the swing shift too, but comes in early to eat our sandwiches because she's always hungry.'

'Not true,' Helen said, although she *was* eating a sandwich. 'It's just that Pete can drop me off so I don't have to drive, and as for Marty, everyone who goes out with him knows the score. He's quite open about not wanting a permanent relationship and if you look around the town most of the women he's been out with are still friends with him. In fact, it was Marty who introduced me to Pete.'

Emma, although curious about this Marty—maybe he

was a GP who did visits at the hospital—turned to Helen, asking when the baby was due.

'Another three months and I'm already so uncomfortable I wonder why I thought it was a good idea.'

She paused, then added, 'You've got twins, is that right?'

'Small town,' Joss explained when Emma looked surprised, but she smiled and agreed she did indeed have twins.

'Three years old, and wild little hooligans already. I'm just lucky I've got my father to help with them.'

'He minds them while you're at work?' Helen sounded slightly incredulous as she asked the question, but Emma just nodded.

'Even does night duty when I'm on night shifts,' she said.

She didn't add that it had been her dad's idea she have the children—well, *a* child it had been at that time, having two had been a surprise.

Dad had taken very early retirement when she'd all but fallen to pieces—well, *had* fallen to pieces—after Simon had died, moving in with her and becoming, once again, a carer to her—a role he'd first taken on when she'd been four and her mother had walked out on the pair of them.

A pang of guilt—one she knew only too well—shafted through her. Dad really should have a life of his own…

Perhaps here…

Soon…

But the conversation was continuing around her and she tuned back into it to find the women discussing unmarried men around town who might suit her.

She shouldn't have been surprised. The remark earlier about her being a possible candidate for the unknown Marty's new woman told her they already knew she was a single mother—single being the operative word.

Small town, indeed.

But before she could protest that she didn't want to go out with anyone, the chat swerved off to the fire. Joss lived out of town on a cattle property and although they were always prepared, she thought this time they'd be safe. She was explaining how they kept the paddocks close to the house free of trees or tall grass when Sylvie came to the door.

'Emma, you're needed on the chopper. It'll put down here to collect you. You have about ten minutes. You know where the landing pad is?'

Emma nodded confidently in answer to Sylvie's question but inside she felt a little nervous. Although, as an emergency department doctor in a small town, she knew she'd be on call for the search and rescue helicopter, and she'd been shown over it by one of the paramedics, she hadn't had much time to take it all in.

By which she really meant she'd refused to think about it. She'd done the training originally to help her overcome her fear of heights, and although she knew most rescue crews got an adrenaline rush at the thought of a mission, her rush was more one of trepidation than anticipation. Yes, she could do her job and do it well, but no amount of training or practice would ever stop the butterflies in her stomach as she waited to hang in mid-air, suspended from a winch.

'—party of older children with special needs from the unit at the high school,' Sylvie was explaining as they left the room together. 'They were walking the coastal path, just this end of it. Apparently, the wind turned suddenly and the fire came towards them, so you can imagine the panic. We know one child with asthma is having breathing difficulties. No idea about the others but they're stuck where they are and will have to be evacuated.'

Beach rescue, no winch!

Her tension eased immediately…

Even inside the hospital Emma could hear the helicopter's approach and hurried to collect the black bag that held all the drugs she could possibly need. But she checked it anyway, relieved to see a spacer for an asthma inhaler, a mask for more efficient delivery of the drug, and hydrocortisone in case the child was badly affected.

Outside, she waited by the building until the bright red and yellow aircraft touched down lightly. Then, ducking her head against the downdraught from the rotors, she ran towards it.

The side door slid open and an unidentifiable male in flight suit and helmet reached out a hand to haul her aboard. She'd barely had time to register a pair of very blue eyes before she was given a not-so-gentle nudge and told to take the seat up front.

She clambered into the seat wondering where the air crew were, but there was no time to ask as the man was already back behind the controls, handing her a helmet with a curt 'Put it on so we can talk', before lifting the aircraft smoothly into the air.

Emma strapped herself in, settled the bag at her feet and pulled on the helmet with its communication device.

'I'm Marty,' her pilot said, reaching out a hand for her to shake. 'And I believe you're Emma. Stephen told me to look out for you.'

'Stephen?' She had turned towards him and shaken his hand—good firm handshake—but wasn't able to take in much of the man called Marty. Unfortunately, checking him out had diverted her from working out who Stephen might be.

'Stephen Ransome—he was up a couple of months ago to introduce the family to Fran. He's my foster brother. You know he got married?'

Steve Ransome was this man's foster brother? Why?

How? Not questions she could ask a stranger so she grasped his last bit of information.

'No, I didn't know, but I'm so pleased. He's a wonderful guy and deserves the best.'

'He is indeed,' Marty agreed, and Emma turned to look at him—or at what she could see of him in his flight suit and helmet.

Tanned skin, blue eyes, straight nose, and lips that seemed to be on the verge of smiling all the time.

So, this was Marty, subject of the hot gossip and, apparently, the local lover-boy!

Foster brother of Steve, who ran an IVF clinic in Sydney and had been her specialist when she'd decided to use Simon's frozen sperm to conceive the boys.

Simon...

Just for an instant she allowed herself to remember, felt the familiar stab of pain, and quickly shut the lid on that precious box of memories.

She was moving on—hadn't that been another reason for the shift to Braxton?

Marty was saying something, pointing out the path of the fire, visible in patches where the smoke had blown away.

She glanced out the window as he manoeuvred the controls to give them both a better view, then straightened up the chopper, intent on reaching their destination.

Marty, the man who didn't do commitment and was open about it...

As she mentally crossed him off her list—not that she had a list as yet—she wondered why he'd be so commitment-shy.

His growing up in a foster family might be a clue.

Had he been born in a disruptive, and possibly abusive, family situation?

That last could make sense...

But he was talking again and she had to concentrate on

what he was saying, not on who he was or why he wasn't into commitment, although that last bit of info was absolutely none of her business.

'There's a coastal path that runs for miles along most of the coast in this area, and people can do long walks, camping on the way, or short walks,' he explained. 'The school mini-bus dropped these kids about five miles up the track—there's a picnic area that's accessible by road—and the idea was they'd walk back to Wetherby and be picked up there. It's a yearly tradition at the school, and the kids love it. Unfortunately, the wind spun around from northeast to northwest and the fire jumped the highway and raced through the scrub towards the path.'

'Poor kids, they must have been terrified,' Emma said. 'Do we know how many there are?'

'Two teachers, a teacher's aide, and sixteen children,' Marty said grimly. 'Hence no aircrew. We stripped everything not needed from the chopper because we'll only have two chances to lift them all off the little beach they ran to. Once the tide comes in, that's it, and not knowing the age or size of the kids makes calculations for lift-off weight difficult.'

Emma nodded. She'd learned all about lift-off weight during the training she'd undertaken in Sydney, necessary training as the rescue helicopter at Braxton relied on emergency department doctors on flights when one might be needed.

They were over the fire by now, seeing the red line of flame still advancing inexorably towards the ocean, while behind it lay the black, smouldering bushland.

Two rocky headlands parted to give a glimpse of a small beach and as they dropped lower she saw the group, huddled among the rocks on the southern end, their hands held protectively over their bent heads as the down-thrust from the rotors whipped up the sand.

'Good kids, did what they were told,' Marty muttered, more to himself than to Emma.

They touched down, the engine noise ceased, and before she could unstrap herself, Marty was already over the back, opening the doors and leaping down onto the sand.

He turned to grab Emma's bag then held up a hand to help her down. An impersonal hand, professional, so why didn't she take it? Jumping lightly to the sand as if she hadn't noticed it...

'I'm a trained paramedic so if you need me just yell,' he was saying as she landed beside him. 'I'm going to juggle weights in the hope we can get everyone off in two lifts.'

He paused and looked her up and down.

'You'd be, what—sixty kilos?'

'Thereabouts,' she told him over her shoulder, hurrying towards the approaching children. One of the adults—probably a teacher—was helping a young, and very pale, girl across the beach.

'Let's sit you down and make you comfortable,' Emma said to the child, noting at the same time a slight cyanosis of the lips and the movement of the girl's stomach as she used those muscles to drag air into her congested lungs.

'I'm Emma, and you're...?'

'Gracie,' the girl managed.

'She's had asthma since she was small but this is the first time we've seen her like this,' the woman Emma had taken for a teacher put in.

'Do you have your puffer with you?' Emma asked, and was pleased when Gracie produced a puffer from a pocket of her skirt.

'Good girl. You've had some?'

Gracie nodded, while the teacher expanded on the nod. 'She's had several puffs but they don't seem to be helping.'

'That's okay,' Emma said calmly to Gracie. 'I've

brought a spacer with me, and you'll get more of the medicine inside you with the spacer. Have you used one before?'

Another nod as Emma fitted the puffer to the spacer and inserted a dose, then found a mask she could attach to the spacer so the girl could breathe more easily.

'Just slow down, take a deep breath and hold it, then we'll do a few more.' Probably best not to mention twelve at this stage. 'See how you go.'

The girl obeyed but while it was obvious that the attack had lessened in severity, she was still distressed.

Marty had appeared with the oxygen cylinder and a clip and tiny monitor that would show the oxygen saturation in the blood. He joked as he clipped it on the girl's finger, and nodded to Emma when the reading was an acceptable ninety-four percent.

The oxygen cylinder wouldn't be needed yet.

Emma drew the teacher aside and explained what had to be done to fill the spacer and deliver the drug.

'Are you happy to do that on the way to the hospital?' she asked, and the teacher nodded.

'I do it all the time,' she said. 'My second youngest is asthmatic. We just didn't think to carry a spacer with us.'

Which left Emma to fill in the chart with what she'd done, dosage given, and the time. The flight from the hospital had only taken fifteen minutes so the child would be back in the emergency department before there was any need to consider further treatment, and she knew from her briefing that another doctor would have been called in to cover for her.

Marty had done a rough estimate of the weight of his possible passengers and had begun loading them into the helicopter. To the west the smoke grew thicker and the fire burning on the headland to the south told them they were completely cut off.

He looked at the tide, encroaching on the dry sand

where he'd landed. He had to move now if he wanted to get back here before the tide was too high.

'I'm taking the sick child and the teacher with her,' he said to the new doctor, wondering how she'd cope being left on the beach surrounded by fire on her first day at work.

'And the teacher's aide who's upset,' he added, concentrating on the job at hand. 'She's not likely to be of any use to you, plus another six children. Will you be all right here until I get back? You have a phone? We're quite close to Wetherby so there's good coverage.'

'I have a phone, we'll be fine, you get going,' she said, waving him away, and as he left he glanced back, seeing her hustling the children towards the sheltering rocks to avoid the sand spray at take-off.

Sensible woman, he decided. No fuss, no drama, she'll be good to work with.

He settled the asthmatic girl in the front seat and strapped in those he could, letting the rest sit cross-legged on the floor.

He ran his eyes over them, again mentally tallying their combined weight, adding it to the aircraft weight so he was sure it was below take-off weight. The next trip would be tighter.

They were off, the children sitting as still as they'd been told to, although the urge to get up and run around looking out of windows must have been strong. The teacher he'd brought along would have sorted out those who were strapped in seats, he realised when the excited cries of one child suggested he had at least one hyperactive passenger.

'Can you manage?' he asked the teacher, who was in the paramedic's seat behind the little girl, and had put another dose of salbutamol into the spacer and passed it to his front seat passenger.

'Just fine,' the sensible woman assured him. 'You fly

the thing and I'll look after Gracie. Deep breath now, pet, and try to hold it.'

The school mini-bus was waiting behind the hospital as he landed, and the aide helped the children into it while the teacher took Gracie into Emergency.

'Most of the parents are at the school,' the bus driver told him. 'I'll take this lot there, then come back.'

Marty nodded, hoping he hadn't misjudged the tide and that he would be bringing back the other children, the teacher and the unknown Emma Crawford.

As *yet* unknown? he wondered, then shook his head. Hospital staff were off limits as far as he was concerned.

Besides which, she was short and dark-haired, not tall and blonde like most of his women.

Most of his women! That sounded—what? Izzy would say conceited—as if he thought himself a great Lothario who could have whatever woman he liked, but it really wasn't like that. He just enjoyed the company of women, enjoyed how they thought, and, to be honest, how they felt in his arms, although many of his relationships had never developed to sexual intimacy.

What colour were her eyes?

Not Izzy's eyes, obviously, but the short, dark-haired woman's eyes—the short, dark-haired woman who wasn't at all his type.

The switch in his thoughts from sexual intimacy to the colour of Emma Crawford's eyes startled him as he flew back towards the beach.

Meanwhile, the woman who wasn't at all his type was attempting to calm the children left on the beach. Three were in tears, one was refusing to go in the helicopter, and the others were upset about not being in the first lift. The teacher was doing her best, but they were upsetting each other, vying to see who could be the most hysterical.

'Come on,' Emma said, gathering one of the most distressed, a large boy with Down's syndrome, by the hand, 'let's go and jump the little waves as they come up the beach.'

Without waiting for a response, she steered the still-sobbing child towards the water's edge, and began to jump the waves herself. A few others followed and once they were jumping, the one who still clung to Emma's hand joined in, eventually freeing her hand and going further into the water to jump bigger waves.

'Now they'll probably all compete to go the deepest and we'll be saving them from drowning,' Emma said wryly to the teacher, who had joined her at the edge of the water.

'At least they've stopped the hysteria nonsense,' the teacher said. 'They work each other up and really...' She hesitated before admitting, 'I was shaken by it all myself, so couldn't calm them down all that well.'

'No worries,' Emma told her. 'They're all happy now.'

Which was precisely when one of them started to scream and soon the whole lot were screaming.

And pointing.

Emma turned to see a man race down the beach and dive into the water, her fleeting impression one of black-ness.

'He was on fire,' one of the children said, as they left the water and clustered around their teacher, too diverted by the man to be bothered with screams any more.

Emma waded in to where the man was squatting in the water, letting waves wash over his head, her head buzzing with questions. How cold was the water? How severe his burns? Think shock, she told herself. And covering them...

'Can you talk to me?' she asked, and he looked blankly at her.

Shock already?

'I'm a doctor, I'd like to look at your burns. I've got pain relief in my bag on the beach.'

She touched his arm and beckoned towards the beach but he shook his head and ducked under the water again.

Time to take stock.

He was young, possibly in his twenties, and very fair. His hair was cut short, singed on one side and blackened on the other. The skin on his face on the singed side was also reddened, but not worse, Emma decided, than a bad sunburn.

If the rest of his body was only lightly burned then maybe waiting in the water for the helicopter was the best thing for him. She tried to see what she could of his clothes—now mostly burnt tatters of cloth. At least in the water they'd have lost any heat they'd held and not be worsening his injuries.

But shock remained an issue…

'Can I do anything?' the teacher called from the beach.

'If you've got towels you could spread a couple on the beach—just shake any sand off them first.'

Not that shaking would remove all the sand, but if she could get him out, lay him down and cover him loosely with more towels, she could take a better look at him and position him to help with possible shock.

The low rumble of the helicopter returning made them all look upward, and Emma was pleased to see the children running back to the rocks.

Pleased to think she could avoid the difficulty of examining him here on the beach, she was also relieved to have help getting the man out of the water.

'Rescue helicopter,' she told him, hoping the words might mean something. 'It will fly you to hospital.'

This time she got a nod, but as she reached out to take his arm and help him to stand upright, he pulled back again.

She didn't argue—he was probably better staying where he was rather than risk getting sand on his burnt skin.

Marty saw the two heads bobbing in the water below

him and wondered what was happening. At least the kids were all over in the rocks.

He hovered for a minute before touching down, checking the seemingly minute area of sand that was still above the incoming tide. It would have to be a really quick in and out.

As soon as he jumped down, the children hurtled towards him, all talking at once. Jumping waves, man on fire, doctor might drown...

He thought the last unlikely but had pieced together the information by the time the teacher arrived to explain.

'He won't come out,' the teacher told him. 'And every time Emma tries to take his arm, he dives away from her. He might be a foreign backpacker and not understand she's trying to help him.'

Marty nodded.

Most of the backpackers roaming Australia had some knowledge of English, but the shock of being caught in the fire could have been enough for this poor bloke to lose it. He pulled a couple of space blankets out of the helicopter and gave them to the teacher to hold.

He turned to the kids.

'Now, all of you sit down on the sand, and the one sitting the stillest gets to fly up front with me, okay?'

The children dropped as if they'd been shot and although Marty doubted they'd stay still long, it should be long enough to get Emma and the man out of the water.

And work out what he was going to do next.

Maybe the man was very small...

Emma had apparently finally persuaded her patient to move towards the shore so Marty had only to go into knee-deep water to reach the six-foot-plus young man.

'I haven't been able to get a good look at his burns but I'd say some of them are serious,' Emma told him, her face pale with worry about this new patient.

She took one of the space blankets from the teacher, who had unfolded the silver material, and wrapped it around the man's shoulders, looking across him so Marty saw the worry in her serious grey eyes.

Grey, huh?

'I'll give him some morphine for the pain, and start a drip.' She turned to the teacher. 'Could you manage the fluid bag on the trip back to the hospital? It's just a matter of holding it above his body and making sure the tube doesn't kink.'

'And just why are you asking that?' Marty demanded as they both helped the man into the chopper and settled him on the stretcher.

She turned and touched his arm, just above the wrist— a simple touch—getting his attention before saying very quietly, 'Because there's no way you can take him *and* me, given how tight your take-off load was already. I'll just wait until the tide goes down and someone can come for me. I'll be all right, although you'll have to phone my dad and let him know what's happening.'

Marty stared at the small hand, still resting on his arm, then studied the face of this woman whose touch had startled him. She met his gaze unflinchingly.

'Well?' she said, removing her hand and concentrating again on their patient.

He shook his head, unable to believe that she'd figured all this out and delivered it to him as naturally as she might tell someone she was ducking out to the shops.

'That's right, isn't it?' she continued, as she calmly inserted a cannula into the man's undamaged hand and attached a line for the fluid. 'The children are upset already, so the teacher has to go back with them. I'm the obvious choice to give up a place.'

'And you're happy to stay alone on the beach?'

Grey eyes could flash fire, he discovered.

'I didn't say I was happy about it, but as I can't fly the helicopter I can't see any other solution. You'll have some chocolate bars in the helicopter—I've never been on one that didn't—so you can leave me a couple, and some water. I'll be fine as long as you phone my dad.'

Much as he wanted to argue, there was little point. He couldn't take off with both of them on board—not safely…

He went with practical.

'There's a cellphone signal here, you can phone your father yourself.'

It seemed a heartless thing to say to a small woman he was about to leave on a deserted beach with bushfires raging all around her, but his mind wasn't working too well.

Something to do with grey eyes flashing fire?

Impossible…

She half smiled as she drew up a calibrated dose of morphine and added it to the drip.

'I could if my phone hadn't been in my pocket when I went into the water.'

'Well, of all the—'

He stopped. Of course, she wouldn't have considered her phone when there was a man in the water who needed her help.

Realising she was so far ahead of him he should stop talking and just do something, he wetted some cloth with sterile water and laid it over the man's legs where the stretcher straps would go, so the burns wouldn't be aggravated.

Or too aggravated.

He tilted the stretcher to raise the patient's legs, then checked on the children—all of whom were still sitting remarkably motionless on the sand near the door.

'Okay, you stay,' he said to Emma, 'but I'll be back for you just as soon as I can. Are you winch trained?'

'I am, but I don't think that'll be possible tonight. Even

if you're still on duty, the chopper will be needed to get the young man to a burns unit,' she told him. 'I'll be fine. It's warm and there's enough soft sand on the top of the dune that will stay dry so I can sleep on that until someone can get back here. Or if the fire dies down, I can walk out.'

Could he read the nonchalant lie on her face? Emma wondered as she satisfied herself that their patient would make it safely to Braxton Hospital, where he'd be stabilised enough for a flight to the nearest burns unit.

But it wasn't really a lie. The twins would be fine with her father, they were used to her coming and going, but—

Damn her phone!

Damn not thinking of it!

'Here's a spare phone and an emergency kit. Chocolate bars and even more substantial stuff, water, space blanket, torch.'

She spun towards Marty and read the worry in his face as he handed her the phone and backpack. He was hating doing this, leaving her on her own on the beach, but he was a professional and knew it was the only answer.

'I'll be back for you,' he said, touching her lightly on the shoulder, and this time she didn't argue, backing away towards the rocks to avoid the rotor-generated sandstorm.

CHAPTER TWO

As THE LITTLE aircraft lifted into the air, she watched it until the noise abated, aware all the time of the part of her body his hand had touched.

It had to be caused by comfort for some kind of atavistic fear, she decided. A reaction to being left so completely alone in a place she didn't know at all.

Ring Dad.

Speaking to her father calmed her down. As ever he was his wonderful, patient self, assuring her the boys were already eating their dinner, having had a busy day helping him in the garden.

Emma laughed.

'I can just imagine their idea of helping!'

'No,' her father said, quite seriously. 'Once I'd explained which were weeds to be pulled out and which were plants to be left behind, they only removed about half a dozen chrysanthemums that needed thinning anyway, and one rather tatty-looking rosemary that looked as if it was happy to give up the struggle to live.'

There was a pause before her father added, 'But more importantly, what about you? You're out near the coast path? I saw on TV that the fire had swung that way.'

'I'm on a beach, and quite safe. I've even had a swim.'

She told him about the man in the water and made light of being left behind, doing her best to give the impression she wasn't alone.

'I'm just not sure what time the chopper will be able to get back,' she told him, 'so I may not be home before morning.'

For all Marty's 'I'll be back' she just couldn't see it happening. The dune at the top of the beach might still be dry, but it would be impossible to land anything bigger than a drone on it.

She spoke to both the boys, who were full of their gardening exploits, then said goodbye.

An emergency telephone would be kept fully charged, but it was not for idle chatter. Who knew when she might need it again?

Marty delivered his passengers to the hospital, following the stretcher with the burns victim into Emergency. He'd radioed ahead to make sure there was a senior doctor on duty, and was relieved to see Matt, another of the chopper pilots also there on standby.

'I'll do the major hospital run,' he told Marty. 'You've had enough fun for one day.'

As he'd spent hours this morning helping out with water bombing the fire, Marty knew his official flying hours were just about up. But his day was far from finished. He left the hospital, getting a cab back to the rescue service base where his pride and joy was kept—his own, smaller, private helicopter.

A quick but thorough check and he was in the air again, this time heading for the seaside town of Wetherby. The man he and all his foster siblings called Pop had levelled a safe landing area for him behind the old nunnery that had housed his foster family, and within ten minutes he was home.

Home. Funny word, that—four small letters but, oh, the massive meaning of it, the security it held, the memories…

Hallie was first out through the back garden to meet him, Pop emerging more slowly from his big shed. Both of them were older now, well into their seventies, but still fit and healthy, always ready with help or advice, or even just a cup of tea. They had been the first people in the world to offer him love—unconditional and all-encompassing love—and were still the most important people in his life.

He lifted Hallie in the air and swung her around, explaining as he swung that he couldn't stay. He'd left a woman on Izzy's porpoise beach and had to get her off while the tide was still high enough to take the jet ski in.

'What jet ski?' Hallie demanded. 'You boys took all your fast, noisy toys when you left here.'

He grinned at her.

'The jet skis at the surf club are bigger, stronger, and faster than any we ever had, poor orphans that we were!' he said, unable to resist teasing her. 'I've phoned a mate to have one fuelled up for me.'

'You're going around there on a jet ski in the middle of the night.'

He had to laugh.

'Hallie, it's barely seven o'clock. We'll be back before you know it. I'll take her straight to Izzy and Mac's as she'll need a shower and some dry clothes. Something of Nikki's will probably fit her. There's not much of her.'

'Then bring her here for dinner when she's dry,' Hallie insisted, but he shook his head.

'She has her own family to get back to,' he said, 'but we have to come back here to get the chopper so I'll introduce you then.'

He turned to Pop.

'Okay if I take your ute down to the club?'

'Just don't run into anything,' Pop growled, and they

all laughed as the ute was ancient and, having survived numerous teenagers learning to drive in it, was a mass of dents and scratches.

Down at the club, while his mate checked the fuel on the jet-ski, he called the emergency phone, and knew from Emma's voice when she answered that he'd startled her.

'It's okay, it's only me, Marty. I'm coming to get you and want you to stand in the middle of the beach and point the torch that's in the emergency kit straight out to sea so I don't run aground on the rocks.'

Silence on the other end told him she didn't know what to make of these instructions, but the jet ski motor was on and he had to get going, this time while the tide was high, not low.

'See you soon, don't forget the light,' he said, and disconnected.

Fortunately, the sea was calm, as it often was when a westerly had been blowing across the land. But his heart raced as he thought of the woman he'd left on the beach— standing there in the darkness, the world behind her ringed with fire. Surely she'd be...

Frightened?

The thought made him smile. He might not know Emma Crawford very well—not at all, in fact—but he doubted fear would be upmost in her mind.

Apprehension, yes, but fear?

He revved the engine, anxious to get to her—frightened or not, it must be an unnerving experience for her, especially on her first day at work!

Emma stared at the phone in her hand.

Had it really rung?

Was Marty serious about coming in by water to get her off the beach—what little of it was left?

Presumably...

She lifted the emergency backpack he'd left with her, took out the torch, and slipped the pack onto her shoulders. She then paced the beach and decided where the centre of it was, waded in knee deep then turned on the torch as instructed, pointing its beam out to sea.

She was just beginning to feel a little foolish when she heard the loud roar of an engine, definitely somewhere in the darkness of the ocean, then light appeared, at first shining across the width of the bay, the motor throttling back but still very loud in the otherwise silent night.

Now the light turned towards her and, as if drawn along the path of torchlight, a large jet ski rumbled her way, the noise cutting as it approached so it drifted right up to where she stood.

Marty was off in an instant.

'On you hop,' he said cheerfully, while she was still considering what seemed like a miracle night rescue.

'Quickly—we need the tide high now,' he added, holding the craft steady in the small waves while she clambered on board.

'Now shove back to make room for me, then hang on tight,' he said, and before she could say thank you, or marvel at the fact that he *had* come for her, he had the craft moving again and they were off, the roaring motor preventing even the most basic of conversations.

But she did hang on tight, very tightly indeed, for they were travelling at what seemed a ridiculous pace, bouncing over waves as they sped back to wherever he'd come from.

Wetherby?

The beach town she and the twins had visited last week?

Was that the closest place?

And was she thinking these thoughts to keep from considering the strange reaction she was experiencing with her arms around a man's body, her breasts pressed against his back—the solidity of it, the different feel...

The maleness...

Not that she'd been clasping a woman's back recently, but there was something decidedly odd going on within her body.

Decidedly odd and totally unnecessary, but just as she considered not holding on quite as tightly, they leapt another wave and her arms tightened around him even more.

Maybe as well as needing a father for the boys, *she* needed a man.

Although friends and relations had been suggesting such a thing for some years now, she'd never given it a thought, probably because she'd never experienced a physical...

What?

She didn't want to call it need, but it was certainly a male-female kind of thing she was feeling right now.

Though this particular man—a commitment-shy lover boy—was definitely not for her.

There was no way she could tarnish the memory of the intense and beautiful love she and Simon had shared with a quick affair to satisfy a...

'Need' did seem to be the word...

Consumed by her thoughts, she was unaware of the silence that had fallen, but the jolt as the jet ski glided up a ramp onto the deck outside the surf lifesaving clubhouse told her the journey was over.

She let go of the body that had started such bizarre thoughts in her head, and dismounted as quickly as she could, although the wet clothes she was wearing made that difficult, sticking to the plastic seat and tangling around her legs.

'Thank you,' she said, as Marty put out his hand to steady her. 'And for rescuing me as well. I'd have been okay staying there till morning, but Dad would have worried.'

'Only Dad?' Marty queried, and it must have been the

tiredness that was creeping over her that stopped her thinking the question at all odd.

'Well, the boys as well, but they've grown up with my erratic hours of work, and my coming and going, and they don't seem to mind. Dad's been there for them far more than I have.'

She'd smiled at him as she'd explained, this small, wet, matter-of-fact woman, and Marty didn't know if it had been the smile or the love she somehow invested in the word 'Dad' that caused an uneasy lurch in his usually reliable stomach.

'This way,' he said, and although he would normally have slung an arm around a woman's shoulders to lead her to the car, tonight he couldn't do it, so he stomped ahead, slightly perturbed, although he didn't do perturbed any more than he did stomach lurches. For most of his life he'd kept his demons at bay by being the joker, the light-hearted mate, just a 'good bloke' in the Australian vernacular...

He grabbed a couple of towels Hallie had thrown into the ute, and handed one to Emma, using the other to dab himself dry before tying it around his waist. Woman-like, she wound hers around above her breasts, though not before he'd noticed the way her wet clothing clung to a very curvy figure.

You like tall, slim, blonde women, don't date hospital staff, and don't do commitment, he reminded himself. And a woman with 'boys' would be looking for commitment. Would need commitment...

'We're both wet through and will be chilled to the bone by the time we get home so I'm taking you to Izzy and Mac's,' he told his passenger. 'Izzy's one of my foster sisters, and Mac, her husband, is the local doctor here in Wetherby. They actually met at the little cove where we rescued the kids, only they were rescuing a porpoise. Their daughter Nikki is about your size, and should be able to provide some dry clothes.'

Sensible talk—that was the way to handle the strangeness he was experiencing, which, as he now considered it, was probably caused by his having to leave her alone on the beach in the first place. It had brought out all his protective instincts, nothing more...

Izzy, obviously primed by Hallie, had Emma through the door and into the bathroom while he was barely out of the ute.

Mac met him on the wide veranda of the centuries-old doctor's house.

'You can use the back bathroom, I've put some dry duds in there,' he said, waving Marty along the veranda, following to ask about the rescues, about the injuries to the burns victim, the hospital network having already filled Mac in on what had transpired during the afternoon.

'At least the temperature and the wind have dropped,' he said, 'and the forecast for tomorrow is rain, so it should dampen what's left of the fires on the coastal fringe, although those in the national park will be harder to stop.'

'Great news,' Marty replied, pleased to have talk of bushfires diverting his brain from its seeming obsession with Emma. He could do bushfire talk! 'The firefighters will get a break, and with decent rain these might be the last of the fires for the season.'

'Let's hope so,' Mac said. 'I'll leave you to have a shower, then Izzy's made some sandwiches. If you want to get straight back to Braxton you can eat them on the way.'

Marty turned in the doorway of the bathroom that had been tacked onto the veranda at the back of the house.

'Thanks, Mac, I appreciate it.'

Mac smiled at him.

'That's what family's for,' Mac reminded him.

Marty took the words into the shower with him and

as the water splashed down over his body he thought of the main one—family. How lucky had he been to have landed with foster parents whose determination had been not merely to provide a home for abandoned or damaged children but to provide them with a family—to meld them into a family in the truest sense of the word—a group where they belonged?

But as he dressed in dry, borrowed clothes, his mind returned to Emma and *her* family—boys, Dad, her—but no wedding ring and no mention of a husband.

Not that it was any of his business, and neither was he interested in finding out more. He tried not to think about the fact that, given the gossip mill that was the hospital, he'd soon know everything there was to know about Emma Crawford, and probably far more than she wanted people to know.

He was smiling to himself as he pushed open the door into the kitchen and greeted Izzy with a kiss.

'No Nikki?' he asked, looking around the room, taking in Emma's appearance in long shorts and a slightly too tight T-shirt, damp dark hair framing her face like a pixie's in a story book.

'Studying with her friend,' Izzy explained. 'Now, Emma's having a cup of tea. Do you want one or do you need to get back to Braxton? I've made sandwiches to go if you can't stay.'

'We'll go but take the sandwiches, not that I expect we'll be able to eat them all because you know Hallie, she'll have a basket of goodies already packed into the helicopter. But thanks.'

He dropped another kiss on her cheek, then bent and kissed her baby bump.

'That's from your Uncle Marty, Bump. I hope you're behaving yourself in there.'

Mac and Izzy laughed, but although Emma smiled, he sensed a sadness in her.

Or maybe it was just plain exhaustion. For a first day at work, it had been a beauty!

'Come on,' he said to her. 'Let's get you home.'

Had he spoken too abruptly—too roughly—that she looked startled and stumbled slightly as she stood up, and her hand shook as she put her cup on the table?

'Are you okay?' he asked, when they'd said their good-byes and were back in the ute.

'Fine,' she said quietly, 'though I'll be happy to get home. It's been a long first day.'

But was she entirely happy to be going home?

Of course she was.

Then why the little niggle somewhere deep inside her that suggested she'd have liked to stay a little longer with Marty's family, sitting in the kitchen, talking about nothing in particular?

She thrust the thought away, aware that it was something to do with being in a new town, and not having had time to make friends, her life revolving around the boys and now work.

'Tired?' Marty asked as they pulled up in the shed behind a huge old building.

'I think I must be,' Emma replied, deciding that would explain all the strange things going on in her head.

'Well, I'll have you home in no time,' he told her as he led the way to where two elderly people waited by a little helicopter. 'Do you have a car at the hospital?'

His hand was behind her back, guiding her through the dark yard, barely touching her, yet the—probably imagined—warmth from his hand was as distracting as the niggle had been earlier.

'Car? Hospital?' he asked again as she didn't reply.

She shook her head, hoping to clear it.

'No, I walk to work.'

'Then I can run you home. The good thing about Braxton is that nowhere's far from anywhere else.'

The small helicopter looked like a toy after the rescue aircraft.

'This is yours?' she asked, glad of distraction.

'My pride and joy,' he told her, 'and the two people standing beside it are my—well, mother and father, Hallie and Pop.'

He introduced Emma, explaining she was new to Braxton.

'I've put a bit of food in a basket behind the seats,' Hallie told them.

'And Izzy packed us sandwiches,' Marty said. 'We might have to stop on the way home for a picnic.'

Everyone laughed, but the picnic idea had taken hold in Emma's head. It was such a short flight back to Braxton, and eating on the way would be awkward.

'If you're driving me home and not in a hurry to get back to your place, we could picnic on my veranda,' she found herself saying as they flew over the mountain range between the two towns. 'The boys will be in bed, and Dad will happily join you for a beer if you fancy one, or a glass of wine if you'd prefer. I think after the day I've had I'll be having one.'

The words rattled out of her mouth, and the pleasure she felt when he agreed was all to do with making friends— well, *a* friend.

And having worked with him and seen him with his family, she knew he'd be a good friend to have.

Or so she told herself.

But he *would* be a good friend to have, an inner voice insisted. Hadn't he introduced one of the nurses to her husband?

Surely she wasn't thinking he might do the same for her? This from the more sensible of her inner voices…

And she didn't really want a *husband*, did she?

The thought reminded her once more of loss and pain—first her mother, then Simon. No, she couldn't go through that again, the pain of loss was just too much to bear. But it *would* be nice to have a father for the boys.

The voices stopped arguing as the helicopter touched down back in Braxton, and Marty transferred wet clothes and the picnic goodies to his four-wheel drive.

Although now a slight uneasiness had crept into Emma's head to replace the argument.

Oh, for heaven's sake! Sensible inner voice to the rescue. You're only going to share a meal with a colleague, what the hell is wrong with that?

'Wow, you live in this place?' Marty said as they drove up the street towards the big house. 'I've often wondered about it because for years it seemed abandoned, then suddenly it came to life again.'

They pulled up outside the old federation house, with its fresh white paint, wide verandas and dark green roof, and Emma saw it through Marty's eyes—the front steps climbing up to the veranda, the wide hall with its gleaming polished floorboards leading off it, living and dining rooms off to one side, bedrooms and bathrooms off the other. And at the end of it the kitchen, already the heart of the home.

'It was Dad's aunt's place and she was ill for a long time before she died. Dad grew up in Braxton—a little further up the hill. The four of us, me, Dad and the boys, had been crammed into a tiny flat in Sydney so when this became available we couldn't move fast enough. I think we'd have come even if I hadn't been able to get the job. Moved here, and just believed something would eventually come up.'

'I doubt any country hospital would turn away a doctor—particularly an ED specialist.'

Having heard them arrive, her father had turned on

the light over the front steps and was waiting at the top of them.

'Dad, this is Marty…' Emma stopped and turned to her companion. 'Do you know, I've no idea of your second name. But my father's name is Ned, Ned Hamilton.'

Somehow they sorted out the confusion, Marty supplying an unexceptional surname of Graham, and explaining about the food.

After which, as always seemed to happen these days, Dad took charge, bringing out plates, and napkins, cold beer and a bottle of chilled white wine, a couple of wine glasses dangling precariously between the fingers of one hand.

Emma took her wet clothes through to the laundry and glanced in at the sleeping boys before joining the party. Her father was telling Marty that he was kept fairly busy by the boys during the day but was slowly reconnecting with old school friends.

'The boys will be in kindergarten from the beginning of next term so he'll get more free time,' Emma put in, but her father and Marty had discovered an acquaintance in common. One of Marty's older foster sisters—one of the first children fostered by Hallie and Pop just over forty years ago—had been at school with Ned.

'Carrie has twins too,' Marty said to Ned—and just when had he found out her boys were twins? She tried very hard not to refer to them as 'the twins' as though they were one entity.

She tuned back into the conversation and found that this unknown woman's twin daughters were in their final year at high school and very experienced babysitters.

'In fact,' Marty said, as Emma poured herself a glass of wine and selected a sandwich, 'I could check whether they're already booked for Saturday week. It's the annual barn dance for the animal shelter just outside town. A barn dance is a bit old hat for teenagers these days so they won't be going to it, but for you, Ned, it would be a chance to catch up with other old school friends, and I'm sure you'd enjoy it, too, Emma. I'd be happy to take you both. I always go.'

Which certainly wasn't a date, Emma realised, while her father was agreeing enthusiastically to this plan, and reminiscing about the good times he'd had at the annual event.

'It's been going that long?' Emma asked, and Marty laughed.

'Your father's not exactly ancient,' he reminded her. He glanced at Ned. 'You'd be, what, mid-fifties?'

'Spot on,' her father replied. 'I took early—well, very early—retirement when Emma needed a bit of help, though for a few years I did a lot of supply teaching, filling in for absent teachers.'

Marty was delving into Hallie's basket as her father explained, and now produced a paper plate piled with home-made biscuits and another with slices of chocolate cake.

'Heavens!' Emma said. 'There's enough food here to feed an army.'

'Or two always hungry little boys who'll love these leftovers.' Her father smiled as he spoke.

'Though, really, Marty should take it,' Emma suggested.

'And deny the boys Hallie's chocolate cake? I think not!'

Laughing blue eyes met hers across the table and for a moment the air caught in her throat, just stuck there, as if she'd forgotten how to breathe.

Of course she could breathe!

In, out, in, out—simple as that.

But it seemed to take forever to get it sorted…

Not that her absence from the conversation was noticed as her father was now exclaiming about Hallie and Pop still being in Wetherby.

'I met them, you know, quite a few times when I was a member of the surf club, and seeing a bit of Carrie.'

'Small towns,' Marty said, smiling again, but this time, thank goodness, at her father. 'Carrie was one of the first children they took in, she was about twelve at the time so she was their first teenager. My lot—me, Izzy and Stephen, both of whom Emma's met—and a couple of others were the last. I think all of us being teenagers together finally convinced them they'd done enough.'

'What didn't kill them made them stronger,' her father remarked with a smile.

'Dad was a high-school teacher so he knows all about teenagers,' Emma explained, mostly to prove to herself she could speak as well as breathe…

The evening ended with complicated arrangements being made for her father and the boys to meet up with Carrie and her twins, the potential babysitters, and her father walked out to the car with Marty while Emma cleared the table and put everything away.

'Well, that was fun,' her father said, wandering back into the kitchen a little later.

The words sent a sharp pang of guilt spearing through Emma.

'I'm sorry, Dad, I've been so selfish, letting you give up your life to help me out, first when Simon died and I lost the baby, and then with the boys. I hadn't realised quite *how* selfish I've been until tonight.'

Her father put his arms around her.

'You needed me back then, so where else would I have been? And wasn't it me who talked you into having the boys, and didn't I promise to look after them for you?'

He kissed her on the top of her head, adding, 'And I've enjoyed every minute of it, but tonight, meeting Marty, and sitting out there just talking about nothing in particular, has shown me how restricted our lives have become.

That was natural when the boys were small and very demanding, and the flat was really no place to be entertaining, but we both need to get out a bit more now, and the barn dance is a splendid idea.'

He was voicing the feeling she'd had back at Izzy and Mac's place—voicing the fact that their lives had become too constrained, too centred around work and childcare.

She moved a little away from him and kissed his cheek.

'You're right,' she agreed. 'It's time for both of us to get out and about. Who knows what's waiting for us out there in the wild country town of Braxton?'

Her father chuckled and they parted for the night, Emma going quietly into the boys' room and watching her sons sleep for a few minutes before dropping a kiss on each of their heads and taking herself off to bed.

Where, exhausted as she was, sleep was a long time coming.

Mainly because every time she closed her eyes she saw an image of a pair of laughing blue eyes.

She'd no sooner banished this image—with difficulty—when the barn dance hove into her mind. Though with Dad going too, the gossip mill could hardly slot her into the ranks of one of 'Marty's women'.

Could it?

CHAPTER THREE

IT WAS SOMEWHERE during this mental argument that she fell asleep, to be woken by two very excited boys telling her God had brought them a puppy.

'We've been praying and praying,' Xavier was saying, while Hamish, usually the leader, echoed the words.

'Praying and praying?' Emma muttered weakly, then remembered the playgroup her father and the boys had attended at a local church in Sydney.

But praying for a puppy?

It was the first she'd heard of it!

The boys were now bouncing on her bed so any thought of going back to sleep was forgotten, while their combined pleas to come and see it dragged her reluctantly out of bed.

The 'puppy', sitting quietly in the kitchen listening to a lecture from her father on a dog's place being in the yard, was the size of a small pony. It leapt up in delight when it saw the boys and lolloped towards them.

And her, where it slobbered enthusiastically all over her pyjamas.

However, that gave her more time to check it out. For all it had, at some time, been well cared for, it was painfully thin and none too clean.

'Sit,' she said, and was surprised when he obeyed immediately. He'd definitely been cared for by someone who'd taken the time to train him.

But a dog?

A strange dog?

'I think we should leave him outside until he's had a bath,' she said, which brought wails from both boys.

'Well, go and play with him on the veranda,' she compromised, following them as far as the door so she could keep an eye on all three of them, mainly the dog.

'We can't keep him,' she said to her father over her shoulder. 'He'll just be something else for you to look after. Besides, he's sure to belong to someone. We can take a photo, put up posters, maybe ring the local radio.'

Her father nodded.

'I'll do all that, and I'll take him to the vet, get him checked out. He might be micro-chipped. But if no one claims him, well, the boys do love him already and he'd be great for them. I've been watching him closely and he's certainly not dangerous. The yard's all fenced and he's big enough to handle two rough little boys.'

Emma shook her head, then realised the dog had taken up far too much time already and if she didn't hurry she'd be late for work.

But a dog?

Were they settling in to country life so quickly?

The ED was quiet when she arrived, not quite late but close, and the chat about the triage desk was of the forthcoming barn dance—apparently one of the big events in the Braxton social calendar.

Maybe the animal shelter would take the dog.

She was about to ask when the radio came on—an ambulance ten minutes out. Sylvie lifted the receiver to her ear so the whole room didn't have to hear, relaying information to Emma as it came through.

'Atrial fibrillation, blood pressure not too bad but pulse of one hundred and forty.'

Emma's mind clicked into gear. Amiodarone drip. The cardiologist she'd always worked with recommended an initial IV treatment of one hundred and fifty mg over ten minutes, followed by sixty mg an hour over six hours and thirty mg an hour over eighteen hours.

But…

'Is there a local cardiologist?' she asked Sylvie, although she was reasonably sure the town would be too small to support one.

'No, but we have a fly-in-fly-out cardio man. He does two days a week in his office in Retford, then flies around about six country towns each fortnight. We usually phone him with any problems, and, without checking to be sure, I think he's due here tomorrow.'

Emma nodded. Presumably she could phone him, as she'd have done in the city, although down there the specialist she'd phoned had usually been in the same hospital or in rooms close by. It was strange the shift from a huge city hospital to a small country one, but the work remained the same.

'Could you get him on the phone for me?' she asked Sylvie as she walked away to meet the ambulance and its passenger.

'It happens every so often,' the patient told her cheerfully, obviously unfazed by the sudden onset of fibrillation. He was a man in his late thirties or early forties, she guessed, and sensible enough to know when he needed medical help.

She walked with the trolley into a cubicle and asked Joss to help their new patient into a gown then get an ECG started, a blood sat clip on one finger and a cannula in his arm.

'Do you see the visiting cardiologist?' she asked her

patient, now introduced as Rob Armstrong, who nodded, while Joss bustled about, sticking pads for the electrodes on the man's body.

Sylvie walked in with a phone in her hand, and Emma moved outside the cubicle to take the call.

After introducing herself, she told him about the patient, whom he apparently knew quite well.

'And what would you do?' he asked, and she felt a rush of pleasure. Many specialists would simply dictate their preference.

She told him what she'd do, and was even more delighted when he said, 'Well done, you! I love knowing efficient ED doctors. It makes for a far better outcome for the patient. Go ahead exactly as you thought, and I'll be there tomorrow. Unfortunately, he's got one of those stubborn hearts that will probably need cardioversion to shock it back into normal rhythm but we always try the drugs first. It's up to you, and available bed space, but I can do the cardioversion in the ED if you decide to keep him there.'

A few pleasantries, a promise from him to phone later for a report, and he was gone. A nice man, Emma decided. She'd look forward to meeting him.

In the meantime, she had a patient to see to. Joss had already taken a list of the medications he was on, and Emma was pleased to see blood thinners on the list.

'We need to take some blood for testing before we attach the drip, and a chest X-ray—'

Damn, she hadn't asked the specialist if he wanted an echocardiogram as well.

Decided to leave it. She'd ask him when he phoned and could do it then if he wanted one.

She wrote up the details of the drug delivery, and, as a radiographer came in with the portable machine, she explained it to Joss.

'No worries,' Joss assured her. 'I've been here long

enough to have seen Mr Armstrong a few times now. He's lucky the cardiologist is coming tomorrow. When he can't have the cardioversion within forty-eight hours, he has to go on drugs to keep him as stable as possible for about a month, not that he complains.'

She hesitated and Emma had a feeling she was being assessed.

'Actually, he's a great guy, Rob Armstrong—that's our patient—he's an engineer with the local council. Single too.'

Emma frowned at the nurse.

'And I might be interested in that information, why?'

Joss wasn't the least abashed by Emma's cool demand.

'Oh, just that you're single, and those boys of yours—well, I think boys probably need a father, you know, to kick a football around with and stuff—so I was just saying…'

'Take blood for testing then start the drip,' Emma told her, but Joss's smirk suggested she hadn't spoken nearly sternly enough.

Because that little seed of an idea that the boys might need a father had been slowly spreading its roots in her mind?

Because she'd found meeting men in the city fraught with danger and doing just that had been one of the reasons she'd been happy to move to Braxton?

So what if it had been? She was fairly certain it wasn't written across her forehead.

And she certainly wouldn't be eyeing up patients as prospective husbands—very unethical—although in a small town most of the men she was likely to meet would be prospective patients!

Yet here she was, on only her second day at work, with someone doing a bit of very unsubtle match-making.

And adding to her confusion over what exactly she did want in the future…

Seeking distraction, she phoned Retford Hospital to enquire about the man with the burns.

He was doing well, she was told, mostly second-degree burns, and he'd now been identified and a friend tracked down. He was, as she'd suspected, a backpacker, walking the track on his own after his friend had picked up casual work at the last village they'd visited.

The person on the other end of the phone already knew who she was—did small town gossip travel from town to town so quickly?—and enquired how she was enjoying Braxton, laughing when Emma explained it was only her second day.

But the conversation made her feel…as if she belonged? As if she'd somehow come home?

Weird!

Not that she had time to consider the strange feeling of belonging, for the day got busier, with a farmer coming in with the skin on his left hand lacerated from being caught in a baling machine he was fixing.

'Not an everyday thing in a city hospital, I bet?' he said to her as she cleaned the wound and stitched the tattered skin back together.

'No, it's not,' she agreed, but it wasn't only the type of accident that was different. The man's cheerful good humour was like the friendly phone call she'd had earlier. Somehow people seemed to have more time to chat, or perhaps felt freer to talk than they did in the city.

From time to time she checked on Mr Armstrong, but she had no time to think about the man as anything other than a patient.

Although he *did* have an engaging grin, and the kind of rugby-player build that made her think he probably *could* kick a ball.

Not that ball-kicking ability would have been top of her list of desirable qualities in a father for the boys—

Not that she had a list.

But as she walked home later that day, she was slightly startled to find herself thinking about a list. Well, not actually a list but what she *might* want to consider necessary attributes in a father for her boys.

Was she being silly, thinking this way?

Had growing up without a mother—wonderful though Dad had been—sown the seed about wanting a father for the boys?

But a father for the boys would also be her husband.

Was she ready for that?

For love?

Because, in all fairness, that's what it would need to be…

She shrugged off the thought and had got to the gate before she'd reached any conclusion in the matter.

And now the 'puppy' was stopping her, standing behind the gate so she had to shove hard to open it, reminding it that this was her home not his.

'You're just passing through,' she told him firmly, as he showed apparent delight at her return by standing on his hind legs to lick her cheek.

'Here, boy!'

The male voice that wasn't her father's startled her, but the dog must have heard authority in it for he immediately stepped back from her before gambolling away towards the house.

Emma was moving in that direction herself when clear shouts of 'Mum, look at us,' had her turning towards the big mango trees that lined one side fence.

When she'd left for work the previous day, her father had been in the process of assembling a double swing set. She'd arrived home in the dark last night but now she could see what the excitement was about.

'It's like seeing double,' she said as she walked towards

the trees where two identical teenage girls were pushing two small, identical boys.

'These are our friends,' Xavier told her.

'They're called Milly and Molly,' Hamish added.

The two girls laughed.

'Mandy and Molly,' one of them explained. 'I'm Mandy.'

'And I'm Molly.'

They'd stopped pushing the swings and moved towards Emma, holding out their hands as they introduced themselves.

'Marty thought you might be looking for babysitters—well, *a* babysitter but we come as a pair, although we don't charge double.'

Molly—or it might have been Mandy—was explaining this but Emma's brain was still getting over a jolt of recognition. It had been Marty's voice that had called 'Here, boy'—Marty Graham, who didn't do commitment so certainly wouldn't make even a secondary list for a possible father for her boys!

But if his voice was here, so must he be.

The girls were pushing the swings again, so there wasn't anything to keep Emma under the mango trees.

Nothing at all—

'Emma, I've made a fresh pot of tea.'

Her father's voice this time.

She had to go and join him and…

Well, whoever was with him.

Yet try as she might, she couldn't figure out the reluctance that weighed her down as she made her way towards the house.

Marty stood as she approached the table.

'Have you had a busy day?' he asked, and she heard sincerity in his voice. But it wasn't the tone of voice or even the words that held her in limbo on her approach to the table.

Something else—something she didn't understand—had stopped the world for a moment. She could see the low table set with tea things and leftovers from Hallie's basket, with another chocolate cake added to the feast. And there was a woman, sitting smiling at her, speaking words Emma couldn't hear.

Because of Marty?

Couldn't be!

He took her elbow, leading her forward, introducing her to his sister Carrie, mother of the babysitting twins, and probably maker of the new chocolate cake.

Marty dropped his hand, and the world righted itself again, so she was able to smile at Carrie and tell her how happy the boys seemed to be with her girls.

'But it's a bit of a shock,' Marty said, his blue eyes smiling at her in a quite unnecessary way, 'seeing the four of them together. I thought I was seeing double—which I suppose I was—but it was weird.'

'Exactly my reaction,' she told him, but switched her attention to Carrie as she spoke so she didn't have to dwell on the blue eyes.

Dwelling on blue eyes was a definite danger—she knew that as certainly as she knew her own name, even if she had no explanation for the knowledge.

'Tea?'

Her father held up the fresh pot and Emma nodded, taking the chair Marty had pulled closer to the table while she was battling to stay focussed. Carrie was telling her how amazing it had been to meet up with Ned again and, glancing at her father, Emma rather thought he considered it special as well, for he was smiling at the attractive, dark-haired woman as she spoke.

Emma settled back in the comfortable cane chair her father had inherited with the house, and sipped her tea. It was a pleasant, unexpected distraction after a busy day, but seeing her father chatting away to their visitors, she felt again the stab of guilt that the demands of the boys had kept him from the normal social interaction a retired man might expect.

Especially a younger retired man...

Not but what bringing her up had probably stopped any normal social interaction long before she'd had the twins...

She finished her tea and stood up, intending to take her cup to the kitchen, explaining she'd better start on the vegetables for the boys' tea.

'Sit down,' her father said—not quite an order but close. 'And leave the cup, we can sort it later. I've already asked Carrie and Marty to stay for dinner—we'll have a barbecue. I bought lamb chops and sausages today and you can throw a salad together while I cook.'

'I'll give you a hand, Ned. I love a barby,' Marty said, and as he pushed back his chair and moved away from the table, Emma dared a sneak look at him.

It wasn't that he was drop-dead handsome or even, to her way of thinking, all that sexy, but something about the man drew her to him.

The lure of the unattainable?

Was it easier to moon over someone totally unsuitable than to go through the 'getting to know you' procedure with another man? Was that what was causing her uneasiness over Marty?

Uneasiness?

Yes, uneasiness! She was damned if she was going to call it attraction.

'Don't you agree?'

She came out of the fuzz in her head and was wondering just what Carrie had been saying to her when her phone buzzed.

'Sorry,' she said to Carrie. One glance told her it was the

hospital, and as she stood up and moved a little apart to take the call, she saw Marty walking back around the veranda.

'Duty calls,' he said, waving his phone at her.

'I'm wanted too,' Emma told him, before heading for the kitchen to tell her father.

Marty watched her slip away before hurrying down the front steps and out to his car.

Should he wait for her?

Offer to drive her?

It would be no trouble to drop her back later...

He heard her voice and saw her out in the yard now, saying goodbye to the two little boys, thanking Carrie's girls for playing with them.

'Are you on duty for the chopper?' he asked as she came towards him.

'Seems so,' she said. 'Traffic accident on some road I've never heard of so I'm glad you're the pilot, not me.'

She smiled at him and he knew the blip in his heartbeat was something he had to ignore. For all he'd been startled by his reactions to Emma, she wasn't for him. A woman with children needed commitment...

'I'll give you a lift to Base,' he said, mainly to show the blip and his other reactions they didn't matter and that he could be in her company without ever thinking of her in a non-platonic way.

Perhaps.

'The hospital will have sent whatever supplies you'll need straight to the chopper,' he added persuasively, although he knew he should be organising things so he saw less of her, not more.

She studied him for a moment—a fleeting moment—then shook her head.

'I'll need my car to get home,' she told him in a voice that suggested it was the end of the conversation.

'I'll drive you home, it's no bother. If we're in the same car we can pool whatever we've been told about this accident and maybe work out how we're going to tackle it.'

He wasn't really holding his breath, but when she nodded her agreement, the relief that swept through him suggested he might have been.

'I was told it was a traffic accident,' she said, as they pulled away from the house. 'The driver's badly injured and is still being cut out of the car.'

She paused, then asked, 'Wouldn't an ambulance have been just as quick?'

He glanced towards her, glad she was already mentally attuned to the situation, as he should have been. But, no, he was taking the opportunity to study her.

Just briefly!

Study her and wonder just why she affected him the way she did—this small, quiet woman.

Looking at her didn't help, so he turned his thoughts firmly to what lay ahead.

'With badly injured patients, we often just grab and go. Stabilise them as much as possible but get them into the air and en route to a major hospital as quickly as we can. That's why we take a doctor, so you can work on the patient while we're in the air. Statistically, it's better for the patient.'

'I hadn't thought of that. In the city, the nearest hospital is usually a major one so it's not an issue. What's the nearest one to the crash site?'

'Retford, a thirty-five-minute flight each way.'

'And if the patient needs better stabilisation than we can do on the ground?'

She was good, this woman, thinking her way through all the possibilities.

'Then it becomes a very long night. We bring him—

or her—but we'll stick to him, to Braxton, stabilise him, *then* take him to Retford.'

They'd reached the base and he was pleased to see Emma out of the car as soon as he pulled up, already hurrying towards the open side door of the chopper. He caught up with her and they jogged over together, Mark, his paramedic air crewman putting out his hand to help Emma up.

'And up front is Dave,' he told Emma. 'These are the best two crewmen in the skies. Mark'll give you a helmet so you can listen to the chat.'

He slid into his seat, his mind now firmly focussed on what lay ahead, Dave giving him the latest information from the crash site, and the co-ordinates he needed.

The big chopper lifted into the air, and the sense that this was where he belonged swept over him. It was here, in the air, that he really lived, the muddy waters of his early years receding like the tide so he was whole again.

He thought of his foster sister, Liane, wondering if she'd had some place she could go where all the past was forgotten. Perhaps if she had, she might have lived.

Dave's quiet voice brought him out of the useless speculation, and now he could see the bright arc lights of the emergency services teams revealing a macabre scene of twisted metal wrapped around a substantial tree.

He put the chopper down as close to the scene as he possibly could. Word had come through that the two passengers in the car had been taken to Braxton by ambulance, both suffering from minor injuries.

But whoever was still trapped inside—well, he didn't want to think about it, because the front of the vehicle had concertinaed and pushed the engine back onto the driver.

A fire officer was using the huge cutters to free the man—his gender confirmed on arrival at the scene. Emma was squatting close by the vehicle, checking what the ambos had already done to help the victim—checking the victim himself as best she could, given that a low, heavy branch of the tree prevented her from getting right up to him.

'We need to hook the rear of the vehicle up to the fire truck and see if we can haul it off the tree,' the fire officer told them. 'Problem is we don't know if it will make things better or worse for him.'

'The way the dashboard has come back on him, there could be injury to the femoral artery on both legs,' Emma pointed out, 'so we've got to be ready for massive blood loss.'

She was speaking to Mark, who nodded his understanding, hauling pads and bandages out of one of the flight bags.

'And hypovolemic shock?' Marty muttered, thinking through what lay ahead, the paramedic he'd once been never far away at the scene of any accident.

'Definitely. But we deal with the normal things, check his airway, immobilise him on the stretcher...' she turned around and nodded when she saw that Dave had the stretcher ready behind her '...put pressure on any wounds to slow the bleeding. I'll start IVs in the air and check him over properly, but getting him to hospital as quickly as we can will be the best thing we can do for him.'

The deep growl of the fire engine made them both step back, and slowly—protesting noisily—the vehicle was dragged away from the tree. Marty moved in to help the fire officers who were still working on freeing the patient, helping them fit a block and tackle to the front of the vehicle, already cut free, so they could lift it off the injured driver.

And Emma was proved correct. As the pressure lifted, blood spurted from the man's thighs. Being closest, Marty clamped his hands against the wounds and held tight until Mark and Emma came with dressings.

'Bind it tightly,' Emma said to Mark, then she half smiled. 'Sorry, telling you something you already knew, wasn't I?'

And while Emma bound the man's other leg, Marty fastened a collar around the man's neck while Dave slid a spine board down behind him. Once strapped to that, Emma was happy for them to lift him onto the stretcher.

'Let's get him airborne,' Marty said, hurrying to the chopper, Mark and Dave following him with the stretcher, while Emma jogged alongside, adjusting the oxygen mask the ambos had fitted.

He had the aircraft ready for lift-off by the time Mark confirmed the patient was secure, and as they rose into the air, he glanced into the rear-view mirror in front of him and saw Emma kneeling by the patient, fitting a cannula into the patient's hand, ready for fluid resuscitation.

All in all, it had been a good grab and go—slightly delayed by the problem of extricating the man but they'd still make it to hospital not far outside what the emergency staff considered the first golden hour.

He felt a sense of satisfaction, although another glance in the mirror—another glance at Emma attending to their patient—reminded him the job wasn't finished.

Not yet.

The flight home from Retford to Braxton was uneventful, and beyond Marty congratulating them all on a job well done, there wasn't much chat.

No doubt, Emma thought, because none of them felt confident about their patient's future. His injuries had been horrific, not only the damage to both legs but internal injuries caused by the steering wheel being driven back into his body.

'I'm glad I'm not in Retford Emergency tonight,' she

said quietly, and while Mark and Dave murmured their agreement, Marty was far more positive.

'At least there they had a full team of trauma specialists standing by and he'll be whisked into Theatre probably before we get home.'

'Is he always this positive?' Emma asked, and Mark and Dave laughed.

'He's the world's greatest optimist,' Mark told her.

'Yep,' Dave added, 'his glass isn't just half-full, it's practically brimming over.'

Why? Emma wanted to ask, but the two crewmen were indulging in a 'remember the time' conversation and she tuned out to think about her own positivity, which she believed was fairly strong.

Except when she was tired, or the boys were playing up, or—

No, she told herself firmly, she was a very positive person.

But driving home with Marty, in the close confines of a vehicle, with whatever it was going on inside her body whenever he was near, she was positively confused.

How ridiculous!

She was tired, probably exhausted, that's all it was.

'You tired?' he said, picking up her thought.

'Not really,' she said, though why she denied it she had no idea.

'Liar,' he said softly. 'I can see your head nodding. You're nearly asleep.'

And whatever restraint she'd been managing to hold onto snapped.

'Okay, I'm tired, exhausted, in fact. There, are you satisfied now?'

'Hey,' he said softly, reaching out to touch her arm. 'I didn't mean to upset you. I was just teasing.'

'Then don't,' Emma retorted, although she rather thought she meant *Don't touch me* rather than *Don't tease.*

'I won't again, I promise,' he said, but as she turned towards him she saw a smile hovering about his lips and knew his eyes would be smiling as well.

What was it with this man, that stirred her up so much?

He pulled up outside her house and she hesitated before opening the door, wanting to make amends for her earlier tetchiness.

'I'm having a cup of tea before I go to bed. I find it relaxes me. Do you want something?'

Idiot!

Fool!

Imbecile!

The words raged through her head, but it was as if this man had mesmerised her in some way.

'I won't, thank you,' he said, and an unlikely feeling of disappointment descended like a cloud.

He was turned towards her as he spoke and she turned her head away, hoping her feelings weren't obvious.

Apparently not because now he was getting out of the car and walking around to open her door. Well, hold the door because she'd managed to open it as soon as she'd realised what he was doing.

She slipped out past him, far too close, said thank you and good night and hurried towards the front steps.

He was waiting by the car, a tingling sensation up and down her spine telling her he was watching her go. Sheer politeness to see she got safely inside, she knew that, but...

She turned at the top of the steps and waved, absentmindedly patting the dog who'd heard her arrival and come to stand beside her.

Marty waved back and drove off, while she stayed

where she was and watched until the two red tail-lights disappeared from view—

To be replaced within seconds by the glare of head-lights, and what was unmistakeably Marty's vehicle pulled up in front of her gate once more.

The light was on above the door so she couldn't pretend she hadn't seen him, but as he got out of his car and came purposefully towards her, she felt her heartbeat accelerating as a kind of panic filled her body.

'Something you forgot?' she asked, doing her best to sound at ease.

'Just thought I'd have that cuppa after all. I know we're both tired but we don't have to be up for an early shift, so we might as well relax together.'

The last two words sent shivers through Emma's body, although she knew perfectly well what he meant.

Idiot!

Fool!

Imbecile!

The words ran through Marty's head as he watched Emma bustling about in the big, country kitchen, taking what seemed like forever to make a pot of tea.

Why on earth had he come back?

What had drawn him?

He had nothing to offer this woman, so surely the less he saw of her the better?

Yet the car had barely reached the end of her street before he'd turned back, the fleeting expression of disappointment he'd caught on her face vivid in his mind.

Now he was sitting at the kitchen table while she pushed a cup and saucer, the teapot, milk and sugar, and the remnants of the chocolate cake towards him.

'I'd have thought if your boys didn't finish it off, Molly

and Mandy would have,' he said, pouring his tea but waving away the cake. 'Or this "puppy" of yours.'

'Dad's pretty strict about how much sweet things the boys eat,' his hostess replied politely. 'Especially close to bedtime. And I'm still not sure about the puppy being ours.'

She didn't look at him as she spoke, too busy pouring herself a cup of tea, although how much concentration did that really take?

'He's good with the boys? Your father?'

'The best,' she said, with not a hint of hesitation, but it was there again, a shadow in her eyes, nothing more.

He closed his eyes briefly. Had he turned his car around—come back—for this? An inane conversation with a woman he barely knew?

Not that she was keeping up her end—inane or not. His polite question had been answered—briefly—but she hadn't picked up the conversational ball and lobbed it back to him.

And now, when he looked across at her, she was frowning at him while the dog, sitting like a sentry beside her, studied him closely.

'Why did you come back?' she asked.

He stared at her, willing words to come. Words usually came easily to him, and as for a simple chat over a cup of tea? Well, he considered himself something of an expert!

But how could he tell her he'd seen something in her face, so fleeting he couldn't even be sure it had been disappointment?

Tell her whatever it was had touched him in some way?

'For a cuppa?' he suggested, and tried a smile, but knew it was a feeble effort.

'And?' she persisted.

'I really don't know,' he said, resorting to honesty. 'I just felt we'd parted wrongly, somehow. Felt that I should have had a cuppa with you. I suppose…you're new in town, might need a friend, and I *mean* a friend, nothing more. You've probably heard the gossip—Marty doesn't do commitment…'

Aware he was burbling on, tripping over his words and actually saying nothing intelligent, he stopped.

Emma studied him for a moment, then shook her head, and he read her tiredness in the gesture.

'I'm sorry, you're exhausted. You've had a tough introduction to Braxton. I'll get going—leave you in peace.'

He stood up, drained his cup and set it back down in its saucer.

'But if ever there's anything you need—anything I can do for you—just let me know.'

She half smiled.

'Because Stephen told you to look out for me?'

Relief flooded through him—it was the perfect excuse. Far better than saying, *You looked disappointed that I didn't stay...*

'Of course,' he said. 'But because we're colleagues as well. Up at the hospital, we all look out for each other.'

He could tell by the look on her face that she didn't believe him—well, not entirely—but how else could he explain the uncontrollable urge that had had him turning his vehicle and heading back to her house?

'As I said, if there's ever anything I can do, you only have to ask,' he said, aware that his voice sounded rough.

There was something about this woman…

'Thank you,' she said, oh, so polite, although the words seem to hold—what? Longing?

Definitely something, but what he couldn't define.

He walked down the front steps, feeling all kinds of a fool—coming back the way he had, confused, and slightly unhappy…

'Bye.'

He was at the bottom of the steps now and turned at the word, looking back up at the woman who'd spoken—at the dog by her side. She raised her hand and wiggled her fingers, and a tension he'd never felt before—or not within recent memory—filled his body.

He was tired, that's all it was.

Yesterday had been a big day, today even longer…

Maybe he was sickening for something.

But as he got into his car and drove away, he knew it was none of these things.

Any more than it was to do with whatever she wanted— or didn't want—to talk about.

This was different, internal somehow.

Emotional?

He was pretty sure it wasn't love, because love didn't— couldn't, surely—happen like that, like a thunderbolt from the blue—but whatever he was feeling was something he'd never felt before.

He loved Hallie and Pop and his foster siblings, but that was different. It had grown almost organically as he'd grown within the family.

Which only went to prove love wasn't thunderbolt stuff.

But whatever it was he *was* feeling, he didn't want to feel now…

Definitely didn't want to feel now!

Of all the women in the entire world he should *not* be getting involved with, Emma was at the top of the list.

Emma had children, and children meant commitment.

And he didn't do commitment—at least in his ramblings he'd managed to tell her that much.

He just couldn't *trust* himself to do commitment.

An image he'd thought he'd banished forever flashed clearly through his mind—not the blow itself, or the blood that had flowed after it, but his father's arm rising, slowly, menacing, then deliberately striking downwards.

His own arm, many years later, rising the same way, hitting out at the man—barely a man—who'd stolen his girlfriend...

It wasn't the sins of the father handed down, but the genes...

CHAPTER FOUR

THE FOLLOWING DAYS were busy for Emma, but totally Marty-free. Not that she wanted to see the man who was causing so much confusion in her mind and body, but he'd been such a presence in her first few days at work, she couldn't help but be aware of his absence.

Molly and Mandy had called in after school one afternoon to play with the boys, and Emma had to wonder if it had been prearranged when Carrie came to collect them and joined her father for a beer on the veranda before taking them home.

She couldn't feel anything but pleased that her father had found an old friend, and if she wondered, as she lay in bed at night, just how friendly they might have been in the past, she dismissed the thought as none of her business. At least her father was happy...

And her own social life was improving—slightly. She'd had a drink after work on Friday afternoon with Joss and a couple of other staff, Joss suggesting that she bring the boys out to her farm over the weekend.

'We've a couple of orphan lambs and a poddy calf the boys might like to play with,' she'd said. 'Come tomorrow and stay to lunch.'

Knowing the boys would be delighted with the farm animals, she'd agreed immediately, resolutely ignoring an inner whisper that she'd miss Marty if he happened to pop in.

Something he hadn't done for a couple of days, she had to admit.

And why should he?

He'd produced babysitters for her, found a friend for her father to help him settle back into town, and offered her friendship too—what more could she expect?

Nothing.

Why should she?

Especially when he'd made it very plain that friendship was all he would offer.

But when she arrived back from Joss's place, two exhausted boys sleeping in the back of her car, and saw the familiar four-wheel drive parked outside the gate, why did her heart rate rise, while her mind wondered just how much of the farm mud that had liberally covered the boys had ended up on her nose or cheeks?

'Good morning?' he asked, coming down the front steps and offering to carry one of the boys inside for her.

'Great morning, and I can manage,' she said automatically, *and* stupidly as she couldn't manage—not both boys at once—not now they were getting bigger.

As he'd already unhooked Xavier from his car seat and was lifting him out, she hoped her words might have gone unnoticed, although the eyebrow he cocked at her as she leant in to free Hamish told her otherwise.

'Kids look so innocent when they're asleep,' he said quietly as they stood and watched the boys settle into their cots.

'Only if you don't know what devils they can be when they're awake,' Emma told him, although seeing her children sleep always tugged at her heart.

'I suppose,' he murmured.

The whispered words seemed to linger in the air, although they had been spoken as Marty left the room. His tone had been tinged with something she couldn't identify—sadness?

Regret?

She knew from his footsteps he'd walked out onto the veranda and much as she'd have loved to have a shower—or at least check for mud—before she faced him, she knew she had to follow.

Had he a reason for being here?

Was it to do with her?

'You look as if you had a good time,' her father said, running his eyes over her farm-stained clothes.

'The boys just loved it.'

She looked from her father to Marty, who, she rather thought, was also taking in her appearance.

'Did you want to see me?'

Silly question—what if he said, no, he'd just called in to see her dad.

Although her father had already drifted off, no doubt back to the garden that was becoming a passion with him.

'I did,' Marty said, and, no, her heart *didn't* skip a beat! 'I know it's a bit short notice, but the Mid-Coast chopper has offered to cover our area tomorrow and I'd like to do a winch refresher session. I know you're up to date with your winch protocols but our aircraft is new to you and it's possibly a different winch to one you've used before. We'll all be involved and if we can get through it in the one day—maybe even the morning—we're right for six months.'

He paused, as if waiting for some response, but Emma was too busy hiding the dread she always felt about winch work to answer him. Why it still happened when she was extremely proficient at it she had no idea.

'All the crew do six-monthly refresher training,' Marty continued, 'but we've got out of sync, so if we can all do it together, it'll save having special days for one or two crew members.'

He obviously needed an answer, so Emma managed a nod, then, realising that might be a little wishy washy, went for a word.

'Super!' she said, though it was far from how she felt and was not a word she could recall using before that moment. 'What time and where?'

'Seven, at the base. Best to get started before the wind gets up. We'll just do a lift and lower for each of us and if we've time a quick carry, just clip on and lift then down and unclip.'

He grinned and added, 'Pilots included.'

As if that made it better! Those men threw themselves around in the sky as if it was their playground. Dangling on a rope—well, a wire—thirty, forty, fifty feet above the earth wouldn't bother them at all.

'I'll be there,' she said, then thought of something.

'Can I go first?'

She didn't add, because it would be stillest, instead using the boys as an excuse.

'That way I can get back and spend most of the day with the boys.'

'You could bring them,' the ever-helpful Marty said. 'They might like a flight.'

'No way!' Emma told him, aware of the blood draining from her face at the thought of the boys in a helicopter. Helicopters crashed...

With a promise he'd see her at seven, Marty departed, but not before wondering just how nervous Emma was about her children.

She'd certainly seemed shocked at the thought of him taking them for a ride, though he knew small boys usually loved being airborne.

Did she worry herself when she flew?

Dislike flying?

If so she'd hidden it remarkably well on the trips they'd already taken together.

Although winch training was always a test of a person's mettle. For someone who didn't like heights or flying, it would be a nightmare.

She wasn't due for a refresher—he'd checked her CV and knew she had a couple of months to go—but life was so much easier if they could all do the refresher in one day and with the offer of cover from the Mid-Coast team, it seemed too good to pass up.

But he'd keep an eye on her...

The unspoken words elicited a groan from deep inside his body. Metaphorically or not, he needed to see less of Emma, not more, and keeping an eye out for her?

Definitely seeing more!

It was because he was between girlfriends that he was attracted to her. It had to be that. Nothing to do with the way her eyes would twinkle at him when she laughed, or the pinkness that came into her cheeks when she was embarrassed, or the earnest way she always thanked him when he did the smallest thing for her...

This feeling of attraction was very different somehow.

Caring.

Protective.

That was it; he felt protective of her. Protective was far better than attracted...

And if he found a new girlfriend...

Wasn't there a new female assistant manager at one of the banks?

Hadn't he heard that somewhere?

Plus, if he could get Emma hooked up with someone else, that would be even better. It would remove her from all consideration in the most positive way.

His mind began listing eligible single men—well, eligible men rather presumed their single status...

Rob Armstrong would be good. Marty had heard Rob had been in hospital recently and although he had a bit of trouble with atrial fibrillation, it responded to treatment.

But did it weaken his heart?

Ned had told him about Emma's husband—about his sudden death from cancer six years earlier. Could she handle losing another husband who might die before his time?

And just why, if he wasn't attracted to her, did the unspoken word 'husband' cause constriction in his chest?

He'd scrap Rob, but there was that new bloke on a cattle property further west—rich family sending junior to learn the ropes on one of their smaller properties.

Marty had done a bit of heli-mustering for him. He could drop in and mention the barn dance.

Better yet, he could phone the bloke, ask if they could do their practice lifts out of one of the gullies on his property. Most of his cattle were in the back country so they shouldn't be disturbed. He'd get the bloke—what *was* his name?—to act as the patient and have Emma do the lift. Clinging together at the end of the wire, who knew what chemistry might happen...?

Shane—his name was Shane.

Marty's old vehicle lacked Bluetooth so he pulled over to the side of the road and checked the contacts in his phone. Best to do it right now.

Before he forgot.

Or changed his mind...

Hiding the dread in her heart at the thought of the winch training session, Emma went in search of her father, finding him digging in the old vegetable garden out the back.

'Did you really have a good time today?' he asked shrewdly, and she smiled.

'Well, the boys did but I rather think Joss had been doing a bit of unsubtle match-making. A friend of hers, an engineer at the local council who'd been in hospital earlier in the week, also called in and it seemed a long way out of town for just a casual visit.'

'Nice bloke?' her father asked, so casually Emma had to smile.

'Nice enough,' she said, 'but that's all. Besides which, he's a patient.'

She sighed, and sat down on a corner stump that held the sleepers for the raised beds in place.

'Simon was so special, Dad, it's hard to get interested in someone else.'

Laughing blue eyes notwithstanding, she added silently.

'Do you ever think that Simon might have been so special because you had so little time together? Your marriage was still fresh and wonderful; still full of new experiences like getting to know each other, sharing tales about your lives, making plans for the future, and building dreams together.'

Emma looked at the man who'd left the work he'd loved at fifty so he could be with her during the weeks before Simon's death. Just there, in the background—ready to support her when she needed it and to hold her when the knowledge that she was losing Simon became too much to bear.

Been there, too, for the extra sadness that had followed it but she pushed that thought away, not wanting to remember her emotional and physical collapse.

He'd done some supply teaching when she'd returned to work, but he'd been there for her whenever she'd needed him, needed someone to comfort her—to just be there...

'I don't know, Dad,' she said, finally coming around

to considering his question. 'You might be right. But I do know I'll never love like that again.'

Her father kept on digging, and a cry from the house told her one of the boys was awake—and no doubt intent on waking his brother.

'I'll go. And I know I've said I'll be on deck for the kids at weekends, but I'm afraid I've got a winch training session tomorrow. We're starting early so hopefully I'll be home for lunch. Did you have anything planned?'

'Nothing I can't do with the boys. Carrie asked us all up for lunch so I'll go on ahead and you can join us if you get home in time. I've got the address in the house. Will give it to you later.'

Which kind of finished that conversation.

But was Dad right?

Had her marriage been so special—her love so strong—because it had been cut short?

Because they hadn't had time to grow niggly with each other over squeezed toothpaste tubes—although Simon had always been practically fanatical about squeezing from the bottom, whereas she just squeezed from wherever got the toothpaste out the quickest.

Hmm…

The morning dawned fearsomely bright with the promise of a still day, light winds forecast for the afternoon.

With any luck, they'd be home by afternoon, Marty decided, but would that be all good?

Carrie had phoned to invite him to lunch and insisted he come after the training session, however late that might be.

'I've asked Ned and Emma and the boys, but I guess she'll be out with you, being hauled up and down in your practising. But do come.'

Because you don't really want to be with just Ned for

too long, or because you're doing a bit of unsubtle match-making between Emma and me? Marty wondered.

Surely not? Carrie knew his views on commitment and marriage and she'd be the first to realise that Emma needed both.

But the sun was bright and he left all thoughts of later behind as he headed out to the base. Shane had agreed they could use his property and Marty would fly all the staff out there, then share the hovering duties with Matt.

Mark, Dave and Emma all arrived at the same time, only minutes after he'd driven in, Matt arriving close behind them.

'Okay, flight suits and helmets on, all of you,' he said, and heard Emma groan.

'Problem?' he asked, smiling at the grimace on her face.

'Only that I look like a balloon in a flight suit,' she muttered. 'One of those balloons clowns tie into funny shapes at kids' parties. It's okay for you tall people, but for us ver-tically challenged, it's not much fun.'

He grinned at her, but had to turn away to hide laughter when he saw what she meant. The suits did come in two sizes—small and large—but he knew they were for small and large men, not for diminutive women. With the ends of the legs and arms rolled up, and the belt cinched tight, she did kind of resemble a tied balloon.

'And why am I the only doctor here?' she demanded, obviously still grumpy.

'You're the only one with winch training. The others need to do the full course and somehow the hospital ad-ministration can't seem to find the time to send even one of the other ER doctors down to Sydney for it. It's prob-ably why they were so happy to get you. Mac's trained, so we've used him in emergencies, particularly if the incident is over towards Wetherby.'

'Hmph,' was the reply to that, but as she'd now added

her helmet and was looking like a little mushroom, Marty busied himself with the chopper.

No way was he going to tangle with a grumpy mushroom!

'We're going to a property out of town, with a good gully,' he explained when they were all ready. 'I'll land you as close as I possibly can, then you'll have to walk in—'

'Or roll in Emma's case,' Dave said, and Emma laughed and punched him lightly on the arm.

They had the makings of a really good team, Marty realised, pleased to be distracted from images of a laughing mushroom.

'I was going to say, so you can get some idea of the lie of the land. Dave and Mark can stay with me, and Mark can do the first fast response drop when you find a good spot. Matt'll sort out the order for the rest of the practice.'

Once in the air, Dave gave Matt the co-ordinates of the gully, and Marty watched as Matt tapped them into his GPS. Ten minutes' flying and he could see Shane's big four-wheel drive parked beside a dam. He landed close by, introduced his crew—Emma pulling off her helmet rather self-consciously he thought.

'Okay,' Matt said, 'let's go, kids. Dave, you act as winch man for Mark, and, Dave, you can do it for me later.'

Emma and Shane followed Matt into the gully, Shane walking beside Emma, who tried desperately to pretend this was just a nice little bushwalk. But the thought of the winch, added to her embarrassment of the unflattering flight suit, was making it difficult to follow Shane's polite conversation.

Though she did learn he kept a thousand head of cattle on his property, mostly breeding cows. The calves he sold off as weaners at about eight months for other people to fatten into steers.

At least that's what she figured from a long, slow conversation that included calving percentages, heifers kept to replace breeding cows, and the problems of getting recalcitrant cattle into cattle trucks.

Matt had signalled to the aircraft and Mark was already on his way down on the winch wire.

'You're up first,' Matt told Emma, and although she'd volunteered to go first, now the time had come she rather wished she hadn't.

Nonsense, she told herself. You've done it dozens of times—you're good at it.

Mark had reached the ground and unsnapped his harness, handing it to Emma.

'You needn't go right into the aircraft. Just strap yourself in, signal you're ready for the winch and Dave will lift you as far as the skids, then drop you back down. Hopefully you'll stay clear of the trees.'

A huge grin had accompanied the last words, and Emma glared at him as she fixed her helmet back in place and took the harness from Mark, adjusting it to her size before climbing into it and strapping in securely. She signalled to lift and up she went, reminding herself again she'd done it dozens of times, and that from what she'd seen of Marty he was an excellent pilot so would hold the aircraft in hover mode as still as he possibly could.

'Okay?' Dave called down to her as she rose above the trees.

'Just fine,' she assured him, even venturing a small wave.

He helped her onto the skids, checked she was okay, then down she went, only too happy to be back on firm ground again.

'Don't unhitch, Marty wants you to do a patient lift.' Dave's voice came through the helmet communication and as everyone was listening she could hardly screech and yell about it.

Matt was handing Shane his helmet.

'I'm lifting Shane?' she couldn't help but yell.

Matt laughed.

'*You're* not lifting him, the winch is,' he reminded her, handing her the strop she would fit around the chest of this total stranger, before clipping him onto her harness. In this way, snapped together, they would be lifted off the ground.

Helmet to helmet, face to face, body to body.

And Shane had the hide to be grinning at her as if he was enjoying himself! It was like sharing a sleeping bag with a complete stranger, only worse because she knew all the crew would be laughing about it to themselves.

She checked all the clips and safety clasps were in place, then signalled with hand and voice that they were ready. Fortunately, their height difference—and Shane's broad shoulders—ensured she was looking at his chin, not directly into his eyes. She shifted the helmet mic away from her mouth and muttered, 'This is so embarrassing,' but she doubted he heard as they were brushing past the foliage of the trees.

In fact, he was looking all around him, as if this was a wonderful experience, put on purely so he could see this little bit of his property from a different angle.

'Lowering now.'

She sighed with relief at Mark's order. Apparently, they didn't have to go right into the aircraft for this lift either.

What she hadn't realised was that Shane's feet would touch the ground first, and he'd automatically put his hands out to steady her as she came down, holding her so close that embarrassment flooded through her.

Maybe the boys didn't need a father, she decided when she'd unhooked, taken off her helmet, and moved a little away from the men so she could recover her composure.

Uncomfortable, that's how she'd felt.

Uneasy, too…

But surely she wouldn't feel like that with all men who touched her, no matter how platonically.

Besides which, the other part of her search for a man— what search?—had been to free up her father so he could have a life, because she knew full well he'd never leave her to cope with the boys on her own.

Considering how much he'd already given up for her, the very least she could do was *look* for a man.

And if she fell in love?

She looked around at the surrounding trees, aware deep inside herself she feared losing herself in love again, while knowing she couldn't cheat a man by not offering it.

The practice continued, Matt and Mark lifting, the helicopter landing and Matt taking over as pilot while Dave and Marty practised.

Shane had settled beside Emma on a fallen log and had been regaling her with tales of bringing the young cattle in to be ear-tagged and, in the case of the young steers, castrated.

It all sounded particularly nasty to Emma, but Shane's enthusiasm was so great she suspected he thought she was as fascinated as he was by the subject of cattle. He was telling a particularly grisly tale of having to use the tractor to haul a dead calf out of an exhausted cow when Marty called to her.

She leapt to her feet and hurried towards him, so thankful for the interruption she could have hugged him.

Until he told her why she was wanted.

'Your turn to be the patient,' he informed her, and as he was still in his harness she knew just who was going to do the lift.

Not that being held close against Marty meant any more than being held close against Shane…

Not really…

Of course it didn't.

He was tightening the strop before dropping it over her head, tightening it again under her arms, clipping them together.

'Okay?' he said, his smiling face and teasing blue eyes so close they could have kissed.

Except their helmets would have bumped together and anyway she didn't want to kiss Marty.

Definitely didn't want to kiss Marty.

Marty was the last man on earth she should consider kissing...

Would consider kissing!

'I said are you ready?'

His voice pierced the tumble of confusion in her head.

But it didn't clear the mess enough for her to speak.

She made do with a nod—bang onto his helmet—and closed her eyes because she knew he'd be laughing at her.

'Lifting now,' she heard Mark say, and kept her eyes closed because she really didn't like to look down—or even up—and for this lift she didn't have to, as Marty was in charge.

They reached the skids and Mark and Marty helped her in. Her head cleared and she hoped she wasn't blushing at the thoughts she'd had. Marty hadn't chosen her to lift, but was simply getting all the crew back on board. The winch wire and harness were already going back down for Dave, and peering out cautiously Emma realised Shane was back in his vehicle, bouncing his way across the fields towards the homestead.

Yet some wilful thread of disappointment wound its way into Emma's brain—Marty *hadn't* chosen her.

And why *should* he have?

No answer, any more than there was to the even more personal question of whether he'd felt what she'd felt, clipped so close their bodies had been touching.

Had the sudden warmth of her body transmitted itself to his?

Or had it been his that had warmed hers…?

Had he chosen Emma to lift for personal reasons?

Definitely not, he told himself as he settled back into his seat, quite happy for Matt to fly them home, as he really needed to think.

It had been a mistake, of course. He'd known that the instant he'd tightened the strop around her. Given their situations, *an*d the weird sensations he was experiencing in her vicinity, clipping her up against his body was the last thing he'd needed. It was feeling her softness despite all the harnesses and flying suits. It was catching the woman-scent of her, and seeing the clear, pale skin on her cheeks colouring slightly—with embarrassment?—and the dark, slightly curling lashes that framed her eyes.

He knew women, by some mysterious process, did curl their lashes, but he rather doubted, with the boys to be got up and fed before she'd left for the exercise, she'd have had time to curl her lashes this morning.

If she ever did.

Somehow he thought of Emma as a 'take me as you see me' kind of woman, rather than the eyelash-curling type—

But what did he know?

She was as much a mystery to him as she had been when he'd first met her.

Oh, he knew bits of her story, knew she was a loving mother to her boys, knew how much she relied on her father. Apart from that, he suspected she felt guilty about her reliance on her father, and would like to free him up in some way.

But would her father move on—and out—and leave her to cope on her own?

He doubted it.

'We're home, flyboy!' Dave said. 'Can't take the early morning start, eh?'

The rest of the crew were already climbing out, Emma in the lead and almost at the equipment shed.

He smiled to himself.

She'd want to get out of the flying suit as quickly as possible, given how much it embarrassed her. Another little insight into this woman who, for some reason, was occupying far too much of his thinking time.

And would be occupying even more of it over lunch…

'I'll see you at Carrie's,' he said, as she left the shed he was entering.

She gave him such a startled look he had to add, 'You are coming, aren't you? Carrie was furious when I told her about the winch practice and I had to promise her I'd have you back in time for lunch.'

She frowned at him.

'*You're* going to Carrie's for lunch too?' she demanded, sounding so put out he had to smile.

'Well, she *is* my sister,' he reminded her, causing the frown to turn into a scowl as she hurried away from him.

He was right, of course. Carrie *was* his sister, and he possibly had lunch with her every Sunday, but right now she wished he wasn't going. Or, failing that, that she could somehow cry off.

But she could hardly not go—it would be rude. When he turned up Carrie would know the exercise was over. Besides which, she really wanted to go, mainly so she could play with the boys and let her father catch up with his old friend.

She drove home in a daze, her mind once again such a mish-mash of thoughts it was impossible to untangle them.

Her father, the boys, a ball-kicking man, Marty—no, Marty definitely didn't fit into the slot—Carrie and her father, and what to wear to lunch, though why she was worrying about that minor detail when the rest of her life was so unsettled she had no idea.

Jeans and a top—there, that was one worry gone. She had that nice blue top she'd bought before leaving Sydney—perhaps not with jeans but her white slacks. White slacks when she'd be out with the boys? No, definitely jeans—

'We waited for you so we'd only have to take one car,' her father said as she walked up onto the veranda where the boys were explaining to the ever-patient dog that he had to stay and guard the house, although Xavier, Mr Persistent, was saying, 'But Molly and Mandy would love to see him.'

She left her father to sort out the dog and hurried through the house to shower and dress. The green top her friend Sally had given her might look better with the jeans…

Annoyed with herself for such dithering—since she'd had the boys getting dressed usually meant pulling on whatever was closest and relatively free of food stains. And even more annoyed because, although she hated to admit it, she knew it was the fact that Marty would be there that was causing the dithering.

Why he, of all men, should be affecting her the way he was, she had no idea. Could it be because she knew nothing could come of it? Not that she wanted to start regular dating, as in going out with various men. That would be bad for the boys. Wouldn't it?

But how else would she find a man?

She sighed. All she wanted was one man—one who'd want her enough to take the boys as well—a permanent, happy-to-be-with-her man, a friend to share her life, a father for her boys, but definitely not a commitment-phobe.

The green top made her eyes look green—a greyish green for sure, but better than dull grey…

CHAPTER FIVE

LUNCH WITH CARRIE turned out to be a party—a small party admittedly but more than a casual lunch. Mac and Izzy were there—well, like Marty, they were family—and another couple who were friends of Carrie's from her work in the local government office.

And had the tall, bespectacled man Carrie introduced as Neil been asked especially for her—Emma—or had he kind of latched onto her because he didn't know anyone else?

'Neil's the local agronomist, and he's not been in town very long,' Carrie had said by way of a succinct introduction, and although Emma's mind connected the job description with agriculture, she really had no idea what he might do.

The polite thing to do was ask, and as Molly and Mandy had taken her boys off to play in the garden, and she and Neil were kind of in a space of their own, she *did* ask and was soon being treated to a lesson on crop yields and safer farrowing methods for free-range pigs.

She looked desperately around for someone to rescue her, but her father was talking to Carrie's friends, while Mac had taken charge of the barbecue and Izzy was helping Carrie produce bowls of salad and plates of meat. Which left Marty, who was actually watching her, and must have been aware of her predicament as he was grinning with malicious delight.

She threw a murderous frown in his direction and suggested to Neil that they look at the garden, knowing how easily her boys could create a diversion.

Neil seemed a trifle taken aback, for he was in the middle of an extremely complicated—to Emma—story about a horse that had been cast in its stall. But he followed her—albeit reluctantly—out to the garden, where Marty had now materialised and was kicking a football with the boys—the two girls acting as goalies for the hectic game.

A side kick from Marty brought the ball to Neil's feet and although even Emma's instinctive reaction would have been to kick it back, there it sat.

'Kick it here,' Hamish shouted.

'No, here,' Xavier insisted.

But in the end it was Emma who kicked it, not to either of the boys but to Molly—or perhaps Mandy…

Yet the incident stayed with Emma for the rest of the day. At lunch she'd managed to sit down between her father and Izzy, Neil opposite her at the table, explaining something about mung beans to Mac, who was obviously a lot better at looking interested than Emma had been.

But Neil, although she had no doubt he'd been invited to meet her, wasn't the subject of her preoccupation. No, it was Marty kicking the football right to Neil's feet that had disturbed her.

Not because Neil hadn't kicked it back—she'd been talking to him long enough to realise he probably hadn't even noticed it—but that Marty had tested him in that way.

Because it *had* been a test.

Yet try as she might, she couldn't recall ever mentioning to Marty her vague idea that a ball-kicking man might be good to have around for the boys' sake…

Had he divined it?

Read her thoughts?

Had she told Joss and it had become hospital gossip?

She had no idea, yet she knew as well as she knew her own name that Marty had kicked that ball as a test...

Neil claimed her when lunch was finished, and, desperate for a conversation that didn't involve farm animals or crops, she asked if he was going to the barn dance the following weekend.

'Oh, yes,' he said, adding with obvious pride, 'I'm going to be the auctioneer. I did a bit of cattle auctioneering when I was in Queensland—mostly Brahman crossbreeds where I was stationed. They're big beasts and tick-free, which is essential in those parts.'

Emma hid an inner sigh as she just knew she'd soon know more about Brahman crossbreeds than she'd ever needed to know.

But Neil surprised her.

'If you're going, maybe you can act as my assistant,' he suggested, beaming at her as if he'd just conferred a great honour on her. 'Just passing me the slips with the information about the animals to be auctioned and such.'

'Wouldn't you have them in a pile on the lectern?' she said, possibly a little snappishly as the thought of spending the entire evening discussing various aspects of agriculture filled her with horror.

But Neil was undaunted.

'You're right, but perhaps you could spot the bidders. You know, let me know who won each lot.'

'You need someone who knows the locals for that job,' a voice behind Emma said, and the little hairs standing up on the back of her neck told her as much as the voice did.

Marty.

Relief at being rescued made her turn to him, smiling far too brightly.

'You sound as if you've had practice,' she said, moving a little closer to him.

Unconsciously hoping Neil might see them as a couple?

She could feel embarrassment colouring her cheeks that she'd even *thought* such a thing.

And as for using Marty, of all people, as a cover?

Hardly fair...

'Emma?'

Lost in thought, she'd missed whatever conversation had been going on between Neil and Marty, but apparently one of them had included her in it.

'Sorry,' she said. 'I was distracted by the boys.'

Which she now was, as Hamish was attempting to hold the ball behind his back—not easy for someone only three feet tall—while Xavier howled and dashed around him, this way and that, as Hamish twisted and turned.

'Got to halt the war,' she said over her shoulder as she moved to separate the two, who were now rolling on the ground, wrestling with each other, the ball forgotten.

Molly and Mandy arrived at the same time she did, but she smiled at the girls as she separated the boys.

'You girls deserve a break,' she said, holding the boys close to her. 'While you two rascals can walk around the garden with me. I'm sure if we look hard we can find a caterpillar or a snail or maybe even a grasshopper.'

They prepared to race off but she was quicker, grabbing one hand of each of them to keep them anchored to the spot.

'We need to walk quietly so we don't frighten the caterpillar.'

So, with the boys now tiptoeing, they set off to search Carrie's generous-sized garden, squatting down now and then to lift a leaf or check a low-lying branch.

'You left me listening to that man talk about sow farrowing!'

The note of reproach in Marty's voice as he came up

behind them made Emma smile, but as the boys had also heard his voice and were greeting him with a chorus of 'Marty' and demands that he help them find a caterpillar, she had no choice but to let him join the hunt.

They were at the far end of the garden when Carrie called, 'Ice cream for whoever wants it,' and the boys shot off.

Emma looked at the man who could not only kick footballs but had the endless patience required for caterpillar searches.

'You're so good with children,' she said suddenly, 'so why the no-commitment rule? Why not marry and have some of your own?'

She looked into his eyes, no longer laughing but filled with a great sadness.

And for a moment she thought he might speak—might tell her what had caused it, what held him back.

But he shook his head, then touched her gently on the shoulder.

'It's just something I decided a long time ago,' he said quietly. 'Something to do with history repeating itself, which we see so often in life.'

She should let it go at that, she knew, but his words were so bleak and she could feel such pain emanating from his body.

She put her hand on his where it still rested on her shoulder.

'How long ago?' she asked, and he gave a huff of laughter that held no mirth, although his eyes looked better now—almost smiling at her.

'Too long, lovely lady,' he said, then he bent his head and kissed her, ever so lightly, on the lips, running his hand through her hair as he added, 'Way too long to ever change my mind about it.'

And he walked away.

Emma watched him go, one hand pressed against the lips he'd just kissed, her body tingling from that, oh, so light touch.

He's not for you, her head said bluntly, while her heart grew heavy in her chest, and a longing she barely understood filled her body.

But her head was right—hadn't Marty said as much?

He was not for her...

Hell's teeth! What had he been thinking, kissing Emma?

Though it hadn't been a real kiss—

Then why had his toes curled?

Okay, so no more kisses, not even unreal ones...

He headed for his car. He'd call Carrie later and apologise for leaving without saying goodbye to everyone. At least they were all out the back in the barbecue area, eating ice cream.

Except Emma.

But when he turned his head, he saw that she, too, had moved, so hopefully no one would see or even notice his strategic retreat.

Except Izzy, of course. It was nearly dinner time and he'd just returned from the base where he'd been doing some work on his own chopper—something that up until today had always soothed him—when Izzy phoned.

'You left very suddenly,' she said.

'Stating the obvious, Iz?'

'Well, you did! It's Emma, isn't it? Emma and that stubborn streak of yours about commitment. Honestly, Marty, of all of us, I thought you were the most sensible—the most stable—and you were Hallie and Pop's kid from the time you were five or six, so *they* were your parents, *that* house was your home—your life.'

'Leave it, Iz,' he said quietly, and she did because they had all *always* respected each other's boundaries.

'So tell me about That Man,' she said, and he knew she was talking about Neil.

'Got caught by him, did you?' he teased. 'I can't think why Carrie invited him.'

'For Emma, of course,' Izzy replied, 'although Carrie mustn't have known him well—just that he wasn't downright ugly and was single. She couldn't possibly have had a conversation with him. He spent half an hour telling me how young boars sometimes have difficulty mating and how a boar's penis is shaped like a corkscrew.'

Marty roared with laughter, only stopping when Izzy said frostily, 'It's all very well for you to laugh. I couldn't get away from him. Mac was there, pretending to clean the barbecue, but he was secretly enjoying it so much he didn't want to rescue me.'

Marty apologised but Izzy was having none of it.

'You're still smiling, I can hear it in your voice. How is Emma? Did she get over being stranded on the beach? Is she enjoying Braxton? Those boys of hers are a handful, but Ned seems to be able to handle them.'

'He does, but I suspect it's starting to worry Emma that he gives so much of his time—his life really—to her and the boys. I'm sure that's why Carrie asked Neil to the party. I think she'd like to get Emma married off.'

'For her sake or for Emma's?' Izzy asked, and Marty laughed again.

'You don't miss much, do you?'

But he was more relaxed now. Talking about Carrie and Ned and a possible romance there had got Izzy off the subject of his commitment to remain single.

Izzy was the most perceptive of his siblings—probably because she lived close by and saw more of him than the others did.

But for all that Pop had been the father figure he had followed and still adored, his memories of the fear and rage he'd felt towards his birth father were still too strong, too vivid, to ever be forgotten.

And that man's genes were embedded deep within him. So he had no intention of ever putting them to the test…

Emma collected her tired and grubby boys after the ice creams had been consumed, telling her father to stay on and enjoy himself.

'The boys and I both need a rest,' she added, as Carrie helped out by insisting Ned stay on.

But although the boys, once bathed and free of sticky ice cream, went peacefully off to sleep, and she tried to rest, she remained awake, staring at the ceiling, her mind—and other bits of her body—remembering the kiss.

Not that it was a real kiss, she kept reminding herself, but if it wasn't real, why did even remembering it make her lips tingle?

But the no-commitment thing had been laid out, made plain to her in no uncertain terms. So tingly lips were about all she'd ever get from Marty—tingly lips and friendship— she was pretty sure that was still intact.

She sighed, and because the ceiling wasn't giving her any answers she gave up pretending to rest and went into the kitchen. She'd have a baking afternoon, fill the biscuit tins, maybe make some meals that could be frozen for nights when she didn't feel like cooking.

Not that she cooked that often in the evening, but if she was going to push her father further into whatever social life Braxton held for men his age, then she'd have to get used to it. Carrie's friends had mentioned a bridge club and her father had always loved a game of bridge.

He arrived home as she finished washing the pots and pans that didn't fit in the dishwasher.

He picked up a tea-towel, but she took it out of his hands.

'There's football on the telly, go and watch it. We came

to Braxton for a change and I've started my changing with a new job and new friends at work, so it's time you started yours. I'm going to take over more responsibility for the boys and if I'm not here, I'll get the girls, or one of them, to babysit. For a start, you should join the bridge club.'

He took the tea-towel out of her hands and lifted a wet pot.

'I've already said I'd go to the quiz night at the bottom pub on Tuesday night,' he told her, smiling as she looked surprised. 'And spoken to Molly and Mandy in case you're held up at work.'

'Well!' Emma said. 'Good for you!'

And she reached out and hugged him, the pot caught between them, tears pricking at her eyes.

'I can never thank you enough for all you've done for me and the boys, and for just being there for me through so much.'

He finished his task, slipped the pot into a drawer, then turned to face her, reaching out to touch her cheek.

'I wouldn't have been happy not being there,' he said quietly. 'Hadn't you ever realised that?'

She shook her head, a couple of tears escaping now. Swiping them away, she smiled at him.

'I don't suppose I had, but now we're living here, and the boys are nearly ready for kindy, it's time you had a life of your own.'

He smiled back and kissed her on the forehead.

'I will,' he promised, 'but for now get out of my kitchen. You're probably putting things back in the wrong places. I thought after the big lunch we might just have cheese on toast for dinner.'

'Sounds great! And I'll cook it. Cheese on toast is something of a specialty for me.'

A shuffling noise from the direction of the boys' bedroom told her at least one of them was awake. And if one was, the other soon would be. Hoping to spend some alone time with whoever was awake, she hurried in, grabbing Xavier as he prepared to climb onto Hamish's cot and bounce him awake.

'How about you and I do some painting on the veranda?' she said quietly, carrying him out of the room before he had time to make a noise.

'Finger-painting?' Xavier asked hopefully, and after shaking away the knowledge of just how much mess that would entail, she agreed.

It was a quieter week in A and E, and with Emma working an early shift she was able to be home with the boys by three. Most days she would then shoo her father out of the house, insisting he do something for himself.

'I'm playing snooker on Thursday night,' he protested.

'Not enough,' she told him. 'Go to the library. I know you take the boys there for story-time on Tuesdays but that's hardly a peaceful, fruitful visit. You used to love poking around in libraries, and now you're back in Braxton, you can read up on the history of the place. I doubt you had much interest in it when you were young.'

He smiled at her.

'Actually, I did. I must have been a complete nerd because the library was my favourite place and it has always had a great local history section. I'll see what I can find out about the history of this house because it must have been one of the first built here in town.'

The briskness in her father's footsteps as he crossed the veranda told her he was pleased to be free, and she smiled to herself.

Maybe if she could prove to him that she could juggle work and the boys by herself, she wouldn't have to worry about finding a man. She was making playdough while she considered this and telling herself that of course it would work.

After all, many single women coped with work and a family—coped very well in most cases. She just had to show her father that she could, too.

And the heavy feeling in her heart as she thought about these things was to do with the loss of the man she'd had—nothing at all to do with a vague idea that maybe she, too, could do with a man around the place.

Footsteps across the veranda—her father returning so quickly?

'Anyone home?'

Marty!

'In the kitchen,' she called back, but the comings and goings had woken the boys from their afternoon sleep, and her only reaction to Marty's 'I'll get them,' was one of relief.

At least she could wash the sticky dough off her hands, and probably her face, before he came in.

But when he did come in, a beaming boy on each arm, the dog at his heels, her heart stood still.

Maybe she did need a man, a voice in her head whispered. A man to make a family—father, mother, children, and a dog—surely the picture-perfect family?

So, a man—

Just not this one, another voice pointed out. He wasn't available.

Somehow they were all around the table, Marty making a pot of tea while Emma rolled the dough in flour to lessen the stickiness and divided it into two pieces.

'It's green,' Hamish pointed out, quite unnecessarily.

'Very green,' this from Marty as he put the teapot on its stand in the middle of the table.

'We can make frogs,' Xavier said, sheer delight in his voice and face.

'Out on the veranda, and not until you've had your snack,' Emma told them, getting up and washing her hands again—and, no, green food colouring didn't come off with soap and water.

She found biscuits and sultanas for the boys, poured each of them a glass of milk, then sat down to have a cup of tea, Marty already having found mugs, small plates and the biscuit tin.

Yes, maybe a husband would come in handy some-times. But no more than that. She could easily manage without one.

'Your hands are green,' Hamish told her.

'Really?' she teased. 'I thought they were purple.'

'No, definitely green,' her more serious son, Xavier, assured her.

But the lure of green hands ended the boys' conversa-tion as they scoffed down their snacks, drank their milk and headed, green balls in hand, for their play table on the veranda.

'Too much food colouring?' Marty asked.

He was seated opposite her, across a wide, old, kitchen table that really wasn't wide enough. But she had other distractions right now.

'Dad does all this stuff so casily,' she said, sighing and running her green fingers through her hair to push it off her face. 'I do so want to set him free—to get him out and about, and leading a life of his own—but he worries about how I'll cope. And then there's the boys—growing up without a father, especially when they reach puberty, and start asking questions. I know heaps of kids do grow up without a father, but what if they feel cheated later?'

She paused, shaking away the thoughts tumbling through her head, then looked across the table at Marty.

'I really do need a man,' she said, the words burst-

ing from her lips before she realised just how desperate
they sounded.

Not to mention pathetic!

Although who better to tell than a man who wasn't interested in her himself?

Wouldn't it be handy to have his opinion on the subject?

'I know I should be able to cope on my own, and I'm
sure I could, but it's making Dad see it.'

Marty was sipping his tea, but looked interested enough
for her to continue.

'If I had a man, then Dad would feel it was okay to get
on with his own life because he wouldn't be leaving me
alone. I'd thought of it—not hard, but there'd been a tiny
seed of an idea—back there in Sydney. I'd been thinking it might be good for the kids to have a father. It's only
since I've been up here and seen Dad with people of his
own age that I realise how selfish I've been not to have let
him go before now.'

'I don't think it was a matter of you letting him go,
but more he wouldn't have left you on your own,' Marty
pointed out.

'That's the problem.'

She was about to say more but noises from the veranda
had Emma on her feet.

Green froth around the dog's mouth explained what had
happened, and as Xavier was wailing, it was his playdough
the 'puppy' had eaten.

Emma divided the remaining dough, ignoring Hamish's
protests, and they settled down again, but she knew the
game was losing their attention and was relieved when
Marty appeared with their two cups of tea.

'If we sit here, we can watch them,' he said, hitching
a cane table closer with his foot. He set down the tea and
brought over two chairs.

Emma gave a huff of laughter and half smiled as she said, 'You can see why having a man around would be easier.'

Marty looked at the woman who was causing chaos in his mind and body, agreeing with the idea she needed a man but for different reasons. If she was married he'd no longer be interested in her—he hoped—because he'd always avoided the unnecessary complications of dating a married woman. As far as he was concerned, it just wasn't done.

But all her talk of having a man around didn't seem to be making her happy. In fact—

'You said that as if, while it might be easier as far as managing the boys goes, *and* freeing up your father, you'd see it as a nuisance—a penance of some kind. Something you'd be doing solely for your father and the boys and not for yourself.'

She frowned at him over her teacup.

'Would it matter why I wanted him?' she asked.

'It might to him,' Marty pointed out, and she frowned again.

'Why?'

He studied her for a moment.

'Well, from all you've told me, you could hire a housekeeper. It's a big house, so she could live in, be around for you and the boys, satisfy your father that there was someone there for you.'

'But…' She shook her head as if trying to dislodge the words she needed. Tried again. 'But she wouldn't be a *father* to the boys.'

'You haven't thought this through at all, have you?' Marty asked, more than slightly bemused by the situation. 'If this unknown man is to be a father to your boys, he'd have to be your husband. You should be thinking of a man for yourself, not the boys. Thinking of what *you* want first.'

He saw the colour creep into her cheeks.

Embarrassment or anger?

'I do know I'd have obligations,' she said, obviously embarrassed now. 'I'm not completely stupid. I'd probably even enjoy the kind of closeness sex brings.'

She'd dropped her voice before mentioning the 's' word but the boys were further down the veranda now, wrestling with the dog.

'And love?'

'What about it?' she demanded, looking directly into his eyes, as if daring him to continue the conversation.

He shrugged, sure she knew exactly what he meant.

They sat in silence for a minute, then she reached out and touched his hand where it lay on the table by his teacup.

'I'm sorry, it's just the love thing, the risk of it. I don't know if I could do it again. But I shouldn't argue with you of all people. You're the only real friend I feel I've made so far in Braxton.'

Marty's hand burned from the touch but he knew he was an inch away from quicksand.

'It's what I hang around for,' he said, hoping he sounded far more disinterested than he felt. 'Just someone to be snapped at, and thank you for the friend part. Friends are precious.'

Unsure he could maintain his air of detachment, he stood up, collected both cups, and walked through to the kitchen.

'I'd better be going,' he said as he returned to the veranda. 'Only called in to say I'm happy to drive you and Ned to the barn dance on Saturday night. I'll come by at about six-thirty. It's a twenty-minute drive out along the Wetherby road. Wear jeans, check shirts, straw-in-mouth kind of gear.'

He paused before adding, 'Oh, and we all bring our own picnic supper. Izzy and Mac will be joining our group, so

Carrie will probably arrange who brings what. She'll be in touch.'

'We'll be ready,' Emma said, but all emotion had been wiped from her voice, and her face was pale and still.

Had he hurt her with his talk of love? The thought made him uncomfortable in a way he didn't want to think about.

Deep down uncomfortable…

A whole new emotional discomfort he'd never experienced before…

Love?

No way!

'Then I'm off,' he said, and called out goodbye to the boys.

That gave her time to get to her feet and come to the top of the steps.

'You're right, friends are precious,' she said, taking his hand and holding it as she reached up to kiss his cheek. 'Thank you for being mine.'

He walked down the steps, his mind keeping pace with his feet. I will not touch my cheek. I am not sixteen, and bowled over by a first kiss. And I won't turn around, for all I know, she's watching me.

He lasted until he reached the gate, when he did turn, and wave, and if his hand accidentally touched his cheek as it dropped back into place, well, that wasn't all that adolescent!

CHAPTER SIX

SATURDAY FINALLY ARRIVED, and although Emma was secretly dreading this first social event of her life in Braxton, she was excited as well.

And, no, she told herself firmly, it had nothing to do with seeing Marty again.

He'd been conspicuous by his absence at the hospital all week, although she knew two new patients in the post-op ward had been brought in from outlying properties by the rescue helicopter.

She'd even looked out for him in case he came to visit the new patients, then chided herself for caring.

But as she made a large salad on Saturday afternoon, and phoned Carrie to ask if she needed to bring plates and cutlery, her excitement grew.

Because she'd be seeing Marty?

She blanked the thought, replaced it with the knowledge that her father would enjoy meeting up with old school friends again, and maybe get involved in more local activities. Marty had been right, she could get a housekeeper, even part time. That would free up her father to pursue a new life.

They'd work out a schedule to give him more free time.

She was in her bedroom, looking through her wardrobe

for something that would pass for a country shirt, when her father called from the hall.

'Ta-da!' he said, grinning from ear to ear and looking utterly ridiculous in a too-small hat with pigtails hanging from it.

'I don't think it's a back to childhood party,' she told him when she stopped laughing.

He took it off and handed it to her.

'It's for you. I found it in a junk shop and I've wiped it out with antiseptic, though I doubt, from the look of it, it's ever been worn. Do try it on.'

She pulled the hat onto her head, arranged the pigtails so they fell across her ears, and bowed to her delighted father.

'Great!' he said, and he went off to get dressed himself, although when she saw him, he didn't look much different to his usual self in tan chinos and, yes, a checked shirt, but he had tied a bandana around his neck and then produced from behind his back a hat with corks dangling from it.

'We'll make the perfect Aussie couple,' he told her, offering her his arm and sweeping her into a wild dance down the hall.

'Hey!' she finally said. 'I've got to finish getting ready. You could put the salad in the big basket and pack some cold drinks into a cool box. Marty will be here before we know it.'

And he was, coming up the front steps to tell them he already had Carrie in the car, and ask if they were ready.

He roared with laughter at Emma's hat.

'That's priceless!' he finally said. 'You'll fit right in.'

She said goodnight to the boys, and reminded the baby-sitters to call her cellphone if there were any problems, then followed the men to the car.

The drive took them through some of the burnt-out bushland, legacy of the fire, and although it made Emma feel a little sad, her driver, the eternal optimist, pointed out green shoots already sprouting from some of the trees and bushes.

'The Aborigines used fire to regenerate their land,' her father said. 'They did it carefully, in patches, so there was always fresh food for the animals and fresh seeds and nuts for themselves.'

The road wound through the mountains, then opened out onto green farmland.

'We turn off here—the sanctuary is just down this lane,' Carrie explained.

And soon they began to see the animals, horses so old they moved slowly but were probably still loved by the families who could no longer keep them.

Goats and donkeys abounded, and Emma was delighted.

'Do they allow visitors? Could I bring the boys out here?' she asked, and Carrie laughed.

'Of course you can. It's how they make most of their money,' she explained. 'You pay a small admission charge and there are set visiting hours, but with busloads of school kids coming, as well as families at weekends, they get a fair bit. The barn dance and auction top it off, and usually that money goes towards building repairs.'

'What's the auction about?' Emma asked. 'What gets auctioned?'

'The animals,' Marty said, breaking a silence that had seemed to be too long.

'You can bid for any of the animals, and whatever you bid goes to that animal for the year. I think Mac got the three-legged goat his first year here.'

'Poor Mac,' Carrie said. 'He hardly knew what had hit him when he was thrust into this family.'

'Hardly knew what had hit him when he met Izzy,' Marty pointed out, and Carrie agreed that their romance *had* been something special.

But ahead Emma could see lights, and hear music, and soon the lights showed her the largest barn she'd ever seen.

'It looks like more like a three-storey building,' she said, and the others agreed.

'Bloke who built it had a combine harvester and several other large farm machines. He contracted out to farmers who didn't want to keep expensive machinery sitting around for most of the year when there was someone who would come in and do the job. He knew Meg, who runs the centre, and knew her premises were growing too small, so he left the place to her in his will—the whole property.'

'It was a wonderful gift,' Ned said, looking around, while Emma's attention was on the barn and the people gathered about a bar just inside the doorway.

She was sure she'd spotted Neil and was wondering how she could get through a whole evening without being caught up with him when Carrie said, 'Oh, no, it's Neil. Emma, I do apologise for inviting him for lunch, but I'd only spoken a few words to him in the corridors at work and thought he'd be okay.'

'I'll keep him occupied,' Ned offered. 'Maybe not all night because I'm here to dance, but I'll keep watch and if he nabbles you, Em, I'll steer him away. I'm actually quite interested in the agricultural produce of the area. Things have changed a lot since I grew up here.'

It didn't take long for Emma to realise she was really enjoying herself. Many of the staff from the hospital were there, and she was whirled from one country dance to another.

To her delight, she saw her father was also enjoying himself, sometimes dancing but more often deep in conversation with men and women his age—no doubt old school friends.

'This was the best decision we've ever made, me and Dad,' she said to Marty when he appeared from nowhere and claimed a dance. 'Just look at him, he's having the time of his life.'

Marty looked over to where Ned was engaged in a spirited dance with Gladys from the milk bar, talking and laughing at the same time.

'How he's got enough breath to talk beats me,' Emma said.

'Does it matter?' Marty asked, teasing blue eyes looking down into hers.

'Of course not,' Emma managed, although she knew her face had grown hot and her whole body had reacted to that look.

Marty pulled her closer.

'I'd like to whisk you away behind a deserted hay bale,' he murmured in her ear.

Emma recovered enough sense to retort, 'If you could find one—deserted, I mean.'

But her mind wasn't completely on the conversation. Some distance away, sitting quietly on a rug-covered straw bale, Izzy was looking far from well.

Emma looked around, and saw Mac dancing on the other side of the barn.

'Let's go see Izzy,' she said to Marty, who'd been slowly drawing her closer and closer in his arms.

He began to protest, but Emma was already moving away, wending her way through the revellers to where she'd seen Izzy.

'Are you okay?' she asked, when she reached the flushed and slightly shaky woman.

'I think so,' Izzy replied. 'Just suddenly didn't feel well. I probably shouldn't have been rollicking around so much on the dance floor and it's made me a bit dizzy, as if my head's still whirling.'

But Emma was already checking her out. Some swelling of the feet and ankles—fairly normal in pregnancy—

but as she took Izzy's hand she saw it was also swollen, her wedding ring biting into her finger.

She slid her fingers up the swollen wrist to feel for a pulse—definitely high—and turned to Marty, who had appeared beside her.

'Get Mac to come over, take his car keys and get his car as close to the door as you can, then ask Dad if he'll drive your car and Carrie back to Braxton. It could be pre-eclampsia and we should get Izzy to the hospital in Braxton as soon as possible just in case.'

Memories threatened. Memories of shock and fear, but she pushed them away. Izzy needed her to be at her best.

To Izzy she said, 'You'll be fine. It's a precaution, but you have enough medical experience to know if it *is* pre-eclampsia you need treatment right away.'

She hoped she sounded calm and efficient but inwardly she was a mess. Had she made a promise she couldn't keep; would all be well for Izzy and the baby? And what had she been doing, fiddling around with a pigtail hat when she should have been putting an emergency bag of drugs in the car?

Mac arrived, his face tense and strained, although he was so gentle and loving with Izzy, Emma felt like crying.

'Possible pre-eclampsia?' he asked, touching his wife's face where fluid had collected.

Emma nodded.

'I'll get Marty to drive your car, you can sit in the front, and I'll sit in the back with Izzy and do whatever I can to make her comfortable.'

'I could do that,' Mac protested. 'I'm a doctor, too.'

'And she's your wife—that's enough pressure for you. And Marty knows these roads better than anyone, but you'll still have your car in Braxton when you need it.'

As she could see Marty beckoning from the door, she got the party moving, Mac lifting Izzy into his arms as

though she were a featherweight and striding urgently towards the door.

The music had stopped and people were stepping
back—leaving room for him to carry her swiftly to the
car. Ned caught up with Emma.

'You okay?' he asked, and she smiled and gave him
a quick hug, aware he, too, was remembering what had
happened to her.

'Right as rain,' she told him. 'You'll take Marty's car
back to town—and Carrie?'

Her father nodded.

'Get going, and good luck,' he said, pacing beside her
as far as the door.

Mac had settled Izzy into the rear seat, her feet up and a
pillow collected from somewhere placed behind her back.

Emma scrambled into the footwell, where she would
be close to Izzy and able to keep an eye on her condition.
She had to focus on Izzy now—to the exclusion of all else.
The past was the past.

'Let's go,' she said, and Marty needed no second telling.

The drive, along winding mountain roads, seemed endless, although they must have made it to the hospital in
record time. Marty had given Mac the relevant phone numbers to call so by the time they pulled up at the emergency
doors, they had not only a trolley and staff waiting but
Izzy's obstetrician.

Emma hung back as Izzy was wheeled away, to be examined, treated, and have decisions made about her condition and the safety of both her and the baby. There were
so many variables—and so many risks—connected to the
condition, Emma found herself shivering as she followed
the parade into the ED.

'I think I should go and get Nikki.'

Just when Marty had caught up with her, Emma wasn't
sure, but when he materialised beside her she wasn't al-

together surprised. He made a habit of it, the materialising thing...

She turned to him and nodded.

'You're right, I think she'd like to be here. You'll be, what, a couple of hours? I can explain to Mac—'

'Couple of hours be damned, I'll fly over. I'll phone Hallie to let her know I'm coming and what's going on, and she'll track Nikki down.'

He paused, then smiled—the kind of smile that Emma wished had been for her.

'Come to think of it, Hallie will want to be here too, and I think Izzy might need her.'

He really was a special person, Emma thought as Marty dashed off. Always thinking of others, thinking ahead then working out the best way he could help.

As special as Simon?

The thought was so startling she stopped in her tracks, shook off her straying thoughts and walked swiftly into the emergency room, where Izzy was being examined.

Except she wasn't there. Mac met her at the door.

'They've decided to deliver the baby, she's been wheeled up to theatre for a Caesar,' he said, his voice tight with strain. 'She's only thirty-one weeks, but the foetal heartbeat isn't that great. She's had anticonvulsant medication and steroids to help the baby's lungs develop more quickly, but her obstetrician doesn't want to wait.'

'Thirty-one weeks? Braxton PICU won't be able to keep the baby. He or she—'

'He,' Mac put in. 'We only decided at the last scan that we wanted to know, and, yes, I'd been thinking the same thing. Where will they send them?'

'I haven't been here long enough to know,' Emma told him. 'But I'd say Retford. It's the major hospital in the region and as it's attached to the regional university I would think they'd have a top-class PICU.'

Mac gave a huff of laughter.

'I actually know that, having sent a baby there myself. Shows the state I'm in.'

'As does the fact you're standing here chatting with me. I know they'll have to prep Izzy for the op, but shouldn't you be up in Theatre, waiting for her?'

Mac's face paled.

'Of course,' he said, his voice so hoarse Emma could read the fear he felt for his wife.

'They'll both be fine, so go,' she said to him, giving him a little push in the direction of the theatre.

Should she follow?

Could she follow?

She'd been battling to keep focussed from the moment she'd crossed the barn to sit beside Izzy, battling to keep away the memories that were threatening to flood her brain and render her totally useless. Thinking about Marty to distract herself?

But they could no longer be pushed back, and as she walked along the corridor towards the theatre she remembered being wheeled in, still numb from Simon's death, not really aware of anything that was happening around her, let alone within her body.

She turned, seeking privacy in the ER tea-room, quiet at night with only a skeleton staff on duty. She fiddled with the kettle so if anyone came in she'd have her back to them and at least *look* busy.

And now she let the memories flood in. The mad dash to the hospital, pre-eclampsia—the dreaded word—being muttered somewhere outside the fog that was in her head.

Decisions being made by experts because this had been one shock too many for her. Bed rest not helping, and a Caesar the only option.

But her baby, Simon's baby, hadn't lived and now the tears she hadn't been able to shed then because Simon's death had left her empty—now those tears, the tears for her baby, rolled down her cheeks.

'Has something happened? Izzy? The baby?'

Once again Marty was there, behind her this time. She swiped away the tears, aware she must have been staring at the kettle for at least an hour.

Probably longer…

'They're fine, as far as I know,' she said, turning to find not only Marty in the room but a teenager Emma assumed must be Nikki, with Hallie close behind her.

'We should hear soon,' she told them. 'I was thinking tea if anyone wants one. You might like coffee, Marty. Or is Matt on duty? Because the baby will be too premmie for Braxton so they'll all have to be flown to Retford.'

He didn't answer, too busy studying her face, so many questions in his eyes she had to turn away and wipe her face again before greeting Hallie.

'And you must be Nikki,' she said, holding out her hand to the teenager. 'I've got some clothes of yours I should have returned earlier.'

'Keep them,' Nikki told her. 'Mum bought me new ones anyway.'

She spoke brightly but her face clouded over at the thought of her mother.

'How is she? Will she be all right? And the baby?'

'Everyone will be fine,' Hallie announced, and the certainty in her voice not only made Emma smile but also eased some of the hard edges of the grief that had struck her so suddenly.

'I'll organise the chopper to take them both to Retford,' Marty said. 'We'll take a PICU nurse and can take Mac too.'

He looked at Hallie.

'Good idea,' she said. 'We'll wait until we've seen Izzy

then Nikki and I can take Mac's car to Carrie's, spend the night there, and drive down to Retford in the morning.'

Emma shook her head.

'You're some organised family, aren't you?' she said, and Hallie laughed.

'We had to be,' she said. 'We had eight kids with us at one stage. How many with your lot, Marty?'

He counted them off on his fingers.

'Steve, me, Izzy, Lila and Liane—that's five, hardly any at all.'

'And more trouble than all the rest put together,' Hallie said sternly, but Emma saw the twinkle in her eyes and wondered if that group—her last lot of foster children— had maybe been her favourite.

Marty knew he had to leave, but the sadness and the sheen of tears he'd caught on Emma's face made him want to comfort her—to hold her, even, though that could never be. If ever there was a woman who needed commitment it was Emma.

'Let's get up to Theatre. Both mother and baby should be cleaned up by now and we can all say hello before I have to fly them away.'

He led the way, hoping Emma would follow and he'd have a chance to speak to her while Hallie and Nikki spent a few moments with Izzy.

But it was not to be.

When they all trooped into the small recovery room where Izzy lay pale but smiling, and Mac was hovering protectively over a humidicrib inhabited by quite a robust-looking baby, Emma was nowhere to be seen.

He left the family there, knowing he had work to do, knowing too that a PICU nurse would be accompanying them on the flight so there'd be no need for Emma.

Yet wanting to see her, find out about that awful sadness he'd read in her lovely eyes...

It's none of your business, he reminded himself as he headed for the base. An ambulance would bring his passengers out there, and he had to be fully prepared for the flight.

Extra fully prepared for he'd be carrying precious cargo—family cargo.

Family...

Emma had watched them all go off to see Izzy and the baby but she couldn't follow, because, although her tears no longer flowed, she didn't want the misery she'd been feeling to taint the delight of a new birth—even if it was a premmie one.

So she walked home, and even found a smile when she saw the light burning at the top of the front steps, welcoming her back.

Home.

She nodded to herself, aware that this old house, with its high ceilings and large airy rooms, the warm family kitchen and the untidy garden with its mango trees, had become just that—a home.

And that being the case, she decided as she climbed the steps, she had to stop thinking about Marty Graham. He wasn't for her, they both knew that, so if she wanted a man in her life—for the boys' sake *and* to free up her father—she'd have to start sifting through the available men in the town.

She walked inside, checked the boys in their beds, and read the note her father had left on the kitchen table. Carrie had driven him home and taken Molly and Mandy home with her. Boys quiet all night, had fun at the barn dance, talk in the morning.

It was a comforting note, but the fact that he'd had fun

then had had to come home to mind her children, drove home the need for her to find a man—or a housekeeper.

A housekeeper who could kick a football maybe?

She made a cup of tea, having failed to make one at the hospital, and took it with her to the front veranda, where she settled on the top step to look out at the sleeping town.

So far she'd met three available men, the meetings engineered by helpful friends or colleagues. There was the engineer, Rob Armstrong—a nice enough guy but she kind of suspected he might be holding a torch for Joss, and although Joss was happily married, he'd shown absolutely no interest in her, Emma.

Neil didn't need consideration, although maybe she was being a trifle unkind. There'd be some woman somewhere out there who'd love to know how many tons per acre a good mung bean crop should produce, he just wasn't Emma's cup of tea.

She drained the real cup of tea and sighed. She was fairly certain they'd done their winch practice on Shane's property so Marty could engineer a meeting between her and Shane.

Shane who?

Had she ever heard his surname?

Not that it mattered, just thinking of their possible wedding photos—hers and Shane's—with her looking like a midget beside him, was enough for her to know he wasn't worth pursuing.

This was ridiculous. None of these men had shown the slightest interest in her, and even if one had, how fair would it be to use any one of them as a distraction from Marty?

Marty, whose smile warmed her heart, whose touch sent shivers down her spine, and who was definitely not available...

She sighed, stood up, and made her way to bed.

At least all those 'man thoughts' had helped her shut away the feelings of loss that had hit her so hard at the hospital.

And she didn't really need a man. A housekeeper would be far better. The boys could kick footballs at kindy and school, and, anyway, she'd been quite good at soccer at school herself.

She'd kick footballs with them!

And just to prove she could, next morning saw her at the park down at the bottom of the hill, where children of all ages congregated to play—football kicking being only one of the activities.

She'd pushed the boys down in their stroller, although they'd both protested they were big enough to walk. Which they were, but she'd doubted they'd be happy walking back up the hill when they were tired from their play.

A cone-shaped, spider-web climbing frame soon became a favourite, and they were carefully negotiating their separate ways across the ropes when Marty turned up, sent on from the house by Ned.

'I just called in to give you an update on Izzy and George,' he said, smiling and waving at the two boys as he spoke.

'George?' echoed Emma.

Marty turned to grin at her.

'Exactly what I said, but I'm assured old-fashioned names are coming back,' Marty told her. 'I suppose we should be glad it wasn't Alfred.'

Emma laughed, although when she thought about it…

'Actually, I don't mind Alfie.'

'You *can't* be serious!' Marty said, then he dived forward to scoop up Xavier as he fell towards the soft sand beneath the climbing frame.

Emma watched as he set a far from worried little boy

back on the ropes, then stood back as another adult rushed towards his child.

An older child, a boy of about seven, was trying to push his sister off her perch above him, and as Emma watched the girl fell and the man hauled what was presumably his son off the ropes and smacked him, yelling at him for his actions at the same time.

Marty stepped forward, fists clenched, but Emma caught his arm.

He shook her off, but her touch must have calmed him down for he walked away, but not before Emma had seen his face, ashen with shock.

Or memories?

She gathered up her boys, who'd stopped climbing to look at the sobbing child, and followed Marty to where he'd dropped down onto a bench under a shady tree.

Should she say something?

Ask why it had upset him so badly?

Or did she need to ask?

He'd been a foster child, presumably taken from his family.

Because of an abusive father?

'I should have stepped in,' he said.

'And done what? Punched the man in front of his children? Met violence with violence in front of a dozen children?'

She sat beside him and rested her hand on his knee.

'I think he smacked the boy more out of shock than anger. He saw the girl fall and reacted. He was comforting both children when we left.'

Marty nodded, then moved his shoulders as if to shift a burden.

'I know no one likes to see a child being smacked, but why did you react to it like that?' she asked, though she doubted she'd get an answer. For all his outgoing, friendly manner, he was a very private man.

He didn't answer for so long she thought he wouldn't, but then he said, very quietly, 'There was violence in my home—my birth home. My father had an uncontrollable temper and flew into rages at the slightest provocation.'

He'd been looking into the distance but now he turned to her.

'It's in me, too, Emma, that rage. It's in me too.'

'Nonsense,' she said calmly, but he was already on his feet.

'Who's for ice cream?' he called to the two little boys, who were back on the climbing frame.

He got the response he wanted when they ran towards him, and he took a hand of each to lead them to the ice-cream van that was parked, almost permanently, on the other side of the park.

'I'll bring them back safely,' he said to Emma.

She smiled at him and said, 'I didn't doubt it for a minute—there's no one I'd rather trust my boys to than you, Marty Graham.'

But as she watched them walk away, she sighed.

Was friendship always so complicated?

Or was this friendship more complicated than usual because, deep down, she'd have liked it to be more than that?

Of course, it was, but her feelings towards Marty were so tangled up with who they both were—she remembering the pain of a lost love and he, now she understood, fearing his own genetic heritage.

Could love flourish when they both had the darkness of the past to contend with?

Could she take the risk...?

CHAPTER SEVEN

GOING TO WORK seemed something of an anticlimax after the excitements of the weekend, but once there Emma found it soothing to be back in a familiar environment, and even welcomed the rush of the busy morning—patients who hadn't wanted to waste their own precious time over the weekend in the local A and E came rolling in with a variety of complaints.

'Half these people should be visiting their GP,' Helen, no doubt suffering broken sleep patterns given her advanced pregnancy, grumbled.

'Or have come in earlier,' Emma said, having just admitted a small girl with a severe headache and the suggestion of a rash appearing on her body.

'Has she had her meningococcal vaccination?' Emma had asked the concerned parents.

'Oh, no, we don't believe in that kind of thing,' the mother had replied, while Emma had cursed under her breath and hoped it was just an infection that could be cleared up with antibiotics.

But she'd ordered a lumbar puncture to collect a sample of cerebrospinal fluid and in the meantime put the child on a strong antibiotic drip. And she'd spoken to the mother about the importance of vaccinations, not only to protect

the individual child but to stop many childhood diseases
reaching epidemic proportions once again.

She knew the woman hadn't listened—knew also it
wasn't because she was concerned for her child. No, this
particular parent had made a stand and had no intention
of changing her mind on the subject.

Recognising a lost cause, and admitting to herself that
everyone was entitled to their opinion, Emma had walked
away, though inwardly seething. Aware she couldn't meet
another patient in that state, she'd headed for the tea-room
to calm down.

Only to find Marty ensconced in the most comfortable
armchair. In fact, the *only* comfortable armchair, the room
seemingly furnished with odds and ends of rejected chairs
no one else wanted.

She glared at him and he held up his hands.

'Hey, what have *I* done?'

Sat in the chair I wanted.

No, she couldn't use such an inane excuse for her temper.

She made herself a coffee—instant.

'One day I'll buy a decent coffee machine for this place,'
she muttered to herself.

'Someone would probably pinch it,' Marty said laconi-
cally from the depths of the armchair. 'Is it instant coffee
that's got you all steamed up or something else?'

'Of course it's not instant coffee, although I hate the
stuff,' she stormed. 'It's parents who don't believe in vac-
cinating their children. Honestly, Marty, they must never
read a paper, never listen to the news to not know how
much danger they put not only their own child in but other
children in too. I know they have good reasons or beliefs,
but if they'd ever seen a child with meningococcal—a child
who's lost a limb, or his hearing, or even died, surely they
would agree it's better to be safe than sorry.'

He smiled the lazy smile that did funny things to her heart.

'As you said, they have their reasons or beliefs, and they've freedom of choice because we're not a police state—yet.'

Resisting an urge to throw her coffee at him, she settled into the next best chair, comfortable enough if you knew to sit on the left side so the loose spring on the right didn't get you.

'Maybe we should be in some instances,' she muttered darkly, although she knew she didn't mean it. 'Anyway, what are you doing here?'

'Brought you a family update,' he said, not smiling now but she knew from his eyes he was still amused by her tantrum. 'Mother and baby are both doing very well. The local GPs in Wetherby have offered to cover the hospital for Mac so he can stay down in Retford for as long as he feels he's needed. Hallie and Nikki will stay on for the week. I'll work out when I'll be off duty, so I can fly down and take them home.'

'So all's well that ends well,' Emma said with a smile. 'That's terrific. Will they transfer the baby here when he's old enough for us to cope with him in our PICU?'

Marty shook his head.

'I don't know for certain, but as he'd still be an hour away from their home if he's here, I can't see the point. They might as well stay there until he's due for discharge.'

It was a nice, normal conversation, so why did Emma feel it held undercurrents she couldn't understand?

She drank her much-maligned coffee, improving it slightly by dipping gingernut biscuits into it, so aware of Marty across from her, her nerve endings were screaming.

He'd lapsed into silence, which made things worse. Marty was usually good at casual banter—far better than she was. Having worn out the coffee conversation, *and* parents who didn't vaccinate their children, she had no idea where to start a new one.

Marty had sat forward—perhaps he was going to help out with some idle chatter.

Gossip, local news.

No such luck, for he fixed those blue eyes, serious now, on her face, and asked, 'Did you lose a baby? Before you had the twins?'

She couldn't speak, just stared at him. How on earth could he have picked that up?

And what business was it of his?

But she knew that was unfair—he hadn't asked out of curiosity but because he cared, because he was a caring man.

And suddenly it was easy...

'Not long after Simon died,' she told him quietly, glad she'd used up all her tears for the baby the night they'd brought Izzy in. 'I was stressed, lost in grief, I suppose, and didn't recognise the symptoms. I was only twenty-one weeks, the baby didn't have much chance of surviving and it didn't. She didn't.'

Well, he *had* asked, Marty muttered in his mind. And if staying in the chair—not crossing the room to take her in his arms and hold her—was the hardest thing he'd ever done, then too bad.

'You saw me crying—the night Izzy was brought in?' Emma had paled at his question but her voice was steady.

He had to nod—agree—because he *had* seen the hastily wiped-away tears and his heart had been gripped by pain.

But Emma seemed less upset now, so maybe he hadn't made a mistake in talking to her about it.

She was looking directly at him, and spoke slowly, as if finding the right words was difficult.

'I think I hadn't properly grieved for the baby,' she admitted. 'I was still so lost, still hurting over Simon, so the other night, when it all came rushing back, well...'

She half smiled, and he marvelled at her bravery.

'When something like that happens, at first you're angry—the "why me" thing. I'd been exactly the same with Simon, though more "why him". Then losing the baby, his baby, I felt as if my world had ended a second time and I just shut down.'

She paused, and though he ached to hold her, to comfort her—protect her really—he stayed still and silent, aware she hadn't finished and probably needed to say more.

'In a way it was a good thing, the tears the other night. They released something that had been pent up inside me for too long,' she finished, standing up and crossing to the sink to wash out her cup, returning the biscuits to their tin.

Her movement told him the subject was closed—probably forever. But how could he not love this small woman who had been through so much, yet soldiered on, wanting only the best for her patients and the very best for her boys, her father, her family?

A woman who trusted him with her children...

'I've got to get back to work,' she said, telling him in no uncertain terms that the intimacies were over.

Although...

She'd stopped at the door and turned back towards him.

'And now I've told you my last bit of secret pain, sometime you can tell me yours.'

He was dumbfounded.

'Secret pain?' he echoed, and she smiled and nodded.

'That innocent act doesn't fool me for one minute, Marty Graham. Next time it's your turn to talk.'

Emma returned to work in a more positive state of mind. She'd vented her anger and shared something very personal with a friend—something she hadn't done for a very long time.

A friend?

The tiny whisper in her head was nothing more than wishful thinking. Marty was a friend, full stop.

Fortunately, before that devious voice could whisper again, she was diverted by two patients, herded into A and E by a large and obviously angry man.

'Bloody idiots,' he said, waving his hand towards the two teenagers who'd sunk down onto the nearest chairs, blood visible on the hands that held their respective heads.

'Fighting in the school grounds—which is banned,' the man continued, 'and over which football team is the best, of all things. What does *that* say about sport?'

Helen was there, leading one of the combatants towards a cubicle, while Joss appeared to take the other one.

'I think it's only minor damage—a lot of blood from head wounds, but we need to get them checked out,' the man said, then, as if remembering his manners, he held out his hand.

'I'm Andy Richards, assistant sports master at the high school. You're new here, aren't you?'

Emma took his hand—a nice firm hand.

'I'm Emma Crawford, and, yes, I'm new in town.'

He studied her for a minute.

'You're not by any chance Ned Crawford's daughter?'

Emma nodded.

'Do you know my father?'

Andy grinned at her.

'No, not had the pleasure, but if I've heard one story about what Ned and my father got up to in the "old days"—' he gave the words inverted commas with his fingers '—I've heard a dozen. Dad hasn't been well lately, which might explain why he hasn't realised Ned's daughter is in town. I know he'd love to meet you.'

'Then maybe he'd also like to see my father,' Emma suggested. 'He's back in town with me. I'm a single mum so he looks after my boys when I'm at work, and generally takes care of things. But I know he wants to catch up with old friends. I'd better see to your two lads now, but if you give me your father's number, Dad can give him a call.'

Andy produced a pen and a rather grubby piece of paper from his pocket and jotted down a number.

'I live there too—with Dad,' he said, and she had a feeling he was telling that bit to her, not as a message to her father.

She put the note in her pocket and hurried to the first cubicle, where Angie had cleaned up a forehead wound and was busy putting plastic strips across it.

'I don't think it needs stitching,' she said. 'What do you think?'

Emma agreed with her and left her to finish the dressing. But the second combatant had come off the worse for wear, a cut close to his eye definitely needing stitching, and he had enough bruising on his face, especially near the temple, for Emma to decide a CAT scan was necessary.

'It's purely precautionary,' she told their patient. 'I'll put a temporary dressing on that cut until after I've seen the scan.'

Not that the scan would make any difference to her treatment of the wound, but she felt it was more urgent than a few stitches.

She left Joss with him to arrange the scan, then crossed the room to explain to Andy what they were doing.

'It won't take long, but if you need to get back, we could phone when he's ready to leave.'

Andy shook his head.

'I'll stay—duty of care and all that.'

She smiled at him.

'Something we're all only too aware of these days,' she agreed.

It was close to an hour before she'd finally stitched the cut, and between patients had stopped a few times to speak to Andy. He seemed a really nice guy, and if he lived with his father, maybe he *was* single—

What on earth was she thinking?

Was she really stalking the single men of Braxton?

Hadn't she decided she could kick a football with the best of men?

And that she'd get a housekeeper to free up her father? After all, she could afford one…

Or was she using the 'single men' idea in her head to stop her thinking of Marty?

Some questions had no answers.

The days flowed smoothly after that, and Emma realised she was getting into the routine of the hospital, fitting in as she learnt the ways that things were done, and feeling comfortable at work. She'd found she liked being part of a smaller hospital where the different departments all mixed far more than they did in city hospitals.

And it was easier to follow the progress of a patient she'd admitted than it had been in the labyrinth of wards where she'd worked before.

Yes, all in all, it was great.

Until late on Friday afternoon, when one of the coast-guard officers called the emergency line.

'We've got a seaman badly injured on a large container ship east of Wetherby. I've alerted helicopter rescue but we'll need to drop a doctor on board to check him out before he can be moved.'

Emma sighed.

If there was one thing she hated more than winch practice it was being winched onto the deck of a moving ship. Not that she'd done it for real, but the practice sessions on Sydney Harbour had been terrifying.

But it was her call. The doctor who'd come in on the swing shift was too old for helicopter work but would cover her in A and E.

She took the phone.

'How badly hurt? And do we know how it happened?'

'They've come through some bad weather and it's still a bit rough out there, but he was checking the chains on the containers when one moved and trapped him somehow. We're thinking crush injuries to his legs and chest, and probable internal injuries.'

She *had* to go!

She thanked the man absentmindedly, her mind racing as she thought of drugs and equipment she might need. She could already hear the helicopter approaching but by the time it put down she was ready for it, scrambling on board with Mark's helping hand.

Mark handed her a flight suit and helmet, and she hurriedly pulled them on, replacing the sneakers she wore to work with the sturdy boots, her pair now marked with an E for Emma.

And lastly the helmet.

But she no sooner had it strapped into place than Marty's voice came blasting through it.

'Are you up to this?' he demanded. 'Have you had marine rescue training? Mark's a qualified paramedic, he can go down to the boat if you're not sure.'

Put out by his doubts about her ability, her replies were naturally tetchy.

'Yes, I am up to it,' she snapped, 'and, yes, wonder of wonders, I've done marine rescue training, and if you think landing on a small motor boat on Sydney Harbour in gale-force winds is easier than landing on the massive deck of a container ship, then you've never tried it.'

She paused before remembering the last bit of his conversation.

'And although Mark's a great paramedic, just maybe someone who's had a container land on him actually needs a doctor.'

A silent clapping from Mark made heat rise to her cheeks. She'd broadcast her conversation to all of them, rather than holding the button that would have taken it only to Marty.

'Stop it,' she hissed at Mark, who was grinning with delight.

'No way,' he whispered, his mic well away from his lips. 'The boss needs to be put in his place now and then. He's far too protective of all of us.'

Which, Emma decided as she tightened the straps on the harness that would hook her to the winch, was probably a good thing.

And another good thing was that it wasn't personal. Marty behaved protectively towards all his crew, not just her.

They saw the slowly moving vessel within minutes of crossing the coastline, and Emma watched as it grew bigger and bigger. Then it was beneath them, Marty matching his speed to it, holding the chopper at a steady pace above a mark the crew had painted on the deck. Mark clipped her and her bag to the winch before opening the side door, and after a quick prayer to any god that might have been hovering nearby, she sat in the doorway, took a deep breath, signalled she was ready to go and began her careful descent.

The wind wasn't as strong as she'd expected, but it gusted unpredictably, teasing her with a push or shove every now and then.

The crewmen awaiting her were close now, their excitement rising in their voices. Someone caught her legs and guided them down onto the deck, where Emma unclipped herself and her bag and sent the wire back up for the stretcher.

None of them had had any doubt that it would be needed.

Her patient lay in the shadow of the towers of containers, and Emma could see the one that had moved slightly out of alignment, apparently pushing him against the next, though what he'd been doing between the two she couldn't fathom.

Not her problem.

One of the crewmen, wearing a uniform that suggested rank, explained what had happened in careful English, then added, 'He was conscious at first, but then not. I do not think his head was injured, but he is not speaking.'

Even before examining the extent of his injuries, Emma could believe he'd passed out because of pain. Which was better as far as she was concerned. Giving pain relief to a patient likely to be heading straight into Theatre was always tricky.

She knelt to examine the man, lifting temporary dressings off his legs, shuddering at the damage that had been done.

Airway!

His breathing was rapid but shallow and his lips slightly blue. It hardly needed the misalignment of the trachea to tell her the cause.

Tension pneumothorax.

She found the needle she needed and inserted it into the second rib space on the damaged side, drew up some air into the syringe, then carefully withdrew the needle, leaving the cannula in place.

Air rushing out told her she'd done the right thing, although she knew this was only temporary relief for the blood vessels in the man's chest. She secured the tube, fixed a loose dressing over it, and checked his blood pressure.

Far too low, but the best thing she could do was get him on the stretcher and into the chopper, where she could work on him as they flew him to hospital.

With the help of the crew, they slid the two sides of the stretcher under him and clicked the parts together, then wrapped him in the protective wings and fastened the straps that held him securely in place.

Worried that a vertical lift might injure him further, she radioed up to let Dave know she was sending him up, attaching four straps to the winch wire, and signalling to lift.

As ever, it seemed to take an age for the winch wire to descend again for her, but when it did, a crewman handed it to her and she slid the little seat between her legs and clipped on, signalling again to lift.

By the time she unclipped back in the helicopter, Mark had the stretcher secure and a cannula inserted in the man's hand, ready for fluid resuscitation, and an oxygen mask on his face.

'Braxton or straight to Retford?' Marty asked.

'Retford,' Emma told him, aware that the Braxton Hospital didn't have the surgical teams the man would need.

Working carefully, she and Mark removed the man's boots, cutting the laces to ease them off his feet before cutting away his socks and the tattered clothing on his legs. They irrigated the wounds, squirting most of the loose debris away, but had to resort to tweezers for the deeper pieces.

'It's a mercy he's unconscious,' Mark said as they wrapped clean dressings around the injured limbs. The tibia was broken on both legs and from the position of the break, Emma suspected the fibula would also have suffered. But the breaks were above the ankles, which would make surgery and recovery simpler.

His thighs were less damaged.

'Probably because his right hip bone and pelvis bore the brunt of the pressure,' Mark said, but for all the IV fluids they were pumping into him, his blood pressure remained worryingly low.

Had a major blood vessel been impacted when his chest had been caught by the great weight? But wouldn't he have already bled out if that was the case? The question tormented Emma.

Should they put down in Braxton first so a surgeon could open him up to look for a rupture?

'ETA Retford thirty minutes.'

Marty's message decided her. Retford was definitely the best option.

She radioed her findings to Retford Hospital, adding her suspicion about internal bleeding, so was pleased to see a crash team waiting as they touched down.

The man was rushed straight into Theatre, and she sat in the doorway of the helicopter to complete her paperwork. One copy had accompanied the man, but this second sheet was required for the Search and rescue service records.

'You want to come and see George?' Marty asked, dropping down to sit beside her.

Did she?

Her boys had been premmie, but only by six weeks, but she'd still spent enough time in a PICU to know she didn't really like the places. There was always a positive vibe, and few premmie babies were ever lost, but the sight of the wee mites in their cribs brought back memories of the baby she had lost—the baby who had been too small to save.

'No, thanks,' she said, but probably so long after he'd asked the question that he'd guess what she'd been thinking.

'No worries, but I'm popping in to see the family, so

why don't you go over to the canteen? Dave and Mark will be there. We'll leave in thirty minutes unless there's another callout, in which case I'll contact you.'

He jumped to the ground and walked away, leaving Emma feeling very alone, and more than slightly put out.

Normally, Marty would touch her shoulder as he passed her, or at least turn around and wave if he was walking away.

Had she let him down, not going to see George?

Oh, for heaven's sake, get your head on straight, she berated herself. There was no reason on earth why Marty should wave or touch her shoulder. In fact, it was far better that he didn't because if either thing had happened it would have affected her body in ways she didn't want— her shoulder would have felt warm where his hand had been, while a wave, or the smile that always accompanied it, would have sent shivers down her spine.

But physical reactions stemmed from attraction—that's all it was. After all, he was an attractive man—hadn't half the women in town been attracted to him at some time?

And if it was attraction, then all she had to do was resist it…

Marty headed straight for the PICU, knowing at least one of the family would be there.

Mac and Nikki were.

'Hallie's taken Izzy to get some clothes—little essentials like underwear and nightdresses and stuff to wear during the day,' Mac explained.

'And I'm in charge of George,' Nikki announced. 'Of talking to him, I mean. You have to talk to the babies, did you know that? I've been telling him about Wetherby and how we'll play in the sand when he gets a bit bigger and how I'll help him make sandcastles with moats around them and even volcanoes.'

'Might be a while before you get to volcanoes,' Mac put in drily.

Marty laughed, then bent to examine his new nephew.

'He certainly looks good, given how premmie he is,' he said, and Mac nodded.

'He's the unit champ already,' he said, and the note of pride in Mac's voice pierced through a special shield Marty had wrapped around his heart.

No babies! he reminded himself, but he knew the wound remained and always would.

But Nikki was pointing out his tiny toes, and Marty found a smile for this girl he'd known since she'd been born.

'You were in a crib like this, and you had even tinier toes,' he told her, and she laughed.

Which was a good way to leave them, Marty decided.

'Well, I'd better get the crew back to Braxton,' he said, kissing Nikki and patting Mac on the shoulder. 'Give Izzy my love, and Nikki, tell Hallie to phone me when you're both ready to go home.'

'I can phone you. I do have a phone, you know,' Nikki told him, so he was smiling as he left.

Still smiling when he reached the chopper to find Emma sitting where he'd left her.

'Didn't you want refreshment?' he asked, and she looked up as if he'd startled her.

Her eyes met his and messages he couldn't understand seemed to flash between them, messages that made him feel hot, and light-headed at the same time.

Made him want to close the distance between them in long strides and take her in his arms...

Kiss the eyes that sent him messages...

Was he nuts?

This was Emma.

Emma, who'd already suffered two terrible losses in her

life. No way could he cause her more disruption. Yes, he was attracted to her—maybe very attracted to her—but...

But what?

Love?

He shook his head in an attempt to clear it, aware that this wasn't the first time that word had filled it when he thought of Emma...

She watched him walk towards her, feeling such a mix of emotions she didn't have a clue which one dominated.

Attraction was in there for sure, but it was more than that. It was something deep inside her gut, some instinct that was telling her stupid things, telling her this man was important in her life and—worse—that she wanted him there.

He *is* in your life, stupid, she told herself. He's a friend, a colleague, almost a relation if Ned's friendship with Carrie leads to something more...

He'd reached her now, and settled himself beside her in the doorway.

'Tell me?'

It was gently asked, his voice deep and slightly husky, and it would have been foolishly naïve to ask him what he meant.

'I met Simon, my husband, when I started work as an intern in the ED of a big Sydney hospital. He was senior staff and I knew he'd barely notice me, but he did. I'd already noticed him—thought him wonderful, and although at the time that was more hero worship of a junior to a very accomplished man, I found out he *was* wonderful. He was everything a top ED specialist should be—kind, caring, compassionate yet firm with drunks and time-wasters.'

She glanced at Marty, wondering how he was taking this—really wondering why he'd asked...

'Tough competition for any bloke coming along now,' he said, and she felt a little spurt of anger.

'Well, it shouldn't worry you, because you're not, are you?'

'Not what?' he asked, all innocence.

'Competition! You don't do commitment, remember?' she snapped. 'Now, do you want me to finish or not?'

Talking about Simon had stirred up the memories she usually kept tucked carefully away in a box in the back of her mind, but now she saw him in her mind's eye, striding through the ED, flashing a smile here, touching a shoulder there, always so equable, so patient—always with time for everyone.

Especially for her.

Always for her...

'Please,' Marty said, and it took her a moment to remember what she'd asked.

Could she go on?

Best if she did.

Hadn't Dad been telling her she should talk about the man she'd loved, if only for the boys' sake?

'We got married; I kept working until I fell pregnant then Simon began to get headaches, not telling me at first—not, in fact, until he'd seen a specialist, had all the scans and tests, and been told he only had six weeks to live.'

Try as she might, she couldn't shut the box of memories now and her eyes blurred with tears.

'I've told you most of the rest—the "why me" reaction that is purely selfish, then living with a loved one's pain, feeling his suffering and knowing I couldn't ease it, pretending all the time that life goes on when, really, it doesn't—it stands still, seemingly forever...'

'And the boys?'

The question was so out of left field, so startling, she forgot her tears, and just stared at the man who'd asked it.

'You were pregnant but you lost that baby,' he reminded her gently, moving closer to put his arm around her shoulders.

The pain she'd been feeling receded.

'I think the day Simon had the news, he went to see Stephen. They'd been contemporaries at university. Simon and I—we'd talked about our family, what we'd like in the way of kids. We knew we wanted more than one, so just in case I ever decided to have another one, he had some sperm frozen.'

Emma paused, wondering if talking about stuff you didn't want to talk about really was cathartic, because somehow now she was feeling better.

'For a long time after I'd lost the first baby, having another just wasn't on the agenda. I was still grieving for Simon and for his baby—our baby—as well, so I'd completely forgotten the frozen sperm.'

She paused, thinking back to that momentous day when Dad had suggested using it.

And smiled.

'Dad suggested it, promised to help, to mind the baby while I kept on working. It was three years after Simon's death and I must have been ready, because suddenly it was the best idea I'd ever heard. I went to see Stephen and the rest, as they say, is history. The very best part of it was that I conceived not one but two babies.'

Marty drew her closer and clasped her hands in his, aware how hard it would have been for her to tell this story. But she'd been through so much loss and pain *his* heart hurt, thinking about it.

But now he understood her detached approach to the

search for a father for the twins. She'd suffered too much to want to love again—to risk that terrible pain...

So he sat and held her, felt her warmth, knew whatever it was between them could not continue.

Except for friendship.

That he could provide...

CHAPTER EIGHT

BY THE TIME they touched down at the base in Braxton, Emma was well and truly off duty.

'You want a lift home?' Mark asked, as the pair of them stripped off their flight suits and hung them on the pegs in the big shed that was the headquarters of Braxton Search and Rescue.

But Marty was right behind them, and he spoke before Emma could reply.

'Don't worry, I'll take her, it's on my way.'

'Do I get to choose?' Emma muttered, then realised it was a stupid thing to have said. She'd far rather Marty drove her home, although wouldn't it be better if she went with Mark?

No temptation that way, no time to study the way Marty's hands held the steering wheel, the precise but effortless way he drove; no need to sit there revelling in the warmth that just being close to him always provided. No need to torture herself.

Especially after the way she'd poured out her heart to him!

But while these ridiculous thoughts tumbled through her head the matter had been decided. While she'd been thinking of his hands on the steering wheel, and whether or not she regretted telling him about Simon, he'd answered her question with a sharp, inarguable 'No'.

Feeling aggrieved, she followed him out to his vehicle, clambering into the big four-wheel drive.

'Where does Mark live?' she asked, still put out by his making her decision for her.

'Way out the other side of town and he'll have his wife and kids waiting for him. They always hear the chopper go over so they know exactly when he'll be home.'

'Is this your subtle way of telling me he's a married man? Warning me off?'

He didn't answer, so she added, 'Anyway, I already knew that. He's told me all about his family.'

Marty sighed, then pulled over to the side of the road and turned off the engine.

He stared out through the windscreen for a few moments then said, 'I can't keep doing this.'

As he was still studying the road ahead and perhaps the bush that surrounded them, Emma could only see his profile and it wasn't telling her anything.

'This what?' she asked, and he turned towards her, reaching out as if to touch her.

'*This*,' he said. 'This being close to you, finding excuses to be near you, aching for you in every cell in my body but knowing I've no right to even be touching you.'

Emma turned to fully face him and caught his hands in hers.

'Why haven't you?' she asked. 'Just tell me why.'

He shook his head and went back to staring out the windscreen.

Heart pounding, Emma undid the clasp of her seatbelt and manoeuvred across the seat to get as close as she could to him.

She put her hand on his cheek and turned his face towards her, then leaned forward and kissed him on the lips.

They were warm, his lips, but still, and for a long, dreadful moment she thought she'd done the wrong thing—totally wrecked whatever it was they had.

Or didn't have…

Then his lips responded and he turned his body, reaching out to draw her close, to hold her in an iron clasp while his lips devoured hers, feasting on them—a starving man finding food…

Her heat matched his, burning in her body, lips opening, tongues tangling, little moans coming from one or other of them, maybe both, Emma didn't know.

She only knew that this was what she'd wanted, yet hadn't wanted, what she'd missed, but hadn't wanted to miss.

The engine noise of an approaching car broke them apart, and they both straightened in their seats, *both* looking through the windscreen now, panting slightly.

The car passed and Marty started the engine of his vehicle, pulling carefully back onto the road.

Emma re-buckled her seatbelt, too confused to speak, hardly daring to look at the man who'd aroused such fire in her.

But was it only fire?

Need?

Lust?

Or something more?

Fire and need would be okay. Maybe even lust. They could have an affair, try to keep it quiet. They spent so much time together anyway, maybe it would go unnoticed…

Except by her father, who would be the one minding the boys while she was with Marty, which would mean putting more responsibility on him when she was trying to free him up to live his own life.

'I can't have an affair.'

She blurted out the end result of all her torturous thoughts as Marty pulled up outside her house.

'It wouldn't be fair on Dad. Especially now when he's just begun to have a little bit of social life himself.'

Marty turned towards her, one side of his mouth lifting in a rueful smile.

'I was about to say the same thing,' he said, reaching out to cup her cheek in one hand and rub his thumb across her undoubtedly swollen lips. 'I couldn't do that to you. Couldn't have you join the list as "another one of Marty's women" because you are way, way more than that to me.'

He shook his head, not smiling now.

'So, we're stuck, aren't we?'

Unless it wasn't an affair, the treacherous voice in Emma's head whispered, and it was her turn to shake her head. Getting married again was a sensible, practical idea for her and she had no doubt she'd grow to love the man she married.

In time...

But the thing she didn't want was passion, because that way heartbreak lay...

Yet whatever it was that had flared between her and Marty was definitely passion, the kind, she feared, that would deepen and spread like wildfire through her body, steal the heart she'd have to grow again, and fill her life.

Which meant commitment—the one thing Marty didn't want.

She leaned across and kissed his cheek.

'Thanks for the lift,' she said, and slid out of the car.

Marty drove home, his body throbbing, his mind in turmoil as anger at his foolish action raged back and forth.

He'd stopped the car because the urge to kiss the woman

he'd been with—to hold her in his arms and feel her body against his and, yes, to kiss her senseless—had been so strong he'd feared he'd have an accident if he'd kept driving.

Had it been Mark's offer to drive Emma home that had lit the touch-paper?

Or had it happened earlier when he'd walked back to the chopper and seen her sitting in the doorway—watching him. Something he couldn't read in her eyes. Something he couldn't read yet still excited him.

Then she'd told him about her husband—about Simon's death—had poured out her heart to him and he'd…

What?

Whatever, he'd stopped the car to cool down—to get his head together—and the damn woman had kissed him.

Not just kissed him but responded to his kisses with white-hot fire that had burned through his body like a fever.

Which left him where exactly?

Apart from frustrated as hell…

He'd just have to avoid her whenever possible, quite easy, really, a lot of his flights didn't involve a doctor…

He remembered her little boys, their hands placed so trustingly in his when they'd gone for ice cream, and he thought his heart might break.

But his sudden surge of temper just before that happy moment had reminded him genetics ruled.

Okay, so he probably wouldn't have hit the bloke for smacking his kid, even without Emma's touch on his arm, but he'd wanted to…

Yet hadn't Emma said, even after seeing that, that she'd trust him more than anyone with her boys?

Could he get past the so hated, yet still so vivid image of his father's raised arm, his mother falling with the baby…

Could he deny his genes?

* * *

Refusing to think about what had happened in the car and adamant not to dwell on her reaction to Marty's kiss, Emma had marched into the house determined on action.

'You're home early,' her father called to her. 'The boys are still asleep.'

'That's great,' she said, joining him in the kitchen where the sight of him, ironing board out, carefully ironing small T-shirts strengthened her resolve.

'What afternoons does the bridge club meet?' she asked.

'And why would you want to know?' he asked, not looking at her as he folded the now ironed shirt into a neat square.

He was *so* much better at this housework stuff than she was!

'Because I'm about to employ a housekeeper,' she announced. 'I've been thinking it over for a while, and now we've settled in up here, it's time I made a move. Not full time, I wouldn't think, but a few days a week, and, no, it's not for your sake but for mine.'

'I'm not good enough?' her father teased.

'You're too damned good,' Emma retorted. 'So much so I've taken you for granted for far too long. I know I would never have coped alone when Simon died, let alone even thought of having children, but I'm fine now, and you need your life back.'

'But—'

Emma held up her hand.

'No, don't tell me how much you've loved doing it or any other nonsense. I know you love the kids and me, but we can't be your whole life, not anymore. You deserve better than that, Dad, and it's your turn now.'

Her father picked up another tiny shirt, smoothed it flat on the ironing board, and carefully pushed the iron across it, and only when it was done and folded, sitting on top of the small pile, did he look at her again.

'I *have* enjoyed it,' he said, smiling at her. 'Every last minute of it, although we've had some hairy times, haven't we?'

Emma smiled at him, thinking of the night Xavier had had croup, and her father had been on a rare night out and she'd driven to the house where he'd been having dinner with friends to leave Hamish with him before taking Xavier to the hospital.

'Some,' she admitted.

She made herself a sandwich and a cup of tea then retired to the room they'd allocated as an office in the big, rambling, old house. Setting the snack down on the desk, she pulled out the book where they kept phone numbers, knowing Carrie's number would be in it.

But Carrie was in Retford, and possibly in the PICU where no phones were allowed...

Would Joss be home? She'd be off duty by now, and as she'd grown up in Braxton she'd be sure to know someone who'd know someone who might be able to help.

Joss put her on to her mother, Mrs Carstairs, who was only too happy to recommend a couple of women, giving Emma the names and numbers, and adding, 'Christine, the first one, probably needs the money most,' she said, 'and she's wonderful with children. She used to work at the childcare centre until the new regulations came in about all helpers needing at least six months at a training course before they could work there. All nonsense, of course, because six months at a college doesn't help you comfort a child who's not feeling well, or tell you when a child needs a cuddle.'

Emma smiled at the woman's disgust but she understood what she was saying, although she was pretty sure these days the college courses for early childhood education would include a fair amount of work in kindergartens, spending hands-on time with children.

As predicted, Christine was delighted at the idea and, yes, she could call around at Emma's house in an hour, by which time the boys would certainly be awake, and hopefully in good moods after their sleeps.

Research time…

Emma opened her laptop and searched for childcare wages. She'd known for some time she'd have to get a local accountant but had been putting it off. If she was going to become an employer, she'd need him to work out things like superannuation. But at least that could wait until Carrie got back, or she could ask the nurses at work. Right now, she had to pin her father down to what day the bridge club met, and whether he wanted to take up bowls again.

And if, at the back of her mind, there was a whispered suggestion that employing a housekeeper could also free her up to have more of a life outside work and childcare, she ignored it.

Although that Andy Richards had seemed a nice guy…

And wouldn't finding someone else, even on a temporary basis, help her ignore her futile feelings for Marty?

Probably not, but at least she could try…

Marty flew back to Retford a few days later in his own chopper to collect Hallie and Nikki, delivering them safely to Wetherby and deciding to stay the night.

Sometimes a bit of time with Pop in the shed, a night in his old bedroom, and a chat about nothing in particular with Hallie got his head straightened out. But it was not to be. Although he felt relaxed and happy in his old home, he also realised the problem that was Emma would never straighten out.

The best strategy, as he'd decided after the fateful kiss, was avoidance and although he dismissed moving to another base—he's miss his family too much—if he kept busy, and found another woman to squire around town, then surely he wouldn't see too much of her and that would be that.

But fate conspired against him.

He thought Carrie's birthday celebration, on a Saturday night, would be okay because the girls were throwing the party for her. Marty knew Carrie was seeing a bit of Ned so he would be there for sure, and without the girls to babysit, Emma would be stuck at home.

Of course, that was before he'd heard about Christine, or learned that she was always happy to do extra hours, babysitting.

Neither had he heard about Andy.

Well, he knew Andy, had been at school with him, and although they didn't see much of each other these days, they were still quite friendly.

Until his old school-mate arrived at the party with Emma, so it was a double shock. Seeing Emma, and, what was worse, seeing her with another man—particularly a man he liked and respected...

He prayed for a callout, because there was no other way he'd get out of his sister's birthday party. But no matter how many times he checked that his phone was turned on and, no, there'd been no missed messages, no call came.

So he made himself useful, filling people's glasses, passing around the canapes the girls had prepared, chatting to Pop and Hallie, and Carrie's friends from school. Avoiding Emma and Andy and the group of locals who would normally have been his chosen company at any party.

But there were only so many glasses to be filled, and the canapés ran out so he sought refuge on the back veranda, only to back away through the door when he saw one of his nieces out there in the passionate embrace of what was probably a spotty youth.

He could leave.

He'd done his duty.

He found Mandy—so it was Molly on the veranda—in the kitchen and was about to say goodbye when his phone buzzed in his pocket.

He dug it out and positively beamed at it.

'Have to go, pet,' he said. 'Lovely party, say goodbye to your mum for me.'

He kissed her cheek and slipped away, hurrying out the back way, so it wasn't until he reached the gate that he realised someone was coming down the steps behind him.

'Can you give me a lift?'

Of course, it was Emma!

'Isn't anyone else ever on callout duty at that hospital?' he demanded, as heat and despair battled in his body.

'Nope,' she said, far too cheerfully. 'You're going to be stuck with me for a couple more months, at least while Paul's still having chemo.'

The reminder made him feel terrible. Paul Robbins, father of four, had been diagnosed with lymphoma and although it was one of the less aggressive forms of the disease, he still had to undergo some treatment.

'What have you heard?' he asked, as he opened the vehicle door for her.

She turned to look at him as the interior lights came on, her face a little pale.

'Possible heart attack, maybe stroke. It was a very confused call, out on some road I've never heard of where there's no ambulance access. An old man in pain—a hermit of some kind? Somewhere between here and Wetherby, is it?'

He nodded, shutting the door as she settled in and hurrying around to the driver's side.

'Ken Irvine, he's an old timber cutter who lives out in the bush.'

* * *

Emma had squashed herself as close to the door as possible in case the urge to touch Marty—just to feel the warmth of him—was made harder by an accidental brush of clothing. She'd been watching him—surreptitiously, she hoped—all evening, whilst keeping up with the conversation between Andy and the people he knew.

After all, *she'd* invited Andy, bumping into him down town where she'd been shopping for some new jeans. Thinking, hoping, *needing* a distraction from the man she couldn't have…

Yet the minute Marty had walked in, she'd known it wasn't going to work—that no matter who she saw, or met, they wouldn't ever banish the memories of that kiss.

Which was ridiculous, because that's all it had been—a kiss!

'Do you know the place?' she asked as the silence stretching between them reached snapping point.

'From when I was a kid,' he said. 'I remember going out there the first time with Pop. You could only drive to within about six miles of his hut, then walked in the rest of the way. He had a horse and cart, would you believe, and would drive you back to the car in that. He'd once felled huge cedars in the forest, but now he pulls out old fallen timber and cuts it for firewood. Nowadays, the track gets you to within about two miles of the hut, but he still has the horse and cart to haul the cut wood to your car.'

'How does he exist?' Emma asked. 'What does he do for food? Does he take the horse and cart to town?'

'Until recently he did, although I've a feeling he's stopped coming—maybe his horse died. One of the home care people goes out from time to time to check on him, and he's had a phone connected so he can order anything he needs and someone in town will always take it out. I've sometimes taken my little chopper in there—actually took it in with a couple of friends a year or two ago to clear a space big enough for the rescue helicopter—but on the whole, he'd far rather people stayed away.'

They'd pulled up at the base, where Dave was waiting for them.

'As far as I can make out, they don't know what happened but he'll probably need to be brought back to town for checking,' Dave said. 'He should be kept in town now. He's far too old to be out there on his own.'

Dave looked from Marty to Emma.

'If you've got Emma, do you need me?' he asked. 'It's only that I've left my eldest looking after the younger kids and the baby's not that well.'

Emma looked at Marty—he was the boss in these situations.

'It's fine with me,' she said, and he shrugged.

'Me, too,' he said, but Emma guessed it wasn't all that fine.

Was he wanting to spend as little time with her as she was with him?

Dave had brought her bag from the hospital so she climbed in, settling in Mark's seat, and wondering if Marty would suggest she move up front.

He didn't, which really didn't bother her, although as they flew through the night she realised she wouldn't have minded seeing the forest at night, looking for animals the searchlight might pick out.

It was a short flight, and they landed not far from a small shack, where a light flickered uncertainly.

An old kerosene lantern, Emma realised when she followed Marty into the shack.

Ken had managed to crawl to where the phone stood on a small table, but once there had obviously collapsed. She knelt beside the old man's body while Marty held the lamp a little closer for her.

'This light won't do,' he said, setting the lamp down on the table where the phone must have been. 'I'll see what I can find.'

But Emma knew it wasn't necessary to have more light. Ken was barely conscious, his pulse thready and his breathing raspy and shallow.

Yet he had the strength to grasp her wrist.

'Don' take me from me home,' he whispered. 'Le' me die in me own bed.'

'Marty,' she called softly. 'Can you help me lift him onto his bed?'

He appeared beside her.

'Surely we should be lifting him onto a stretcher?' he asked, and she shook her head.

'He called for help,' Marty persisted.

'I'll take his legs,' Emma said, ignoring his protest.

She leant down towards Ken.

'We'll lift you onto the bed, it shouldn't hurt.'

For a moment, she thought Marty would argue, but in the end he knelt and gently lifted the man into his arms, dispensing with Emma's services and carrying him to the old bed in a corner of the room, wrapping a faded quilt around him to keep him warm.

Emma followed, bending to examine him, seeing the distortion of his face that told of a stroke, the blue colour of his lips, and the old man's struggle to breathe.

She took Ken's hand in both of hers, and held it tightly.

'This is a beautiful, peaceful place,' she said quietly.

Ken smiled.

'Built it all meself,' he told her, and she could still hear pride in the weak, quavery voice.

'Found the clearing when I was cutting big stuff, saw the creek nearby, and knew it was for me.'

The words took a long time to come out, and were indistinct at best, yet Emma knew the old man wanted her—or them—to understand.

'Been a good home,' he said. 'Good life.'

His eyes closed and it seemed as if he dozed, then the hand Emma still held squeezed her fingers.

'You won't leave me?'

Emma gently returned the pressure.

'No way, Ken. Marty and I will be right here.'

The rheumy eyes opened and he looked at her and smiled, a tremulous spread of blueish lips over tobacco-stained teeth.

'Never thought I'd 'ave a pretty girl with me when I died,' he joked, and Emma had to fight to hold back tears.

Had Marty sensed her distress that he joined the conversation?

'Every bloke deserves a pretty girl to be with him at the end,' he told Ken. 'Really, it's the only way to go.'

But although Ken smiled, Emma had heard the tremor in Marty's voice, and knew he, too, was affected.

Marty had found a stool and he'd pulled it over so he sat close to Emma by the bed, and he talked softly, reminding Ken about his visits here. And now and then Ken added memories of his own, about the bush around his hut, the animals who'd shared his life here, deep in the forest.

'You were lucky the bushfire missed you,' Emma said at one stage, and the old man, whose breathing had become raspy and uneven, shook his head.

'Gullies east of range don't burn,' he managed between faltering breaths. 'Worked it out.'

And he smiled...

He was breathing still, deep breaths followed by a pause...

'Cheyne-Stokes,' Marty whispered, and Emma nodded.

In the past it had been known as the death rattle but,

whatever its name, they both knew it meant the end was in sight.

The crackle of Marty's radio broke the silence, and as he stood to go outside to answer the call, Emma said, 'I can't leave him.'

'As if we would,' Marty retorted softly, before disappearing into the darkness.

He was back within minutes, sitting down again beside Emma.

'If there's a call I'll have to go,' he said quietly, and she nodded.

'I suppose me too if I'm needed.'

Marty didn't answer, but he slid his arm around her waist and they sat together, keeping vigil over the old man, both praying they could stay so he had company on his last night on earth.

'So talk to me,' Emma murmured to Marty when the old man had drifted into a deep coma. 'Tell me why no commitment? You're a warm, loving person, you're good with kids, why the rule?'

He was silent for so long she began to think he wouldn't answer, then he took his arm from around her waist and held her free hand instead, moving his stool just a little away from her and Ken.

'My father killed my mother, Em,' he said, barely breathing the words so she had to strain to listen, certain Ken wouldn't hear them.

'He killed her and the baby she held in her arms. He lifted up his arm and struck her. I watched her fall and heard the silence—a silence so loud I've never forgotten it. I don't remember if he knelt to touch her, to see if she was dead, although looking back I knew she'd hit the corner of the table in her fall. My father ran howling from the room—gone—and no one knew until I don't know how long later when I was in hospital and someone told me he was dead.'

She used the hand he held to draw him closer.

'You were how old?'

They were both whispering, the words disappearing into the darkness of the hut.

'Five, from what I've pieced together and what Hallie found out when they took me in. Yet the sight of him with his raised arm lives with me day and night. It's there inside me, Emma, the same way as his genes are. I know I have his temper, I've felt it surge inside me from time to time—quick, hot, unthinking—and I wouldn't want to put someone I love at risk.'

'But Pop was your father for far longer than your birth father was around,' Emma pointed out. 'I know debate rages over nature versus nurture but surely you've been far more influenced by Pop than by your birth father.'

'In every way except genetically,' he argued, then he drew back from her. 'Anyway, that's the story. You asked, and now I've told you, okay?'

Only it wasn't okay at all. In fact, Emma wanted to cry. Wanted to hold him in her arms and tell him it was nonsense, that she knew him well enough to know he'd never harm another human being, maybe any living thing. But she sensed he wouldn't listen, and she knew for sure that other people would have tried—Hallie and Pop in particular.

And if Hallie and Pop, who'd raised him and loved him unconditionally, couldn't convince him he was wrong, how was she, who barely knew him, going to succeed?

Although she didn't *barely* know him at all. She might not have known him long, but she did know he was special. He was caring and compassionate, kind, and friendly, and fun to be with. He was special…

CHAPTER NINE

KEN DIED AT three and, swallowing a sob, Emma consci-
entiously wrote it in her notes. Marty had collected the
stretcher from where he'd left it by the door and together
they gently lifted the frail body onto it, Emma wrapping
the quilt around it this time, as if he could still feel the cold.

They carried him to the chopper and secured the
stretcher, then walked together back into the hut, knowing they had to check for any papers he might have, to
dispose of any food, blow out the lanterns, and if possible
secure the hut against any vandals that might make their
way out here.

But the stress of the vigil, their sadness at the old man's
death, and Marty's story had churned up too many emotions and in search of relief they turned to each other,
clasping each other in a vice-like grip.

Their kiss spread fire through their bodies as they
melded together, feeding the hunger that had been raging
between them for too long.

Had it gone on forever, or was it only a matter of minutes before Marty eased himself away from Emma?

'Later?' he whispered.

'Later,' she replied, and it sounded like a promise.

He took one of the lamps outside to where he knew Ken
had kept a meat-safe in the shade of a lean-to, and emp-

tied it of cheese and some bread that had been there long enough to be breeding different types of mould.

Emma had found garbage bags and had handed one to him, so he emptied the weird metal contraption with the wet bags hung over it, and returned to the shack to find other perishables.

'I've put together all the papers I can find,' Emma told him, for all the world as if this was just another day, another job and the word 'later' had never been said. Twice. 'There should be something there about next-of-kin if he had anyone.'

She paused, then added, frowning slightly, 'Should we take his clothes? There's not much and most of it should be thrown away.'

'I think leave them. Someone will come out to see to things out here.'

'Then I'll sweep the floor to leave it tidy,' she said, and had to smile.

'Putting off the later?' he teased, coming closer to her to touch her cheek.

'No, I'm not!' she snapped. 'Now get out while I sweep.'

He walked down to the creek, pausing where he'd sat with Ken in days gone by, then looked back at the shack.

Had Ken been hiding not from people but from life itself?

Was that what he, Marty, was doing—hiding from life, but doing it amongst people, plenty of people so they didn't realise…?

Emma cleared what she could from the little shack, sadness for the old man she hadn't known battling with Marty's explanation of why he wouldn't—in his mind couldn't—do commitment.

Personally, she was certain nurture played a far more important part in a person's upbringing than nature, but she knew from the way he'd spoken that Marty held a deep, primal fear of physically hurting someone he loved.

She'd done some psychology as part of her medical course, but not enough to know if such a deep-rooted notion could ever be dislodged. Certainly, the love he'd received from Hallie and Pop and the loving support of all his foster family hadn't driven it away, so possibly not.

And *that* thought filled her with unutterable sadness…

'Come on, it's time to go.'

Marty's call woke her to the fact they should be moving, and she gathered the little stack of papers she'd collected, and with a last look around the shack headed for the door.

Only to stop, and turn, aware something had caught her eye, yet unable to place it. She looked around, certain she'd seen something that might be important—just a glimpse—turned again and caught it, an early sunbeam catching on glass, high up on the wall—a photo!

She hurried back and lifted it off the nail where it was hanging, not stopping to investigate as Marty already had the engine revving and she knew she had to go.

Blow out the lamp and go…

But once on the chopper, belted in, she had time to wipe the dust of ages off the glass and take a proper look at the picture in her hands.

A photo of a woman—young, and rather beautiful— beautiful in that haunting way as if the image could be labelled sadness.

It was the eyes—the look in them—that gave that impression—a polite half-smile on lovely lips, but such sadness in the heavy-lidded eyes Emma could feel it in her chest, her heart…

She turned it over, looking for a name, but the back was bare. Yet somehow she was sure she knew this woman.

Or did she only know the feeling the woman portrayed? Nonsense!

Why should *she* be sad? She had the boys, her father, a job she loved, and she'd made sure over the years to keep her memories of Simon to the happy times.

These she had tucked into that box that she stored in the back of her mind, and if she took it out and sifted through them from time to time, well, that was only natural surely.

But permanent sadness like this woman had been feeling?

The slightest of bumps told her they were back at Base, an ambulance waiting to take Ken's body to the hospital. She'd already learned they only used the hospital landing site for emergencies, sparing patients and staff within the building unnecessary noise disturbance.

She undid the stretcher straps, then stood aside as two ambos came in to take over. She grabbed her bag and clasping the paperwork she'd found—and the photograph— against her chest, she jumped lightly down and walked towards Marty's vehicle.

And now the memory of 'later' returned to the forefront of her mind.

'My place?' he said as he opened the door for her, and she'd probably have said no if he hadn't touched a finger to her chin and lifted her head so he could look into her eyes.

And she into his, so what she saw there took her breath away.

She nodded, and slid in, wanting to be close, to feel his heat and wonder how his skin would feel against hers.

He pulled up in front of a small house, set in a wild cottage garden that would be a riot of colour in the daylight.

'Hallie does my garden,' he said as he helped her out, and she knew they were just words to keep him going until they were inside, because the hand that held hers was shaking, and her own body was tight with tension.

They barely made it through the door before they were kissing again, Emma desperate to learn the taste of him, to run her fingers through his hair, across his back—learning the feel of him, needing all her senses to take in this man, needing to drown in him…

A voice in Marty's head shrieked warnings, but it was too far away to be clearly heard. Emma was so soft in all the right places, so pliant as he moved towards a wall to give them some support, and he knew she needed this as much as he did.

They fumbled with each other's clothes, while their lips maintained a desperate contact. Then her breasts, bare, soft and warm, were pressed against his skin, while her hand had slid down his belly, easing down his jeans, to hold him, hard and hot, in her hands.

He found her heat, already moist, and lifted her so her legs clamped around his waist, and he could slide into her, death adding passion to the frantic coupling—the act an affirmation of life.

She cried out as he groaned his own release, and she eased back against the wall, still clasped in his arms, breathing hard, trembling slightly.

So he held her, her head resting on his shoulder, until the trembling ceased, and his own breathing steadied. Then, for a little longer, for this was Emma, and this *could* not be because—

Because he loved her?

Hadn't he dismissed that thought way back in their friendship?

So why now had he discovered it anew right now?

The idea was so astonishing he shook his head to dislodge it, but the movement did little more than make Emma move in his arms—still close but not so close she couldn't rearrange her clothing and do up the buttons on her shirt.

So, he, too, pulled clothes into place, his fingers not

quite steady as the enormity of what he—they—had just done hit him with the force of a boxer's punch.

'I know there's no commitment,' Emma said quietly, moving away from him. 'It was just something we both needed at the time.'

Yet he read pain in her eyes—knew she needed more…

What could he say?

I love you?

Would she feel she had to love him back?

When he knew full well how much love had hurt her in the past, and how she didn't want to risk it?

They walked out to the car.

The short ride home was agony for Emma. She knew she'd want him again—want to make love with him properly next time—want to do it slowly, unhurriedly, delighting in discovering the man inside the clothes, delighting in his discovery of her…

Tiredness, that's all it was. She'd sat beside him in the vehicle often enough without wanting to rip his clothes off, so of course she could sit beside him again.

Would sit beside him again.

Had to sit beside him again…

She looked down at the photo she'd left in the car, seeking distraction in its beauty and sadness.

Had Ken loved her, this woman with the hauntingly sad eyes?

Had *she* loved him in return?

And had their love been doomed, as hers and Marty's was?

Love?

She looked harder at the face in the picture, turning it to show Marty when he got in.

'I found this,' she said, and he took it from her hands to look at it.

'She's lovely,' he said, passing it back, no mention of sad eyes or unrequited love.

'Might have been his mother,' he added.

No, she was too young to have been his mother—the clothing told Emma that much. She'd seen a similar dress in another photo somewhere—a photo of her paternal grandmother perhaps? They'd discovered boxes of old photos when they'd moved into the old house…

She was so engrossed in the distraction she'd provided for herself that she was startled when Marty pulled up at her front gate.

She opened the door and turned to thank him—well, to look at him really but she'd thank him as well.

He was staring straight ahead, his face so still it might have been carved from marble—a bust that was titled, 'Say Nothing'.

She thanked him anyway and slipped out, heading for the gate and, now that she was home, praying that the boys would still be asleep and she could tiptoe into her bedroom and maybe get an hour's rest before they woke.

Puppy—why hadn't they found a real name for the huge dog? Puppy was just ridiculous!—was there to greet her, and she patted him gently then sent him back to his bed on the veranda.

Making it safely to her bedroom was one thing, but she desperately needed a shower, and as the bathroom was close to the boys' room that was hardly an option right now.

'One day I'll put in an en suite bathroom,' she muttered to herself, sinking down onto the bed and flopping back, staring at the ceiling, at the wall opposite her bed, at the portrait of a woman that had hung there when they'd moved in and which she'd decided to leave hanging there.

She sat up, looking more closely, then knew, tired as she was, she'd have to stand up and look more closely.

Standing in front of it, she shook her head, unable to

believe the coincidence. The artist had put a glint of laughter in the eyes of the woman as he'd painted her—maybe they'd been talking, joking—but the dress was certainly the same as the one in the photo, and the heavy-lidded eyes were unmistakeable.

She'd always assumed it was a portrait of her great-aunt, the woman who had left the house to her father because she'd never married, never had children of her own.

Because of unrequited love?

Because Ken Irvine hadn't asked her—or had he asked her and been turned down?

Not by her, if the sadness in her eyes in his picture was any guide.

Separated by her family perhaps, so she'd lived on alone, a lonely woman in a large house that should have been filled with children's laughter, while deep in the forest Ken kept her near him in a picture on his wall...

It's all nonsense, she told herself. You're tired and your imagination's gone into overdrive. You should give up doctoring and write romance novels if you can come up with such a story so quickly.

Or was it something else that had fired her imagination?

Had the picture been symbolic of—?

No!

Perhaps?

No!

Although it could be, couldn't it? Symbolic of her and Marty...

Except Marty didn't love her, and she wasn't sure she loved him.

Not definitely sure...

Go to bed!

CHAPTER TEN

OFF DUTY FOR the day, Marty drove carefully back to his little house on the top of the hill.

From the day, aged fourteen, when he'd started work at the local Wetherby surf shop, he'd banked every penny he'd earned—drawing out what he needed for gifts for family members at Christmas or birthdays or sometimes a bunch of flowers for Hallie, but squirrelling the rest away with one aim in mind.

Eventually he'd have enough for a deposit on a house— *his* house, his *home*.

He'd once joked to Mac that he'd learned more maths working out how to get the best interest on his money than he ever had at school.

So why, as he dumped the rubbish bag from Ken's shack into his wheelie bin and walked into his house, did he not feel the usual thrill of possession—the pride of ownership— that the house usually gave him?

Because it was empty?

Ridiculous. *He* was here, wasn't he?

Was it because the air retained a faint scent of Emma?

He shook away *that* memory. It had been something they'd both needed, an affirmation of life—nothing more...

No, it was the house itself that bothered him. It seemed

to echo with the same kind of…not exactly sadness but definitely emptiness as Ken's shack had.

He touched the walls he'd painted with such care, walked through to the kitchen where appliances he'd chosen himself stood neatly on their shelves.

Maybe it was because he was hungry.

He pulled some bacon from the refrigerator and set it under the grill, turning the heat up high so it wouldn't take forever. Made himself a pot of tea—not for him a tea-bag in a cup—he had enough of that at work. No, Hallie had instilled in him that tea came from a pot, pointing out that you could always pour a second cup, or even a third, if you felt like it.

Hallie…

Was Emma right when she talked about nature and nurture?

Hallie and Pop had certainly nurtured him, and taught him not only the skills he'd need to live a successful life but the values to lead a good life.

Which he had—in his own way, right up until Emma Crawford had walked into the picture and everything had become so convoluted in his mind he didn't know where to start thinking about it.

And desperately wanting to make love to her again—to make love, not just have sex—was not the answer.

More a problem that he'd just have to ignore and hope it would go away.

Because, for all the nurturing he'd received, he knew that, in a flash, nature could take over. It hadn't happened for years but it *had* happened, the first time when he'd been at high school and an older boy had been teasing Liane.

He hadn't seen the red mist that he'd read about in books, hadn't seen or heard anything, although he knew there'd been shouting. He'd simply charged in, fists flailing, more missing than connecting but throwing enough lucky ones for the boy to end up with a black eye and a broken nose.

During the weeks he'd been suspended from school, he'd gone to work with Pop, too young to drive the big rig then but keeping him company, and Pop had never once spoken of the incident, just chatted on as Pop did when he was driving, pointing out places of interest, taking Marty to towns he'd never visited before.

But Pop was basically a quiet man, so there had been plenty of silence for Marty's head to think about what had happened, and about his reaction. To think about his father, and worry that he was like him...

And at the end of the two weeks' banishment, Hallie had packed his lunch and put it in his backpack, kissed his cheek, and sent him off with the others as if nothing had ever happened.

Their attitude had confused him and it was only years later that he'd spoken to them about it.

'What could we say that you weren't learning for yourself? You were bright enough to work out you had to find other ways to react, and better ways to protect your family and friends.'

She'd looked at him across the table with its teapot full of endless cups of tea and smiled.

'And you did, didn't you?'

She'd been right. He'd learned to walk away, taking a sibling or friend with him—to turn his back on bullies instead of becoming a bully himself.

Which had been fine until girlfriends had entered his life—and one had left his life for another bloke and—

What had he been?

Eighteen?

And yet he hadn't actually hurt the bloke for all he'd wanted to...

* * *

Emma woke at midday, surprised she'd slept at all, until she read the note Christine had left on the kitchen table.

'We've all gone to Wetherby for the day. Hallie and Pop are cleaning out the attics and have found some toys the boys might like.'

And in a different hand, 'Might make a day of it and bring you back fish and chips for dinner. Love Dad.'

Disappointment shafted through her, though maybe, her practical self told her, it was hunger. But as she made and ate some toast and drank a morning coffee, she did feel a little disappointed that she couldn't talk to her father about the photo and the portrait on her wall.

She'd checked it again when she'd got up—holding the two close together—and she was sure they were images of the same woman.

But who?

The great-aunt she'd never met?

She phoned Carrie, but got an answering-machine and assumed she'd probably gone on the jaunt to Wetherby as well. The people carrier she and Dad had bought when she'd been expecting the twins would certainly hold everyone.

And leave room for toys.

Anyway, Carrie would be too young to know much. Someone's grandmother, that's who she'd need to find.

Joss?

Joss's mother had produced Christine, and Emma still had the phone number.

But what to say?

Do you know the woman in this photo?

Surely that would be far too personal—and too intrusive because, dead or not, she'd still be meddling in Ken Irvine's affairs.

She sighed, deciding to give up thinking about the photo at least until she'd talked to her father…

But not thinking about the photo created a vacuum in her mind and, naturally enough, into it rushed the other revelations of the night.

If she thought only about Marty's story—about his mother's death—and his determination not to risk hurting anyone he loved, maybe she'd forget what had happened later.

Hardly possible as her body tingled just *not* remembering it.

She'd go to work. That would stop her thinking about anything outside the job at hand. And although she had no idea just how her work roster stood at the moment, never having worked out how the rescue helicopter hours fitted into the general work timetable, there'd always be something she could do, even if it meant attacking the mountains of paperwork that multiplied on her desk in the small office she shared with the other ED doctors.

Except Marty was the first person she saw when she walked in.

'What are *you* doing here?' she demanded, before realising he was surrounded by young men and women and she'd embarrassed herself far more than she'd embarrassed him.

'Ah, Emma, just the person we needed,' he said, with such a bland smile she wanted to hit him. 'These are a group of medical students from Retford university. We always take some for work experience so they can see a smaller hospital in action, and although we don't wish for accidents it's an opportunity for them to see how the search and rescue team operates.'

Emma smiled feebly at the four young women and two young men who made up the group.

'Emma,' Marty continued, 'usually joins the rescue team when we have a callout that requires a doctor.'

'And is she trained the way you say you're trained?' one of the young women asked, flashing such a dazzling smile at Marty Emma wanted to hit her.

Or *him,* for he was smiling right back at the questioner, all daring charm.

'Of course,' he said. 'We had a training day only last week. Every member of the team has to update their skills twice a year.'

The young woman looked as if she'd have liked to have been at the training day, and Marty's smile suggested he wouldn't have minded at all, but one of the men was now asking, 'Don't most SAR teams have their own doctors on staff? Wouldn't it be better carrying a doctor who knows what he's doing?'

He realised what he'd said, blushed, and turned to Emma.

'Sorry, ma'am, that came out wrong.'

'Indeed it did,' Marty replied, not bothering to hide his delight at both Emma's and the young man's embarrassment. 'But we're a very small operation, situated at a small country hospital because from here we can cover a far wider range than we would flying out of Retford, for example. Originally this service was connected to the Lifesaver's movement with sponsorship from big business, and we still get that sponsorship, although we get some government help as well.'

'So all doctors here at Braxton can be on call?' the young man persisted, and Emma took pity on him.

'In areas where there are no doctors employed by search and rescue operations the local doctors, usually from the emergency department, are used. I think one of the reasons I got this job was because I'd been trained for SAR missions, and had done winch training, underwater rescue, which is great fun if ever you want to get into SAR, rescues off moving targets like ships at sea, the lot.'

The young man looked at her in admiration.

'I wish we'd been here for that training day you had, it sounds like fun.'

Emma's eyes met Marty's across the young heads, and the slight nod he gave told her that he, too, was thinking of Ken. But they were young and idealistic, these students, and didn't really need to know about sitting by someone's bed waiting for them to die when all your years of training and experience had been about helping people live...

A wave of tiredness swept over her and she knew she'd have been better off staying at home and trying to sleep, no matter what thoughts would have run in circles through her head.

'Will you join us for lunch? We're just off to continue this discussion in the canteen then we're taking the hospital bus out to the base to show them around.'

Emma would have loved to say no, but there'd been the hint of a plea in Marty's voice, and if he felt as tired as she was feeling, he would need help to field the students' questions.

The young man who'd asked the question—Alex, she'd discovered—made sure he sat next to her at the long table, and Emma smiled to herself as she saw the young women crowd around Marty.

Like moths to a flame, she thought, and realised that, quite apart from his commitment problems, he would be a dangerous man to know well because he *was* kind and interesting and always willing to help, but anyone who loved him would live in a constant state of jealousy which would surely eat away at the strongest relationship.

Anyone who loved him?

No, no, she *definitely* didn't.

Couldn't!

So why was she probably turning green as he patted a beautiful young blonde on the hand?

Why did her stomach scrunch when he smiled at the hot brunette?

Damn the man! He'd bewitched her. He'd made it quite clear right from the start—and had definitely confirmed it last night—that he wasn't available for any kind of commitment, then he'd taken her with a passion that had imprinted him not only in her mind but on her body.

The problem was that she'd responded with equal intensity and although she had known full well it had been nothing more than just sex, her body tingled even thinking about it.

CHAPTER ELEVEN

THE STUDENT GROUP, and Alex in particular, begged her to come out to the SAR base with them, but she pleaded work and hurried back to the ED. She knew, given time, she'd get over the heart lurches and galloping pulse every time she saw Marty, but until that happened, avoidance was definitely the answer.

Sylvie greeted her with relief.

'We're having one of those days when it's dead quiet for an hour, then everyone comes at once. Could you see a lass in cubicle one who's complaining of stomach cramps?'

Emma was only too glad to be occupied, and she made her way to the cubicle where a very young woman, a teenager, in fact, was crying copiously into a handful of paper tissues the nurse on duty had given her.

The lass was very overweight and was probably bullied mercilessly at school.

The nurse introduced Ebony to Emma, then muttered something about work to do and departed, so Emma helped the still-crying patient onto the examination table.

Even under layers of clothing unsuited to the warm weather, once Ebony was lying supine, a possible cause of the stomach cramps became obvious.

Not wanting to cause further distress, Emma checked Ebony's blood pressure—good—pulse, a bit rapid but no cause for concern, and took some blood for testing—*and typing*, although she didn't say that out loud.

She was feeling Ebony's swollen stomach when the girl yowled in pain.

Emma held her hand, noted the time, then said gently, 'Did you know you were pregnant?'

Colour drained from Ebony's face, leaving it as white as the pillow case.

'Dad'll kill me,' she said, and Emma closed her eyes momentarily in a silent *Please don't let it be Dad* prayer.

'Do you have a boyfriend?'

A miserable nod of the head.

'Once I did but then he was just like the others and laughed and called me Fatty.'

'But you had sex with him?' Emma was watching the clock as she spoke—the contractions, for that was surely what they had been, were still widely spaced.

'Only a couple of times.' The defensive reply must have brought unwanted memories for Ebony began to cry again.

She felt Ebony's abdomen, finding the shape of the foetus, then, speaking quietly, she explained she'd have to examine her.

The nurse had reappeared, and together they removed Ebony's jeans and knickers.

Even a quick glance showed the cervix had begun to dilate. This baby was coming.

'The cramps are telling us the baby is on the way. It will be a while yet—' please let it not be too long, her head whispered '—so is there someone you'd like to have with you. What about your mum?'

Hope battled the tears in Ebony's eyes.

'Do you think she'd come?' she asked. 'She'll be mad at me, you see. She mightn't want to come.'

'Would you like me to phone her and explain?' Emma asked, then watched the emotions play across Ebony's face.

Mum would be mad, but she did want Mum, but then Mum would tell Dad, although Mum could usually fix Dad when he was angry. They were as easy to read as the pages of a book.

Finally, Ebony nodded, and Emma took the file with the name and address on it so she could phone the mother, leaving Ebony with the nurse.

'The cramps?' Sylvie asked. 'Is she pregnant?'

Emma nodded. 'Could you arrange to have her taken up to Maternity, while I phone her mother? Poor woman, although maybe she's had her suspicions.'

Sylvie was already on the house phone, arranging the transfer, so Emma made the call from the privacy of her office.

Mrs Challoner, Ebony's mum, was not nearly as surprised as her daughter.

'I kept thinking maybe that was it,' she said, 'but at that age they hate you asking questions and with all the sex education they get at school I thought she'd know if she was—or even suspected it—and she'd talk to me.'

'I'm sorry,' Emma said. 'But perhaps she didn't know. If she's usually a bit irregular she probably put it down to that then forgot all about it.'

'Or was so terrified she shut it right out of her mind,' Mrs Challoner said, a break in her voice telling Emma how upset she was—not, Emma thought, about the pregnancy, but about Ebony not talking to her.

'I'll be right up,' the anxious mother said. 'Where will I find her?'

'Come to the emergency department. We're transferring her to Maternity but it sometimes takes time and if she's still here, she'll be happier going up there with you than on her own.'

'Bless you,' Mrs Challoner said. 'I'll be there as soon as I can.'

Bless you.

What a lovely thing for someone to have said, Emma thought as she made her way back to Ebony to assure her that her mother was on the way.

Two words—but enough to reassure Emma too. This mother would stand by her child and probably bring up her grandchild.

And for a moment she wondered what it would have been like to grow up with a mother.

She shook the thought away. Dad had done his best to be both mother and father to her, and as far as she was concerned he'd done a damned good job.

But would her boys grow up and wonder what it might have been like to have had a father?

Should she get serious about finding a father for them?

Somehow that task seemed slightly distasteful now.

It was all Marty's fault...

Marty had finished with the students and was back in Ken's shack, flying out in his own chopper on what should have been time off. The old man had prided himself on keeping it clean, but he'd probably been failing for some time, and Marty wanted to make sure it was as spruce as Ken would have had it in the early days.

Yet walking in brought memories of Emma—of her closeness as they'd sat waiting for the old man to die, of her softness later when they'd found relief from the trauma that came with any death, back at his house...

He cleared and cleaned almost maniacally, aware his burst of energy was a way of not remembering. And when he was finally happy that Ken's little home looked as it had when the old man had been younger, he went out into the bush, picking red gum tips and yellow bottlebrush, dark green fig leaves and some trailing creeper.

He arranged them all in a big old coffee can, just as Ken

had done, and set them in the empty fireplace. They'd dry out there, and still look good—a dried arrangement, Hallie had told him they were called.

He checked the cleared area around the shack for rubbish and loaded it all into the chopper.

Then he walked towards the little creek that gurgled and splashed its way down the mountain, and sat on the log where he had sat at least a dozen times with Ken, listening to his stories of the bush, picking up a lot of the older man's ideas about life and how to live it—about being true to oneself, and owing nothing to any man.

And love?

Thinking back, he couldn't remember discussing love with Ken, although he'd been there often as a teenager when love—or more probably lust—had never been far from his thoughts.

'What would you have said, Ken?' he asked of the man who was no longer there.

But try as he might, Marty couldn't imagine what Ken's response would have been, and as the creek had nothing to tell him either, he walked back to shut the door of the shack and took himself, reluctantly, back to Braxton.

Reluctantly because he was off duty and being off duty gave him more time to think, and while he might now be out of the shack and his memories of Ken's life, the fact remained that he'd had unprotected sex with the one woman in the world he would hate to hurt.

Maybe it would be okay...

She was looking for a father for her boys, so she was probably on the Pill...

Surely she was on the Pill?

Yet, somehow, he was pretty sure she wasn't.

Emma was too organised, too methodical, to look beyond going out with any possible candidates in her quest. She was conservative, would take it slowly, not rush into anything—

Which meant she'd go on the Pill when she was ready to commit to a man, not take it all the time just in case.

Concentrate on flying, he told himself, but he knew he could fly this little toy in his sleep.

Nevertheless, he did concentrate, more to block out the other thoughts, and he landed at the base, carried the rubbish bags to the skip, cleaned out and refuelled the chopper, and even gave it a wash.

'Too much time on your hands?' Dave called to him. 'You can help me do a stocktake, then while I clean out the chopper you can take the list to the hospital and bring back the stock.'

No way! He was avoiding the hospital.

Only surely Emma wouldn't be there—not after pulling an all-nighter.

And he *did* need something to do.

Emma had sent her patient up to Maternity, put staples into the split head of a teenager, and dug a bead from the nose of a kindergarten kid.

Deciding, as she wasn't supposed to be on duty that day, she could have a cup of tea, she escaped to the tea-room, desperate to have a think.

Why hadn't it occurred to her earlier?

Why did she have to wait until a pregnant teenager came in before she considered her own situation, and the fact that she'd had unprotected sex with the one man in the world she shouldn't have?

But her mind grew cloudy so thinking of the possible consequences got muddled up with the remembered warmth—no, heat—the act had brought with it.

She made a mug of tea, grabbed a couple of biscuits from the never-empty tin, and sat down to muse.

Well, to think really, mostly about consequences of actions, but there was more musing than thinking going on.

Marty's arrival put paid to both. Her mind went blank and she could only stare at him.

'You shouldn't be here,' he said, and she recovered enough to point out, 'Neither should you.'

Then he was sitting on the sofa beside her, close but not too close—annoyingly not too close, but she wouldn't think about that either.

'Oh, Em,' he said, and even the shortening of her name made her feel warm. 'I'm so sorry. I didn't think, I didn't ask— Hell, what if—?'

She put her hand on his knee, wishing he was closer, knowing the wish was stupid.

'It's as much my fault as yours, and it's highly unlikely that there'll be any fallout so don't worry about it.'

'Not worry about it?'

His voice had risen and she touched her finger to his lips to hush him, then grew hot and breathless as he slid his tongue along it and closed his lips against the tip, sucking it gently.

It took a mammoth effort but she finally removed it.

'We can't do this,' she said, and if she sounded desperate, well, that was just how she felt.

He shifted, nodded, shrugged, stood up, then reached down to touch her cheek.

'You *will* tell me if you're pregnant,' he said, his voice harsh with an emotion she couldn't read.

She nodded, not at all sure she would.

If it happened, and that was one huge if, she'd think about it then—think about what was to be done, what would be the best way forward. But not today. It would be like when Simon had been dying and she would only let herself think of one day at a time.

Although that had been totally different—back then it had been death she'd been desperately trying to hold off.

But life?
A new life?
She had no idea how she'd feel about that.

CHAPTER TWELVE

EMMA HAD PUT the possibility of being pregnant completely out of her mind, and tried, unsuccessfully, to do the same with Marty.

He seemed to be around more than usual, bobbing up in the tea-room at unexpected times, coming in with a patient when usually Mark and Dave would bring them in.

So, a week or two later, when she heard the helicopter fly over—its distinctive noise far too recognisable by now—she fully expected to see him when it returned. The gossip in A and E was something about a road giving way—the result of the rain they'd had during the week after the bushfires causing a landslide effect.

She was hearing snippets of theories about why this sometimes happened, but not really taking much notice as it was a busy morning.

Until Mark walked in, with a list of equipment and drugs needed for restocking.

'You not on the chopper for the landslide mission?' she asked.

'Kicked off by Marty,' he said. 'Matt's flying, and Dave will act as winch man. Marty wants to go down.'

'Marty wants to go down?' Emma repeated the words as ice-cold fear swept through her body.

'He's still a qualified paramedic—jolly good one too—

but he knew he was a better pilot than anyone else around here when we first got the chopper, so he took it on.'

'But why would he choose to go down now?' she asked, although she already knew the answer.

The rescue must be tricky, probably dangerous, and knowing Marty now, she also knew he wouldn't let his crew put their lives at risk.

And definitely not crew with families.

'Where is it? What's happened?' she demanded of Mark, when he'd ignored her first question.

'Out on an old timber road. Some new folks have recently bought a property out that way and want to turn it into a holiday camp for children—you know, farm animals and horse riding and milking cows.'

But Emma couldn't care less about the cows right now, or the new people.

'Apparently,' Mark continued, 'Pop was taking out a load of cattle for them. These days he only does the odd job like a small mob of cattle, or sometimes in his covered trailer a load of furniture for someone. As far as I know, the road slid out from under his cabin in the prime mover and he's stuck there, with the cabin of the prime mover balanced over the edge of the slide, the trailer weight and cattle the only thing holding it from plunging down the slope.'

Mark was still talking but somehow Emma's mind had stopped at the word 'Pop'. That's why Marty was going down the wire. Of course he would, with Pop in danger.

She *had* to be there.

Had to be sure he was safe…

She looked frantically around the ER—not busy but it could be any moment. She checked her watch. Still an hour before she was off duty. She checked the rosters. Paul was taking over from her and she knew, since his return to full-time work, he was always looking for overtime.

She phoned him, told him what was happening, and although she had no way to explain why she needed to be at the accident, he seemed pleased enough to cover for her.

'Be there in ten,' he said, and she blessed the closeness of everything in the small town.

By the time he arrived she'd found out exactly where the landslide had occurred and how to get there.

She raced home and was thankful to see their car was out front. Dad and the kids were probably down at the park. Once inside, she wrote a note explaining where she'd be, changed into jeans and boots, a tough checked shirt, and headed off towards the collapsed road.

She knew she shouldn't be doing this, because onlookers—and that's all she'd be—were a nuisance at any accident, to say nothing of what havoc vehicles could cause on an already weakened road.

A police car blocked the road long before she could see anything, except the helicopter hovering above the trees further ahead.

'You can't go further, miss,' the policeman told her.

Emma hesitated for a second, then told her lie—a small lie but a lie nonetheless.

'I'm a doctor, I was told I might be needed.'

'You'll have to walk and it's a good mile, uphill most of the way.'

As if that mattered. She just had to be there.

She thanked the man, then, sneaking past, off the road now and through the bush above it, she eventually saw the back of Pop's truck.

But the scene that eventually met her eyes was horrifying.

The cabin of the vehicle hung precariously, tilted downwards, over nothingness. The cattle in the trailer were restless, and getting increasingly so, making the prime mover shake, but it was obvious to Emma that if they were removed, the loss of their weight would send the whole thing plunging into the gully.

As well as police cars and fire service vehicles closer to the accident, she saw a large crane, although that had apparently been stopped from moving closer for fear its weight would make things on the unstable road worse. Men were uncoiling a thick wire from the crane, maybe intending to hook it to the rear of the truck as extra anchoring weight.

But more horrifying than all of it—the dangling truck, the increasingly restless cattle—was the sight of Marty, in his flight suit, half in and half out of the cabin.

Emma crept closer, unable to stop herself, willing the man she loved—yes, okay, that was finally sorted out— to stay safe.

Was Pop wedged in there somehow that it was taking so long to get him out?

A rumble beneath her feet gave warning that time was running out, and the rest of the road was about to follow the earlier slide into the gully. She could hear Marty's voice but it was too muffled to hear the words, so she stood, hands clasped tightly, lips firmly shut so she didn't make a noise and distract him.

Reaching Pop had been no trouble at all. Matt was holding the hover well, and he, Marty, had missed the worst of the tall timber branches on the way down but now Marty couldn't work out how to extricate his father.

He'd leaned far enough in to release his seatbelt, but the old man—his dearly loved Pop—was only semi-conscious— shock possibly—and could do little to help.

Trapped as he was in the cabin, there was no way Marty could get a strop around him, so it would have to be a manual lift. The problem was, the door was jammed so it meant hauling a solidly built, seventy-something-year-old man through the window.

And a dead weight at that.

If he got a firm hold on Pop, and asked them to unload the cattle, the truck would plunge down the gully, and he could lift Pop free as it fell.

Or, and it was a big or, the combined weight of himself, Pop and the truck could pull the helicopter down with it, crashing it into the trees.

Couldn't risk it.

He kicked at the door, more in frustration than in hope he might shift it, and to his surprise it flew open, Pop tumbling out.

Dave on the winch must have seen what had happened and dropped Marty lower, so he was able to grab at the only father he'd ever really known and hang on tight, wrapping his arms and his legs around Pop's unresponsive body.

He signaled to lift, and as they rose said to Pop, 'If you can, hang onto me, that way we'll be doubly safe.'

But shock and maybe a head knock when the cabin tilted had the old man out cold.

They rose slowly with the double weight, the wire twisting so Marty thought he caught a glimpse of Emma by the roadside.

He couldn't look again, his full attention needed to get Pop to safety. Then Dave was there to haul them up onto the skids, checking Marty was okay before dragging Pop into the chopper.

Marty crawled in himself, unhooking from the winch wire, fingers trembling now he realised just how close run it had been, his body shaking from the strain of the lift.

Below them they could see the cattle being unloaded, then hear, above the engine noise, the roar as the land beneath the road plunged into the gully.

He strapped in and sat there, trying hard to quell his

tremors, while Dave settled Pop on the stretcher, the old man now awake and complaining that he was perfectly well and didn't need Dave's fussing.

But Marty was trying to remember what he'd seen. It couldn't have been Emma.

Could it?

Or had he conjured her up because he'd been thinking of her—thinking of Pop, of fatherhood, and right along that train of thought to Emma and the boys.

With relief battling rage within her, Emma drove back to town as fast as she dared on the winding mountain road.

Hospital or base?

Surely they'd take Pop to the hospital to have him checked over, although she knew Marty would prefer the base, where he could see to the old man himself.

The chopper was so far in front of her when she cleared the trees she couldn't see it, but decided to go straight to the base.

And there he was, helping Pop down out of the side door, steadying him as they walked across to the hut, talking, talking—probably questioning him about how he felt.

Emma stayed in the car and waited, aware she didn't belong here—shouldn't be here—should be anywhere but here, really…

But she had to see him, touch him, make sure he was all right, so there she stayed.

He must have seen the car for eventually he walked towards it. She got out as he drew nearer, knowing the metal walls around her weren't enough to contain her rage.

'Emma, what are you—?'

'What in heaven's name did you think you were doing?' she yelled at him, before he had time to complete his question. 'You could have been killed! Eventually they'd have got a wire attached to the back of the truck and hauled it backwards, there was no need for you to put your life in danger like that. You frightened me to death.'

'Or the road could have given way first,' he said quietly, touching her shoulder.

One touch and the rage abated, leaving her feeling so weak she wanted—no, needed—to lean against him, to feel him against her, to be one with him as surely they were meant to be.

And perhaps he felt the same as he folded his arms around her, held her close, dropping kisses on the top of her head.

'I'm sorry you were frightened,' he murmured, 'but...'

He paused and moved a little away from her, one finger tilting her chin so he could look into her face.

'But how could I expect you to accept me as a father to your children if I could not save my own father?'

She pulled away from him, anger rising again within her.

Anger and something else.

Hope?

'What did you say?' she demanded, looking into the blue eyes she knew so well.

Smiling now, though warily...

'I'm asking you to marry me—if you'll have me. Asking because I love you—I think I've loved you from the day we met. But I was so hung up on the past, on my birth father, I resisted it with all my strength, but I can't resist it now. You were right, Pop's my real father, and a better role model no man could ever have. I realised that today when I thought I might lose him. And if I lost him, would I lose you? Or would you marry me out of pity? So many thoughts, Em, but all of them of love.'

He paused, then added, fairly tentatively for someone who'd been talking non-stop, '*Will* you marry me?'

Emma stared at him, trying desperately to assimilate all

she'd heard, but the only words that meant something were the early ones, the 'I love you' ones. Words she'd never expected, hardly even dared hope she'd hear on Marty's lips.

She smiled and shook her head, and had moved closer to kiss him when her head shake obviously bothered him.

'You're saying no?'

'That was disbelief,' she said, smiling as she put her arms around him. 'Disbelief that you'd love me when I've only recently realised just how much I love you. I was so afraid, you see. Afraid of love—of loving again. I thought if I made it all about the boys...'

'It wouldn't hurt?' he whispered.

And he held her close again, so they only broke apart at heavy footsteps approaching, and Pop's gruff voice saying, 'If it's all the same to you two, I'd like to get home sometime today. Hallie will be worrying.'

'You can't go home!' They spoke together, then Marty took Emma's hand and he said, 'You need to go to the hospital to be checked out, probably kept in for a while in case you have concussion. *We'll* take you there.'

'Hmph!' Pop said, looking at the pair of them hand in hand in front of him. 'Hallie reckoned this would happen. I just hoped you wouldn't be so stubborn as to not see what a gem you'll have in Emma.'

He smiled at Emma then leaned forward and kissed her cheek.

'He gives you any trouble, my girl, you come straight to me. I've been sorting him out anytime these past thirty years!'

And Emma laughed, and hugged the man who was to become her father-in-law, then Marty took her hand and they headed for her car.

In the end, she dropped them both off at the hospital and went home to tell her father what was happening— and to ask about the woman in the photo.

'That's your great-aunt,' he said. 'The woman who left us the house.'

'Do you know her story? Did she ever marry?'

Her father frowned, thinking back.

'No, she didn't, but I seem to remember there was a man, someone who felt he wasn't right for her.'

'No wonder her eyes look so sad,' she said, thinking how close she'd come to having that same sadness in her eyes.

When Marty arrived, determined, it appeared, to ask her father's permission for her hand, she waited until the excitement was all over and they were sitting on the veranda on their own.

She showed him the two photos, and told him the story.

'Bloody hell!' he said. 'To think that could have been us if I hadn't finally come to my senses.'

Emma laughed.

'It wouldn't have been us,' she said. 'You once told me I should want a man for myself, not just for the boys, and it took me a little while to accept that. Until I realised that, more than anything, I only wanted—still want, and will always want—you.'

He kissed her then and she relaxed into the kiss, glad they'd not only found each other but had finally found their way to love.

EPILOGUE

THE WHOLE FAMILY was gathered, Lila and Tariq flying in laden with gifts for everyone, Steve and Fran were up from Sydney with their baby Chloe, Carrie and the twins, all three looking beautiful, Izzy and Mac, with George, usually held in Nikki's arms, the centre of much attention as the very latest addition to the family.

Emma and Marty had decided, after much deliberation, to hold the celebration at the old nunnery where the Halliday family—as the locals called them—had grown up.

And there were dozens of them, all present to see the last of the brood safely married off.

Emma dressed in the little flat Pop had fixed up for Izzy when she'd brought Nikki home from hospital—Nikki, the birth daughter of Liane, the sister who hadn't survived her horrendous early childhood.

And Dad was with her in the flat, helping with the last-minute touches, fastening the pearls he'd given her as a wedding gift—pearls that had been his mother's.

'Why didn't my mother take them?' Emma asked, and watched him closely for they rarely spoke of her mother.

'She felt they were yours,' he said. 'She wasn't bad, or uncaring, Emma, she was just a square peg in a round hole and she had to escape or die. She loved you and in her own way loved me, but once she'd met Helena and realised what true love was, she couldn't live a lie anymore. Helena took her back to Europe, to Hungary where she was from, and from there they roved the world—or that had been the plan when they departed.'

'She never thought to keep in touch?'

Her father drew her close and hugged her, heedless of creases in the soft green dress Emma was wearing.

'She said that that would make it too hard for all three of us, and she was probably right, for it would have awoken memories that hurt both of us.'

He paused, then added, 'Have you missed her?'

Emma eased away from him and looked into his eyes.

'Not for a minute. You've been all I've ever needed and more as far as parents go.'

She kissed his cheek.

'Now, let's go and get this wedding over with,' he said. 'Knowing Hallie, she will have organised a tremendous spread, and everyone will be getting hungry.'

They walked down the stairs and out into the big back yard, where Marty and his family would have played so often. And the family had obviously been busy, for the rather saggy old grape arbour had been fixed and covered with fresh flowers, and a carpet laid beneath it.

And there was Marty, waiting for her, Stephen beside him as support, while Hallie held the hands of two little boys, dressed in smart new clothes for the occasion, Puppy, with flowers in his collar, sitting docilely beside them.

'It's Mummy,' Xavier yelled, and everyone turned to watch her and Dad walk towards them, the two boys, obviously under strict instructions from Hallie, standing very still.

It was Marty who'd insisted they be part of the wedding party, because, as he'd explained, he was marrying all three of them. Well, four of them it would be by the end of the year—but only she and Marty knew that.

And in that flowery bower, looking out over the town towards the sea, they committed to each other, repeating words that echoed down through the mists of time, yet still had the power to bring tears to the eyes of the onlookers.

'You may kiss the bride,' the celebrant declared at last, and as Marty bent to kiss her, the boys broke free, rushing towards Emma, who knelt to hug them both, before Marty lifted them, one on each arm, and turned to his family and all their friends.

'My new family,' he said, and the pride in his voice, and the promise it held, made Emma smile through blurry eyes.

* * * * *

A SURGEON TO
HEAL HER HEART

BY
JANICE LYNN

MILLS & BOON

To all those caring for loved ones with chronic illnesses.

CHAPTER ONE

"I'M TELLING YOU, that man has the hots for you."

At her co-worker's words, the corners of nurse Carly Evans' lips inched upward. Still, she shrugged as if the comment was no big deal. She needed to fight the excitement Rosalyn's claim incited, not give her heart free rein to jump up and down with joy.

Jump up and down? Ha. More like her heart was somersaulting worthy of a world-class medal.

The same flip-flopping routine her heart went into any time she thought of the hospital's newest general surgeon.

Not that she had a right to feel that way. Not when she couldn't do one thing about her heart's acrobatics or any hots Dr. Stone Parker might have for her.

Stone.

Just thinking his name, how his eyes, his mouth had immediately crinkled with a smile when they'd met hers on this morning's rounds, had her blood pounding. The erratic rhythm practically demanded a giddy schoolgirl dance with fists thrust into the air.

Maybe her friend should be saying Carly had the hots for Stone.

She did.

For all the good it would do her.

Which was the problem.

She'd have been better off if she'd never met Stone, never felt the way he made every nerve cell inside her hum with life.

That she wasn't free hadn't been a problem, until she'd met him. Now…now, she was torn and hated herself for it.

Closing the medicine cart and nearly dropping the medications she'd just taken out, Carly took a long, steadying breath, and grimaced.

"Uh-huh, I saw that so don't go pretending you're immune to the man." Rosalyn's dark brown eyes glowed with eagerness at Carly's tell-tale motion. "I've seen you two talking, the sparks that fly back and forth. You like him, too. Admit it."

Wasn't that the same as saying she liked to breathe? How could any sane, straight woman not like Stone? The man was gorgeous and the total package.

Just over six feet tall, dark brown hair with the slightest hint of curl, green eyes that twinkled when he smiled, and a face that had inspired numerous fantasies… Yeah, Stone was 'likable'.

Just a tad.

"He seems to be a great doctor and, of course, he's a good-looking man." Understatements of the year. "I can appreciate that, just as most females, including yourself, can," Carly pointed out, using all her willpower to keep her voice level, cool, and as unaffected as possible. "But that does not mean I 'like him' like him."

Like liking Stone was a waste of emotions she didn't have to spare.

"Honey, you're protesting too much." Chuckling, Rosalyn practically rubbed her hands with glee. "Admit it. He makes you all hot beneath your nursing uniform."

Carly rolled her eyes at the nurse she'd worked side by side with for the past five years. Rosalyn was a big-hearted African American woman raising four teenagers with her mechanic husband. There was no one Carly would rather work with than the long-time med-surg nurse.

Except maybe for this moment. None of her other co-workers would initiate this particular conversation.

Squaring her shoulders, Carly stared straight into her friend's dark eyes.

"I'm sure Dr. Parker is a very nice man." He was. "I enjoy our conversations very much." She did. "But whether or not he has the hots for me is totally irrelevant." Sadly, the truth. "I'm not interested in a relationship with him, or anyone else, outside these hallowed walls." Also, sadly, the truth.

Inside the hospital walls Carly was a very different person from who she was outside them.

Inside these walls she could focus on being a shining light to her patients and cling to the shadows of the Carly she'd once been.

Part of her worried *that* Carly was shriveling into nothingness to disappear forever. Which might be why she enjoyed time around Stone so much. He gave her glimpses of a younger, carefree version of herself.

Made her insides spark as if trying to relight a fire that used to brightly burn. In her fantasies, it still did.

In the real world, that fire couldn't be relit. Unfortunately.

"Why is that?"

Carly jumped at the question that came from behind her. Literally and figuratively. *What? How?*

She'd been expecting Rosalyn to respond, not the familiar masculine voice that had the effect of morphing her insides to melted butter.

When had he walked up behind her?

Why hadn't Rosalyn told her?

Or at least given some indication he was on the medical floor and within earshot? She had to have seen him behind Carly.

Rosalyn had set her up, playing matchmaker.

Slowly, Carly turned to face the man she'd just been talking about.

Insides quaking, she stared into the most beautiful green eyes she'd ever encountered. So green she could almost be convinced the color was the result of contact lenses. If she'd had any doubts, he was now close enough to put that question to rest. All she could see was gorgeous bright green eyes, the color of spring bringing life back after a long cold spell.

Dark, long lashes fringed his eyes, giving them a surreal look that only added to his already handsome face. No doubt about it. Stone was easy to look at.

She opened her mouth, meaning to tell him something, anything, but not the truth.

The truth was something she kept private. Something she didn't talk about with her co-workers because she needed to keep her life compartmentalized. At the hospital, she worked hard, was free to laugh with her co-workers and patients, to just feel normal and pretend life was grand.

She wouldn't let home creep into work.

She couldn't.

Not if any part of her was to survive.

Compartmentalization was her friend and kept her sane.

"Yeah," Rosalyn added, her amused gaze bouncing back and forth between Stone and Carly.

Her co-worker was definitely having Cupid inclinations. In another lifetime, Carly would have welcomed her help, would have welcomed a man like Stone being interested. Welcomed and been over the moon. But that wasn't where she was and probably wouldn't be for years.

Lord, she hoped it would be years.

The alternative was unthinkable.

Stone's gaze cut to the grinning nurse who was watching them with the eagerness of a movie-goer. All she needed was a seat and some popcorn.

"Rosalyn, would you mind getting a warm blanket for Room 207?" he asked. "That's what I stepped out to do, but fortunately I ran into you lovely ladies."

Carly was one hundred percent sure "fortunately" was not what she'd call him overhearing her and Rosalyn's conversation.

Heat flooded Carly's face and she glanced down at her tennis shoes, staring at the neon-green laces. Good work shoes were the one luxury she allowed herself. With the long hours she worked, good shoes mattered.

"Yes, sir." Rosalyn grinned at him, and then winked at Carly. Chuckling, she took off toward where the blanket warmer was located. "Just you remember what I said, Carly Evans," she called without turning around. "It would do you some good to think about that."

Carly was pretty sure her cheeks were as red as her scrubs. Maybe more so as her scrubs were a little faded from too many washings.

When Rosalyn was out of earshot, Stone turned back to Carly. One side of his mouth lifted in a wry smile. "I didn't intentionally listen in, but will admit that I'm intrigued by what I heard. You mind explaining?"

She minded. "How much did you hear?"

"Enough to know I want to hear more."

Being careful not to spill Room 204's medication from the cup, Carly put her hands on her hips. "Which tells me nothing."

"How much could I have overheard?" His eyes twinkled.

Good grief, he'd heard everything. Was the fact that he was standing behind Carly why Rosalyn had mentioned him in the first place?

"Not a lot." Carly decided to go for nonchalant. Nonchalant was good and meant she didn't care what he'd overheard. He didn't know her private thoughts, nor would he ever. "Rosalyn had a theory about you. I told her that her theory was pointless as I wasn't interested in anything beyond friendship."

"Which is where I asked why you weren't interested." His lips twitched, his eyes sparkled, and he was enjoying that he'd caught her having a conversation about him.

"Yes," she said for lack of knowing what else to say, a little flustered by the fact Stone didn't mind that Rosalyn had said he had the hots for Carly. Which meant what?

That he did have the hots for her?

He'd flirted, but he was such a good-natured person, talking with everyone, so she'd consoled herself that her talking back was harmless, that nothing would come of their shared conversations. He wouldn't really be interested in her outside of having a little fun at the hospital.

He was a gorgeous doctor. She was just her. An overworked, over-stressed, financially stretched nurse doing all she could to provide care for her seriously ill mother.

"You didn't answer my question," he pointed out, his intent gaze warning she'd been fooling herself on thinking their conversations didn't mean anything.

Her pulse drummed rapidly at her temple.

"I wasn't having a discussion with you," she reminded him, knowing she had to get her thoughts, her reaction to him, under control. Better to stay in denial than to acknowledge what she couldn't have, what she couldn't let herself have. "You weren't a part of the conversation you interrupted."

She wanted to be irritated with him, but how could anyone be upset with him when he had such an all-encompassing smile on his face? A smile that crinkled the corners of his eyes, dug dimples into his cheeks, and made his eyes sparkle?

Good grief. The man was incorrigible. And so gorgeous. And so out of her reach. Still, the way he made her feel was addictive, like a magic spell that gave everything a shiny glow.

A shiny glow she'd like to bask in, but life had other plans for her. Plans that didn't include time for a dalliance with the most intriguing man she'd ever met.

She arched a brow and shook her head. "Some would say eavesdropping was rude, you know?"

His left dimple dug a little deeper. "I'm part of the conversation now."

She rolled her eyes upward. "Not by my choice."

He laughed. "You saying I'm holding you here against your will?"

Carly shrugged. "Obviously not. If you'll excuse me?" She went to push past him.

"I won't."

Eyes wide, Carly stopped, met his for once serious gaze. "Pardon?"

"I won't excuse you," he clarified. "Not this time. Eavesdropping was rude. You're right. But since I was the topic of conversation, surely I'm forgiven for jumping in?"

Her insides shook so that she still might end up spilling those meds she held yet. "There's no rule that says I have to forgive you for butting into my conversation."

"Even when the conversation is about me?"

"Especially when the conversation is about you."

He chuckled. "You should have dinner with me tonight and let me convince you to forgive my so-called rudeness. Plus, we can discuss why my having the hots for you doesn't matter because it matters a great deal to me."

Guilt hit Carly. This was her fault. She should have put a stop to whatever sparks Rosalyn said were flying between them but she'd not dared to believe he was really interested in her.

Sure, he'd gone out of his way to start conversations, asking her things he could have asked any hospital employee. He'd sat back in the break room with her a few times while she'd quickly swallowed down whatever she'd packed from home.

His sitting with her while she ate should have made her horribly uncomfortable, but instead she'd found herself regretting how quickly her short lunch break had slipped by while they'd talked. He'd asked about her favorite parts of Memphis and, drawing upon her childhood and college memories, she'd told him. No need to tell him that for five years she'd not been to any of those places. Surely, they hadn't changed that much in such a short time?

Then again, she'd changed that much.

Aged a hundred years, at least.

But for all that, she'd thought their interactions innocent. She'd figured Stone had svelte, glamorous women lined up in droves out there in the real world. Talking with Carly was just a fun way to pass time when he was at work.

Had she really believed that?

Or had she refused to believe anything else because she enjoyed his attention and hadn't wanted to give it up?

She didn't lead on men when she had no intentions of following through. So if he was interested then, yeah, she had to put a halt to it right now.

Carly's throat tightened as she said, "Our discussing that would be an utter waste of both of our time."

"I've time to spare."

"That makes one of us." She seriously doubted he had much time to spare, either.

His dark brow arched. "You're too busy to go to dinner with me tonight?"

"Absolutely." She took off toward her patient's room, but he stayed in step beside her.

"Tomorrow night?"

"Busy."

Her answer seemed to waylay him for a few seconds, but then, still beside her, he asked, "Surely you make time to eat, Carly? I'll take you to the restaurant of your choice and promise to have you home at a decent hour." He waggled his brows and gave another crooked smile. "Unless you want me to keep you out past bedtime, that is."

Oh, my. Not going to happen… But, oh, my, oh, my, oh, my.

She ate in quick snatches after getting home, usually soup or a peanut butter and jelly sandwich while Joyce filled her in on the day's events.

Carly liked uneventful days.

Days in which her mother didn't have any angry outbursts or falls or screams of pain or significant declines in her failing health. It had been so long since Carly had eaten out at a restaurant that she didn't have a favorite. Money was tight. Eating out was expensive. There would be time for such luxuries later, after her mother's life succumbed to her illness.

Just as there would be time for relationships. For real relationships and smiles and going to restaurants with handsome men.

The odds of a man as fabulous as Stone ever asking her to dinner again was next to nil, but, even so, dinner dates, or staying out past bedtime, had to wait.

Carly prayed that would be many years down the road. Those snatches of good spells with her mother were worth everything. They were getting further and further in between, but on a day of clarity Carly's heart filled with enough joy to tide her over until the next brief glimpse.

Thoughts of her mother, of the fact she wasn't free to

date, that to pretend otherwise with Stone was wrong, made a new wave of guilt hit her. She'd been wrong to ever let things get to this point, but it was too late to undo that now. Other than to put an abrupt stop to his interest.

As difficult as it was going to be, she had to cut all ties with Stone.

"I eat," she admitted, not that that was in question. She stopped mid-hallway to glare in as much annoyance at him as she could muster. "But not with strangers."

"I'm not a stranger," he clarified, not seeming fazed by her glare.

No wonder. It wasn't easy to glare at a gorgeous man smiling and trying to convince you to go to dinner. Maybe he could see right through her, could see that everything female inside her responded to him. Maybe he saw how much she longed for a different set of life circumstances that would mean she could have her mother and a relationship. No matter. That wasn't the life she'd been given and she wouldn't bemoan things she had no control over.

"And, we have eaten together," he reminded her, his grin full of charm. "In the break room at lunch when I'm lucky enough to catch you there. Plus, we've been working together for almost a month. We are not strangers."

He made a valid argument, but none of which made any impact on why she couldn't go to dinner.

"A whole month since you came to work at Memphis Memorial? Time does fly." To make her point, she glanced at her watch, then gave him the sternest expression she could muster. "My patient is due his medication and I am going to administer it now. Thank you for the invitation, but my answer is no and won't change." She met his gaze. "I'm sorry if I ever gave you reason to think otherwise."

He looked ready to say something more, but didn't attempt to stop her when she moved past him to hightail her way down the hospital-floor hallway.

No matter. She could feel his gaze as she hurried to escape into her patient's room and away from the most disconcerting man she'd ever met.

Tony had sure never gotten her worked up the way Stone had in the month she'd known him.

One month, four days. That was how long Stone had been at Memphis Memorial.

Not that she was counting.

She shouldn't be aware the man existed outside that he was a doctor at the hospital where she worked.

But she was aware.

Too aware.

With that thought she bit the inside of her lower lip and fought the urge to cry a little. A lot. No matter.

She had a good life, had her mother, anything beyond that would have to wait for a day she prayed never came.

Stone Parker wasn't sure how he'd misread what was happening between him and Carly Evans.

He'd thought they shared a connection, that she felt the spark he felt when he looked at her.

Today was the most direct conversation they'd had about what was happening, but he'd never tried to hide his interest, and he'd thought it was reciprocated. From the moment he'd met her, he'd gone out of his way to bump into her. She'd been pleasant. Cheerful. Smiling a lot. Had often had a sassy rebuttal to things he'd say. Had she just been being friendly? Polite?

After hearing her comment today, he had to wonder.

With her soulful brown eyes that held so much emotion, her silky chestnut hair she kept pulled up in a ponytail, pouty full lips, and almost fragile features, she'd caught his attention his first day at the hospital.

And held it.

He enjoyed their conversations, enjoyed sitting with her in the break room while she grabbed a quick lunch.

Although he'd yet to ask her out due to finishing up his move, settling into his new job and home, working three of the four weekends he'd been in Memphis and having to go home the previous weekend for his parents' anniversary, he'd planned to see if she was free for the upcoming weekend.

Not once had he questioned whether or not she'd say yes. He'd swear she was interested, that she enjoyed their light, fun conversations as much as he did.

Just the previous day, he'd asked her friend Rosalyn about her. Surprisingly, Rosalyn hadn't been able to tell him much about Carly's personal life. They'd worked together for five years, Carly didn't attend any of the hospital's social functions, rarely talked about family and never about anyone special.

None of their other co-workers had been able to tell him anything more.

He was a young healthy man who'd been used to an active social life since his divorce. Staying busy, active, was how he'd kept sane after Stephanie had left him. The fact his social life had been on hiatus from the move and job change was probably why he got so twisted up inside when he looked at Carly.

Although thinner than his usual taste, she was a beautiful woman, had a great sense of humor, and a quick smile.

When she smiled, his breath caught.

Rosalyn was right.

He had the hots for Carly.

Although he'd been in several relationships since his divorce, they'd all been light, fun, about mutual pleasure. From the moment he'd met her, Carly had tugged at something deep that made him question the meaningless relationships he moved in and out of with the ease of a broken heart that didn't allow anything more.

Memories of the past hit him, freezing him in place and making him question his interest in Carly.

Was she playing hard to get? Had he misread her? Or was there something more going on?

CHAPTER TWO

"SORRY I TOOK so long to bring your medicine," Carly apologized to the elderly man lying in the hospital bed.

Although partially dozed off, he wore a thick pair of glasses, along with oxygen tubing and a nasal cannula. He opened his eyes and stared in her direction, blankly at first, then with vague recognition.

Carly was used to that reaction. Wasn't it one she saw with increasing frequency from her mother?

Just as she did at home, Carly pasted on her brightest smile.

"I don't need medicine anyway," the man muttered grumpily and without making eye contact.

"Your medicine helps keep your heart in rhythm and will help get you out of this place and back home soon."

The man snorted. "I don't have a home."

Carly had been taking care of Mr. Taylor for three days, knew his personal history, and understood his frustrations that his family felt he could no longer live alone. With forgetting to eat and frequent falls, he couldn't.

"That's not what your daughter told me when she was visiting yesterday," Carly reminded him.

"She lied."

Carly handed him the plastic cup that held his pills. "You don't live with her?"

He thought a moment, then shook his head. He didn't say more, just took the medications.

"Is there anything else I can get you, Mr. Taylor?"

"A new body."

Carly smiled. She'd heard that many times over the five years she'd been a nurse.

"I wish I could," she admitted. She wished she could do a lot of things when it came to making someone well.

Especially with her mother's Parkinson's and dementia.

What she wouldn't do for there to be a cure to such horrific diseases that robbed one of their mind and body.

She checked his vitals, made sure his nurse-call button was within his reach, and left his room to check on another patient.

Mrs. Kim. A lovely little lady who'd had a surgically excised abscess on her chest. Due to the amount of infection and her weakened system, she'd been admitted for a few days for intravenous antibiotics to make sure the infection was knocked and to build up her strength.

Mrs. Kim's family had been taking turns staying during the evenings and night, but during the daytime her family worked and the woman was usually in her room alone.

Carly popped in frequently to check on her.

Most of the time the pleasant woman would be enthralled in whichever game show she was currently watching, but the vision that met Carly's eyes had her pausing in the doorway.

Looking distraught, Mrs. Kim was crying. Stone was at her bedside, holding her hand, offering comfort. Carly couldn't make out his exact words, but she could feel their soothing balm.

Could feel her own eyes watering in empathy at Mrs. Kim's distress.

Mrs. Kim grasped his hand in hers and was voicing her frustration over the wound that refused to heal in her chest, over how it was keeping her from her very busy life, and how she missed her two cats.

Whatever he said, Mrs. Kim weepily smiled, pulled his hand to her lips and smacked a kiss there.

"Thank you."

She said more, but Carly couldn't make out the words, just saw the woman's lips move and then Stone throw his head back and laugh.

A real laugh. One that reverberated through Carly. Made her long to share such a laugh with him.

How long had it been since she'd laughed like that? Carefree through and through? With all her worries set aside in the joy of the moment?

Since she'd felt any real, all-the-way-to-her-soul sense of joy?

No, that wasn't fair. She was happy, appreciative that she had her mother to go home to every day. It was what she wanted, what she'd choose given the choice. Every day was a blessing and to be cherished.

She did cherish life. She was *not* just going through the motions.

Thinking she'd come back later to check on Mrs. Kim, she turned to go, but the movement caught Stone's eye.

"Carly?"

Pasting a smile on her face, she stepped into the hospital room.

Ignoring Stone, she met her patient's gaze. "Hello, Mrs. Kim. I wanted to make sure you didn't need anything. I see you're in good hands."

Mrs. Kim's hand was locked between Stone's and the woman smiled. "Very."

"Is there anything you need?" She checked the woman's IV settings and vitals. Feeling Stone's gaze, she did her best to breathe normally, to function normally, and not make some total klutz move.

"Just to get better so I can go home."

"We're working on it," she promised, then wondered if she should have deferred to Stone.

She'd never gotten the impression he was one of those high-ego docs, but she'd only known him a month.

One month, four days.

Okay, so she was counting.

He didn't seem to mind her having answered for him. Possibly because he was too busy watching Carly's every move. As a doctor concerned about what his patient's nurse was doing? Maybe, but his expression was more inquisitive, as if he was trying to figure out what made her tick.

Good luck with that, she thought.

Actually, she was pretty dull. She worked and she took care of her mother. There wasn't time for anything more.

Just ask her ex-boyfriend.

"I'll be back in a little while to check on you," Carly promised, heading out the door.

When she reached for the handle, she couldn't resist glancing back. Her gaze collided with brilliant green.

His gaze holding hers, Stone smiled.

Something kicked in her chest.

Hard.

It might have been her heart skipping a beat or giving the strongest one in its twenty-seven-year history. Either way, she felt a little dizzy.

Carly's lips parted, because she should say something, right? The man moved her in ways she'd forgotten she could be moved.

Or had never known she could be moved.

But nothing came out of her mouth and she scurried out of the room, before she did something crazy.

Like admit that the problem with Stone was that he made her long to explore all the emotions sparking to life inside her.

But she wasn't free.

She needed to forget Stone.

Which was easier said than done since she saw the hospital's prized new surgeon every day she worked and every time she closed her eyes.

Stone wasn't wrong. He wasn't sure why Carly had said no to going to dinner with him, but she was as interested in him as he was her.

Desire had flashed in those eyes of hers.

Desire, longing, and so much more.

Which left him in a quandary.

He'd been rejected before, didn't have any desire to set himself up for another woman to walk away from him. But he needed to know why she'd said no when her eyes were begging him to sweep her off her feet.

"Hello," Carly called as she walked into her quiet house. The same house she'd grown up in. The same house she'd probably live in the rest of her life. "I'm home!"

She was. The small once white, but now faded, house was home, was where her heart and lots of wonderful memories were. Memories of better times when her mother had been well, full of spunk and energy, sharp-witted and capable of doing anything she wanted.

But those days were long gone.

For once Carly had gotten off work on time so hopefully her mother would still be awake, would hopefully be clear-minded, and not in the fog her memory often got enveloped by.

Joyce, her mother's nurse, came around the hallway corner and into the living room. "Busy day?"

Carly smiled at the sixty-something woman with gray hair she kept cut short and in loose, no-nonsense curls. A pair of thin gold-rimmed glasses sat on the bridge of her nose. She wore a Rolling Stones T-shirt with a big tongue on it and baggy, faded, rolled-up jeans that exposed slim ankles and flat white sandals.

Carly smiled. She and Joyce had an agreement the nurse wouldn't wear a uniform. She wanted her mother to feel she had a friend, not a medical professional. Joyce appreciated not having to don scrubs any more, too, as she'd done so for almost forty years prior to "retiring".

"They all are," Carly said, putting her handbag on the small dining table in one corner of the room. "But that's okay. I like to be busy."

"Which is a good thing because goodness knows you have enough on your plate for three people." Joyce tsked, shaking her head. "You need to slow down a little, and enjoy life before it passes you by."

"I'm fine." She was. Really, she was. So why did Stone's face pop into her mind and doubt fill her heart? She. Was. Fine. "There will be time for slowing down long before I'm ready." Which squeezed her insides and put things into proper perspective. "Speaking of which, how was Mom today?"

Joyce's expression tightened. "Not great. Getting her to eat is a major ordeal these days."

Carly winced. She knew from her own attempts to get her mother to eat. She seemed to have lost the will to live. "But she did eat?"

"She got her feeding tube meals, but by mouth." Joyce shook her head. "She just doesn't want anything."

Carly nodded, knowing the nurse would have done all she could to get as many nutrients into Carly's mother as possible.

"She struggled to communicate today," Joyce continued. "Not that she tried saying much, but, when she did, understanding her was more difficult than normal. And most of the day she called me Margaret."

Carly's grandmother, who'd passed away years ago.

Taking a deep breath, Carly nodded again.

"But in other news," the older woman began on a false hopeful note, "Gerald texted to say he picked up ten lottery tickets and one was sure to be a winner this time."

Rubbing the back of her neck, massaging a knotted muscle, Carly smiled. Joyce's husband struggled with a lifelong gambling problem. These days, he limited himself to no more than ten tickets in each week's Powerball lotto.

"He says when he wins we're gonna put your momma somewhere real fine and move you out of this place."

Carly shook her head. "First off, I'd never let you do that and, second, I don't want to move. You know this is where Momma wants to be. I'll keep her here as long as I am physically and financially able."

Always. She'd always keep her mother at home. She hoped and prayed.

Joyce waved her hand. "You know what I meant."

She did. Joyce wanted to help, as did Gerald, to lighten Carly's burden. But Carly had this. Precariously, but she was making ends meet. She'd worry about sorting out all the tangles and knots later…hopefully, much later.

"Thank you for all you do. Nothing more is needed." She hoped it never was. "Just you taking care of Momma."

Joyce made another loud tsking sound. "I don't do nearly enough."

"You're here and that frees me to work without worrying about what kind of care Momma is getting. That's huge." As she thought about how different life would be without someone she trusted to care for her mother, Carly's eyes misted. "If I don't say thank you often enough, please know how grateful I am that I met you while doing my clinical rotation at the nursing home where you worked."

Joyce's eyes filled with love. "You say thank you about every other breath, and you know the feeling is mutual.

Gerald and I love you and Audrey." The woman hugged Carly in a big bear hug, gathered her belongings, and got ready to leave. "Don't work too late into the night. You have to rest, too, you know."

Carly nodded. She worked a side job for an insurance company going through medical claims. The more claims she processed, the better her extra pay. While sitting next to her mother's bed, she'd work late tonight, processing as many claims as she accurately could.

"See you bright and early in the morning," she told the woman she truly didn't know what she'd do without.

Carly peeked in at her mother, saw she was resting, and went to the bathroom to grab a quick shower. When she'd finished and was dressed in old gray sweats and a baggy T-shirt, she checked her mother again, then went to make herself a sandwich before logging into the insurance company's website.

Work waited. It always did.

But when she went back into her mother's room, Audrey was awake.

"Hi, Mom. How was your day?" Some days her mother would answer. Some days her mother just stared blankly.

"S-same a-as a-always-s." Although slurred, her mother answered, which made Carly's heart swell. Did she know who Carly was today?

"Mine, too. Busy, busy, busy. Some of my patients are the same ones I mentioned to you last night, but I did have a couple of new ones." Carly never gave names or identifying information, but chatted about her patients. She tried to make her stories interesting, to give her mother a link to the outside world as often as she could.

Audrey rarely left the house these days. When she did it was usually to go to a doctor's appointment.

Before Carly knew it she was telling her mother about

walking in on the new surgeon and how he'd been holding his patient's hand, comforting her.

"I-i-is h-he h-h-handsome?"

"Gorgeous," she admitted. "He's also very kind and funny. The man makes me smile."

Realizing she was going on too much about Stone, she glanced at her mother.

Her mother who was staring oddly at her. "Y-you l-like h-him?"

Oops. Not the first time today she'd been asked that.

But, unlike at the hospital, to her mother, she nodded. "He seems like a great guy."

"Y-you sh-should g-go out with h-him."

Her mother knew her. If she thought Carly was Margaret, she'd be scolding rather than encouraging her mother to cheat on her father.

"Mom, he's a doctor. I'm a nurse. How cliché can you get?" She tried to keep her voice teasing and fun and similar to conversations they might have had during Carly's teenaged and college years when Carly had dated, when she'd been wrapped up in Tony and thought he was her forever person. "Besides, Stone's way out of my league."

"Wh-why?"

"Because he's such a great catch."

"S-so a-are y-you."

"You, my dearest mother, are the tiniest bit biased." Carly stood, bent over and kissed her mother's cheek. While her mother was with her, really with her, Carly wanted to milk the moment for every precious second. "Truly, he's out of my league. Even if he wasn't, it would never work."

"Be-because of m-me?"

"Of course not," Carly gasped. Never would she want her mother to think such a thing, never would she want her feeling guilt over Carly taking care of her to the ex-

clusion of everything else. It was a privilege to take care
of her mother. One Carly treasured and had never thought
twice about…until Stone.

Darn him. That he made her discontent with the status
quo was enough that she should dislike him.

"To-Tony," her mother began.

Despite the slight thrill that her mother's memory was
working at the moment, Carly stopped her. "Tony was an
idiot and I was lucky to be rid of him."

She was. Any man who couldn't understand that Carly
had to take care of her mother, that her mother came first,
well, he needed to hit the road. She'd needed Tony's support; instead, he'd resented everything about Audrey.

"Tony has nothing to do with why Stone and I would
never work. He and I are just not physically or economi-
cally compatible. That's all."

"I-if h-he th-thinks that then y-you are b-better off
wi-without h-him."

"Exactly." Before her mother could talk more about
Tony or Stone—why on earth had Carly mentioned him?—
Carly launched into a tale about another patient, exagger-
ating to make the recounting more entertaining.

Because tonight her mother looked at her and saw her
daughter. Sometimes that wasn't the case.

Sometimes it was all Carly could do not to cry.

Sometimes she did cry.

But not tonight. Tonight she smiled and enjoyed talking to the weak woman lying in the hospital bed that took
up a good portion of the bedroom.

Tonight her mother was mentally her mother.

"Any regrets?"

Having just stepped out of a patient room, Carly spun
toward the sound of Stone's voice near her ear and almost
collided with him.

"About what?" she asked, stepping back because of his close proximity. He wore dark navy scrubs that made his green eyes pop.

She glanced up and down the empty hospital hallway. Although the nurses' station was within view, no one was paying them the slightest attention.

"Not going to dinner with me last night." His voice teased, but his eyes asked real questions.

"Not a single one." The truth. She prized the evening she'd spent with her mother until she'd dozed off and Carly had worked on insurance claims late into the early morning hours.

Stone's sigh was so dramatic someone should give him an award. "Pity."

Despite knowing the best thing was to walk away, to not encourage him in any shape, form, or fashion, she couldn't resist asking, "Why's that?"

His gaze locked with hers, sparkled like an emerald sea. "We'd have had a good time."

She rolled her eyes. "Spoken like a true man."

"Meaning?"

"Men automatically think you getting to spend time with them means you'll have a good time." Tony had thought that. "That's not always the case, you know."

His grin was quick. "We should test that theory."

Step away, Carly. Don't get pulled in by his charm.

"By?" she asked, unable to follow her own advice, and wondering how long they could linger in the hallway prior to someone taking notice.

"Going to dinner with me tonight."

Her gaze met his. "I've already told you no to going to dinner tonight."

"That was yesterday. Today's a new day."

"My answer hasn't changed."

"It should."

Rosalyn stepped out of a patient room, glanced toward Carly and Stone, and stopped to stare.

"That's a matter of opinion," Carly quipped.

Obviously, Rosalyn's opinion ran more along the lines of Stone's. Grinning big, she gave a thumb up.

"Your opinion is that you should deprive yourself of dinner with me?"

"Deprive myself?" Carly snorted, then shook her head at Rosalyn. "I'll survive just fine if we never go to dinner."

Turning, Stone shot a grin at Rosalyn, who smiled back, then headed toward the nurses' station.

"You won't know what you're missing."

Shifting her weight, Carly squinted at him. "Is that supposed to bother me?"

His eyes flashed somewhere between serious and teasing. "It should."

"Why?"

"Because there's something between you and I."

Her breath caught. She felt it. He felt it. Thoughts of her mother were all that kept her from throwing herself at the mercy of whatever he wanted. She had no time for a relationship, no energy for a relationship. Everything she had, and more, was already claimed.

"You're wrong." She smiled tightly. "There's nothing I want from you."

"Why don't I believe you?"

Because I'm a horrible liar and usually pride myself on being a person who tells the truth, but with you…

She didn't want his pity. Or his rejection if he felt the same as Tony had.

"I don't know," she replied, not meeting his eyes. "Why don't you?"

"Because you're not telling the truth."

She hadn't expected him to call her bluff, and her gaze shot to his. "How dare you say such a thing?"

"Because it's true."

She lifted her chin in indignation, partly feigned, partly real, at his arrogance. "So your word gets taken as the truth, but not mine?"

"In this case, yes."

"What an ego you have, Dr. Parker."

"Stating facts doesn't make me egotistical."

Carly put her hands on her hips and glared at him with the sternest look she could muster. Not an easy thing to do when he was grinning at her with his brilliant smile and twinkling eyes.

"Is there a point to this conversation?"

"Just enjoying your company." His tone was teasing, but the glint in his eyes said he told the truth.

If she were honest, she'd admit she was enjoying his company, too. Which was ridiculous considering what their actual words were. Was she really that desperate for any scrap of his attention?

"I've work to do." She glanced down the hallway and caught Rosalyn and a nurse's aide watching them.

"Am I interfering with your work, Carly?"

"Yes." Carly's head hurt. Or maybe it was her heart.

"How so?"

"You're distracting me."

His eyes danced. "You're admitting you find me distracting? Finally, we're getting somewhere."

She bit the inside of her lower lip, then shook her head. "Dr. Parker, I shouldn't be having lengthy personal conversations while on the clock."

"Which is why you should go to dinner with me tonight. We could have lengthy personal conversations to our hearts' content."

She wanted to. She wanted to say yes, go to dinner with him, and stare into his eyes all evening. Longer.

But, even if she could, how unfair would that be to him? Very. To lead him, or anyone, on was wrong.

She should tell him, should apologize for smiling when he sat with her at break, for laughing at his corny jokes, for looking at him and longing for things outside her grasp.

But she couldn't find the words, so she hurried away, dodging into a patient room to avoid both the man she could feel watching her and her two co-workers anxiously waiting to question her.

She didn't think of herself as a woman who ran from her problems. But, at the moment, running from temptation, and the questioning thereof, seemed the best course of action.

CHAPTER THREE

"CAN I HELP you with that?"

Carly peeped at Stone from over the top of the box she carried through the hospital corridor. He'd changed out of his navy scrubs into his own clothes, black trousers and a green polo shirt that perfectly matched the color of his eyes. She fought sighing in appreciation. The man should be in movies, not a hospital operating room.

"I've got it," she assured him. "Thanks anyway."

Ignore him and maybe he'll go away. Not likely, but maybe.

"That box is bigger than you are."

The sturdy box was more bulky than heavy. Inside were expired medical supplies the hospital couldn't use. Carly had gotten clearance from upper management to take the expired supplies home with her. No one at the hospital knew about her mother, but they did know she sat with someone on her days off work.

There might not be a thing she could use. But Carly would go through the box, pull out what she could use, and take the rest to a free health clinic for the uninsured that could hopefully make use of the items.

"You look like it's all you can do to keep steady. Quit being stubborn and let me help you, Carly," Stone insisted, his voice sounding off a little.

He had a point. Plus, Carly's fingers ached from gripping the box so hard and she was curious why his voice wavered. "Fine."

He took the box from her with an ease indicating it weighed no more than a feather, then beamed as if he'd done something amazingly chivalrous. Whatever had caused the waver, he was all smiles now.

"Lead the way."

As in to her car.

She didn't want Stone to see her reliable, but old sedan. Whereas most people didn't notice the little details in Carly's life that hinted things might not be fairy tales and roses, that sharp mind of his would question things she didn't want questioned.

She didn't want him making her question things.

Pushing the hospital door open and holding it for him, she sighed. "Of all the people who offered to help, it would have to be you."

"If I didn't know better, I'd think you didn't like me."

"I don't know you well enough to like or dislike you," she said as she made sure the hospital door completely closed. "I only know you from the hospital and what little interaction we've had here."

"I keep trying to correct that."

"You want me to know you well enough to dislike you?" She pretended to misunderstand in hopes of redirecting the conversation. Besides, he deserved a little taking down.

Rather than look offended, he laughed. "I'm hoping you'll swing the other way and like me."

Fighting a smile, she narrowed her gaze at him. "But you're admitting there is a distinct possibility I won't?"

"It's not been a big problem, but you wouldn't be the first." He cut his eyes toward her. "For the record, I'd prefer you like me."

"Noted," she said, keeping a step ahead of him as they crossed the employee parking lot.

"Go to dinner with me, Carly."

He was asking her again. How could something be so unbelievably dreamy and such a nightmare at the same time?

"I can't." Part of her wanted to. Part of her wanted to grab her box and run.

Despite how she'd hightailed it from him earlier, she didn't run from her problems. She dealt with them head on and chin up.

Just as she had with Rosalyn and the nurse's aide's teasing questions about Stone.

"Because?" he prompted.

Because she had to relieve Joyce. The retired nurse was wonderful, never complained if Carly worked overtime, but, otherwise, Carly always came straight home.

"Are you involved with a married man?"

Almost tripping, eyes wide, Carly spun toward Stone. "What? Are you crazy? Of course not. What would make you think that?"

His gaze, not so twinkly at the moment, stared into her eyes. "No one knows anything about your private life, yet you say you're busy."

She glared for real. "Because I'm not interested in you that means I must be sneaking around with a married man?" She rolled her eyes. "Get over yourself, Dr. Parker."

He winced. "That's not what I meant."

"It's what you implied and I don't appreciate it." Was that what he'd taken away from the short bits of time they'd spent together? That she was a woman who would mess around with a man who'd vowed himself to another woman?

"I'm sorry. That's not what I meant to imply."

Hanging onto her anger proved difficult when his apology was full of sincerity. Frustrated with herself, she put her hands on her hips. "Then say what you mean."

He shifted the box. "Regardless of what I say, I upset you."

"You should take the hint and not say anything, then."

"What's the fun in that?"

"What's the fun in upsetting me?" she tossed back and took off toward her car in a fast walk.

"You're right," Stone said from right behind her. "I take no pleasure in upsetting you. The truth is I want to do the opposite."

"You want to take pleasure in upsetting me?" She pretended to misunderstand, again. She felt contrary and purposely misunderstanding gave her a little reprieve. Asking if she was seeing a married man! The nerve. "Thanks, but no, thanks."

Okay, she might be latching onto that to throw a wall between them. She needed whatever shield she could find to protect her from the charm he exuded.

Digging her key out of her pocket, Carly unlocked her old economy sedan, then hit the button on the car-door panel to unlock the back doors. She opened the backseat door, tugging a little extra hard where the door often stuck, then stepped back for Stone to put the box onto the seat.

He made sure the box wasn't going anywhere if she slammed on her brakes or took a curve a little fast, then faced her. "Is it me, then, or men in general?"

"Is your ego so big that you just can't fathom I'm not interested?"

He closed the car door and moved to where he stood right in Carly's personal space. "My ego isn't that big and if it had been, you'd have corrected that."

Ouch.

"What I'd like," he continued, "is to know why you

say you aren't interested when I'd put money on the fact you are."

Hands digging into her hips, she glared. "You'd lose your money."

"Would I?" His question was gentle rather than mocking. "I'm not sure what changed yesterday, Carly. I'm not blind. I've seen how you look at me. It's the same way I look at you. With interest. If my delay in asking you out is the problem, know it wasn't from lack of interest. On the days I haven't worked, I've been traveling back and forth from Atlanta to settle up everything with my move."

Any spunk Carly had left her like a deflating balloon.

Any woman would be flattered at Stone's attention. If his ego had been huge, it would be with good reason.

And she was flattered by his attention.

But his attention was a distraction she didn't need because she had to stay focused. Losing focus could mean everything falling apart and she couldn't allow that to happen.

Plus, how could she in good conscience involve any man in her crazy life? Just look at how Tony had balked and her mother hadn't been nearly as needful at that time.

She closed her eyes. "It would be simpler if you'd move on and forget whatever interest you have in me."

"Do you remember when we first met?"

Stone's question caught her off guard. Her eyes popped open and she stared at him.

"You were coming out of the medical supply room and bumped into me," he continued, his gaze searching hers. "You almost fell over yourself apologizing." A soft smile played on his lips. "I thought you were the prettiest thing I'd seen in a long time."

Vanities were not something Carly had the time or money to indulge in. She kept her hair in a no-maintenance style of long and natural to where she could pull it up and not bother with highlights or salons. She hadn't worn make-up since college. Money was too tight for such frivolities. His calling her the prettiest thing stirred up a thousand butter-flies in her belly.

"I think that right now."

His words set every butterfly into fluttery flight. Oh, my. Carly gulped.

"You must have had your eyes closed a long time, then." She fought to keep from putting her hand over her stomach.

Studying her, he shook his head. "You were in these same blue scrubs, but had on different shoes. Your laces were bright orange rather than neon green."

He remembered what she'd been wearing when they first met? That her shoe laces had been a different color?

"You are a lovely woman, Carly."

To which she could only say, "Thank you."

Embarrassed, feeling a little shaky at the knees, Carly glanced around the employee parking lot and caught sight of a co-worker curiously looking her way, the nurse's aide who'd been with Rosalyn earlier.

The woman called out, "Goodnight."

Carly waved and wished her a good evening as well, then frowned at the man still standing too close.

"She's a wonderful person, but does tend to gossip. No doubt, everyone will know you were at my car with me."

"Then we should give them something to talk about." The eye-twinkle was back.

Horrified, Carly shook her head. "No, we shouldn't."

She needed her job, couldn't risk anything creating waves at her place of employment. Not even the tempta-tion in Stone's eyes.

He sighed and raked his fingers through his hair. "You're right. Sorry. I seem to have a one-track mind where you're concerned. Give me your address. I'll fol-low you home and carry the box inside."

"Not going to happen." No way would she be able to explain to Joyce why a handsome doctor had followed her home. Carrying a heavy box in wouldn't begin to satisfy the protective older woman's curiosity.

As for Stone's one-track mind, why was her body heating up at the possibilities of what he'd meant?

"Are you capable of saying yes to anything I suggest?"

Yeah, she was being ornery. For her own safety and sanity. His, too.

"Probably not," she admitted, giving a wry smile.

"I'm a pretty straightforward guy. I'd like to date you, Carly. I've been trying to get to know you and thought we were until yesterday. If my overhearing your conversation with Rosalyn upset you that much, I truly am sorry." His tone was appropriately repentant. "I want to take you out, talk with you, dine with you away from the hospital, and eventually kiss those lips of yours that I find myself thinking about way too often."

Insides shaking, heart pulled into a tug-of-war between need and want and guilt, Carly closed her eyes. "I can't do this."

"You can't talk to me?"

"I can't hear you say those things," she clarified, not opening her eyes. In a tug-of-war of its own, her mind raced between logic and emotion and loyalty to her mother.

Stone wanted to date her. Stone wanted to *kiss* her. She'd not been kissed in so long. Not since Tony.

Suddenly the need to be kissed, to feel like a woman, to feel alive and wanted and young, burst free and filled every cell of her being to overflowing.

Which was what made Stone so very dangerous to all she held dear.

He could make a total disaster of her life.

"Because?"

Had his voice been closer? She thought so, but she didn't

open her eyes to check. She couldn't look, couldn't see whatever was in his magnificent green eyes.

Stone tempted. Tempted her to want things she shouldn't want.

Couldn't want.

Couldn't have.

Which didn't seem to matter because she was a woman with normal urges and he made all those urges come on full force whether she wanted them to or not.

Probably the rest of her life she'd look back and wish circumstances had presented her with the option to throw caution to the wind with Stone Parker.

To forget the pain of Tony turning his back on her.

To embrace all the warmth and urges Stone stirred.

Because she'd like him to kiss her. Had not been able to stop the late-night thoughts about what it would feel like to be kissed by him.

Now, he'd said he wanted to kiss her.

How was she ever supposed to get him out of her head when he'd verbalized things she'd fantasized?

"Carly?"

His voice was so close, her name whispered against her cheek.

"Hmm?"

"Open your eyes."

She bit the inside of her lower lip. "I can't."

"There's a lot of things you say you can't do, lady."

"Exactly. You should run."

"I don't believe there's anything you can't do."

He was definitely closer. She'd swear she just felt his breath tickle her ear.

"For the record," he continued, "I'm not going any-where."

The brevity of his words dug in deep, breaking through barriers that were best left alone.

"Not unless you tell me to," he clarified. "Then I will leave you alone, because I'm not some psycho stalker, just a man wanting to date a beautiful woman."

Tell him to go away.

Tell him sticking around is futile.

Tell him...

Stone's lips brushed against her hairline, near her ear. Soft, gentle, tentative. Not a sexual kiss, but one full of longing and question and space. Space that gave her control of what happened next.

Carly's eyes shot open, stared into his eyes, and she wondered at what she saw there.

Desire, confusion, so much she couldn't label.

"Tell me you aren't curious, Carly. Tell me I'm crazy when I look in your eyes and see a kindred desire. Tell me to put you in your car, watch you drive away, never think of you again, and I'll try to do just that."

Tell him.

Not to do so would be selfish.

Self-destructive.

But her lips refused to cooperate so she said nothing.

"Tell me what you want, Carly."

She didn't know what she wanted.

Not true. She wanted him to do exactly what he'd said he wanted to do. She wanted him to kiss her.

Crazy.

She wasn't free to have a relationship. To pull some unsuspecting man into her chaotic life wouldn't be fair.

Plus, with two jobs and her mother, she barely slept as it was. Where would she fit in a relationship?

She opened her mouth, determined to tell him she only wanted a professional relationship, that he needed to forget about her and whatever it was he thought he'd seen when she looked at him.

So why did she hear her address spill from her lips?

She was crazy. She couldn't let him into her house, couldn't let Joyce or her mother hear his voice.

Surprise lit in his eyes, then, with a smile, he nodded. "I'll follow you home and carry in the box."

What had she done?

And why?

Because she wanted to know what it felt like to kiss Stone?

It wasn't as if she were actually going to kiss him.

Only in her deepest darkest late-night fantasies and even then she barely gave her mind license to imagine Stone's lips against hers.

She'd made a horrible mistake by giving him her address. Just what did he think it had meant? If he was thinking he was staying the night, he was going to be in for a rude awakening when he realized an invalid woman also lived at Carly's address.

Carly got into her car, leaned forward, and rested her forehead against the steering wheel.

Clearly, she'd lost her mind.

Or maybe, because she hadn't been able to verbalize the reasons why they could never be, her subconscious had taken control, and was going to confront Stone with the harsh reality of why he needed to forget her.

That harsh reality had certainly scared off the last man Carly had brought home.

Had Carly given Stone a bogus address?

If she had, Stone couldn't say he'd be surprised.

He hoped she hadn't, but had to wonder. She'd thrown it out at a point where the last thing he'd expected was an invitation to her home.

She hadn't technically invited him to her house, but hadn't that been what giving her address to him had essentially been?

As he'd only moved to Memphis a month before and was still learning the city, he programmed the details into his GPS and noted she only lived six minutes from the hospital and about fifteen from him as he lived over the bridge on Mud Island.

At least, he'd know pretty quickly if she'd told him the truth. And if she hadn't?

Well, that should tell him that she wanted him to leave her alone.

Only she didn't want that. He knew she didn't.

She hadn't even been able to say the words.

He'd flirted with her at the hospital on more than one occasion. She'd flirted back. Not overtly, but her smiles and sassy eye flashes and little laughs at his jokes had all been leading up to something. What had happened yesterday that had her scurrying back?

No matter how many times he replayed the conversation, he couldn't fathom what had put her on the defensive.

Not quite liking the looks of the run-down neighborhood and having been warned not to go wandering around parts of Memphis he was unfamiliar with, Stone questioned again if Carly had given him a made-up address. He turned onto her street, and, best as he could tell, the houses on the street were small, older, but decently cared for.

His GPS told him he'd arrived at his destination and he pulled up his SUV outside a small once-white frame house that even in the dark he could tell needed some major TLC. Much more so than the surrounding homes.

That surprised him.

Carly was meticulous in her care of patients and all that she did at her job. To ignore upkeep on her home didn't fit what she believed about her. He could be wrong, but he struggled to wrap his mind around the neglect that registered.

He wouldn't have guessed her to live in the house of obvious worst repair on her street.

Then again, maybe she rented the place and her land-lord was the slacker.

As a nurse, she made a decent salary to where she could afford to move if she was renting and things weren't up to par. If she had some long-term lease that had her trapped in the run-down house, maybe he could call on a lawyer friend to get her into something better maintained.

He would help her find another place.

A place closer to his on Mud Island.

There was another car, a much newer sedan, parked in the drive beside hers. Did she have a roommate?

She must have just pulled into the short gravel driveway right before him as when he turned off the SUV's engine and opened his door, Carly got out of her car.

"You really didn't need to do this," she said immediately, before he could ask about the other car. "Yes, it's bulky, but I would have gotten the box inside without any problems. I was doing just fine before you came to my rescue."

"No need to risk hurting your back when you have me."

Whether she wanted him or not, he planned to help Carly because he suspected more was going on than met the eye with the woman who'd captured his imagination.

CHAPTER FOUR

Stone was at Carly's house.

Now that he was there, what was Carly supposed to do with him?

Let him carry the box to her porch and send him away?

It was what she wanted to do, what she was tempted to do.

Somehow she didn't think he would agree to it though. He had that "let me be your knight in shining armor" look that she'd seen in the movies her mother enjoyed watching, but that Carly had never seen in real life.

Until now.

If Stone went inside, it was quite possible her mother would be asleep and Carly could avoid that explanation. But Joyce would be there and ready to head to her home to spend the evening with her husband.

Joyce seeing Stone would raise questions. From Joyce, but perhaps more so from Stone.

Maybe she could have him set the box just inside the doorway and get him back outside prior to Joyce realizing they were there. Before Stone realized there was someone else in the house.

Unlikely, but she could try.

Or she could just tell Stone everything.

Which made her stomach hurt.

She didn't want him to feel sorry for her or feel obligated to offer help. The past had taught her people might think they wanted to help, but most only offered idle words.

She had this. She could take care of her mother.

She could, she was, and she would.

Or was it that she was afraid he'd pull a Tony?

Wasn't that what she actually needed him to do? What would be best for her and Stone?

So, why was she hesitating?

"It's no problem," Stone assured her, pulling Carly back to their conversation as he lifted the box out of her backseat.

"Thank you." She shut the car door then moved ahead of him to unlock her front door.

She turned, wondering if Stone would be agreeable to drop the box in the foyer and leave.

Maybe she was a runner after all, because if she could escape this moment, her tennis shoes would be getting a desperately needed workout.

Stone carried the box, stopped just inside the doorway and asked, "Where would you like me to put this?"

She pointed to a small wooden bench that had once upon a time belonged to her long-gone grandparents. "Right there is fine."

He set the box down. "What's in this thing, anyway?"

"Stolen goods from the hospital."

His eyes narrowed.

Nerves still shaking up her insides, Carly grinned. "Gotcha."

His lips twitched. "Maybe a little."

"It's expired hospital supplies that were going to be tossed," she admitted, wondering if she was strong enough to toss him out the front door before Joyce saw him. The nurse must have been tied up with Audrey or she'd have already greeted Carly.

Stone glanced toward the box. "What do you do with the supplies?"

She shrugged. Best to stick with the truth. "Use what I can and donate the rest. Let's go back outside." *Please*. "I think I left something in the car."

"Oh." He turned toward the front door, but they were too late.

"I thought I heard voices in here," Joyce said, entering the room, then stopping when she spotted Stone.

Carly's stomach dropped.

Startled, Stone glanced toward Carly, then back at the woman who was gawking at him as if she didn't believe her eyes. She must not have because she was adjusting her glasses as if they'd stopped working.

Quickly recovering, Stone stuck out his hand. "Stone Parker." He flashed his amazing smile. "I work with Carly."

"You're a nurse?" Joyce's gaze went back and forth between them.

Carly inwardly cringed at the questions in the older woman's eyes. Joyce was trying to figure out who Stone was and why he was there. Maybe she even thought he was trying to replace her as Audrey's sitter. As if.

"He's a doctor," Carly clarified to make sure there was no doubt Joyce's job was not in jeopardy. Far from it. Carly needed Joyce every moment she could afford her.

"You're a doctor?" Joyce asked, sounding a bit incredulous. "Sign me up for some healthcare. I think I'm way past due for my physical."

Heat infused Carly's cheeks at Joyce's off-color remark.

Stone's smile dug his dimples deep into his cheeks. He was probably used to such comments from women of all ages. "I'll have to give you my card so you can schedule an appointment."

Joyce's eyes twinkled. "You do that."

"Nice shirt, by the way."

Joyce looked down at the vintage Kiss T-shirt she wore with the four band members in full make-up and leather garb framed in a fiery circle. "Thanks. My husband and I were music buffs in our younger years." She glanced over the gold rim of her glasses. "I have quite the collection."

"Stone helped me carry in a box of supplies the hospital was getting rid of," Carly said, trying to explain his presence.

Joyce nodded toward the box. "I see that."

"But he has to go now," Carly added, not meeting Stone's eyes but staring at his forehead instead.

His brows veed. "I do?"

"Yes, you do."

Disappointment clouding his expression, he frowned. "Oh."

"Unless you'd like to stay for dinner," Joyce offered, obviously thinking she needed to keep Stone there. "I could whip something up."

Ha. Carly would like to know what the woman could whip together. She'd not been to the grocery store that week and wouldn't for another two days. Not until after payday. Even then, it would be meager shopping as her mother's neurologist had started her on a new medication that month hoping to better control her tremors. The new medicine hadn't been covered by insurance and Carly had dipped into what little she had put back for a rainy day. If the medicine helped her mother, it was worth whatever the cost.

"Since I couldn't convince Carly to go to dinner to keep me from dining alone, dinner here would be great."

Carly shot him a dirty look. That was a low blow, she mentally willed him to hear.

"Carly wouldn't go to dinner with you?" Joyce sent her an "Are you crazy?" look. "Why not?"

"You know why not."

Please don't say anything about Momma. Please. I don't want Stone involved.

"I could've stayed late. I wouldn't have minded."

How tacky did it sound to say she couldn't afford her to stay late? Especially not this month.

"I have to ask you often enough when I'm stuck behind at work," she reminded her. "I don't expect you to work late here so I can go to dinner with a new co-worker. That wouldn't be fair."

"Work?" Stone asked, obviously confused.

"What's not fair is you not going to eat dinner with this young man. I insist you go."

Although confused and obviously enjoying Joyce taking his side, Stone looked as if he was trying to connect all the dots. Hoping he wouldn't was futile.

Carly was exhausted by it all. Her long work day. Stone and all the crazy emotions he made her feel. Her mother's illness. Joyce and her motherly concern that Carly wasn't having the life she deserved.

Who got the life they deserved?

Not many. Maybe not anyone.

Overall, Carly was content with life. She had enough to pay the bills—barely—and she had her mother. That was all that mattered.

"You should listen to your mother."

Stone thought Joyce was her mother?

"Joyce isn't my mother, or even blood kin, although I do love her as if she is family." Carly took a deep breath. "My mother has late stage Parkinson's disease with dementia and requires full-time care. Joyce stays with Momma while I am at work."

"And would have been glad to stay this evening so you could go to dinner," Joyce jumped in to say. "You need to get out more. You're way too young to spend all your free time locked away inside this house."

Advice Joyce gave several times every week, but that didn't change a thing. Carly chose to live her life by taking care of her mother. Her only regret was that her mother was so ill.

Bracing herself for what she might see, Carly brought her gaze to Stone's face, expecting the worst, probably because of Tony.

"I agree with Joyce." His gaze searched hers, a million questions shining in the green depths. Most of which centered around, "Why didn't you tell me about your mother?"

Carly bit the inside of her cheek.

"You are way too young, and beautiful," he added, his eyes not wavering from hers, "to be locked away. For whatever it's worth, I'm sorry about your mother."

His empathy was something Carly didn't want. Not that she preferred him to be cold or callous, just that…well, she didn't want his pity.

Wasn't that part of why she kept her private life private? That, and she wanted to just be happy at work without anyone judging her for doing so when her mother was so ill. Being down and out wouldn't change her mother's illness, so Carly chose to pretend life was grand when she was at the hospital. She could smile and laugh and not feel judged for feeling joy. It helped her feel…normal.

"It's not as if I feel locked away." She didn't. She felt blessed to take care of her mother, to have the time with her that she did. "This is my home. I like it here."

She'd grown up within these walls, had once played in the small backyard. Her, her mother, and her grandparents. She'd had a carefree childhood, not understanding how poor they were or how hard her mother worked to make ends meet after her grandparents had died. Her mother had been diagnosed with Parkinson's Carly's senior year of high school, but that hadn't stopped her from working or living her life. Not initially.

Carly had moved away for college, but when, during Carly's senior year at university, her mother's disease had progressed, causing her to leave her job, Carly had moved home. She'd had to. Her mother had needed help with expenses as she'd been on the verge of losing the house to her mortgage company.

Through endless hours of hard work, Carly had saved the house, taken over her mother's limited finances, and worked as much overtime at her waitressing job as she could to make headway on the enormous burden of medical bills, the expenses of keeping up a house, and all the other bills that had seemed to hit her from every direction. Plus, she'd maintained her grades, gone to clinicals, and somehow found time to study for her nursing board examination.

That had been just over five years ago. Although Carly's income had jumped upon graduation, her mother's health had continued to deteriorate and her expenses had skyrocketed. Audrey had been unable to stay home alone for the past three years and been mostly bedridden for the past year. Although taking a huge chunk of Carly's income, Joyce had been a life-saver and was worth every penny.

To keep treading water and making a little progress from time to time, Carly worked her hospital job, worked from home reviewing the claims for a large insurance company, cared for her mother, and slept whenever she could squeeze in a few hours. Things were tight and Carly often felt she was barely managing to juggle all the bills, but it could be worse. She could be sinking rather than treading the surface.

Or even worse, she could not have her mother.

She wouldn't complain.

"Of course, you do, dear," Joyce assured her, coming over and giving Carly a quick hug. When she pulled back, she gave Carly that motherly look that made her feel as if she were five rather than a grown woman. "I'll stay with Audrey and you go have a nice meal."

Five or twenty-seven, Carly started to protest.

"I don't have plans tonight. Gerald has his bowling league and won't be home until late," Joyce countered before Carly could get started. "I'll be going home to an empty house, so I'd gladly stay for free."

Joyce had offered to come in to help Carly on numerous occasions, offering not to charge anything for her time. She truly had become like family. Still, Carly had hoped she'd never have to take the woman up on her offer. She didn't want handouts.

She shook her head. "I can't ask you to do that. You already do too much."

"You didn't ask. I offered." Joyce glanced toward Stone, gave him an appreciative once-over. "Actually, I insist. Go relax for an hour or so, Carly. I'd just gotten your mother changed as you were getting home. She fell asleep as I redressed her. She isn't likely to wake any time soon. I can heat some soup and catch the news here just as easily as I can at home. Go."

Carly bit the inside of her cheek. She couldn't say yes, could she? The expression on Joyce's face said the woman wasn't leaving without an argument. "You're sure you don't mind?"

"Positive."

"We could bring back dessert," Stone offered, his gaze focused on Carly, except to flash a quick smile to the older woman.

Joyce smiled at him in a way that made Carly wonder if the woman was seeing wedding bells and a solution to Carly's financial woes, just in case Gerald's lottery numbers failed to produce miracles again this week.

"I like your fellow already, Carly. He knows the way to a woman's heart. Dessert."

Carly started to correct Joyce, to tell her that Stone was not her fellow, but she wouldn't believe her, so what was the point?

Carly turned toward Stone. "Fine. If you'll give me fifteen minutes to check my mother, change out of my uniform and freshen up, I'll go to dinner."

"Take all the time you need. In case you haven't figured it out, I'm not going anywhere."

Telling her heart not to believe him, that he didn't know what he was saying, Carly stepped into her mother's bedroom.

The rhythmic rise and fall of her mother's chest was reassuring. Joyce was right. Her mother wasn't likely to wake any time soon. Generally, Carly came home, ate leftovers or something cheap she could rustle up, then logged in remotely to the insurance company and worked until whatever time her mother woke. Generally, she woke around midnight, was awake for about an hour, and then was out again for the rest of the night. Carly usually headed to bed at whatever time her mother dozed back off.

Last night had been a blessing that her mother had been awake, aware, and communicative. A rare treat.

With Joyce at the house, Carly could go to dinner. She had several hours' worth of insurance claims to go through, but she could do that when she got back and just not sleep as much. Who needed sleep, right?

Besides, she owed Stone an explanation, to verbalize that at least now he knew why a relationship between them was impossible.

Which she could do right now without their going to dinner. So why wasn't she?

Right or wrong, she was going to dinner with the man she'd fallen asleep and dreamed of the night before.

God help her.

* * *

"Is your mother why you said no to going out with me, Carly?" Stone asked the moment they got into his SUV.

His high-end fancy SUV with leather seats and more gadgets than a spaceship.

"There goes your ego talking again," she said flippantly, thinking that just the contrast in their vehicles should warn she shouldn't be with him.

They were as different as day and night.

"You didn't answer my question."

"Sure, I did," she countered, buckling her seat belt over the black trousers and plain rust-colored blouse she'd pulled from the back of her closet. She'd half expected the car to automatically buckle her in.

"Pride isn't why I'm asking," he assured her, pushing a button on the dash and starting the vehicle.

But maybe pride was why she felt so inadequate sitting in his "all the bells and whistles" SUV. Ugh. She didn't like what that said about her.

He punched in some letters she didn't catch on the GPS on his dashboard. He made sure there weren't any cars coming, then pulled away from her house and onto the street.

"There's lots of reasons why I've said no."

"Such as?" He turned the car down a street, then made another quick turn, following the directions from the car's navigation system.

Carly stared out the window, realized they were headed toward downtown.

"My life is full," she finally answered.

"Not in a good way."

Walls shot up and she glared across the car. "That's a matter of opinion. For the record, I wouldn't change it."

Because the only way her life was going to get easier

was if something happened to her mother. God forbid. Her mother was everything.

"I understand that…" Stone's tone softened as he pulled the car into a restaurant parking lot "…but it is unfortunate you live as if you're a hermit."

Looking around at his restaurant pick, she realized he'd chosen one she'd mentioned during one of their lunches.

Julio's. Of all the ones he could have picked, why this one? Totally her fault. She'd been the one to mention Julio's.

"Don't pay any attention to what Joyce said." Or to what she said, because Carly couldn't believe they were at the restaurant where she'd worked during high school and university. "I think she may just be trying to scope out more work hours."

Guilt slammed her for suggesting such a falsehood. Joyce wasn't doing any such thing. Ugh.

He turned the ignition off and turned toward her. "I didn't get that impression."

Because he was astute and there hadn't been any reason for him to get that impression because Joyce was an angel.

Carly reached for the door handle. "Let it go. It's my choice, Stone, one I am happy to make."

After all, her mother had always worked hard, had done everything she could to be there for Carly, to provide for her physically and emotionally. All without help from Carly's father. Carly had no complaints.

She'd had a great childhood where she'd been loved and had loved. That was more than many people ever had.

So what if her twenties had been heavily laden thus far? If Carly was lucky that load would be carried into her thirties, her forties even.

Because she was not ready to let go of her mother.

Some nights, while she worked on her laptop and would get distracted by her mother's grunts and groans, she'd question that, wondering if, when her mother's time came, she'd be able to let go, knowing that her mother's pain had eased and she'd never hurt again. Then Carly would put the thoughts from her head, because she didn't want to think about when that horrible day arrived and how she'd deal with the loss.

She wasn't sure she could deal with losing her mother.

As they reached the entrance of the restaurant, he asked, "Do you do anything for fun, Carly?"

"Of course." But she didn't look at him.

"Name something."

"Sitting with my mother."

"That doesn't count."

"It should. There's no one else I'd rather spend time with."

"Outside your house," he redirected his question, "do you do anything for fun?"

"Joyce has already told you that I don't go anywhere, so that isn't a fair question."

"I like Joyce. She seems like a great lady."

"She is. I don't know what I'd do without her," Carly admitted as he opened the restaurant door for her. "She is a life-saver."

"My guess is that you'd manage," he said, smiling as she hesitated outside the restaurant entrance. "You seem the type to make things work no matter how much stress you endure in the process."

Which was one of the biggest compliments Stone could have given to her. She wanted to be independent, to handle things herself. It was what her mother had done, while healthy and capable, and it was what Carly strived for.

"Thank you," she told him and meant it as they entered the restaurant. Carly's stomach twisted at what she knew was likely to come. Or maybe she'd get lucky and all the people who'd known her would have moved on, just as she had. After all, she'd not been inside the restaurant for five years. "If I've come across as whiny—" she glanced around the restaurant and took in the bluesy atmosphere and smells that instantly filled her with nostalgia "—that wasn't my intention."

"You're not whiny. Far from it. I just stated my observation." He leaned forward and told the hostess, "Two."

Carly didn't recognize the young girl, nor had she seen a single person she recognized. She relaxed a little. A lot changed in five years. Not Julio's décor or atmosphere, though.

Same wooden tables with their battery lit candles. Same high-back chairs that were only semi-comfortable. Same rust-colored seats in the booths that lined one wall. Same jazzy blues playing softly in the background. She breathed in a deep breath. Same yummy garlic and tomato sauce smell.

Her stomach growled. She covered her belly with her hand and turned to see if the growl had been so thunderous that Stone had heard.

If so, he didn't point it out, just smiled and said, "I've been watching you for a month."

"That's creepy," she scolded. All the while her insides danced with a nervousness that had nothing to do with being creeped out and everything to do with the fact she was the object of this gorgeous man's attention.

"Not that I haven't told myself the same thing since overhearing your conversation with Rosalyn, but there's a comment that will deflate a man's ego in a hurry."

"I'd say your ego is just fine."

"Possibly not after the beating you've given it over the past two days."

"I enjoy talking with you at the hospital but we can't have a relationship outside the hospital," she pointed out. "I'm sorry if I let you think that was a possibility."

He studied her. "Because of your situation?"

She nodded. "Yes."

Holding a couple of menus, the hostess motioned for them to follow her. She seated them at one of the booths. Carly had always liked the booths and thought they were cozy and perfect for a date. Not that this was a date. Or maybe it was. She wasn't really sure.

When they were settled into their seats and the hostess had moved on, Stone asked, "Isn't the fair thing to give me the facts and let me decide for myself?"

He made a good point. One she couldn't think of a single argument against.

"I suppose." She stared at her menu.

"So why didn't you?"

Good question.

"I don't know." She stared at the menu harder, marveling that it was the same as when she'd worked there, other than an increase in prices.

"Not good enough."

Not glancing up, she shrugged. "It's the only answer I have."

"Dig deeper, Carly. Why didn't you let me make the choice for myself?"

He studied her so closely that she didn't have to look to feel the intensity.

"We all have baggage, Carly," he assured her. "Just different-sized suitcases."

Carly bit the inside of her cheek. He wasn't going to let this drop, which meant she really did have to dig deeper, and when she dug, she didn't like what she saw.

Lowering her menu, she met his gaze. "I was afraid to give you that option and set myself up for disappointment," she said, watching to see how he reacted to her admission.

"How would I disappoint you?"

Good grief, the man pushed. Why wasn't their waitress interrupting to get their drink orders?

"My life is full. Despite that I am with you now, this

isn't typical. Nor can it be. I rush home from work and am there until I go back to work. I don't have time for dating or becoming involved with someone. I just don't," she emphasized the words, "and won't."

Then the waitress joined them, chatting away about what a lovely evening it was and could she tempt them with some fresh bread, which of course she could. She took their drink orders, then disappeared again.

"Maybe we can be friends."

Stone's words surprised Carly. "Friends?"

He reached across the table and took her hand. "Let's be friends. I get the impression you could use one."

His hand was warm around hers, but not warm enough to explain the fire moving through her body.

Fire that wasn't friendly.

Not by a long shot.

A flashback of him talking with Mrs. Kim, of how comforting his voice had been, how the woman's expression had eased, how they'd both ended up laughing, struck Carly.

Maybe Stone was right.

Maybe she did need a friend.

She'd had friends during college, but she'd put everything on hold to take care of her mother and work. Slowly, one by one, friends had faded away. Now, Carly had her co-workers, Joyce, and her mother.

"You want to be my friend?" The possibility didn't seem feasible. Why would he want to be her friend? Especially when she had little to offer a friendship?

"Let's be clear," he clarified, clasping her hand more firmly. "I want to be your lover."

Oh, God, had he really just said he wanted to be her lover?

"But I'll take being your friend if that's what you're willing to give."

CHAPTER FIVE

CARLY GULPED. HER LOVER. She hadn't been kissed in years, hadn't been touched in years.

Until meeting Stone she hadn't realized just how much she'd missed having someone touch her, want her.

Crazy. That was how Stone made her feel. Absolutely crazy.

"I'm not a very good friend," she admitted. She probably hadn't been a very good lover, either, but he didn't need to know that.

The waitress set their drinks on the table, then a basket of fresh bread.

When she was gone, he asked, "How so?"

"Friends require spending time together. I don't have time. As tempting as the idea of having someone in my life is, it simply won't work. To even try means robbing time from somewhere where I don't have time to spare. No matter how we sugar-coat the facts, they are still the facts. Tonight is an aberration that can't happen again."

He squeezed her hand. "No more serious talk. If tonight is an aberration, then let's make the most of it. What would you like for dinner?"

Glancing at the menu, her gaze landed on her favorite. Her mouth watered just at seeing the description. "The parmesan-crusted chicken is amazing."

His gaze lifted from the menu. "After your recommendation, I've come here a time or two, but haven't tried that yet."

"You should," she encouraged, hoping the amazingness of the dish hadn't been one of the things to change over the past five years, too. "Or you can get something different and I'll share my chicken."

Stone's smile set the butterflies back into motion in her belly.

"Deal."

Satisfied from the delicious meal, Stone stared across the table at the woman who fascinated him more and more. "So did your dad leave before or after you were born?"

Not immediately answering, she frowned. "I thought we weren't having any more serious conversation."

"We're not. At least not along the lines of our earlier conversation," he clarified, not wanting the relaxed atmosphere between them to dissipate. "Feel free to say pass on anything you don't want to answer."

He watched the play of emotions flash across her face and expected to hear, "Pass." Instead, she took a sip of her water, then gave a real answer.

"My dad wasn't ever in the picture," she began. "How did you know?"

"The lack of photos of him in the living room. There were lots of you, some of you and who I assume is your mother, and one of you with your mother and an older couple. Grandparents?"

She nodded. "He and my mother were never married. They lived together for a short while, before she moved back in with my grandparents, the house where we still live, actually. He was a construction worker and only stayed in an area long enough to finish the job. Then he would move to the next place, which is exactly what he did. I'm not sure if he offered to take my mother, but she stayed in Memphis. A month or so after he'd left, she discovered she was pregnant, and let him know. He told her he was sorry, sent money for an abortion. As far as I know, he has no clue that was never an option for her."

Amazed that Carly had revealed so much when he generally had to push for the tiniest tidbit of personal information, Stone reached for her hand, again. Raw emotions tossed his stomach's contents like a tumultuous sea at the feel of her small hand tucked beneath his.

"I'm glad that was never an option."

Carly smiled. A real smile and one that made Stone's chest tighten.

"The feeling is mutual."

Her smile made Stone long for a lot of things, things he might not ever have with Carly. His gut instinct told him to be patient and she would come around.

Exactly what all he wanted, he wasn't sure. He didn't see himself going down the marriage path again. But he would like a relationship with Carly for however long their attraction lasted. Besides, when Carly did start dating, she needed to experience life, freedom, rather than settle into a new commitment such as marriage or motherhood.

She'd clearly missed out on so much life had to offer.

During their friendship, he'd like to show her, give her, some of those missed-out-on things.

"So now that you know all about me, tell me about you," she turned the tables.

Turnabout was fair play. Not that Stone had much to hide, but, as he'd told her, every person came with baggage.

His was of the "ex-wife who'd walked out on their marriage" variety.

But he wasn't going there. Not tonight.

"Middle child of a middle-class family who live in the middle of nowhere."

"That's a lot of middles."

He nodded. "My dad's a dentist." He smiled, flashing perfectly straight white teeth. "My mom worked at the post office for twenty years, then decided she wanted to be a stay-home mom to my baby sister, who was ten at the time and not interested in having Mom around all the time."

"Ten? How old is your sister now?"

"Twenty. My oldest sister is thirty-five."

Carly's eyes widened. "Fifteen years? That's a big age gap. And, you're in the middle?"

He nodded. "I've not mentally delved into how Jenny came into existence. What kid wants to think about his parents' sex life? But I got the impression she was a surprise. Have you ever thought about tracking down your birth father?"

Carly shook her head. "Not once." At his look, she shrugged. "That may sound weird, but my mother was a very good mother. My grandparents, the best. I was a happy, content child. I never felt the need for anything more than what I had, because I had all the things that count. Plus, my biological father had his shot to be involved in my life and sent a strong message when my mother told him about me."

Stone flinched on the inside. Yeah, they all had baggage. Truer words had never been spoken.

"What?" she asked, obviously seeing more on his face than he'd meant her to see.

"You're an amazing person," he said, honestly.

Brow arched, she asked, "Because I had a good childhood?"

"That you are content with what you had," he clarified. "What you have. A lot of people would be bemoaning all they didn't have, that they were saddled with an ailing parent at such a young age. You seem to embrace all life throws at you."

"Ha. Embrace is not the right verb. I have my moments of boohooing and major pity-parties, especially when Mom is having a bad day. Don't think I don't or that there aren't times that I question why."

"You wouldn't be human if you didn't." Stone laced their fingers. "I'm glad you have me to help you now."

He would help her. He might not have been able to help Stephanie, but he could help lighten Carly's load, to add brightness to her life.

Carly winced. She didn't want to lean on anyone, didn't want to depend on someone to be there and them not be, and it to topple her world.

She was doing just fine on her own. Maybe that was partially why she'd kept the world shut out.

To depend on someone meant risking being let down, meant risking a weak link in the wall. She couldn't do that. Not when it came to her mother.

She had to make sure everything that could be done was being done. That she was doing her best to take care of her mother.

Carly didn't elaborate on any of that. She just ignored Stone's comment and changed the subject. "I would like to really bring Joyce dessert, if that's okay?"

"We can order one of every dessert on the menu if that's what you'd like to do."

Carly smiled as she imagined Joyce's delight at the silly gesture. "Really?"

He picked up the dessert menu. "There's four options, so we should bring her one of each. That way we're sure to get something she'll like. After all, it's thanks to her that I didn't have to eat alone."

Carly pinched every penny. Part of her cringed at the idea of wasted money, but the thought of Joyce's smile, of being a part of something that would bring happiness to her face, tempted way more than logic weighed in.

"I'd like to do that," she agreed, not bothering to point out that if Stone didn't want to eat alone, he'd never have to. Innumerous women would line up to keep him company. "I can pay half."

She'd have to cut corners elsewhere, but doing something sweet for Joyce would be worth it.

His brow arched. "Do you think I'd let you pay when I'm the one who offered to bring dessert?"

"You didn't offer to bring four desserts. I don't mind helping cover the cost."

"I'd mind if you did. Let me do this, Carly. It's not much and I want to." He waggled his brows. "We'll call the extra three desserts an investment."

Suspicion rallied in her belly. "An investment?"

"I want Joyce to like me."

Taking air into her tight chest hurt. "Because?"

"You and I are going to be friends. I can't have the person closest to you not liking me or she might not want me around."

Her head spun a little. "You plan to be around?"

His gaze didn't leave hers. "You said it yourself. Friends spend time together. I don't expect our friendship to be otherwise."

"I can't ask Joyce to stay late so I can spend time with you. Please don't think that's what tonight is leading to."

She sure couldn't afford to hire Joyce for extra hours. Doing so just wasn't in the budget. Not even if Carly forwent sleep and worked round the clock.

"Joyce doesn't have to stay late."

Carly stared, trying to figure out his game. "Then how?"

"Where there's a will there's a way." He didn't look concerned, just smiled that casual grin of his and motioned to their waitress so they could order four desserts to go.

Stone pulled into Carly's gravel drive and turned off the engine. She sat in the passenger seat, fiddling with her seat belt.

"Thank you for tonight."

"Even though I had to practically coerce you into going?" he teased, turning toward her.

"Hopefully you understand my reasons."

He considered her comment, then, "Partially."

"Well, it was a lovely evening, and I appreciate the opportunity to feel…somewhat normal, outside of work. Thank you."

Stone wondered what she had been going to say and searched her face, trying to see deep inside her mind, to know everything she was thinking, feeling.

"Any time, Carly. Any time."

She smiled, but it quickly disappeared.

"Shall I go in with you to give Joyce her desserts?"

She flinched. "You bought the desserts. Sending you away doesn't seem quite fair."

He'd hoped Carly would realize they could be friends, could make this work. Obviously, she wasn't on the same page. Not yet.

His gaze not wavering from hers, knowing what her answer was going to be, he asked, "But you'd rather I not come in?"

Carly took a deep breath. Insurance claims. Her mother. Bills. Answering the questions Joyce was sure to have. Berating herself for going to dinner with Stone. She had a long, long night ahead of her.

"As I said, tonight has been lovely." It truly had. A night she wasn't likely to forget any time soon and would replay over and over in her mind. A night where she felt like a semi-normal twenty-seven-year-old female. "If it's all the same, I'd like to say goodnight out here."

"It's not all the same, but I realize you worked a twelve-hour shift today and have to be exhausted."

He had no idea.

"So when I say goodnight, do you mean as in verbally saying goodnight or can I kiss you?"

Carly's heartbeat jumped into overdrive and she gripped the seat belt tighter to keep her hand from shaking. "How am I supposed to answer that without making things awkward between us?"

He considered her question a moment, then asked, "So I should have just leaned over and kissed you?"

His having done so would have been straight from a fantasy, but also a complication neither of them needed.

"Do friends kiss each other goodnight?"

"Good point." He stuck out his hand. "Goodnight, Carly. Thank you for going to dinner."

Carly's gaze dropped to his hand. He meant for her to shake it? Fighting confusion, she glanced back up.

He was going to shake her hand, not kiss her goodnight. Okay. Made sense. Hadn't she been preaching they couldn't have a romantic relationship all evening?

She put her hand in his and shook it in the strangest handshake. His grip was firm and gentle at the same time.

Calming and disturbing.

Warm and hot.

Right, yet all wrong.

"Are you working tomorrow?" he asked, still gripping her hand in a continuation of the awkward handshake. Why was he hanging on? Why was she?

She shook her head. "Today was my last of three on."

Not that she wouldn't be working over the next three

days she had off from the hospital. She'd pull twelve-plus-hour days for the insurance company.

"I'd like to see you tomorrow. Before you tell me you can't, let me assure you that you can. I'd like to come by here after I finish at the hospital."

She bit the inside of her cheek, then ordered herself to stop. She was making a raw spot with how much she'd chewed at the area that day. Of all the ways of dealing with stress, she needed to find a nervous tic that was less self-destructive.

Stone wanted to come there tomorrow evening. Normally, she'd either be sitting with her mother or working, usually both.

"I'm not much of a cook if you're fishing for an invite to dinner." Cooking would mean going to the grocery store, which would mean getting Joyce to sit with her mother and dipping into her rainy-day fund. Which she'd already done once that month for her mother's new meds.

"I could pick up something for us. Just tell me what your mother eats."

"That isn't necessary. Besides, she chokes easily so is on a high nutrient, thick liquid diet."

His thumb brushed across the back of her hand in a slow caress. Were the lightning bolts of awareness shooting through her supposed to be friendly? They weren't. More like an assault on her nerve endings, setting them on high alert.

"Getting Mom to take in anything by mouth is a chore." Not that she and Joyce didn't do their best every single meal. Continuing to take in meals via normal methods was important mentally and emotionally—for her mother and for Carly. "She gets most of her nutrition through her feeding tube, unfortunately."

How ill her mother was seemed to finally click, and Stone's grip on her hand tightened. "I'm sorry, Carly."

The pity in his voice raised walls of annoyance. She didn't want his pity. She didn't need his pity.

Taking a deep breath, she made herself step back, made herself allow him to express his empathy without her going on the defensive. Hard to do because she'd had years of keeping her chin held high.

"It is what it is."

He sat quietly a moment, then asked, "It's okay if I bring you dinner?"

Carly's chest ached at the sincerity in his voice. He wanted her to say yes. He wanted to spend time with her.

She had so much work to do.

But if she had to sit up all night without sleeping, it would be worth it to spend more time with Stone.

"You realize I can't have a normal friendship with you? That you're wasting your time if you're hoping for something more?"

"What's normal, Carly?"

He made a good point. What was normal? Were there any easy, perfect relationships out there? When she'd dated back in her university days everything had seemed easy, but maybe that hadn't been a true reflection of life. Not that they were talking dating. They weren't. They were going to be friends.

Friends with Stone.

"I suppose it wouldn't do any good to offer to give you money to cover my portion?" she asked, conceding to his request against her better judgment.

"You suppose correctly." His smile was so bright it almost lit the car. His dad must be a fabulous dentist. "I'll see you tomorrow evening."

She pulled her hand free and opened the car door. Before getting out, she hesitated. "If you don't show, if you change your mind about our friendship, I'll understand."

He opened his door, came around, took the dessert bag

from her and walked her to her front door. "If I don't show, call 911 because something major happened on my way here."

Staring into his green eyes, she nodded, but still didn't quite let herself believe.

"Goodnight, Carly. I will see you tomorrow."

With that, he bent, kissed her cheek, and whistled as he walked back to his car.

Carly stared after him long after he'd driven away in his fancy SUV, wondering what in the world she'd gotten herself into and why she hadn't stopped it.

Why she'd ever let it get started to begin with.

She couldn't blame Stone.

She'd been the one to know the crazy details of her life. Yet she had spent time with him, had a few flirty conversations, given him her address.

Wanting him as her friend hadn't motivated any of those things.

Her suddenly come-to-life raging hormones that had been dead for five years had taken over her brain and body.

CHAPTER SIX

THE NEXT MORNING, Mrs. Kim's wound wasn't any better.

Stone ordered a new culture, added an additional intravenous antibiotic and talked with her family about keeping her at the hospital longer.

He spent most of the day doing routine procedures, but did have a more intensive mastectomy scheduled for the afternoon.

Every time he was in between high concentration, his mind drifted to Carly.

She had a lot more going on than met the eye. He wanted to lighten her load. He just wasn't sure how to go about it without offending or pushing her away. She was as touchy as the most delicate flower. If he pushed too hard, she'd wither and refuse to let him in.

"So how did your conversation the other day go with my favorite nurse?"

Stone glanced up from the hospital computer at Rosalyn and he grinned. "She's my favorite nurse, too, you know?"

"Oh, I know." Rosalyn laughed. "Not going to tell me details, huh? Neither would she and I've asked her more than once."

"Some things are better kept private."

Rosalyn's eyes brightened. "Oh?"

"Not those things," Stone quickly assured her. "We've decided to be friends."

Rosalyn frowned. "I'm not sure if that makes you the world's dumbest man or her the dumbest woman. Or both."

He chuckled. "Nothing wrong with being friends."

"Except for when you both want more."

"What makes you think Carly wants more?" Yes, his question was self-serving because he wanted Rosalyn to confirm what he knew deep in his gut. Carly was interested in him, but didn't think she had time. He'd just have to make himself so useful that she'd realize his being around made her life better, easier.

Rosalyn tsked teasingly at him. "You're showing your 'more than just want to be friends' interest," she accused.

"Which you already knew since you were the one informing Carly I had the hots for her."

She gave him a "so what?" look. "I didn't hear you denying it."

"Nor will you."

A pleased smile spread across her face. "Carly is a hard worker, always positive, never complains about anything, nor says anything negative about anyone. But sometimes, when she thinks no one is looking, I see the truth on her face and get the impression she has a hard life."

Rosalyn wasn't wrong, but it wasn't Stone's place to fill in the gaps.

"That said, in the five or so years I've known her, not once has she been distracted from her job."

"Now she is?"

"Oh, she's still an excellent nurse, one of the best, but for the past month she gets dreamy-eyed."

It was Stone's turn to smile. "Wonder what happened a month ago to put that look in her eyes?"

"I wonder." Rosalyn's face took on a motherly expression. "All I have to say is you'd better not hurt that girl 'cause I think someone must have done a real number on her in the past."

Carly hadn't mentioned someone in her past, but certainly there could have been. Stone didn't like the idea of a man in Carly's past, especially not one who'd hurt her. Maybe her mother had always been ill and the effects of that was what Rosalyn had picked up on.

"I've no intention to hurt Carly." Quite the opposite. He wanted to make her life better. To take away the darkness and fill her world with sunshine. As much sunshine as he could beam her way when she was dealing with such a tragic situation. She needed his help whether she knew it or not.

Rosalyn's almost black eyes narrowed in warning. "Some pain isn't from intentional infliction."

"Point taken." Not that he didn't already know firsthand. He'd never meant to hurt Stephanie, but had. Or was it the opposite? If only she'd let him help her, how different would their situation have been?

"Just you be good to that girl or stay away from her is all I'm saying."

"Yes, ma'am," he assured Rosalyn. "Now tell me about my new surgical consult in Room 210. An abdominal pain?"

Carly stood from the chair next to her mother's hospital bed and stretched her aching muscles. She'd worked late into the night, set her alarm and gotten up early to work several hours, then fed and bathed her mother, got her out of bed and into her wheelchair, and taken her out for a stroll down their bumpy sidewalk.

She hated her mother being cooped up in the house all the time, but, even with the mechanical lift, getting her in and out of her bed was becoming more difficult.

Eventually, Carly wasn't going to be able to manage

and would have to have more help. Either that or put her mother in a nursing home.

She hoped it never came to that.

Sometimes that was the only option. However, she was a nurse. She knew how to provide her mother's care. Though she just might reach the point where she didn't have the resources to do so in the manner best for her mother.

If that day came, Carly would have hard decisions to face. Decisions she didn't know how she'd make.

She glanced at where her mother slept. She now slept more than she was awake. Which could be a side effect of her medications as much as a symptom of her disease. Either way, Carly appreciated the moments when her mother was awake, lucid, and not in horrid pain.

Like earlier that day when they'd been on their stroll.

Although her mother had called her Margaret, she'd enjoyed the fresh air, had commented on the squirrels they'd seen, had told Carly they needed to hire someone to fix the loose boards on the front porch railing.

Audrey hadn't used the front door in years as her handicap ramp was located on the back of the house, but obviously she still paid attention. The house needed new paint, gutters, landscaping, and a new roof. Just for starters. Every time it rained, Carly feared that that would be the time the iffy-looking roof finally gave in to the weather.

She glanced around her mother's bedroom at the dingy paint, at the photos of the two of them that hung on the wall, at the dresser that held the same perfume bottles from half a decade ago.

"Wh-what a-are y-you th-thinking?"

Her mother's words were low, soft, garbled, but Carly's ears were trained to understand her speech.

"That I should spruce this place up."

Her mother shook her head. "Don't th-think y-you n-need to do th-that on m-my a-account."

"I was thinking more for my account. This place looks exactly as it did when I was in elementary school."

"I-I'm t-too old for ch-change."

Interesting. Was her mother saying that because she truly liked being surrounded by the way things had been or because change confused her?

"You're not that old," Carly countered, smiling at her mother and wondering if she knew she was Carly or if she thought she was Margaret.

Her mother chuckled, making Carly's heart swell.

"I-If you're a-as o-old as y-you feel th-then I-I'm a-ancient."

Carly bent and kissed her mother's cheek. "It's the medicine making you feel that way."

"I-It's my b-body ma-making me f-feel that w-way," her mother corrected. "H-Help me s-sit up."

Carly did so, raising the head of the hospital bed, then repositioning her mother's pillows. She fed her mother as much as she could get her to eat by mouth, which was only a few bites, then fed her the specially formulated liquid meal via her feeding tube.

"Is there anything I can get you? Anything you want?" Carly asked her mother that question every day. Her mother almost always gave the same answer, saying she was fine and didn't need anything.

That day she had Carly's jaw dropping.

"A g-grandk-kid."

Carly stared in disbelief. She'd never heard her mother say such a thing. Or even hint at such a desire.

Not knowing how to respond, Carly gave a shaky laugh. "This one may take a little time as I'll need to find a sperm donor. Plus, there's that whole incubation-for-nine-months thing."

Her mother shook her head. "D-don't do it l-like I—I did. F-find a-a man wh-who'll st-stick around."

"Okay, Mom."

"Th-that d-doctor f-friend, m-maybe."

"Stone? Er… Dr. Parker, I mean?" Carly gulped and didn't meet her mother's still-shrewd gaze. She really shouldn't have gone on about Stone the other night. No wonder her mother was getting ideas. Especially if Joyce had mentioned Carly going to dinner with him. Carly hadn't asked her not to, but had hoped she wouldn't. "I… we're just friends, Momma, but…he is a nice man and a wonderful surgeon. And kind. He's very kind. I like that about him."

There she went on about Stone again. She really needed to stop doing that.

When Carly looked up, her gaze collided with her mother's. But her mother just smiled and closed her eyes. Within seconds her breathing had evened out, indicating she'd drifted into sleep again, leaving Carly to consider their conversation.

She couldn't recall her mother having mentioned grand-children. Not even once. At least not in a manner other than a passing thought that some day Carly would make her a grandma. That had been years ago. Back when they'd both thought Carly's life would be very different.

When they'd thought Audrey's life would be very different.

If only some pharmaceutical company could come up with a cure. Carly would give most anything to see the strong, vibrant woman her mother had once been.

Maybe some day a cure would exist, but, realistically, Carly knew any such treatment wouldn't be in time to save her mother.

Tears pricked her eyes. *Stop it,* she scolded herself. She had no time for self-pity. Especially when the woman lying in the hospital bed never showed any. No complaints, just acceptance that life was what it was.

Was there a connection to Carly having mentioned Stone and the sudden request for grandchildren? If so, her mother would be sadly disappointed. Last night with Stone had been wonderful but Carly didn't expect anything more. Probably, truth be told, the best thing that could happen would be if Stone realized how problematic her life was and forgot she existed.

Certainly, that would be best for him.

After running through a few stretches to protect her spine, Carly sat back down in the chair next to her sleeping mother's hospital bed. She glanced at her watch, wondered where the morning had gone, then dove back into the insurance claims.

Tedious work, but someone had to do it. Since she could work from home and had some control over when she worked, Carly was the woman for the job.

When a knock sounded at her door, Carly jumped, almost dropping her laptop.

She hadn't realized just how much time had passed.

Which was to her advantage because if she had, she'd have been distracted with wondering if Stone would show or not. Would have been anxiously listening for sounds of his arrival and wondering if she was being foolish.

He'd come.

Well, it was possible someone else was at her door, but it was unlikely. She didn't have company. Just Joyce, herself, and her mother were ever at the house.

But Stone had come. He'd said he would and he had. Her crazy life hadn't scared him away.

Standing up, stretching once again because of how long she'd been curled up in the chair and the fact her legs were numb, she then headed to her front door.

Her heart pounded and she felt breathy.

As if she were running a race rather than casually walking through her house.

She stepped up to the front door. Through the screen window, she could see Stone.

A very gorgeous Stone.

The man was really too good-looking to be real. Those eyes belonged to some paranormal hero in a supernatural television show.

And his mouth. A lush, kissable mouth that curved into such an amazing smile. Must come from being a dentist's son.

Friends. They were just going to be friends. Nothing more.

This was okay. Sort of.

"I see there's no need for me to call 911," she teased, opening the door. Then, taking in the number of bags he held, she frowned. "Good grief, how much do you expect me to eat?"

He grinned. "I decided to cook dinner, rather than bring take-out."

She blinked. He was going to cook? "Which doesn't answer my question. Do I look like I have that big of an appetite?"

He laughed. "You're perfect just as you are, so whatever your appetite, it suits you."

Perfect. Her. Ha.

"If I didn't know better I'd think you were Irish and blessed with the Blarney Stone."

His grin was breathtaking. "I wasn't sure what you had in your kitchen," he admitted, "so I bought everything I'd need."

What if she didn't want him in her barren kitchen?

What if take-out felt less personal than him cooking?

What if she was so glad to see him, that he'd shown up, that she wanted to throw her arms around him and hug him? As a friend, of course.

"I don't know what to say."

"I'd say 'thank you', but you should probably wait until after you've eaten." He waggled his brows. "My mother and sisters are good cooks. I'm a decent cook, but make no promises on edibility."

"What are we having?"

"Homemade spaghetti and meatballs, garlic bread, and I brought a couple of different wines to choose from."

She rarely drank alcohol as it tended to make her sleepy, but she nodded. "Sounds good."

"Point me to your kitchen and I'll go back to get the rest of the bags."

She blinked. "There's more?"

"I told you, I wasn't sure if you'd have all the ingredients. Now, give me directions on which way to go."

She pointed down the hallway. "The house is only two bedrooms, so I doubt you'd get lost, but the kitchen is the first door to the right."

"Perfect."

She followed him into the kitchen, watched a little in awe as he set down the bags on her once bright yellow Formica countertops. "Can I help?"

"I'm counting on it."

That was good because she couldn't imagine just watching him work while she did nothing. How awkward would that be?

"Just tell me what to do."

"Come here."

Not knowing what he planned, she came close to where he stood, gasping when he wrapped his arms around her waist and pulled her to him.

With the embrace, she halfway expected him to kiss her, but instead he just grinned down at her.

"Did you think about me today?"

A zillion times. Plus, I'm pretty sure my mother wants

us to give her grandchildren and she's not even met you.
"Was I supposed to?"

His thumbs tracing across her low back, he laughed. "You are such an ego-buster."

His fingers were magical because all kinds of things were happening inside her body. Would it be wrong if she closed her eyes and just pretended this was so much more?

"Sorry." She was smiling back at him. How could she not? "I didn't know thinking of you was a condition of our friendship."

"Thinking about each other is definitely a condition of our friendship."

"I'll keep that in mind tomorrow and make sure I think of you at least once."

He chuckled. "You do that."

His hands rested low on her back. His body pressed hard against her belly. Carly's knees wobbled. Had to have because she leaned into him.

She looked at him, parted her lips, waited in anticipation of whatever he had in mind when he'd pulled her close.

He stared into her eyes, then grinned as if nothing out of the ordinary was happening. Maybe it wasn't.

"I'm going to grab the other bags. You mind unpacking these?"

"I…" She glanced at the bags he'd put on her countertop. "Sure."

With that he was out of the room. When she heard the front screen door open and close, she sighed.

Okay, what had that been? A friendly hug?

Stone paused on Carly's front porch and took a deep breath. What had he been thinking to pull her into his arms?

When he'd gotten her there, he hadn't wanted to let go, had had to force himself to step away.

Because when he'd looked into her eyes, he'd seen

awareness. Physical awareness. And curiosity. She'd wondered if he was going to kiss her and the idea had intrigued her.

Which had done crazy, stupid things to his insides.

Like make all his blood rush south.

He couldn't kiss Carly. No matter the look she'd given. She needed their friendship and he'd give it to her.

A few loose boards on the porch caught his eye and he mentally tallied what he'd need to fix them.

He'd get the rest of the groceries, cook Carly dinner, and make a mental list of things he could help with around her house.

Carly took in the bags on her counter. More bags than she'd bought at one time in years. Maybe ever.

Why was Stone doing this?

Catching the tender flesh of her inner cheek between her teeth, Carly forced herself to stop over-thinking and began pulling fresh vegetables from the grocery bags.

When Stone had said he intended to cook her homemade, he'd meant homemade right down to the sauce apparently. Wow.

He made two additional trips out to his SUV and by the time he'd finished, her countertops were full.

"There's no way we can eat all this."

"We'll eat more than you think."

She glanced at all the food they'd unpacked. "I don't eat this much in a month."

"Which explains why you're so thin. You need to eat more."

He thought she was too thin? She glanced down. She wore loose black yoga pants and a baggy cotton gray T-shirt that was one of the most comfortable items she owned. Not as nice as his khaki trousers and expensive navy polo, but much more practical for how she'd spent her day.

"So much for your perfect comment earlier," she reminded, holding her hand up to stop him when he went to explain away his comment on her figure. "Doesn't matter. I've always been small framed. I take after my mom that way."

He leaned back against the countertop. "Will I meet her tonight?"

She had already wondered that, had wondered how she would explain Stone's presence when her mother woke.

"I'm sure you will."

"Good. It's obvious how much you adore and admire her. I can't wait to meet her."

Protectiveness hitting her, Carly hesitated. "She's been ill a long time. She's not the woman she used to be. Not on the outside."

"Mentally, she's good?"

"Sometimes," Carly told him, deciding to be as open as possible. Why not? He'd soon see for himself how ill her mother was. "Parkinson's disease is her main issue, but she has some vascular dementia as well, possibly from mini-strokes a couple of years ago or maybe from medications or the Parkinson's itself. The doctors aren't sure. More often than not, she thinks I'm her mother, Margaret. Sometimes, she's with me, knows me, and is my mother."

Stone winced. "I truly am sorry you have to deal with this."

There went the pity.

"Don't be," she told him, without looking directly at him because she didn't want to see that in his eyes. "Some people don't have mothers. Feel sorry for them. I'm lucky because I have mine."

There were a few moments of silence, then he said,

"You make me feel as if I should call my mom and tell her how much I love and appreciate her."

Carly's eyes prickled with a little moisture at his sentiment. "You should."

"I'll do that."

But he must have meant later, because, rather than whip out his phone, he began washing off vegetables and whistling a tune she recognized but couldn't put her finger on.

"How can I help?"

"Find a cutting board and a sharp knife."

Carly found an old wooden cutting board and the sharpest knife she owned. Stone didn't look overly impressed. To his credit, he didn't say a word, just took the proffered items.

"I'm going to need a skillet for the sauce and a pan to cook the pasta."

"Right." Carly began digging in the cabinet, found a pan and an old cast-iron skillet that had been her grandmother's.

"That'll do," Stone said, eyeing her offerings. "Nice skillet."

If he said so. She could only recall a handful of times of having used the heavy thing. Memories of her mother using it to cook breakfast and the scent of bacon filling the entire house flashed through Carly's mind. The memory made her smile. She'd had a great childhood and was lucky.

"I take it you really do cook?"

He shot her a mischievous look. "Not often, because what's the fun in cooking for one?"

Not a lot. Which was why she lived on soups a lot. She could make a crockpot of soup and eat on it for a week. It was fairly healthy, easy to make, and inexpensive.

"We both know that if you eat alone it's by choice." She watched as he spread out items on the cutting board.

"The same could be said for you."

"I have a different set of circumstances," she reminded him. "I can't be out. I'm needed at home. I want to be at home," she corrected.

"I've said it before, but where there's a will there's a way." He held up an onion. "Do you have a food processor?"

She held up her hands. "Just these, and a blender if that would work?"

"I take it you don't cook a lot."

"Not much."

"Since I know you usually bring your lunch to work that surprises me."

"Maybe I'm just not a fan of hospital cafeteria food."

"Our hospital's food is pretty good."

Carly couldn't argue. On the few occasions she'd eaten in the cafeteria, it had been well prepared.

Carly's watch alarm went off. "I'm going to bail on you for a few minutes. Maybe longer."

His brow rose.

"I keep Mom on a schedule—that way she gets proper nutrition. I wasn't thinking about the time when I offered to help. Not that I'd likely have been much help, anyway."

"Not a problem. Do what you need to do."

Before leaving the kitchen, Carly mixed the high calorie and nutrient food packet prescribed for her mother's feeding tube. She took out a small container of fresh fruit and blended it to a thick liquid consistency.

"Sorry, I'm bailing," she apologized again.

"It's probably better if you aren't here to watch." He winked. "You might be one of those who flip out if the cook licks the spoon."

"You don't?" she said in a faux-horrified voice.

"Leave now so you can keep thinking that."

Carly laughed, grabbed up the tray she'd put her mother's meal and supplies on, and left the kitchen.

When she went into her mother's room, Audrey was awake, which instantly struck Carly with guilt.

"Sorry, Mom, I didn't realize you were awake or I'd have been in here."

Her mother didn't say anything, just eyed the tray. "N-not h-hungry."

Which was the same thing she said at every meal. If not for the feeding tube, her mother would have withered into nothingness long ago.

"Try to eat a little." Which was the same thing Carly said at every meal. "We have to keep your strength up."

Sighing, looking exhausted, her mother nodded. Although her tremor made feeding herself almost impossible, Carly always let her mother attempt to before taking over the process. More food ended up on her mother than in her, but she wanted some normalcy to her mother's life.

Not that her daughter putting an adult-sized bib on her was normal.

Carly secured the bib, protecting her mother's gown, and her bed coverings. "Do you want me to get you out of bed to eat or do you want to eat here?"

She always gave her mother the choice. Getting out of the bed tired her out tremendously, but on the occasions her mother wanted to get out of the bed for her meal, she always seemed to eat a little more.

Plus, Carly wanted her out of the bed as much as possible. The more her mother felt like getting up, the better.

Today wasn't going to be one of those occasions, though, as her mother shook her head. "T-Too t-tired."

Which was how her mother felt most of the time. Still, between Joyce and Carly, they always got her out of bed at least once and put her in her wheelchair. On pretty days, they'd go for a short walk. Others they'd just push her into the living room to watch television or sit to talk to Carly or her caregiver.

Removing the food for the feeding tube, Carly put the bed tray over her mother's lap. Then, she put the small dish of thickened fruit on the tray, along with a special spoon that was supposed to help prevent food from spilling due to her tremor. It helped a little.

Her mother stared at the food for a few moments, then, seeming to will herself to do so, she slowly and shakily scooped up a bite and made it to her mouth.

Not on the first try, but she did get some of the puréed food there.

Carly wiped the dribble of food away from her mother's chin. "That was great, Mom. I know it's a lot of effort, but it makes me happy that you're eating."

Her mother didn't say anything, just slowly proceeded to take a few more bites. Carly cleaned spills in between each bite because she couldn't stand to see her mother, who'd always prided herself on her neat appearance, with globs of food stuck to her face.

After five or six bites, her mother dropped the spoon onto the tray.

"Full already?" Carly kept her smile in place. "Can't you try just one more?"

Her nursing experience had taught her that the more 'normal' things her mother did, the better her prognosis.

Which was why she or Joyce brushed and styled her mother's hair daily, why they put lipstick on her, why they kept her in pretty nightgowns Carly had picked up at the local second-hand store.

Expression tired, her mother shook her head.

Wishing she could have gotten her to eat more, Carly flushed the tube, administered the meal, then flushed the tube again. Then, she sat, talking to her mother, mostly about the more interesting insurance claims. Carly didn't reveal any personal information, just whatever the incident was that had triggered the claim. Some of the more interesting ones would get a smile from her mother, but her mother rarely spoke during the chit-chat.

"Wh-what's th-that sm-smell?"

Yeah, Carly was smelling it, too. Wonderful, mouth-watering smells drifting their way from the kitchen.

She'd gotten so wrapped up in her mother she'd completely forgotten about Stone.

How could she have forgotten the hunk in her kitchen?

First biting the inside of her cheek, she met her mother's curious gaze and then shrugged as if her next words were no big deal.

"I...uh... I have a friend over for dinner."

CHAPTER SEVEN

DESPITE CARLY'S ATTEMPT at nonchalance, her mother wasn't buying it.

No wonder. Carly hadn't had company, not counting Joyce and a few home-health nurses, in years. Not since Tony.

Her mother's eyes widened.

"A man," she added, because she knew what her mother's next question was going to be. "But don't get any ideas because we're just friends."

The former fatigue on her mother's face lifted significantly. "H-help m-me in—in my wh-wheelchair."

Her mother wanted to get out of bed a second time that day? Carly's heart swelled with joy. And maybe a little anxiety. She knew why her mother wanted out of bed.

"Yes, ma'am."

Carly repositioned the hospital bed to where it would be easiest to use the lift. She positioned everything just so to make that transition as smooth as possible, then assisted her mother into the chair.

"Maybe you'll want to eat with us," Carly suggested, slipping soft, fuzzy house shoes onto her mother's socked feet. "Seeing how much food he brought, I'm sure there is going to be plenty."

"Wh-who is h-he?"

"A surgeon at the hospital. He moved here about a month ago. I told you about him when we were talking the other night. Remember?" Carly kept her voice light, cheerful, but hopefully not overly so. After her mother's comment about a grandchild, she didn't want her pulling Stone into that equation. "He's a great guy. Everyone likes him."

Why was she defending Stone? If her mother didn't like him, what did it matter? He was a co-worker, someone who wanted to be her friend.

It did matter.

A lot.

She wanted her mother to like Stone.

Which was why Carly was nervous as she straightened her mother in the wheelchair, made sure her gown was nice and neat, finger-styled her mother's hair back into place, then pushed her to the living area.

Hearing her moving about, Stone called from the kitchen, "Dinner is almost done."

"Smells good," she responded, glancing at her mother. If she could, Audrey would be out of her chair and into the kitchen quick as a flash. "Stone," she called, taking her clammy hands off the wheelchair grips and wiping them across her yoga pants. "When you can, I'd like you to meet my mother."

"Let me take the bread out, turn the sauce down to simmer, then I'll be right there."

Wondering why she was so edgy at the prospect of her mother meeting him, Carly fought the urge to wring her hands. Instead, she wrapped her fingers around the wheelchair grips while she settled her mother into "her" spot in the living room. A prime open area where there was no furniture, just worn hardwood flooring.

Against a wall was a television that was as deep as it was wide, attesting to its age. A small loveseat-size sofa and a sturdy wooden rocking chair that had been Carly's grandmother's were also in the room. In the far corner was a small round dining table with three chairs. The fourth spot was reserved for her mother, although she rarely felt up to eating meals at the table. A wooden bench was pushed against a wall. Pictures of Carly graced the wall. Her first birthday. Her sweet sixteen. Her high-school graduation shot.

There were a few family photos taken at a local department store that featured Carly and her mother. And Carly's favorite, which was a photo of her grandparents, her mother, and Carly sitting in her mother's lap. Both of her grandparents had died from natural causes within a few years of the photo.

Other than getting rid of a recliner and sofa that had matched the loveseat to make a spot for her mother's wheelchair, the room hadn't changed in years.

What had Stone thought of her home?

Had he judged her the other night when he'd dropped off the box? If so, he'd still come back.

With groceries to cook a meal.

Did he feel sorry for her? Was that what his real interest was? She was his charity project?

If Stone didn't like her home, he could leave. If it wasn't up to his standards, he could leave. If he pitied her, well, he'd better keep it hidden or she'd boot him. She didn't need or want his, or anyone's, charity.

If her mother didn't like Stone, no big deal.

She'd say goodbye and life would go on. He was a co-worker. Possibly a friend. A fantasy all kinds of things.

She positioned her mother to where she could see the television and the hallway where Stone would appear.

"Y-you've n-not br-brought a m-man h-home s-since T-Tony," her mother pointed out, watching Carly too closely for comfort.

She'd not brought anyone, male or female, except Tony, home in years.

"Remember he's just a friend, Momma," Carly reminded her. Okay, so Carly was struggling with remembering that herself. Maybe she needed to convince herself that he felt sorry for her so she could use anger to push him away.

"A very good friend," Stone added as he walked into the room, bent, and held out his hand to Carly's mom.

Intentional movement was a major problem for her mother and that seemed to hit Stone after his hand was in the air a moment longer than it should have been. Rather than wait on Audrey to shakily respond, he lowered to a squatting position, placed his hand over hers, and looked Carly's mom straight in the eyes.

"It's very nice to meet you, Ms. Evans." His smile was enough to dazzle anyone. His dad should use him as an advertisement; make him wear buttons promoting his dental practice. "I've heard a lot about you from Carly."

Carly's mother's gaze cut to her. "Sh-she's not s-said m-much about y-you."

"That's because I'm new in town and she's still trying to figure me out." Stone's charm was on full blast. Plus, he was still squatting, holding her mother's hand.

"Wh-what's sh-she go-going to f-find?"

Stone chuckled, then his expression took on a more serious look. "I'd like to say all good, to assure you there was nothing that wasn't pure white in my past, but we all have skeletons in our closets."

Carly found his comment odd as he'd made that implication previously when speaking about baggage. She couldn't imagine Stone having many skeletons in his closet and if he did they were probably the plastic, non-scary Halloween version.

Her mother studied him a few moments from behind

her glasses, her gaze shrewd and assessing. Then, in testament to how much his being there motivated her, she cradled his hand between her trembling ones.

Carly fought gasping. Movement was painful for her mother, was awkward and shaky and difficult. Yet, she patted Stone's hand between hers as if it were the most natural thing in the world.

Maybe it was.

Just like that, Stone captivated her mother.

"I've cooked spaghetti and meatballs, my grandmother's recipe. Can I tempt you to join us?"

To Carly's surprise, or maybe not surprise since Stone had cast a spell over her mother, Audrey said yes.

Without slurring.

That her mother had already eaten the few bites, had had her feeding-tube meal, and still wanted to taste Stone's cooking had Carly wanting to kiss him.

Okay, maybe she'd wanted to kiss him before that, but definitely she owed him for the spark of life he'd put into her mother's eyes.

Stone unlocked the wheelchair, pushed Audrey over to the small wooden dining table on the opposite side of the room, and situated her at the table.

"She chokes easily," Carly reminded him when Stone started dipping some food out. "She can only have thickened liquids to keep her from aspirating."

"One b-bite is-isn't go-going to h-hurt m-me," her mother insisted, sounding annoyed at Carly. "I-If i-it g-goes d-down wr-wrong, th-there's a d-doctor h-here."

There was that.

Carly was more worried about aspiration pneumonia than her mother choking, though. It wouldn't take much for her food to end up in her lungs rather than her stomach. Even with the puréed bites, it was a risk.

"Can I help you?" Carly's teeth sank into the tender

area on the inside of her cheek. Maybe, just maybe, her mother would chew every bite well and her throat would work properly and prevent aspiration.

Her mother shook her head. "H-him."

Stone shot a look to Carly, one that asked permission. Carly nodded.

To his credit and Carly's relief, Stone used his fork to mash up the spaghetti to a mushy consistency. When he was satisfied with it, he took a small amount on his fork, managing not to get any pieces of the crumbled hamburger meat, and offered it to Carly's mother.

Audrey closed her eyes. Pleasure on her face, she chewed slowly for a long time. Neither Carly nor Stone said anything, just watched her, ready to jump into action at the slightest difficulty.

When Audrey opened her eyes, she smiled. "A m-man wh-who c-can c-cook is h-hard to f-find."

Stone grinned. "Unfortunately, I only have a few meals in my repertoire. I'm a quick study, though."

"B-bet y-you are."

Stone fed her another small mushed-up bite.

Carly watched in fascination at how her mother responded to him. She only ate a handful of small bites, but, as she'd already eaten some of the fruit and had her feeding-tube meal, Carly was impressed.

Her mother hadn't taken in that much by mouth in a long, long time.

"I may have you over every meal," Carly mused.

"That can be arranged," he offered, eyes sparkling and a grin on his face.

Carly's mother's gaze went from Stone to Carly and back again.

Carly's cheeks heated.

She didn't want her mother to get ideas. If Stone wasn't

careful her mother would be picking out names for grand-kids before he left that evening.

Somehow, she didn't think that was what he'd had in mind when he'd said he wanted them to be friends.

Carly took a bite, redirecting her mind so she didn't blush. At the burst of deliciousness in her mouth, she glanced toward Stone in true appreciation.

"Dinner is excellent," she praised, trying not to let her surprise show. Then again, she should have known the meal would be superb. No doubt, anything he did was. "Thank you."

This was the Carly who had caught Stone's attention at the hospital. A smiling one. A laughing one. Her mother sat with them, but said very little while he and Carly ate and talked.

He told tales about his family, recounting a few humor-ous tales of his two sisters that had both Evans women laughing.

"Yeah, Jenny is a troublemaker, for sure."

"No wonder with you as her mentor," Carly pointed out.

"I might have taught her a thing or two." He winked. "Either way, we're both very different from Paula. She's the serious one of the bunch."

"What does she do?"

"She's an infectious disease specialist in Atlanta. Works for the CDC."

"A doctor?" Carly asked, looking genuinely impressed.

"Yes. She's more into research than dealing with ac-tual people."

"What's Jenny interested in?"

"Boys."

At Carly's raised brow, Stone continued.

"She's twenty, but isn't sure what she wants to do when she 'grows up'. Or if she wants to grow up."

"It must have been difficult to grow up in the shadow of you and your sister, constantly being compared to two overachievers."

"Paula is the overachiever, not me."

Carly's gaze narrowed. "Have you ever failed at anything you've set your mind out to do?"

"More often than I care to admit." That squeezing pain he always got when thinking of Stephanie shot across his chest. To redirect the conversation away from his biggest failure, he gestured to the table. "There's quite a bit left."

Carly looked at the large glass bowl he'd filled with spaghetti, at the basket he'd put garlic bread into.

"You want to take it home?" she offered. "I'm sure I can find some containers."

He shook his head. "I'll be in surgery most of the day tomorrow so I'll grab something at the hospital. If it won't go to waste, I'll leave it here."

"Something that tastes this good won't go to waste," she assured him. "Joyce is going to think she's in heaven when I share."

He flashed his dentist's kid smile.

"By the way, Joyce about fell over herself at her desserts." She smiled. "She had to taste them all here and made me take a bite of each, too."

He knew he liked Joyce. "Did she have a favorite?"

"The lava cake."

"Sounds good. We should have done dessert last night."

"No way." She shook her head. "I was much too full to have dessert."

"But you did try a bite of each?"

Carly's lips curved upward. "She insisted."

"Did you have a favorite?"

"The apple cobbler." Her face filled with remembered pleasure. "The ice cream had melted into a soup, but it was still fantastic."

"Wh-when w-was th-this?" her mother asked, her gaze going back and forth between them.

Carly's look of pleasure morphed into one of guilt.

"Stone followed me home last night after work so he could carry in a box." Carly's voice was overly bright. "You were asleep, but Joyce met him and stayed so we could go to dinner. Stone brought her back four different desserts from Julio's." Carly smiled. "Wasn't that nice of him?"

"J-Julio's wh-where you w-worked?"

Carly had worked at the restaurant where they'd gone? Why hadn't she said anything?

"Yes, but I didn't see anyone I knew." She cast a nervous glance toward Stone. "Everything looks the same except for the people working there."

Her mother nodded, then looked Stone dead in the eyes. Her eyes were a similar shade of honey brown as Carly's, only sharper, shrewder. "Wh-what are y-your in-intentions?"

Stone hesitated. He and Carly had agreed to be friends, nothing more. Yes, he wanted more, but the bright red glow to Carly's face warned that he needed to proceed with caution on how he answered.

"And that's why I don't normally bring men home," Carly cut in with a feigned teasing tone. "Mom, I told you, Stone and I are just friends."

"Good friends," Stone added, watching Carly's face for her reaction. He got one. Wide eyes and open mouth.

He also got one from Carly's mother. A smile and look of approval.

"Yes, we're becoming good friends since Stone moved here," Carly rushed out, waving off his comment. "Good friends don't have intentions regarding each other except for friendship, Momma."

Confused, her mother's eyes narrowed his way. "M-men don't want pr-pretty w-women for just fr-friends."

"Momma," Carly pleaded, the red back full force in her cheeks. "Stone just cooked us a wonderful meal. Not only that, he fed you. I'm pretty sure you actually like him so no more awkward questions."

"Th-that doesn't m-mean I tr-trust him where y-you are c-concerned. E-Especially as h-he's not an-answered my qu-question."

He'd bet anything Audrey Evans had been a fireball during her heyday. Stone smiled. "I like Carly, ma'am, but as far as my intentions, at this point in our relationship, we are truly friends. We've never held hands or kissed or any of those things couples do who are more than friends."

Which was mostly true. He had brushed that kiss against her hairline, but that hadn't been a real kiss.

He could just as easily have brushed that temple kiss across his sister's forehead. Not true. That kiss should have been innocent, but nothing about touching Carly felt innocent. The brief brushing of his lips against her temple had lit a few fires.

"I do agree that your daughter is beautiful," he continued, holding Carly's mother's gaze. "And I'll admit I wanted to date her. I asked her out on more than one occasion, but we've decided to be friends."

Audrey didn't look convinced. "In-in hopes it w-will lead to s-something m-more?"

Stone's answer was quick and sure. "I wouldn't be opposed, but consider it a privilege to be your daughter's friend."

"Y-you have my bl-blessing to v-visit our h-home any t-time."

"Mom!"

"Deal." Rather than stick his hand out to shake on it, Stone placed his hand over Carly's mother's on the armrest of her wheelchair. "Is tomorrow evening too soon? Or would that be pressing my welcome too far?"

CHAPTER EIGHT

TOMORROW? CARLY'S EYES WIDENED. Maybe her jaw dropped, too. What was Stone thinking?

What was her mother thinking?

No doubt she was having visions of those grandchildren she'd mentioned the other night. Carly's cheeks were so hot they might burst into flames.

"You said you'd be in surgery tomorrow," Carly reminded him, feeling a little surreal.

Stone shrugged. "I was in surgery today. That doesn't stop me from having a life."

Panic filled Carly. She wasn't sure she was mentally, emotionally, or physically prepared to deal with Stone a third night in a row.

Because her responsibilities did keep her from having a life.

A stab of guilt hit her. Not true, just…not true.

"I'm not sure you coming by tomorrow is a good idea," she began, hoping he'd understand he overwhelmed her.

With little effort, he'd topple the precariously held together bits and pieces of her life.

"Th-that's no w-way to sp-speak to a fr-friend," her mother scolded. "Stone i-is w-welcome."

Her mother smiled toward Stone and Carly knew for

sure she was having visions of wedding bells and grand-kids in her near future.

Please don't think that, Momma.

Whatever Stone's reasons for being there, happy ever after wasn't one of them.

Maybe there wasn't any such thing as happy ever after. Certainly, her mother had never gotten one and Tony hadn't stuck around despite their having planned their future together prior to her mother's illness.

"Y-you c-could c-cook d-dinner for h-him."

Because the way to a man's heart was through his stom-ach? Was that what her mother was thinking?

Carly didn't want to cook for Stone. She shouldn't cook for Stone. But how could she refuse after her mother's comment?

She was racking her brain as to what she could possi-bly cook, when he, fortunately, shot that suggestion down.

"Carly has things to do besides cook dinner for me."

Her mother frowned. "Sh-she can c-cook. I t-taught h-her."

Her mother was right. Growing up, they'd cooked and baked together many a night. Never anything fancy, just whatever they were having as their meal. Those times were precious memories.

Happy times that had faded into present reality.

"Mom, Stone isn't doubting my cooking abilities," Carly explained. "He's just acknowledging that I have things to do tomorrow."

"Which is why I'll bring dinner."

Pride had Carly puffing out her chest. Or maybe it was rebellion. "You don't need to feed us, Stone."

"I'd like to feed you." His eyes twinkled and she knew he was flirting, that he didn't care that her mother was watching.

Carly cared. How was she going to explain that he might

have an attraction to her, but even under the best of circumstances that would pass.

Carly's life wasn't the best of circumstances.

"L-Let the m-man f-feed y-you."

Carly drew in a deep breath. "First you feed my mother, now she wants you to feed me." Carly shook her head. "You're too charming for your own good."

His grin said he knew it.

Fighting a smile, Carly rolled her eyes. "Seriously, you do not have to bring food."

She would stop by the grocery and pick up a few items just in case she needed to feed him. Something simple, but that tasted good. Things that if he didn't come by she could stretch and make last over the week.

Not that she didn't have enough leftovers in her kitchen to cover a few meals. Still, she could freeze some of the spaghetti.

Carly's mother stayed with them for another ten minutes before fatigue caught up with her. Carly could see the switch flip as her mother's adrenaline surge at having a man in the house faded. Her tremor and speech worsened and she struggled to keep her head up.

"I—I'd l-like b-bed."

Carly stood to push her mother's wheelchair back to her room.

"Can I help you get her into bed?"

"I got this," Carly assured him, waving off his help.

A few minutes later, she maneuvered her mother via the mechanical lift from the chair into her bed. Perhaps she should have let Stone help. Her mother was usually able to help support a little of her weight. But she didn't usually get up out of bed in the evenings to eat dinner. Exhausted, Audrey was a limp ragdoll during the transfer, leaving Carly with extra work in transferring from the wheelchair.

Working as a nurse, she was used to transferring patients, but there was only so much one person could do.

She got her mother into her bed, got her situated, gave her night-time medications via her tube, then sat with her for the few minutes it took her to go to sleep.

Before leaving the room, she bent down and kissed her mother's cheek. "I love you, Momma."

Her mother's lashes fluttered open and she mumbled, "I love you, too."

Her words were so clear, so reminiscent of what Carly had often heard while growing up, what she had felt every moment of her life, her eyes watered.

She stood at her mother's bedside, not surprised when a tear, then another, rolled down her cheek.

Such a good, good woman to be so incapacitated.

Maybe the neurologist would have some miracle cure at her mother's upcoming follow-up appointment.

Which had her questioning how she was going to continue to transfer her mother in and out of the car.

She'd figure it out. Maybe her mother would be having a good day and it wouldn't be a problem. Maybe.

She swiped at her cheeks, dried her eyes, then pasted on a smile as she went to find Stone.

She'd expected him to still be at the small table, but he wasn't. He was in the kitchen, wiping down the countertop. The clean countertop.

He'd cleared the table and done the dishes.

"I won't promise I got things put away in the correct places, but at least there's nothing you have to clean up."

"I...thank you." Carly stared at him, a bit awestruck. None of the boys she'd dated, including Tony, had ever done anything so sweet and unexpected.

Boys. Maybe that was the difference. Stone was a man. Not that they were dating. They were friends.

"You really didn't have to do that," she continued. "But I appreciate that you did."

"I didn't know how long you'd be. Cleaning up gave me something to do. Plus, I want to help you."

"I could have gotten it after I got Mom to bed. It's not fair for you to cook, plus wash everything."

His smile said cleaning hadn't bothered him in the slightest. "Like I said, I won't promise things are put away correctly. If you can't find something, just keep looking because I stuck it somewhere."

She nodded.

"Speaking of cabinets, if you have a screwdriver, I'll tighten the screws making that door hang down." He gestured to one of the top cabinet doors that hung at a slight angle.

"I can do that," she assured him. She'd been meaning to for weeks. Every time she was in the kitchen and would see the cabinet, she'd think about it. But there was always something more pressing to get done.

"There's no time like the present. Get me a flathead screwdriver, Carly."

She wanted to argue further, but decided it was easier to get a screwdriver. She dug through some odds and ends until she found the tool in her grandfather's small, rusty toolbox that was stuck in the hallway closet.

Rather than hand it over, she scooted a chair to the cabinet, climbed up, and tightened the loose screws. Opening and closing the door, she made sure her repair had completely corrected the problem.

When she went to step down, Stone put his hands on her waist, steadying her.

Supposedly steadying her.

Because his hands on her waist had quite the opposite effect and she ended up losing her balance and grasping his shoulders as she stepped down from the chair.

"Sorry," she apologized, looking up at him, clinging to his shoulders.

"You should have let me do that." His voice was soft.

"I did just fine."

"You did, but I wanted to help you, Carly. Let me do things for you."

She wondered if his attraction had already waned into pity. She didn't want his pity. She wanted his...oh, good grief! She wanted him.

Much more than the boys she'd dated in high school and college. Not that she'd slept with them. Just Tony and he'd been okay, a good enough guy, but nothing spectacular when it had come to the act of sex. Definitely nothing spectacular when it had come to sticking around when her circumstances had changed.

"You cooked dinner and cleaned up afterwards," she reminded him. "You've done more than your share of helping."

Why was she still holding onto his shoulders?

Why was he still holding onto her waist?

Why did she want to lean against him, feel his body next to hers?

"I'd like to do more."

Lord help her, so would she, but that thought was futile.

"We've had this conversation. My mother invited you to stop by tomorrow, but please don't bring food."

"Do you want me to stop by tomorrow?"

She should lie and say no.

She should tell him to stay away so she could get her work done.

She should do a lot of things, but instead what she did was realize her thumbs were caressing the man's shoulders. Realized that his hands had slid from her waist to behind her to her low back.

She bit into her cheek and didn't scold herself for doing so. No wonder she was giving in to her nervous tic.

Stone's hands slid up her back in a slow explorative move that she knew she could stop with a single word.

She didn't utter a peep.

When he reached up and pulled the clip from her hair, letting her long locks tumble free, Carly didn't stop him. He dropped the clip onto the countertop beside him, then dug his fingers into her hair.

"So soft," he said, staring at his hands surrounded by her hair. "I knew it would be like this."

"What?"

"Touching you."

"My hair, you mean?"

"Your hair. You. All of it."

"We're friends," she reminded him, not quite believing he was saying the things he was, touching her as if she were...desirable.

"I haven't forgotten."

"Good friends," she added, quoting him from earlier. A shiver ran down her spine, prickling her sensitized skin.

"Very good friends." His fingers tangled further into her hair, then caressed the back of her neck. "The best."

"That feels good," she heard herself admit, perhaps speaking to keep from moaning with pleasure. Stone's fingers were magic. Pure magic.

"Agreed."

At first, she thought he meant touching her felt good, then she realized her fingers were at his neck, were threading into his dark hair, caressing, touching. So, maybe he'd meant her touching him.

Not that her fingers were magical, but she felt as if she had some type of super power when his skin goose-bumped and a low sound emitted from his throat.

Good. If he was doing crazy things to her she wanted

to do them back, for him to feel the heart-racing breath-lessness too.

Stone lifted her hair away from her neck, bent, and pressed his lips to her throat.

Pinpricks of pleasure covered her skin and Carly moaned.

He nuzzled, kissed, and gently supped at her throat. Carly melted. Her fingers dug into his shoulders for support because she might just puddle on the floor.

"You taste so sweet."

She didn't use any fancy perfumes or lotions. All he could be tasting was soap, water, and her.

He raised his head, stared into her eyes, a thousand questions in his green depths, but one main one that over-shadowed all the others.

Rather than say yes, Carly stood onto her tiptoes and answered.

By pressing her lips to his.

Dear sweet heavens. His lips were soft. Perfect against hers.

Perfect in how they moved, in how they tugged at hers, tasted hers. In how he let her explore his mouth, taste him.

Perfect.

Her fingers still tangled in his hair, pulling him closer. His hands slid to her bottom, lifted her into him.

Need like Carly had never known took over every cell of her being.

On and on, they kissed, leaving Carly practically gasp-ing when their mouths separated by a few centimeters. She stared into his eyes and didn't bother to try to hide how dazed she felt. Trying wouldn't have worked. He'd totally overwhelmed her senses. Overwhelmed her.

Trying to catch his breath, Stone rested his forehead against Carly's and stared into the molten honey of her brown eyes. "That was amazing."

Her lips twitched. "You think?"

He laughed. "Afraid you might inflate my ego?"

"I'm quite positive your ego is already inflated."

One side of Stone's mouth tugged upwards. There was no hiding that she was right. Not with her body pressed against him. "It's your fault."

A small smile toyed at her lips. "I can live with that."

Her response surprised him. He'd expected her to pull away once the kiss ended, for her to have regrets, possibly backtrack and ask him to leave. Instead, her hands were around his neck, her forehead was against his, and she was smiling as if she'd enjoyed their kiss as much as he had.

He could only hope she'd enjoyed it half as much.

"I'm going to want to do that again," he warned, watching her closely.

"I figured as much."

"You're okay with that?"

"I'm just trying to figure out what you're going to tell my mother now that you've kissed me."

He grinned. "You think she'll ask?"

Carly's expression twisted in thought. "Actually, I think you'd better run before she asks you to stay forever."

He couldn't quite hold his smile.

The light dancing in Carly's eyes dimmed and concern took its place. "I don't want my mother hurt, Stone. Nor do I want her to have unrealistic expectations. I don't have time to invest in a relationship. Not a friendship or more-than-friendship relationship."

"Because of your mother?"

She took a deep breath, then nodded. "Asking Joyce to stay extra so I can spend time with you isn't an option."

He studied her face, the tension etched into her expression. She believed what she said. Maybe what she said was true. He didn't want to add to her burden, but walking away didn't seem a viable option, either.

Certainly not an acceptable option.

"We don't have to go anywhere, Carly. We can spend time together here, with your mother."

Looking pained, she shook her head. "She'll get the wrong idea."

"What wrong idea would that be?"

Rose bloomed in her cheeks. "That we might fall in love, get married, and have her grandchildren."

This time the but was going to come from him.

"But we'll know the truth."

"None of those things can happen," she agreed.

No matter what happened between him and Carly, and he was hoping a lot would, there would be no marriage, or children. Been there, done part of that, had the deep scars to prove it.

"As long as you and I know the truth, that we're just good friends, we can make this work if you'll try."

Carly's lower lip disappeared between her teeth a moment, then she let out a long breath. "Oh, there's a million reasons, but I'm not sure any of them are enough to keep me away from you."

Warmth filled his chest. "I think I like that."

She blinked up at him. "What?"

"That you want to be with me that much."

Carly laughed, which caused her body to move against his and Stone fought a groan. Her body fit next to his so perfectly, so succinctly, so excitedly.

"Why wouldn't I?" she asked. "You shop, cook, and clean. Every woman's dream man."

"Not every."

That he knew for a fact. Some lessons weren't soon forgotten.

Yes, he had moved on, had been in several decent relationships since Stephanie, but he'd not let anyone get close.

"If things begin to get complicated, we'll go back to the way things were, just work friends," she suggested.

Had she read his mind? Felt the tension memories of the past stirred?

"Sounds perfect," he agreed. "We'll keep things uncomplicated."

Only part of Stone wondered if things weren't already complicated where Carly was concerned.

CHAPTER NINE

"TWISTER? YOU WANT to play a game?"

If Stone had any doubts, the sparkle in Carly's eyes would have convinced him playing a game was just what she needed.

"But there's only two of us. Who is going to spin to tell us what's next?"

"I downloaded an app to my phone that will 'spin' for us. You think I was going to risk you having a reason not to play?"

"I have reasons why I shouldn't play, but—" she glanced at the game he'd gone out to his SUV to bring into her house "—obviously, none of them are enough to keep me from doing exactly that."

"You'll have fun."

"And you?"

"Tangling up on a mat with you?" He waggled his brows. "Yes, I'm going to have fun."

Still smiling, Carly rolled her eyes. "I'm beginning to wonder how old you really are. Ten or in your thirties?"

"I'm not telling," he teased, leaning forward to trace his thumb over her cheek.

"Sorry. Did I have dressing on my face?"

He shook his head. He'd brought them grilled chicken salads, plus had picked up some fresh fruit for dessert.

He held up the game. "I play to win."

"I've noticed."

He arched a brow.

"You don't seem the type to not get your way often."

"More often than you obviously think." His happiness ebbed a little. "That's life. We win some and lose some. It's all good and what makes us into the people we are."

"I suppose." Her smile wavered, too.

Stone grabbed her hand. "Come on. Let's play." He opened the box, read the instructions out loud, then spread the mat. "You ready?"

She eyed the mat then met his gaze. "Sure. Why not?"

He chuckled. "I'm going to remind you later that you were skeptical of my idea."

"You do that."

Stone took out his phone, opened the game app, and put in the settings. Then, he took off his shoes and stretched his arms over his head, then touched his toes.

"Should I be worried?"

He glanced at her.

"You look like you're preparing for a major competition."

"Should I not be worried? Are you a Twister loser?"

"I've no idea," she admitted. "I haven't played since elementary school while at a slumber party."

"Did you win or lose that night?"

Her lips curved upwards. "I won."

"See, I need to be warming up."

Carly laughed and the happy sound vibrated all the way through Stone, leaving him a little wobbly.

"Fine," she agreed, doing some quick stretches of her own. "Prepare to be out-twisted."

He grinned, then tapped the start button on his phone's touch screen. A computerized voice began giving them random instructions.

"Right foot red."

"Right hand yellow."

"Left hand yellow," the voice continued. "Right foot green."

"Hey, that was my spot," Carly accused when Stone purposely chose the spot easiest for Carly to use.

"I didn't see your name there," he teased.

She playfully narrowed her eyes at him. "You know this means war, right?"

He laughed. "Twister war?"

She nodded, placing her left foot on a different green circle at the phone app's bidding.

"Bring it on," he encouraged, purposely stretching beneath her arched body to put his foot on an open green spot on her opposite side.

Laughing and bumping into each other, they continued to play, intentionally tangling with each other as much as possible.

"I'd forgotten how much fun this game was," Stone mused close to her ear, their bodies twisted around each other's to keep their hands and feet on the appropriate colored circles.

"Oh? Has it been a while since you've played?" Carly stretched to put her left hand on a yellow circle, very aware of how her arm brushed against Stone's arm.

"Last time I played was at a college party." He'd not thought of that in years, not until earlier that day while at work, trying to figure out how he could get Carly to relax, to laugh, have fun without their leaving her house.

"Were you much of a partier in college?" she asked as they bumped against each other to put their right feet on different blue circles.

"I partied my share, but was never a diehard partier if that's what you're asking." He'd always felt he had a good balance of fun and hard work in his life. Apparently,

Stephanie hadn't thought so. "What about you? Were you a partier in college or were you taking care of your mom then, too?"

Carly put her right foot on the called-out green circle, trying to focus on their conversation and not how her body rubbed against Stone's.

"I had a great high-school experience. Most of my college days were good, too. Mom didn't get so ill until my senior year. Even then, she didn't require around-the-clock care, but just had reached the point she could no longer work and was in a financial mess. I moved home to help with expenses and drove back and forth to university."

Carly and Stone both shifted to put their left feet on yellow circles.

"That couldn't have been easy, working, going to nursing school, and taking care of your mother."

"It wasn't bad." She truly sounded as if it hadn't been. "I loved my mother very much and wanted to take care of her. I only wish I could do more to help her."

He stared at her in amazement. "Surely you realize how much you're doing compared to what most kids do?"

"Most kids aren't trained nurses. I am. Besides, it's not anything that she wouldn't do for me."

"What are you going to do when she reaches the point you can't take care of her here?"

Carly shrugged. "I don't know. I try not to think about that, to just focus on taking care of her a day at a time the best I can."

His heart ached for her, for what she'd been through, what she was going through, what she would go through as her mother's condition worsened.

"You're the strongest woman I've ever met, Carly Evans."

Her gaze jerked to his. "Then you've not met very many

women, because I'm a mess and feel as if I'm barely keeping all the plates in the air most days."

He didn't argue with her, just decided they'd had enough serious talk. When the phone app announced right hand yellow, he reached around her to put his hand on the circle. In the process his body bumped up against hers, just hard enough to make her wobble.

"Hey!" she accused. "I'm on to you, trying to distract me with talk, and then knocking me off my feet."

"You're still on your feet," he pointed out.

She was. How she'd managed to stay balanced, he wasn't sure, but she had.

"No thanks to you."

The app said left foot green. Before Stone could move, Carly bumped him with her bottom hard as she maneuvered her left foot onto the green circle.

"Oops, sorry," she said when he wobbled a little, barely managing to keep from falling.

Her eyes danced with amusement.

"Uh-huh. You're going to be."

She laughed. "Probably."

"Right foot blue."

They both moved hard against each other, trying to get to the closest blue circle. Carly made it first and Stone shifted his body to where he put his foot on the blue circle to her other side.

The position had her bottom cradled against him. It was all he could do to fight his instant reaction.

He forced sobering thoughts into his head, thoughts that would hopefully kill his physical response.

When the app called out their next move, Carly wiggled her body against him as she stretched to touch her right hand to a different yellow circle.

He groaned.

She wiggled again.

"Right hand yellow," she reminded him when he didn't move.

He leaned over her and pressed his chest to her back as he slapped his hand on the yellow circle to her right.

He felt her gulp, was glad that the touch of their bodies caused a physical reaction within her, too.

"Left hand yellow."

Carly stretched to put her hand on a free circle. The only other free circles were two to the far left and one to the far right. Stone went for the far right and did so by looping his left arm underneath Carly's body, allowing him to encircle her torso in a hug of sorts.

"Stone!"

"Sorry, it was the easiest to get to."

"Right."

In their current position, he couldn't see her face but could hear the joy in her voice. He hugged her tighter.

She wiggled her bottom.

"Sorry, I have an itch," she teased.

"I could scratch that for you."

"I bet you could."

"Right hand blue."

They both reached for a blue circle and both lost their balance, tumbling to the floor in a heap of laughter.

Stone rolled, pulling Carly with him so that she rested on top of him rather than vice versa.

Smiling with a carefreeness he'd not seen before, she stared down at him. "If I'm on top does that mean I win?"

Stone groaned. "I don't think you could convince me that you being on top means I'm the loser."

She giggled, then dropped her gaze to his lips. "Maybe we could call it a tie for first place. Then, we'd both be winners."

He arched his neck, bringing his mouth within centimeters of hers, stared into her pretty brown eyes. "I'm good with being tied with you, Carly. In a game, with a rope..."

"You're bad, Stone," she whispered against his lips.

Liking the feel of her pressed against his chest, Stone laughed. "Sometimes."

Smiling, watching him closely, Carly rested her weight on his body, placed her hands on his cheeks.

"Am I too heavy for you?" she asked.

He snorted. "Not even close."

"Good." She closed the small gap between their mouths, gently placing her lips against his.

Stone's stomach turned inside out. His hands automatically went to her low back. Every nerve cell in his body overflowed with testosterone and need for this woman.

For Carly.

Any hopes Stone had had of preventing the hardening in his groin were gone.

All from a sweet, light brushing of her lips against his.

Or maybe it was what shone in her eyes as she stared into his.

The way the color had gone to molten honey, to how he watched her inquisitiveness morph into feminine need. Watched as her gaze filled with desire.

For him.

Despite the boiling need bubbling beneath their surfaces, the kiss stayed slow, explorative, full of questions, full of promise.

Right up until Stone could stand it no more and flexed his hips, pressing against her pelvis in an instinctual move.

"Stone," she whispered, cradling his face with a tenderness that about undid him.

"What do you want from me, Carly?"

She lowered her forehead to his and shrugged. "I don't

know. Sex would complicate things and I'm not ready for that complication. I'm sorry."

He moved his hands up her back, caressing her. "It's okay. I don't want you to have regrets."

Her forehead still pressed against his, she closed her eyes. "I'm going to have regrets, Stone. When I go to bed tonight and am alone and this plays through my mind, I will regret lots of things."

"You're Little Miss Perky today."

Carly smiled at Rosalyn, then shrugged. "Just glad to be alive."

"Uh-huh. A certain handsome surgeon wouldn't have anything to do with that gladness, would he?"

Carly shrugged again. Despite how wonderful Stone had been the past week, she didn't feel comfortable talking about him at work.

Probably because part of her didn't believe he would stick around when her life was so crazy.

Her life was crazy. Crazier than normal.

Because she was getting even less sleep than her normal limited quantity.

Because normally she came home and spent time with her mother, and when her mother wasn't awake, she was working on insurance claims. Every night for the past week, she'd spent two to three hours eating and playing with Stone.

Playing games.

Because every night he brought a new game for them to play.

Silly children's games that had them laughing.

Last night he'd brought Old Maid playing cards. Old Maid.

Was that what she was going to some day be? Had

he been hinting to her to hurry up and invite him into her bedroom?

Not that they hadn't kissed in her living room, and kitchen, her front porch, and in her driveway when she'd walked him out to his car the night before.

What did all those kisses mean? That they were friends who kissed?

The man consumed her every waking thought. And a whole lot of her sleeping ones.

Not that she had much opportunity for those.

Nor would she be catching up any time soon. She was behind on the number of insurance claims she needed to have processed. Way behind. If she didn't get with it, she'd have to dig into her tiny rainy-day fund to pay Joyce's salary.

She had to get with it.

Tonight, she'd send him home early.

It would be easier to tell him not to come, but she couldn't bring herself to do that.

Not when it would mean not seeing him, talking to him, sharing their day happenings, touching him, kissing him. Yeah, she wasn't strong enough to tell him to stay away.

Which was why she'd seen him every night the past week.

She always managed to send him home by ten, but doing so was getting more and more difficult because she didn't want him to go.

But if he left by ten that give her from ten until two to work on claims. She'd sleep from two until five-thirty when she'd get up to get ready for work, spend a few minutes with her mother, before Joyce got there. On the days Carly didn't have to be at the hospital, she slept until seven when she'd get up and feed her mother, sponge bathe, dress, and spend time with her, process as many claims as she could, and try to keep from getting distracted by thoughts of Stone.

Not an easy thing to do.

Today was her last day of four days on, then she'd have another three days off. Three days in which she needed to buckle down and get caught up on her claims so her precarious finances wouldn't collapse.

Fingers snapped in front of her face. "I ask you about Dr. Parker, and you totally go into la-la land. Guess that answers my question."

Carly smiled at the too-wise-for-her-own-good nurse. "I guess it does."

Rosalyn's dark eyes widened. "Yes?"

"We're just friends." At Rosalyn's disbelieving look, she added, "But he is a wonderful man."

"Just friends." Rosalyn snorted. "You keep telling yourself that, honey, if it makes you feel better."

"It does."

Rosalyn laughed, then sobered. "Has he met your family? Do they like him?"

Carly fought grimacing. She never talked about her family. Not ever. But what would it hurt to admit the truth?

"He met my mother." See, that wasn't so difficult. "He charmed her, of course."

"Of course," Rosalyn concurred. "His family?"

Not believing that she was opening up to her co-worker, Carly shook her head. "I've not met them."

"Well, like you said, it's early still."

Rosalyn's smile didn't waver as they shared a look between friends.

Friends. Carly's heart swelled a little. She'd become so isolated that, although she had people in her life, she couldn't have said she had friends.

Her eyes misted a little, and Rosalyn seemed to know her thoughts because the woman pulled Carly to her for a quick hug.

"Now, you go get to work. We got patients to take care of."

CHAPTER TEN

CARLY GENTLY LIFTED the dressing off Mrs. Kim's chest and winced. Overnight the wound had gone from non-healing to angry. Red streaked out from the wound and a purulent discharge oozed from the open gap.

No wonder her patient's vitals had so drastically changed. When Carly had stepped into the room to do morning vitals, she'd immediately known something was wrong.

Mrs. Kim had been stable and Stone's hospital progress notes had said he planned to discharge her today. That wasn't likely to happen.

Her temperature had spiked to one-hundred-and-one-point-two Fahrenheit. Her heart pounded at a hundred and twenty beats per minute. Her skin had a sickly pallor and her eyes just hadn't tracked Carly well.

Before calling Stone to report the changes in his patient, she'd wanted to assess the wound.

The sight beneath the bandage explained everything.

Rather than finish cleaning the wound, Carly stepped back, removed her gloves, and washed her hands. "I'm calling Dr. Parker, Mrs. Kim, before we go further. He may want additional cultures."

The woman nodded. Carly pulled her cell phone from

her scrub pocket and, heart pounding that she was using the direct number Stone had given her, she called him.

Not sure what to expect—would he be happy she'd called him directly or upset?—she filled him in on Mrs. Kim.

"I just finished a lumpectomy and my next procedure was canceled due to a cat scratch on her forearm. Culture the wound, but don't clean or redress it. I want to see. I'll be up there in a few minutes."

Stone shot a quick wink toward the pretty brown-eyed nurse attending to her patient, but verbally addressed the sickly appearing woman lying in the hospital bed.

"Good morning, Mrs. Kim. Your nurse didn't think you looked so well this morning, and I have to agree with her assessment. What happened since I saw you yesterday?"

The feeble elderly woman shrugged. "I got weak."

"Are you hurting?" he asked as he gloved up and moved to her bedside.

"No more than normal," she replied, but grimaced when he pulled away the gauze Carly had used to cover the wound.

Stone wanted to wince himself. Overnight, the wound had reddened and oozed with purulent drainage.

He frowned. "Are you sure that's the same place I checked yesterday?"

Mrs. Kim's tired eyes met his. "That bad?"

"It's not good." He dropped his gaze back to the wound, trying to decide if he wanted to excise it bedside or take her into the operating room. He took off his gloves, tossed them into the appropriate waste bin, then pulled out his phone to call the operating room to check the schedule. He'd had the rescheduled cholecystectomy. Maybe he could slide Mrs. Kim onto the schedule.

"I'm sorry, Dr. Parker, but we're booked solid for anything that's not emergency. Dr. Anderson slid into your canceled slot to do a splenectomy on a post MVA that came into the emergency department."

That decided where he'd be excising the wound.

Hanging up the phone, he turned to Carly. Despite his brain being on Mrs. Kim's wound, his breath caught as he met Carly's brown gaze and she smiled at him.

Breath caught? More like every bodily function halted, leaving him a little dazed.

Gathering his wits, he told her what he planned, what he needed, and then advised Mrs. Kim on what was about to happen.

Carly had done a brief stint in the operating room during her nursing school clinical rotations, but had worked on the medical/surgical floor exclusively since graduation. She loved med/surg. Watching Stone's precise movements as he anesthetized, then opened up Mrs. Kim's wound and cut out infected tissue, she thought she might have missed her calling.

Then again, her fascination might have a lot to do with the surgeon. She'd never seen Stone operate, much less assisted him. The man's hands were steady, skilled, and precise.

While he worked, he chatted with his patient, his voice calm and soothing.

"I'm going to put in a new drain tube then pack the area with antibiotic-soaked gauze."

Carly assisted him as he placed the drain tube.

When he'd finished, he grinned. "Ever think about transferring to the operating room?"

"Once or twice." She didn't elaborate to say that all occurrences had been within the past twenty minutes.

His eyes twinkled and he winked.

Warmth spread through Carly, and she winked back.

Maybe she shouldn't have, but doing so felt right. The happy flicker in his eyes made the whole world feel right.

If only it really were.

"Momma, it's going to be okay," Carly soothed, stroking her mother's face.

Audrey had gotten so agitated Carly had been forced to give her an injection to calm her down to keep her from hurting herself. Something she'd only had to do on one previous occasion.

Carly cried that night, just as she was crying now.

She wasn't sure what had triggered her mother's outburst, her attempt to get out of bed that had ended with her falling. Carly had barely managed to keep her from crashing to the floor.

The fall had upset her mother worse. Audrey had scrambled to try to get up, scratching Carly several times in the process.

Which had never happened before.

Yes, her mother had spells where she didn't know who Carly was, but she had never been aggressive or violent.

"Oh, Momma," Carly sighed, continuing to stroke her mother's face. The injected medication had almost instantly kicked in, calming her, making getting her back into her bed almost impossible.

With a lift belt, the lift machine, and a lot of maneuvering, Carly had managed, but felt the price in her back, neck, and shoulders.

Then there were the scratches on her face and arms. Scratches that stung from the salty tears streaking Carly's face.

Her mother would be mortified if she knew what she'd done. In her right mind, Audrey wouldn't hurt anyone, much less lash out. The woman who'd flayed at her hadn't been in her right mind. She'd been lost and desperate.

Carly leaned forward, resting her head against her sleeping mother's. "Oh, Momma, I'm sorry this is happening to you."

Then the dam broke and the silent streaks of tears became a torrent onslaught. Sobs racked Carly's body.

When her tears had dried, she went to the bathroom, cleaned her face, then called her mother's neurologist. He'd see her later that week.

The previous time this had happened, he'd adjusted medication and that had seemed to help as there hadn't been another episode until the one that afternoon.

Sighing, Carly stared at her reflection in the mirror. She had bags under her eyes. No wonder. She'd sat up until almost four that morning working on insurance claims. She had to get caught up. She had bills looming over her head and if the neurologist changed her mother's medications, who knew what that would cost?

Her mother had awakened just before seven and Carly had started her day over.

Actually, she'd started her night over.

Her night's work, at any rate.

Somehow she'd not processed her claims correctly the night before and none of her work had been saved. Somehow? Exhaustion and distraction would be how.

She had to get her head on straight.

Carly had wanted to throw up and had felt as if she might. Add in that Audrey hadn't known who Carly was, was convinced she wanted to hurt her and that she needed to escape, all equaled a rough morning.

That her mother had turned violent in her attempts to get away from Carly, that she'd had to turn to medication to calm her mother, struck deep.

A straggling tear slid down Carly's cheek and she swatted it away.

No matter. There was nothing she could do about any

of it at this point except to move forward. To stay on task and make the best of what was left of the day. Her mother was asleep and likely would be for several hours, courtesy of the injected medication.

Carly had a lot of work to get done before Stone arrived.

Her gaze met her own in the mirror, took in the dark circles beneath her red-rimmed eyes. Her face was puffy, probably from her crying bout, but maybe from lack of sleep.

"What are you doing, Carly?" she asked herself, not bothering to answer because her answers would accomplish nothing but more stress.

Plus, if she started asking herself questions and answering them, she might have to make an appointment for herself with her mother's neurologist, too.

She shouldn't see Stone that evening. It would take her a big portion of the day to finish the messed-up insurance claims. She needed to get many more than just those done before going to bed tonight. She had bills to pay. Joyce's wages to pay.

Even as she thought it, she knew that when Stone showed up she would stop what she was doing and would spend a few hours basking in his attention.

After all, she had to eat.

And smile.

The man made her smile and right now that seemed like something only a miracle worker could achieve.

Stone was a miracle worker and impossible to ignore.

She would make this work. Maybe she should tell him about the insurance claims.

Why hadn't she?

Pride? Not wanting him to know exactly how financially strapped she was? It wasn't as if he couldn't look around her home, her life, and tell.

Or was it that she didn't want to admit to how guilty she

felt that, rather than working on the claims as she needed to be doing, she snuck a few hours a day to spend with him?

Did that make her a bad person? A bad daughter?

The reflection in the mirror didn't answer, just stared back with glassy, red-rimmed eyes.

"Hello, gorgeous." Stone bent and dropped a kiss on Carly's cheek before walking over to the table to put down the bags of take-out he'd brought with him.

"Obviously, you didn't look at me."

He turned, ran his gaze over her from head to toe. She wore her usual home dress of T-shirt and yoga pants. Her hair was pulled back in its usual ponytail. Her face was make-up-free. She looked tired, her expression pinched, a little haunted.

But the most obvious reason she'd made her comment had to be the scratches across her left cheek.

Scratches that must have been made by her mother. He'd not seen Audrey during a bad spell, other than a few nights that she hadn't known who he or Carly was. Today must have been a bad day. His heart ached for Carly.

He reached out, took her in his arms, and hugged her. "I looked. I liked. I agree with my original statement. You are gorgeous."

Resting her head against his shoulder, she snorted. "You're delusional."

"I do feel that way sometimes when I hold you like this," he admitted, causing her to pull back.

"I knew you'd do this."

"What's that?"

"Make me feel better."

His insides warmed at the compliment. He wanted to make Carly feel better, to make her life better.

"It's probably the freshly baked yeast rolls you are smelling. They smell good enough to make anyone feel better. But I'm good with taking credit for anything that makes you smile."

"Yeast rolls?" She inhaled deeply. "Okay, you convinced me. It's not you." She stepped away from him and began to pull things from the large brown paper bag. "It's definitely the yeast rolls. Yum."

Watching her, he laughed. "Hungry?"

"Starved," she admitted, glancing up as she opened the bread bag and tore off a piece. Her eyes closed and she looked as if she'd just taken a quick trip to heaven. "That is good."

Stone swallowed, trying to clear the knot that formed in his throat. "Remind me to bring you bread every night."

Her eyelids popped open and her gaze met his as she stuck another bite of bread in her mouth. "Sorry. I forgot to eat today. I hadn't realized until just a few moments ago."

He frowned. "You have to take care of yourself or you won't be able to take care of your mother. Then what would she do?"

Her face immediately paled. "You're right. I didn't mean to forget. I was busy and time got away from me."

She didn't need to be skipping meals so Stone was even more grateful he'd brought food.

"You going to tell me about your face?" His gaze lowered, took in the red streaks on her arms. "And your arms?"

She looked away. "I'd rather not."

"Rough day?"

Flinching a little, Carly nodded.

"That bad?" Unable to resist, he reached for her.

"This morning was rough," she mumbled against his chest as she slid her arms around his waist and held him tight, as if she thought she might fall if she let go.

Needing to comfort her any way he could, Stone kissed the top of her head.

"She slept the rest of the day, so I shouldn't be so emotional now." She sighed, then stepped out of his arms and rubbed her hands across her face. "I should be over what happened this morning, but I know her sleeping all afternoon means I will probably have a rough night as she'll likely be awake more than asleep."

Her expression filled with guilt and she moved away from him, removed the last items from the brown paper bag he'd brought their dinner in. "I'm sorry. I shouldn't complain."

Her shoulders drooped a little, as if strained under a heavy load.

"You're not complaining, Carly." Most people he knew would be, would say how unfair life was, would bemoan what she was dealing with. Not Carly. "I asked you about your day and you were telling me."

"It's not what you need or want to hear."

"Not true. I want to hear about you. To know about your life. The good and the bad. Being friends is about more than the good times."

Her gaze cut to him and her lips gave a trembling smile. "Thank you. You are a good man, Stone."

Not that good, but now wasn't the time or place for that conversation. He doubted there ever would be a time or place as he wouldn't want to burden Carly with his problems when she had so many of her own.

"You need me to stay and help with your mother?" he asked as he picked up the brown paper bag and folded it.

She looked at him in surprise. "Why would you do that?"

"To help you."

"Stone, I…"

"We're friends. Friends help friends," he quickly reminded her.

"Like I said, you are a good man. A very good man,

but you don't have to do this." She gestured to the food. "Not any of this."

She was throwing up walls. He could almost visibly see them going up between them and he didn't like it. "We've already had this conversation, Carly. I want to do this, to be with you."

She looked torn, as if emotions were battling within her. "Thanks, but I got this. You want me to get you a drink?"

He regarded her a moment, wondered if she'd always felt the need to carry everything by herself. If pride or strength or conditioning made her feel she had to do this on her own.

Maybe she'd had to and it truly was that she was conditioned to do everything without help. At some point there had been grandparents, but Carly had told him they'd passed before her mother got ill. Other than Joyce, whom she paid, Carly didn't have anyone to lean on.

Which was a sobering thought to someone who had a big family where someone was always sticking out a helping hand.

"I'll take some ice water," he told her, waiting until she'd left to get their drinks before glancing around the room, seeing dozens of things that needed to be done. Things he'd noted each night he'd visited. After how she'd reacted to his offer to tighten the screws on the kitchen cabinet, he'd not mentioned any of the other little things he'd like to do.

"Thanks for dinner, by the way," she said, coming back into the room. "It smells wonderful."

He sat down at the table. "Sure thing. Thank you for the company."

Rather than give her usual response, she just shot him a "yeah, right" look, then asked, "What game am I going to beat you at tonight?"

"You do realize that tying with me doesn't count as beating me?" he teased.

"We didn't tie when we played Trouble, Connect Four, or when we played Old Maid," she reminded him.

Seeing the sparkle he'd come to love in her eyes for the first time since he'd arrived, he grinned. "You won those? Funny, at no point have I felt like a loser."

Carly's smile lit up the small, dingy room that he'd come to feel quite at home in over the past week.

"Sugar-coat however you like," she told him, handing him his water. "But we both know the truth. You just aren't that good at games."

"Or maybe I've been letting you win."

Sitting down at the table perpendicular to him, she regarded him, then shook her head. "Nope. You aren't the type to purposely lose."

"Like I said, I've not felt like a loser."

Except for when he acknowledged that, whether she wanted it or not, Carly needed him and, just like with Stephanie, he was failing her.

Something he intended to rectify.

Carly wasn't going to like what Stone had planned the next evening, but he was determined to help.

Thus, the tool belt and supplies in the back of his SUV. Not that he was a master carpenter, but he'd done enough odd jobs around the house with his dad growing up that he could be handy when needed.

Carly needed handy.

Both her and her house.

After they ate their dinner, he planned to nail down the loose boards on her front porch and around the front porch window. After he got those fixed, he'd sand the peeling paint and freshen up with a new coat.

Grabbing the take-out food bags off his passenger seat, Stone forewent the tools. He'd come back for those when Carly was busy with her mother.

When she met him at the door to unlock it and let him inside, she looked a little frazzled and a whole lot exhausted, just as she had been the evening before.

"You okay?"

"Fine." But she didn't meet his eyes.

His hands were full of their dinner, so he couldn't give in to his urge to pull her into his arms and demand she tell him about her day.

Not immediately. But within seconds, the food was on the dining table and Carly was in his arms.

She let him hold her without uttering a single word of protest. Instead, she rested her head against his chest and leaned on him as if she was too weary to stand.

Just as she'd done the evening before.

Hell.

"I'm glad you're here," she whispered against his chest.

"Me, too," he said and meant. "Me, too."

He held her in silence for a few minutes, before she pulled away, put on a brave smile, and asked what was for dinner.

"Mexican."

"Yum."

"I hope you're hungry because I brought plenty."

"I see that." She gestured to the bags on the table. "We could invite the whole neighborhood over and not run out of food."

He grinned. "You prefer fajitas or burritos or both?"

She dug through one of the bags, pulled out a tortilla chip and popped it into her mouth. "Let's just spread out what you brought and share."

"Sounds perfect."

Dinner had been perfect. Carly and Stone had eaten, laughed, and for a while she'd completely set aside the stresses of the day.

Unfortunately, they crept back in when her watch alarm went off.

"Sorry, I need to go feed Momma."

"Don't be sorry," he assured her, his eyes compassionate. "I understand."

He seemed to.

Which didn't make sense to Carly. She and Tony had dated for more than a year, had planned to get married after graduating from college. They'd talked kids and forever. Yet he hadn't understood when Carly's mother had gotten more ill, when Carly had moved home to care for her.

He'd been mad. Upset. Jealous. Had accused her of not having time for him, of not meeting his needs. She'd tried to make time for him, had done her best to make him feel loved and appreciated, but her mother had come first. Tony hadn't understood. He'd left, started seeing someone else, and hadn't looked back.

Neither had Carly.

Not really.

Tony hadn't been the man for her.

Having met Stone, that was easy enough to see.

Not that Stone was the man for her, either, but he'd made her realize there were good guys out there.

Ha. Barely into this "friendship" and she was classifying him as a good guy. Stone was a good guy.

Some day, when she could devote herself to a relationship, she hoped to find a man like him. Because she didn't kid herself by thinking Stone would still be around. He'd tire of her restricted life soon enough.

She bit the inside of her lower lip.

"Thank you for dinner," she told him, trying not to let her thoughts dampen the joy of his being there. "And for the company."

"That's my line," he teased.

She nodded, then went to the kitchen, mixed her mother's

meal for her feeding tube and a small bowl in hopes she'd eat some actual food, too, not that she had for the past two days.

Actually, she just hoped her mother was herself and knew her, or even if she thought she was Margaret, Carly's grandmother, that would be okay. The angry woman of the past two days was someone Carly wasn't emotionally ready to deal with again.

It didn't surprise her when Stone followed her into the kitchen, his hands full of the containers their food had been in.

"You can leave that and I'll clean up later," she offered, just as she did every night. Not that he let her, but she offered. Part of her understood his need to be doing something besides sit while she was with her mother. Some nights, she was only gone for fifteen or twenty minutes. Some nights, she'd be in the room with her mother for more than an hour. No doubt cleaning the kitchen gave him something to pass the time.

Why did he keep coming back when she had so little to offer?

"Thank you," she told him again as she picked up the food tray, carried it to her mother's bedroom, and said a quick prayer.

Her mother didn't know who she was, but wasn't as agitated as she'd been earlier. Then again, with the way her head kept bobbing, Carly felt it safe to say that the effects of the calming medication she'd given a second day in a row hadn't worn off yet.

"Momma, I have your dinner."

"I—I'm n-not h-hungry."

"You need to eat." Carly went through their normal routine as she set the tray up next to the bed.

Audrey didn't eat anything by mouth no matter how many times Carly tried to get her mother to. She'd refuse the bite, would push whatever Carly managed to get inside out with her tongue, and had even spit at Carly once, covering her with little splatters. Until all the food she'd made was out of the small bowl and on her mother's bib, the tray, and Carly, Carly had kept trying.

With a sigh, she set down the spoon. "I'm sorry you don't feel like eating tonight, Momma."

Carly flushed her mother's feeding tube, then delivered the high-nutrient mixture. Her mother moaned and groaned as if in pain, saying she didn't want Carly to give her the food, saying she just wanted to go home.

"You are home, Momma." Determined to at least put on a happy show for her mother, not that her mother seemed to care, but maybe her mother was still in there some-where. "Guess who else is at our home tonight, Momma? Dr. Parker is here. He's in the kitchen. He brought dinner. You have to get to feeling better so you can eat with us again one evening."

She took her mother's hand, held it, kept talking.

"He's been here every night, Momma. He brings din-ner, then spends time with me and makes me laugh. I know he's out of my league, that there's no future to us, even he's admitted that, but spending time with him is such a joy." She closed her eyes. "He makes me feel good, Momma. Like my insides are lighter and like the whole world is a bit more colorful just because he's in it. We're friends, but—"

"Y-you l-love h-him."

Carly's gaze shot to her mother's face. Her mother who had said very few coherent things the past two days.

She wanted to deny what her mother said. But what would be the point in arguing with a woman whose mind came and went?

Especially when Carly wasn't so sure that her mother's comment was wrong.

"It's hard not to fall for a man like Stone," she admit-ted, wondering at how her heart was pounding, knowing she had to say something to take the wedding bells out of her mother's gaze. She couldn't bear to deceive her mother even when her mother might or might not recall the conversation.

"He's a good man, but, Momma, Stone and I aren't destined to be more than just friends. So, don't go thinking anything more. Even if things were different, if I were able to date freely, I wouldn't be interested in a committed relationship. Some day I want to travel and see the world as a travel nurse, to go places and try new things, like what Tony and I had planned to do. The very last thing on my mind is marrying and settling down."

CHAPTER ELEVEN

STONE SHOULDN'T HAVE gone to check on Carly and her mother. Before he'd started hammering, he'd wanted to make sure Audrey wasn't asleep so he wouldn't be disturbing her. From what Carly had implied her mother had been more difficult the past few days. The last thing he'd want was to wake and, possibly, agitate her.

Or overhear Carly's conversation.

But it was good to know Carly didn't want a committed relationship.

Quietly, Stone moved away from the door, went outside to his SUV. Mind racing and muscles tense, he got his tools and the boards he'd brought.

His hammer struck the nail, driving it deep into the wooden plank. Just a few boards tonight, but he had plans to come back on his day off work. He'd work on spiffing up the porch, the paint, maybe even tackle trimming the overgrown bushes and shrubbery. Although there were signs the yard had once been well tended, it had obviously been years, if not decades ago.

Making minor repairs to her home would help Carly regardless of whether she opted to keep the house or to sell it down the road.

After her mother passed and she was free to do anything she wanted to do in life.

She deserved that. The freedom to explore and see the world. He'd done that. In undergrad, he and a group of friends had backpacked Europe, climbed to the base camp at Everest, backpacked in New Zealand, had even gone on a trip to Antarctica. He'd traveled, been free to explore the parts of the world that interested him most, had done residencies in various cities throughout the country and had done several medical mission trips outside the United States. Yes, some of the trips had been about purging his mind of his divorce, but, still, he'd traveled.

Carly hadn't had the freedom to do any of those things, had never been much further than the outskirts of Memphis's city limits.

He wanted her to have that freedom.

Which made him stop to question himself. She didn't want that freedom. Wouldn't choose that freedom. She wanted every moment she could have with her mother.

Even when she exhausted herself and carried the burden alone.

Still, she was grateful for his help even if she didn't really want to accept it.

Was gratitude what had put that light in her eyes earlier? The light that had made him want to toss the hammer down and take her into his arms?

He hoped not, but the notion wouldn't let go.

Just as the notion that Carly needed his friendship more than she needed him as anything more nagged.

If they became lovers, would they be able to remain friends, afterwards?

He hit his thumb with the hammer, cursed, and stuck the pounding appendage into his mouth as if that would somehow help.

He pulled it out of his mouth and inspected the damage. A little red, but no real harm done.

He straightened the nail he should have hit instead of his thumb, then drove it into the board with his hammer.

If he really wanted to help Carly, they should remain just friends.

At the banging noise, Carly excused herself from her mother despite her reluctance to leave her side.

"What are you doing?" she asked Stone, stepping out onto the porch and staring at where he was hammering nails into a loose board.

"What does it look like I'm doing?" He reached into a pouch on his tool belt and pulled out a nail.

"Um…maybe a better question would be why are you doing what you are doing?"

"It needs doing." He positioned the nail, then drove it into place with a few swift hits from the hammer.

"Not by you. It's not your place."

"My repairing a few things while you're with your mother isn't a big deal, Carly," he pointed out in a tone that warned she was overreacting. He took another nail from his tool belt. "Don't make this into more than it is."

It was already happening. His getting bored with waiting while she cared for her mother. She couldn't blame him. He'd been so patient, so kind with her, so much more so than she'd ever expected. Yet she couldn't stop the sick feeling sweeping through her.

"Repairing a few things?" While he hammered the nail, she took in his tool belt, the supplies he'd carried onto the porch, and tried to keep the panic from her voice. "What are you planning?"

"To do a few things around here."

"I don't need you doing things around here."

He didn't look up at her, just kept working. "Sure, you do."

Carly's hands went to her hips. "If you don't like my home, you don't have to come back."

In response, he placed another nail and hammered it into place. Each hit sent a shockwave through Carly.

"Did you hear me?" she asked, when he reached for another nail.

"I heard."

"Then why are you still doing that?"

Pausing, he glanced up. "It's not a big deal."

Her chin tilted. "It is to me."

"Look, it gives me something constructive to do while I'm here."

"You don't have to be here," she reminded him.

"I want to be here."

His words should have soothed the unease in her, but instead had her hands clenching. "Please don't do this. I don't want to be beholden to you."

The desperation in her voice must have gotten to him, because he stopped working, looked up. "You aren't."

"But if you do this, I will feel as if I am."

He stared a few moments, then picked up another nail, checked the railing, and hammered the nail into place, securing the previously loose board. "I can't help your hangups, but you don't owe me anything, Carly."

"That's not fair to you."

He shrugged. "Doing something to help a friend isn't about fair. If the situations were reversed, wouldn't you do the same for me?"

She would do the same for him. More if she could. But...

She regarded him a moment, then sighed. "How am I supposed to argue with you when you make so much sense?"

A relieved grin slid onto his handsome face. "Because you aren't supposed to argue with me. Go finish with your mother, and then come out here and help me."

Still not quite sure what to make of his having come

prepared to make repairs on her home, she sighed. "You're going to make me work instead of playing games tonight?"

His eyes twinkled. "I've time for both."

Which made Carly's insides flinch.

He might have time for both, but she didn't. How could she tell him that his being there made her life better in some ways and more stressful in others? She was so far behind with processing insurance claims.

"I...okay, Stone. I'll be back when I can." But rather than walk away, she stood, staring at him, wondering how she would ever repay him and if what her mother had said was true.

Definitely, she wanted him.

How could she not?

He was gorgeous and kind and made her feel alive.

"Go," he told her, breaking into her thoughts. "Because if you keep standing there looking at me like that, I'm going to toss the hammer aside and take you up on what I'm seeing in your eyes."

Carly almost instinctively closed her eyes, but caught herself just in time. She didn't want to close her eyes. She didn't care if Stone saw the truth in her gaze.

Not that she was a hundred percent certain what all that truth actually encompassed, but maybe it was time for her to quit pretending that she only wanted to be friends with him.

When Carly got back to her mother's bedroom, Audrey was sound asleep. Carly flushed her feeding tube, because she couldn't recall if she had earlier or not, then removed the dirty bib and cleaned her mother's face.

Although she stirred, her mother didn't wake.

After a few minutes, Carly gave in to the nervousness flowing through her veins and headed to her bedroom.

Once there, she glanced around, trying to envision the

ten by ten room through Stone's eyes. Faded pink walls, an antique full-sized oak bed that had been her grandparents', the matching chest of drawers and oval-mirrored dresser. A rustic chest that her grandfather had claimed had been his grandfather's where Carly had a few quilts and items from her childhood stored.

Not a setting of seduction or romance for sure.

She walked over to the mirror, took in her tired, haggard appearance, the scratches on her face, and frowned.

Nor was she the image of a temptress.

Ha. Far from it.

Going to the bathroom, she had the quickest shower possible, and once out put on deodorant, lotion, and brushed her teeth. She pulled the rubber band from around her ponytail and her hair fell about her shoulders, long and dark and with a hint of wave.

She pulled on a fresh pair of yoga pants and T-shirt, and then wondered whether she should wear something else. He'd only ever seen her in these, a nurse's uniform, sweats, or shorts, and the clothes she'd changed into the night he'd taken her to Julio's.

Walking to her closet, she opened the door, scooted aside her uniforms, and stared at the remaining bits of her former life.

The clothes seemed as foreign to her as if they'd belonged to someone else.

They had belonged to someone else. She felt nothing like the young woman who'd worn fun, fashionable clothes to class and to the social events she and Tony had attended.

Flashes of memories of concerts down by the Mississippi River, of watching the local sport teams play, of hanging on Beale Street with nothing more to do than go from one club to the next visiting with friends and laughing without a care in the world.

Then everything had changed.

It hadn't really been sudden, just that Carly had been in denial of how bad her mother's disease had progressed until her mother had been forced to quit work and confessed what a financial mess she was in.

Carly had begged out of the apartment she'd shared with three girls, moved home, and taken over the bills.

Taken over everything.

And not looked back.

Until Stone.

She reached out, fingered a pumpkin-colored shirt that had once been one of her favorites. She'd always gotten compliments on how it brought out the coloring of her eyes, skin, and hair, when she wore it.

Maybe she should put it on.

"You don't need to do that."

Carly spun. Stone stood in her bedroom doorway, watching her.

"Sorry, I would have called out, but I didn't want to wake your mother."

"I, uh, that's fine." She glanced back toward her closet, thinking she'd taken too long in trying to decide what to do.

Then again, Stone said she didn't need to change. He was right. For what she wanted, she didn't need clothes.

He leaned against the doorjamb and gave a crooked half-smile.

Carly closed her closet door. "Did I take too long to help you?"

"I finished repairing the loose boards, and plan to start sanding them to apply a coat or two of paint. I came in to get a glass of water, then get back to it. I think I can get most of the sanding done tonight."

She was in her bedroom, had been contemplating seducing him, and he planned to sand?

She regarded him. A sinking feeling settled into her

gut. He didn't want her. When push had come to shove, he'd realized she wasn't so tempting after all.

"Stop," he ordered.

She lifted her chin a notch. "Stop what?"

"What you're thinking. You couldn't be further from the truth."

"Then what is the truth?"

He raked his fingers through his hair. "I want you, Carly. A lot. What I don't want is for you to have sex with me out of gratitude."

"You think that's why I…" Embarrassed, she shook her head. "You're the one who couldn't be further from the truth."

"You weren't feeling overly thankful and indebted for my helping you? Because I think you were."

"Yes, I felt thankful for your friendship and your help, but I'm not going to have sex with a man just because he hammered a few nails into my front porch. Besides, from what little I saw, you aren't that good of a carpenter."

He laughed. "Thank you."

Hands on her hips, she frowned. "For what?"

"For being appropriately outraged."

He crossed the room and smiled down at her.

"You want me to be outraged?" she asked, trying to make sense of how he was smiling at her.

"I like your hair like this, by the way. Long, loose, free about your shoulders."

"It gets in the way."

"Of?" he asked, his fingers toying with the strands about her shoulders.

She wanted him to make love to her. Tonight. Now.

The thought hit Carly with the same force as he'd been pounding the nails into the board. They were in her bedroom, he was toying with her hair, and her body was surging with years of pent-up hormones.

She was no seductress. Even with Tony, he'd been the one to initiate sex. But she longed for the knowledge, the prowess, the skills to make this man want her.

No, for him to crave her, need to have her.

Staring at the pulse beating at his throat, she saw him swallow, realized he might be thinking the same thing she was, only was afraid to push because she'd been so adamant that she didn't have time for a relationship. She didn't. They were supposed to just be friends.

Who was she fooling? Just being friends with Stone was impossible.

Not taking whatever he'd give her was impossible.

Acting on instinct, she pushed her hair aside, exposing the curve of her neck, and whispered, "Your lips."

His startled gaze connected with hers. "Carly?"

"Kiss me, Stone. Please, kiss me there." She placed a fingertip on her lips. "Here." This time it was her swallowing. "Everywhere."

"Carly, I—"

"You told me you wanted me," she interrupted, not willing to listen to any arguments he might make. She didn't want logic or reasons why they shouldn't. She wanted him. "You said you wanted to help me," she reminded him, rubbing her palms over his shoulders, slowly and with purpose. "Then help me to forget, Stone. Make me forget everything except you and me. Make love to me like you need me as much as I need you right now."

Stone's brain reminded him of all the things he'd decided while out on her porch.

His brain was no match for Carly's sweet plea.

No match for the raging need that overflowed from him at her words.

Carly wanted him to make love to her, was asking him to do what he desperately wanted to do. The vulnerability shining in her eyes warned that if he turned her down he'd shatter whatever confidence had let her be able to tell him her desires.

Like a fragile butterfly, she was attempting to emerge from the cocoon she'd been hidden in for so long and she was asking him to help her spread her wings.

He felt humbled.

And lucky.

Carly wanted him. Reason left him. Need filled him. Need to give her everything she asked of him.

"No worries about your hair, Carly. It's beautiful, and if it gets in my way, I'll push it aside." He ran his fingers into her hair, nuzzled her neck, felt shivers cover his body. "You smell good."

"I jumped in the shower. I've been working all day, taking care of Mom." Even as she arched into his touch, her voice quivered with a nervousness that made him want to reassure her.

He shook his head. "I don't need to taste soap and water, Carly. I want you on my lips."

"Good, that's what I want." Her fingers dug into his shoulders. "I want to taste you, too, Stone. I feel as if I'll shrivel up inside if I don't have your lips against mine."

He groaned.

Despite how her words thrilled him, he didn't move to her mouth, just continued to explore the curve of her neck, licking and nipping at the sensitive flesh, liking the soft sounds of pleasure in her throat.

His hands slipped beneath her T-shirt, pulled it up over her head. "You're beautiful, Carly. So beautiful."

She mumbled something, but he couldn't make out what, because, gaze locked with his, she reached around and undid her bra clasp and let the scrap of material fall to the floor.

Moving against him, chest pressed against his through

the thin material of his T-shirt, she wrapped her arms around his neck, and pulled his mouth to hers and kissed him.

Hard, passionate, full of heat.

Heaven, he thought. That was what she tasted of. Heaven.

Time faded away. The world faded away.

He caressed her, kissed her, put every bit of her to memory.

She touched him with the same fervor, with the same burning need, as she pulled his shirt off him, stared at his chest with such desire and admiration he wanted to let out a roar of pride.

"How do you manage to look like that and have an impressive brain?" she asked, bending to kiss first one pec then the other.

His muscles tightened to hard knots. "Am I not supposed to be healthy because I have a brain?"

"This…" she trailed kisses down his chest, over his abs "…goes beyond healthy."

"I'll take that as a compliment."

"Yeah, you should, but looking at you makes me feel as if I should put my clothes back on," she admitted, giving voice to her insecurities and bringing out every protective gene in his being.

He cupped her face, forced her to look at him.

"You are beautiful. How many times do I have to say it before you will believe me? Maybe I should show you while I'm telling you." He lowered his hands to her waist, bent to kiss her collarbone. "You are beautiful, Carly." He kissed the opposite collarbone. "So very beautiful."

He bent to the tiny valley between her breasts. Her skin goose-bumped, pebbling her nipples.

His groin strained against his pants.

"You're beautiful, Carly."

"You don't have to keep saying that," she whispered,

gasping a little when he kissed her puckered nipple then took it in his mouth.

"I'm going to keep saying it until you believe me." He kissed her other nipple and showered it with attention while running his hands slowly down her sides. He lowered to kiss the tip of her sternum, her belly. "You're beautiful, Carly Evans."

He lowered further, dropping to his knees to stand before her as, holding her hips, he kissed her belly.

Not quite believing what they were doing, thinking she must be having another fantasy—the best one yet—Carly dug her fingers into Stone's shoulders, whimpered as he brushed his hands over her hips, her bottom, as together they pushed off her yoga pants to let them pool at her feet.

She stepped out of them, kicked them away from where they stood, then rubbed her body against his.

Her thighs clenched at the absolute hardness pressing against her belly.

"Has anyone told you lately how beautiful you are?" he asked as he hooked his fingers into her blue cotton bikini panties to help them join her yoga pants and set about fulfilling his promise to kiss her all over.

Carly trembled, worried her legs were going to fail. She held onto his shoulders for dear life, sure if she were to let go she'd combust from the energy moving through her.

Never had she felt like this. Maybe because Tony had never shown her such complete attention, but she suspected it had more to do with Stone than just how her pleasure seemed to be his number one priority.

The man was an overachiever.

Her body tightened, arched into his touch, and she fought crying out as wave after wave of pleasure rocked her.

"Stone." His name came out husky, sounding foreign

to her own ears. Or maybe that was the sound of all those crashing waves muffling her voice?

He leaned forward, kissed the tender flesh he'd just done miraculous things to. "Has anyone told you how beautiful you are?"

"You're crazy."

"About you." Then he set about proving it again.

Carly's eyes closed and she gave up on holding in the sounds emitting from her throat.

Despite her need to hang onto him for support, her fingers refused to stay still, kneading into his shoulders, his neck, threading into his hair, only to grab hold of his shoulders and dig in deep when a heated spasm the size of a tsunami undid her insides.

Stone didn't stop, not until she clamped her mouth closed to keep from crying out.

"Have. To. Be. Quiet," she managed to say between gasps for breath, stroking her hands over his shoulders, loving the strength she felt there.

He stood, kissed her hard, pulled back, and stared into her eyes. "You're beautiful, Carly."

"Stop saying that," she ordered, dropping her forehead against his chin to shield her eyes from his. He made her feel beautiful, made her feel so good, so unlike anything she'd ever known or imagined.

"Never," he warned. "I'm always going to tell you how beautiful you are."

Not always. She knew that. The day would come when Stone would move on to better things, to women who were free to love a man like him, to a woman who could give him all the things he deserved. The thought caused a painful stab in her chest, but he was touching her again and the pain vanished as quickly as it had hit.

For the moment, Stone was hers to touch, to kiss, to love. So, she did.

* * *

His body collapsing against hers, Stone fought roaring with release, fought shouting out that Carly was beautiful.

But her mother was in the bedroom next to them, and although it was unlikely she'd awaken, Stone didn't want to risk it.

Selfish of him, but he wanted Carly to himself tonight, to sleep with her in his arms, to wake her and make love to her again before the sun came up.

She didn't have to work at the hospital tomorrow, but he was scheduled in the operating room at seven.

Leaving her bed wasn't going to be easy and for the first time ever he considered taking a day off work and just spending the day with Carly.

A short-lived fantasy because he wouldn't cancel a day's worth of surgeries on a whim, but the idea of spending the day with Carly appealed.

"That was amazing," she praised in a breathy voice from beneath him.

Bearing the brunt of his weight to keep from squashing her, he kissed her with a tenderness he didn't recall having ever felt.

Not even with Stephanie, but surely he had once upon a time?

"Hey, Carly?" he whispered against her lips, looking into her glazed-over-with-pleasure eyes.

"Hmm?"

"Anyone told you lately how absolutely beautiful you are?"

Her eyes full of delight, she smiled up at him. "I've heard that a few times lately."

"It's true." More true than she'd ever believe, but he'd keep trying to convince her. He kissed her again. "Can we spend the day together? Not tomorrow, although I wish

I could. I'm booked in the OR all day. But the following day? You could have Joyce to stay here. We could go downtown, walk by the river, visit the pyramid, whatever you wanted to do."

The light in her eyes dimmed and she shook her head. "It sounds lovely, but you know I can't."

"Joyce would say yes if you asked her. I would pay her, Carly."

She tensed. "I wouldn't let you."

"Why not? I'm the one who wants her to stay," he pointed out, hoping she'd see things his way. When she remained tense, didn't say anything, he relented. "We can stay here if that's the only way you'll say yes."

Her tension didn't ease. Instead, she wiggled, indicating she wanted free from under his body. Stone rolled off, propped himself up on his side and watched as she put her T-shirt back on.

Once in her panties and T-shirt, she faced him. "I told you from that very first night that taking care of my mother came first, that asking Joyce to stay extra wasn't an option."

"Because you're so independent and stubborn."

She shrugged. "Maybe, but it's the way things have to be."

"Because?"

"Because it's the way things are."

"The way you choose things to be."

Her gaze narrowed. "I didn't choose this, Stone. Nor did I want this, any of this. I warned you from the beginning, told you I wasn't free for a relationship. You are the one who pushed."

He sat up, took her hand into his before the situation got out of control. "Somewhere this conversation took a turn it wasn't meant to take. I want to spend time with you, but am okay if that time is here or somewhere else. I was making suggestions on ways for us to be together."

Pulling her hand free, she got her yoga pants, put them on, then took a deep breath. "I appreciate that, but it would be better if you didn't."

He frowned. "Better for whom?"

"Me. You. My mother."

He sat up on the side of the bed, searched for his T-shirt. "You think my being here is bad for your mother?"

"It's not good for her."

"That's not what you thought the night I cooked spaghetti," he reminded her. "You said she ate better for me than she had in weeks. You should let me help you more."

She closed her eyes, took a deep breath. "You should go."

"No."

Her eyes widened.

He moved across the small room to stand in front of her. "That came out a bit rougher than I meant, but, no, Carly, I'm not leaving. Not like this. I don't know how things changed from fantastic to tense, but I'm not leaving until things are right between us."

She didn't look at him; her shoulders sagged. "I probably just got overly emotional. I've not had sex in a long time."

"How long?"

She didn't meet his eyes, but admitted, "Over five years."

Five years. She'd been celibate five years. Because she thought she couldn't have a life and take care of her mother, too? Or because she'd not been interested in anyone?

"It's been a while for me, too," he admitted. Despite going a little crazy with one-night stands immediately after his divorce, he'd settled into a place where sex for the sake of sex hadn't appealed.

At the jerk of her gaze to his, he continued, "Not five years, but it has been a while, Carly."

"Why?"

"Why haven't you had sex in over five years?"

Her gaze narrowed. "You know exactly why."

"Your mother?" He shook his head. "Not a good reason."

Her jaw dropped. "How can you say that?"

"Because it's true. Your mother is just as ill right now as she was this morning and last week and a month ago. Yet, tonight you had sex. Why?"

"Because…because you were here."

"Because I pushed you to let me in."

"I don't understand what your point is."

"You've held the world at bay for the past five years, not let anyone in. That's why you've not had sex until tonight."

"Obviously letting you in was a mistake."

Her words struck him with the force of a hot poker, slicing deep into his chest. "Do you mean that?"

She closed her eyes, then opened them slowly and shook her head. "No. I wanted you here tonight, last night, every night you've been here."

"Good, because I don't want you to regret having let me in." He reached out, brushed a strand of hair away from her face. "I'm sorry for upsetting you."

"I'm sorry I got upset. I… I've only been with one man and our relationship was nothing like mine and yours." She took a deep breath. "This is complicated, you know. Our friendship wasn't supposed to get complicated."

"Sex has a tendency to do that."

"Where do we go from here?"

"Nothing's changed, Carly. We're friends, good friends, remember?"

She didn't look convinced.

Stone understood. Despite his words, he wasn't convinced, either.

Everything had changed.

CHAPTER TWELVE

THE BUZZER GOING off indicating that her mother had woken up shouldn't have been a good thing, but Carly welcomed the sound of pending escape.

"I've got to check on her."

Stone nodded, but Carly knew he didn't understand. No one did.

How could they when they didn't live her life?

She started to suggest he go home to get some rest, but he beat her to the punch.

Which didn't really make her feel better.

"I've got to be in the operating room at seven," he told her, searching out the rest of his clothes. "I'll bring dinner when I'm done with my day."

"I have to take Momma to see her neurologist."

"You'll be back before dinner time," he pointed out.

"You don't have to bring dinner," she reminded him, watching as he pulled his underwear, then jeans, on over his lean hips. Totally unfair how hot the man was in a pair of jeans and bare-chested.

What was wrong with her that she was getting hot under the collar so quickly after having been totally satisfied?

Or was that part of the issue? Now she knew what was beneath his scrubs? What he was capable of? That she was getting too attached, too dependent, too used to having him in her life?

Tony had been in love with her, or so he'd claimed for the year before her mother had gotten so ill, and he'd not stayed. She really couldn't expect Stone to stick around when her life was so crazy.

Yes, the past week, they'd made it work, but at what price?

She'd barely slept, her mother kept getting worse, and she'd made more mistakes on her insurance claims than she'd ever made previously all combined.

Even if Stone stuck it out a while longer, she couldn't keep this pace up.

"I know I don't have to," Stone interrupted her thoughts. "But I want to bring dinner and to see you."

His eyes flashed with something she couldn't read, something intense and that warned he wouldn't argue the subject any more. "I'll see you tomorrow evening."

"I think it's time you consider alternative options."

Carly stared at the neurologist, hoping he was going to suggest a treatment that was highly successful.

"Have you checked into any nursing facilities?"

The skin on Carly's face shrunk, pulling tightly across her forehead and cheeks.

"No." She glanced toward where her mother sat in her wheelchair, hating that her specialist broached this subject in front of her, rather than in private. Audrey's eyes were closed and her head slumped over as if she were asleep, but who knew if she was hearing their conversation? "Momma is doing great at home," she assured him, making sure she spoke clearly so if her mother could hear, she'd know Carly had no plans to institutionalize her.

"Is she?"

Carly thought over the past few weeks, at the rapid decline in her mother's health, that she was having so many more bad days than good. "You think she's not?"

"You called and asked for this appointment, Carly. Why?" He leaned forward, took Carly's hand and gave her an empathetic squeeze. "I think you're doing the best you can, but your mother needs more than what you can do."

He was wrong.

"As in what?" she asked, having to force herself to keep her voice calm. "She has constant attention, has had minimal bedsores, definitely a much lower statistical number than the average bedridden person in a nursing facility." She began tossing out statistics. "She has a one-on-one nurse at her beck and call twenty-four hours a day. She isn't going to get that at a nursing facility."

Dr. Wilton held up his hand to stop her rant. "I'm not saying you aren't providing excellent care. You are. But you aren't a nursing facility meant to provide around-the-clock care for a dying woman."

Carly gasped at his adjective. "Don't say that."

He gave a pointed look, one that was full of empathy and pity and a need to fulfill his professional duty to lay out the facts as he saw them.

"Your mother may live years, but, statistically, she isn't going to be with us much longer. Deep inside, your nursing experience will have taught you that."

He was wrong, again. Her nursing experience had taught her that miracles happened all the time.

"She's just had a few bad days, that's all."

Dr. Wilton sighed. "I can't tell you what to do, but my recommendation remains the same. I feel the best thing is for your mother to be admitted to a nursing facility."

"I disagree and I'm not willing to do that."

As if he'd known that was what she was going to say,

he slowly nodded his head back and forth. "What you're doing is admirable, but not in your best interest."

"This isn't about me. It's about what is best for my mother. If you can honestly tell me she will get better care in a nursing facility, then I'll give due consideration to your recommendation. But you can't tell me that because you know I am a trained registered nurse who has the skills to provide my mother with the care she needs in her home where she is going to feel safest and most comfortable. We both know dementia worsens when the environment changes. Moving to a nursing facility might rob her of the few good days she has. I won't do it."

His expression somber, he regarded Carly long moments, then shrugged. "Then let me call in hospice care to help you."

Hospice? Had he lost his mind?

"No. She doesn't need hospice care."

"I didn't say she did."

Ouch. Carly winced. "You think I need help? That this is killing me?" She glared at the neurologist. "I don't find that funny."

"I wasn't trying to be funny. I'm being realistic, using logic instead of emotion, which you aren't able to do due to the circumstances. If this were someone else, you'd advise them the same as I'm advising you."

"I wouldn't," she denied—not if she knew they were doing all that could be done.

"At least think about what I've told you." He printed out a prescription. "This is the new dosage for your mother's medication. I hope it works miracles, Carly. For your sake as much as your mother's."

Carly dropped the prescription off at the pharmacy, sat in the parking lot with her mother for forty-five minutes while waiting for the call that the prescription was ready, then drove back through the drive-through.

"That will be…" The clerk named a price way above what Carly was expecting.

"That much? You're sure? Did her insurance pay anything?"

The woman shook her head. "I'm sorry, but that's what took so long. The pharmacist contacted your mother's doctor about a prior authorization on the medication. Unfortunately, her prescription plan still denied coverage." The woman gave Carly an empathetic look. "Do you want to wait about filling it? Or I could call Dr. Wilton back and see if he could change the medication to something else, something covered by her insurance."

Her mother had already been on all the Parkinson's medications her insurance covered, was still on a few of them.

Carly glanced over at her mother, at the constant tremor, at her glazed-over look that said she just wanted to be in her own bed rather than in the uncomfortable car seat. Carly would like to have taken her mother home rather than her having had to wait to pick up the medication, but she couldn't leave her mother alone.

Nor could she easily buy this new medication.

But what if this was the dose that would make a difference? That would give her more good days?

Carly sucked in a deep breath, mentally figured her bank account, her incoming bills, and knew she was emptying her rainy-day fund with her next words, but said them anyway. "Ring up the prescription. I'll pay for it out of pocket."

The woman nodded, as if she'd known that was what Carly would say. "There is a manufacturing coupon that knocks off fifty dollars. I'll print and apply it for you."

"Thank you," Carly said, thinking she might throw up at how she'd just spent her meager savings. How could a medication cost almost four figures for a mere month's supply, anyway? That it did just seemed ridiculous.

Ridiculous, but still a fact.

She had to get caught up on her insurance claims. Already her next check was going to be a lot less than its usual amount thanks to how much time she'd spent with Stone rather than working.

She'd not done even half her usual number of claims.

She'd barely been maintaining her financial balancing act and this had tipped the scale.

No—spending time with Stone, not doing her work, being distracted from her work, that was what had tipped the scale.

She couldn't afford to keep seeing him.

"How did your mother's neurology appointment go today?"

Carly winced. She didn't really want to think about how the appointment had gone.

Her mother was always exhausted after an appointment and had passed out in the car. Sleep had been a blessing while they'd waited at the pharmacy, and again after Carly had gotten her settled back into her bed.

Moments after which, Carly had had a good cry.

Or was that a bad cry?

Whatever, she'd sobbed for a few minutes. At Dr. Wilton's recommendations. At the cost of her mother's medication. At the fact that she had just enough money left to cover the house payment, car insurance, electric and water, and almost enough to cover Joyce's salary.

But not quite.

She calculated how many claims she'd need to process over the next few nights to keep everything afloat. Actually, today was the last day of the next two-week pay period. Tonight's claims had to be done. Every last one of them. Plus a few more. With no mistakes. She could do it.

If she could get the claims done, with the extra ones, she could just barely make Joyce's salary. And if a single unexpected expense popped up, she'd sink.

But she wouldn't let that happen. She'd made things work this long, had been doing just fine until Stone had stepped into the picture. Now, she just felt exhausted by it all.

Or maybe she was exhausted because after Stone had left the night before, she'd not been able to sleep. She'd kept reliving his coming to her room, his making love to her, the magic he'd spun. Over and over in her mind, she'd replayed his touches, his kisses.

Her mind had raced, making sleep impossible. So, she'd sat in her mother's room and, as much as her distracted mind and body would allow, worked on insurance claims. She'd gotten very few done.

At some point after five a.m. she'd fallen asleep sitting in the chair and had awakened achy and stiff to her mother moaning and crying.

Caring for her mother in a demented state was bad enough; witnessing her in pain was something Carly could barely bear.

Dr. Wilton thought she should put her mother into a facility. No. Just no.

"It went," she answered Stone's question rather vaguely, reaching up and rubbing her tense neck muscles.

What else could she say? That her mother would likely sleep the rest of the evening and not wake until sometime after midnight, if then? That Carly wanted to crawl between her sheets and sleep for hours on end, too, but would instead sit up most of the night working on the insurance claims she hadn't gotten done?

Insurance claims she had to process before going to work in the morning. She had to meet that quota. Not doing so wasn't a choice.

Not if she wanted to pay Joyce.

Plus, she'd need to leave for work a little early to take the blood and urine Dr. Wilton wanted her to collect on her mother to the hospital lab in the morning and still be able to clock in on time.

A heaviness settled onto her shoulders, making her neck hurt worse than it already did from sleeping in the chair, transporting her mother, and the day's stresses.

Stone had just arrived at her house, was unpacking the food he'd brought for their dinner, and putting hers in front of her, but she'd have to ask him to leave. Soon.

"That good, huh?"

Wishing she weren't a Debbie Downer, especially considering the night before, what they'd shared, which seemed like months ago instead of mere hours, she shrugged. "He wants to see Momma back in a week."

Taking a bite of his Greek salad with grilled chicken, Stone studied her. "Did he say why?"

"To go over labs. Re-evaluate how she's responding to a medication he gave her a new dose of today." She told him the name of the new Parkinson's drug Dr. Wilton had put her mother on. She started to tell him how much the medication had cost, but didn't due to not wanting him to think her petty. Her mother's health was the most important thing.

"Routine visit, then?"

Dr. Wilton didn't routinely make Carly bring her mother in again that quickly. He knew how difficult it was transporting her. Carly had seen the concern in his eyes when he'd been examining her mother. She'd heard the concern in his voice as he'd retested her mini-mental status exam and her number had been three points lower than her test just a few months prior.

Although how he could knock points off for her not being able to copy the design or write a complete sentence was a bit unfair in Carly's mind. Her mother's hands shook so badly that of course her design had looked nothing like the one she'd been asked to recreate.

Then again, her mother's scores on that part of the test hadn't changed from her previous test. It had been recall items that had further dropped her score.

If they'd tested her on the day her mother had met Stone, her score would have been higher.

With how she'd been today, no wonder he'd recommended Carly do something different.

Parkinson's disease and dementia were such frustrating diseases individually. Together they were heartbreaking and Carly's heart was doing just that.

"Not hungry?" Stone asked when Carly didn't eat and failed to answer his question. "Maybe I should have checked with you to make sure you liked Greek food."

She glanced at the numerous take-away trays he'd unloaded from the bag he'd been carrying when he'd knocked on her door about ten minutes before. She'd been sitting with her sleeping mother, going through insurance claims, stressing about money, and fighting heavy eyelids.

"Greek food is great," she assured him, flexing her neck from side to side and grateful the stretching of muscles eased the spasm some. "Thank you for bringing dinner. I'm just not that hungry. Sorry."

"Don't be," he replied, studying her. "I'm worried about you. You need to eat more."

His comment caught Carly off guard. Stone was worried about her? How long had it been since someone had been worried about her?

Not fair, she quickly corrected herself. Her mother had worried about her, still did when she was herself. Joyce worried about her, too.

She was worried about herself.

Or maybe she was just too tired to think clearly.

Either way, she smiled and was determined that she was going to keep smiling for at least the next thirty minutes. After that, she'd ask Stone to leave so she could work, then get a little sleep before starting her early morning hospital shift.

She'd thought about asking him not to come over, but hadn't. How could she when it was the first time she'd have seen him after they'd made love? He wouldn't have understood if she'd refused to let him come over.

Besides she had to eat and Stone fed her. At the rate her finances were going, without him she might reach the point of not being able to feed herself.

"I appreciate you bringing this." She waved her hand toward the feast he'd spread out on her dining table.

"I'm still learning what you like and, until I'm sure, I want you to have options."

"Options are good, but I can pretty much eat anything," she assured him.

"That's not what I said," he corrected, his eyes full of a tenderness that somehow fit as much as the mischievous twinkle she often saw there.

As crazy as her day had been, as crazy as her night would be, she was glad he had come back after last night.

"I want to bring things you like," he continued. "Not things you can tolerate without complaining."

She laughed a little and took a bite of the food he'd put in front of her. A charbroiled chicken that had been marinated with a Greek dressing. "Mission accomplished. This is delicious."

It was. Too bad her stomach was so twisted that putting in food just made more knots.

"That's better." He reached out, touched her cheek, then traced his fingertip over her still upturned lips. "I like seeing you smile."

He probably thought her the most boring, miserable

person he'd ever met. She was the most boring person, but not miserable. Not usually. As tired as she was, she was grateful for another day with her mother, for the hope that tomorrow would be a better day, for the hope that the medicine she'd spent her last dime on would work miracles and she'd get her mother back.

She was grateful for the night before with Stone, for his having made her feel so alive, so aware of her body.

The waiting insurance claims called to her. Ugh. She couldn't lose herself with Stone tonight. Not if she wanted to pay Joyce. Not paying her wasn't an option. She couldn't risk Joyce not coming back and she didn't expect her to work for free.

"Sorry." She truly was because, despite the fact that she didn't have time for this, she recognized how good Stone was to her, that he was making an effort. She really did appreciate his doing so. "I'm not the best company tonight." Or ever. "It really has been a long day."

They all were.

How could she explain how bone weary she felt? How every muscle in her body ached with fatigue and from the toll moving her mother had taken? How she had so much work that night that just the thought of it was overwhelming?

She should get started.

When she met Stone's gaze, he was studying her as if trying to figure out a complicated puzzle. She took another bite so he wouldn't think she didn't like her dinner.

"This isn't about last night, is it?"

Meeting his gaze, seeing the uncertainty there, she felt a need to reassure him hit. He was a good man. He didn't deserve her craziness. "I don't regret last night. Do you?"

"Are you kidding me?" he asked. "Last night was amazing. Come on," he surprised her by saying as he stood up from the dining table. He held his hand out. "I want to do something."

Placing her hand in his, Carly arched a brow. Curious, she let him lead her to her small sofa.

"Lie down."

Didn't he know if she lay down she'd be out like a light? She started to argue.

"Lie down, Carly," he repeated, his voice more firm.

Carly's gaze dropped to the sofa. She needed to keep a clear head, to stay awake. Or maybe he meant to… "Stone, my mother is in the next room and there's no door to shut for privacy and—"

The twinkle was back and he laughed. "I like where your mind went, but that's not where mine's at." He waggled his brows. "Not at the moment. But later, after you've relaxed a little, then yeah, I'd like to see if I missed kissing any spots last night."

"You didn't," she assured him, memories heating her cheeks. "I've never been kissed like that."

"Good, I don't want anyone else kissing you that way. Just me."

"They haven't, not even Tony. I…" She cut herself off. No way did she want to talk about Tony, especially not to Stone.

But rather than question her on her ex, he let go of her hand and pointed to the sofa. "Humor me for a few minutes and lie down, Carly. Do this for me."

Curious and compelled to do as he wanted, she lay down, propped her ankles on one armrest, her head on the other.

"Now, close your eyes."

"What?" She frowned. He didn't know what he was asking, how little sleep she'd gotten the past week, but especially the last few nights.

"Do you trust me, Carly?"

She stared at where he stood next to the sofa. Lord help her, she did trust him. She'd never have let him into her bedroom if she hadn't.

"I do."

"Then do as I ask," he ordered in a gentle, but determined tone. "Close your eyes and keep them closed."

Carly closed her eyes, willed herself not to go to sleep, and listened to him move to the end of the sofa. She almost jumped when his hands grasped her shoulders. His brilliant, magical fingers that had touched her all over the night before now applied just the right amount of pressure as they kneaded into her achy muscles.

Dear sweet heavens above!

"That feels good," she told him. "You really don't have to do this."

But don't ever stop, please.

Because his fingers were working the tension out of her neck and shoulders, were working magic through every tight, strained, painful fiber of her body. A different magic from the night before, but that magic was there, too. That magical chemistry seemed to always be an undercurrent between them.

"I feel guilty letting you do this," she murmured, thinking she might go into full-out purr mode any moment. "You worked all day at the hospital. I didn't."

"Somehow, Carly…" his voice was low, as soothing as his hands "… I'm positive you worked harder than I did. Taking care of someone you love who's ill isn't easy."

Something shifted inside Carly. Something sweet and tender and grateful and completely foreign.

Tony had never understood. Not once. That someone as wonderful as Stone did seemed impossible.

"Thank you." Her voice broke a little, but she didn't care. How could she care about anything when her body was going from a tight mess to ooey-gooey butter?

"You're welcome, Carly. Anyone told you how beautiful you are today?"

She smiled. How could she not? "I did get a text saying something along those lines."

"You got that? I wondered when I didn't hear back."

"I was at the neurologist's when it came through and before I could respond, Dr. Wilton came into the room. Then…" Then, she had gotten caught up in what was going on with her mother and had forgotten she hadn't responded. Would he be upset if she told him the truth? "I'm sorry I didn't text back."

"I might question if that was an intentional move with anyone other than you," he admitted.

If Carly didn't know better, she'd think she heard a need for reassurance.

"I'm not into game playing, Stone. I didn't intentionally ignore your text. It was a rough day getting Momma back and forth to her appointment."

"I'm sorry you had a bad day, Carly."

"You being here helps."

It also hurt because she needed to be working. A few more minutes would be okay. Surely. Because his fingers felt so good massaging her tight muscles. His hands felt so good touching her.

"I'm glad this is helping."

"It is. If you're trying to seduce me, it's working."

Whatever she'd thought she'd heard was gone as he said, "I'll keep that in mind for when I am trying to seduce you. This is about you relaxing, on working out the kink in your neck that you rubbed repeatedly throughout what little dinner you ate. Now, be quiet and just enjoy."

It would be difficult not to enjoy this man's hands on her body. His fingers were magic. Magic and wonderful and truly releasing the achiness in her muscles.

She could get used to this, but knew better than to let herself. She'd learned that lesson with Tony.

Not that Tony had ever massaged her neck and shoulders. Not even when he'd been wanting sex had he done anything so giving.

Time with Stone was dangerous and irresistible because he blinded her to everything except him.

What a fool she was.

Maybe she hadn't learned enough lessons from Tony.

No, she couldn't judge Stone from what had happened with Tony. They weren't cut from the same cloth. Plus, she and Stone were friends. There were no long-term expectations.

She wouldn't rely on him and he wouldn't rely on her, because they were temporary.

Why did that thought leave a hollow ache inside her?

CHAPTER THIRTEEN

CARLY'S BODY HAD gone limp over ten minutes ago, but Stone continued to massage her muscles, wanting to make sure when she woke, the tension was gone.

Or maybe he just wanted the excuse to continue touching her. Not as he'd touched her the night before, but a touch meant to soothe.

He smiled at where her mind had gone when he'd told her to lie down. Under different circumstances that would have been exactly why, but exhaustion had been etched on her face. Hadn't she slept after he'd left the night before? Obviously not. Had she been up with her mother or had thoughts of what happened between them kept her awake?

The soft, even rise and fall of her chest confirmed that she'd fallen asleep. Good. She needed to rest.

Stone straightened, then went to the table to clear off the remains of their dinner. She really hadn't eaten much, but obviously she needed sleep more than food. He put the leftover food in Carly's mostly bare refrigerator. Other than her mother's feeding-tube meals and leftovers from the meals he'd brought, the entire house seemed void of food.

Stone got a washcloth and wiped off the small table where they'd eaten, thinking about Carly.

The night before she'd stood at her closet, studying her wardrobe from the past, and he'd seen the pain in her eyes, the indecision and grief for what had once been. He'd wanted to ease that pain.

At the hospital, he saw the person in the photos scattered around this house. Having spent time with her away from the hospital, Stone knew Carly didn't have an easy life despite the easy smile she freely brandished at the hospital.

Other than Joyce, Carly provided all her mother's care. Should he check on Audrey?

Carly constantly went back and forth to her mother's room, even when her mother was sleeping. He quietly entered the room, saw Audrey was still sound asleep.

Despite having been at the house every night for going on two weeks, this room seemed off limits and he'd only been inside a time or two with Carly at his side. He glanced around the small bedroom that was monopolized by the hospital bed. A wooden rocking chair similar to the one in the living room was across from the bed. A plugged-in laptop sat on the floor next to the chair, as did a water bottle with the hospital logo on the side.

Carly spent a lot of time in that chair.

Too much time.

"Wh-who are y-you?"

His gaze shot to Carly's mother and he smiled at the frail-looking shell of the woman from the photos. "Stone Parker. We met last week when I fed you spaghetti, remember? I'm Carly's friend."

She stared blankly. "Who's Car-Carly?"

He knew Carly had been having a difficult time with her mother. But Audrey had seemed very clear-headed on the night he'd met her. The blank look in her eyes told the reality.

"Your daughter. She and I work at the hospital together."

Audrey's eyes closed and Stone thought she'd fallen

back asleep, but she opened them and glared. "I-If you th-think sh-she'll t-take you b-back, y-you're wr-wrong."

Stone wasn't sure who she meant, but didn't speak, just waited to see if she'd say more and hoped she didn't become agitated to where he'd need to wake Carly.

When her gaze met his, tears shone. "D-don't l-leave me a-again."

Her request didn't fit her previous comment, but Stone took her tremoring hand into his. "I'm here, Audrey."

"I—I knew y-you w-would ch-change your m-mind."

"About?"

"Our b-baby. I'm p-pregnant."

She thought he was Carly's father. Stone wasn't sure what to say or do, so he held her hand until, murmuring about their future life together, she fell asleep.

Then he held her frail, shaking hand longer.

Memories hit him.

Once upon a time, he'd been no better than Carly's father. Oh, he'd married Stephanie, had insisted upon helping her, but she hadn't wanted his help or anything else from him.

Yeah, he had some hefty baggage of his own that he didn't think Carly was likely to understand.

Carly woke with a start, letting her eyes adjust to the low light, realizing she'd fallen asleep on her living-room sofa.

What had she been doing…? Stone had been massaging her neck and she'd gone to sleep. Stone. She smiled at the joy that swelled in her heart when she thought of him.

Where was he?

She glanced at her watch, strained to read the time.

Panic hit her. Almost five a.m. Soon her watch alarm would be going off to wake her to leave for the hospital.

She had to draw her mother's labs, get a urine sample

even if it meant catheterizing her mother, plus, get to the hospital early to drop off the samples to the lab.

Her mother! She'd not checked on her or changed her adult diaper or given her feeding-tube meal or… Guilt hit her as she jumped from the sofa.

Recalling all the insurance claims she'd not done from the night before, she winced. She needed those claims. No, not needed. She had to have them. How was she going to pay Joyce when she failed to do her work?

What had she done? Gone to sleep as if she didn't have a care in the world. How could she have fallen asleep?

Maybe she could get a few claims cleared out in the thirty or so minutes before she had to jump into the shower. Tonight, she'd have to stay on task and get lots done even if it meant not sleeping. Maybe she could work extra over the next pay period, balance things until that check came in, and somehow not go under. Maybe. After the almost nine hours she'd slept she ought to be rested up enough to pull an all-nighter.

As quietly as she could, she made her way to her mother's bedroom and stopped in shock in the doorway.

The small bedside lamp was on, casting a golden hue around the room. Her mother slept peacefully.

So did Stone.

His large body was stretched out in the rocking chair, his head leaned back, and his breathing even and steady.

He'd stayed? She'd automatically assumed he'd left after she'd fallen asleep.

Why had he gone to her mother's room?

Had her mother awakened and Carly slept through it?

More guilt hit her. How could she have allowed this to happen?

Even worse, how was she going to get her laptop without waking him up?

Without waking him up? She needed to wake him up. He couldn't be there when Joyce arrived. No way.

Never would she be able to explain away his presence overnight.

Yes, she was a grown woman and could do what she wanted, but Joyce was an old-fashioned woman, which Carly loved about her. Her mother's caretaker would not approve of Stone having spent the night, four desserts or not. Plus, there was that worrying-about-her thing that Joyce did—which hadn't she acknowledged the night before was a good thing?

There were downsides to someone worrying about you. Like a responsibility to not do things that made them worry.

She reached out and touched Stone's shoulder. "Stone? Wake up."

Although appearing groggy, he opened his eyes and immediately smiled. "Good morning, Beautiful."

Good grief. First thing in the morning, her highly stressed, and his smile still rocked her world.

Which was scary.

And unacceptable because look at what had happened the night before.

"You have to leave," she told him in as low a whisper as she could with hopes of still being heard. The last thing she needed was to wake her mother.

"What time is it?" To his credit, his voice was equally low.

She told him. "Please. You have to leave. Before Momma wakes and definitely before Joyce gets here."

He stood from the chair and it rocked back. At some point in the night, it had shifted close enough that it bumped up against the wall.

The smack of the wooden chair against the sheetrock wall thundered around the room.

Carly's breath caught. Her gaze shot to her mother, who seemed oblivious that there were two people in her bedroom, making lots of noise.

"Leave. Now. Please."

His brows veeing, Stone followed her out of the bedroom. "What's wrong?"

"You're still here, that's what's wrong." Angry at herself for the situation she'd let happen, she lit into him. "How dare you spend the night at my house uninvited?"

Shock registered in his eyes.

He raked his fingers through his hair. "You fell asleep and so I checked on your mother. She asked me to stay. I fed her and cleaned her for bed, then sat with her. Was that not the right thing to do?"

He'd fed her mother, cleaned her for bed. Carly's heart pounded, thumping "Why? Why?" over and over. Why would Stone do those things?

"My mother asked you to stay?" was what she asked.

Stretching again, he nodded. "I didn't think you'd mind or I would have left, Carly. I wanted to help you so I took care of your mother so you could rest."

Why did she want to hug him and hit him at the same time?

"I had things I needed to do."

He studied her. "Such as?"

She tilted her chin upward. "How I spend my time away from work is really not any of your business."

He stared at her as if she'd grown a second head. "I know it's early in the morning, but I feel as if I'm missing something. I thought I did something good. Why are you upset with me?"

"Because...because..." She struggled to pull out a concrete answer. "Because I don't want you here."

It wasn't the truth, but it was what spewed from her mouth.

"We can't be friends, Stone. We just can't."

"That doesn't make sense. We are already friends."

"That's just it." She fought to keep her tone low. "We're not friends. Don't you get it?"

"Apparently not because I don't understand why you are upset with me. Are you always like this in the mornings?"

"On mornings when I wake up to find a man stayed at my house all night? Yes, I'm upset. And, because you kept me from doing things I needed to get done last night."

He was obviously confused; his gaze narrowed. "Fine. You're not a morning person. I can live with that and will make a note to let you sleep late in the future. Tell me what things need done and I'll help you this morning. We can knock them out together."

Feeling more and more distraught, partially at the situation she'd let herself get into and partially at how wonderful he was because that was making all this so much more difficult, she shook her head. "You can't help me."

"I'm not a useless person, Carly," he pointed out as if it were news to her. "I have skills and want to help."

"You can't help me." She turned away and wrung her hands. She'd done this. She'd figure a way out of it.

"Carly—"

"Just stop," she interrupted, frustrated by everything about him. "I've told you that you can't help me, so take me for my word. You can't help me." She emphasized each word of the last sentence. "No one can. Just leave."

"But—"

"I need you to leave. Now." She didn't look at him, but could feel his gaze boring into her back.

He must have picked up on her desperation, because after another moment of staring at her he moved closer, turned her around to face him, and kissed her cheek.

"I'll see you at the hospital," he told her. He stopped at the door, his hand on the knob, and turned back to her. "We'll talk after you've calmed down."

The moment he was out her front door, Carly hurried to it, locked the deadbolt, and watched him leave through the little diamond-shaped window panel.

When his taillights disappeared, she burst into tears because this was the last time Stone would leave her home. Because she couldn't let him come back.

CHAPTER FOURTEEN

STONE HAD BEEN in surgery for most of the morning cleaning out an abscess on a patient's leg that had gone horribly wrong and morphed into an infection that might cost the man his leg.

Stone hoped not. He was doing everything he knew to try to save the limb, but the guy's poorly controlled diabetes and decreased circulation weren't helping matters.

Stone rather felt as if he had decreased circulation to his brain himself.

Staying focused on what he was doing had been a mental chore requiring great effort and constant redirecting.

Because he couldn't stop thinking about Carly.

About how she'd looked when she'd awakened him. Wide-eyed, flushed, annoyed, desperate.

She'd been in a panic. Desperate to get rid of him.

"Good afternoon, Dr. Parker," Rosalyn greeted him when he walked onto the surgical floor. "My census shows you've been busy this morning."

He nodded. "Too busy. Is Carly around?"

At his question, Rosalyn gave a knowing smile. "Our manager sent her on break. She's in the staff room."

Perfect. Hopefully, she was alone and they could talk while she ate.

Only, when Stone went into the break room, Carly wasn't eating.

She was frowning at a laptop screen and typing as quickly as her fingers would go.

"Hey, Beautiful."

She jumped at his comment, glanced up, saw him, then, looking perturbed that he'd interrupted, went back to typing. "Not now, please."

Huh? He sat down across from her and watched her work. Her fingers had slowed and when she glanced up, she gave him a pointed look.

"Is there something you need?"

"No."

"Good. Then, if you don't mind, could you go somewhere else?"

"I definitely mind, so maybe you'd better explain this sudden predilection for telling me to leave? First this morning and then, again, now."

Pushing the laptop back, she sighed. "Look, Stone, I don't have time to deal with you right now."

To deal with him? Clearly something was wrong.

"Can I help you?"

"No." Her answer was immediate. Succinct.

"Why not?"

"Because you can't help me. How many times do I have to say that?" Annoyance roughened her voice.

"I'm a man of many talents, Carly. Let me at least try."

She pushed back from the table. "What I need is for you to leave me alone so I can help myself."

Ouch.

"Are you upset I sat with your mother last night?"

"No. Yes." She kept her gaze focused on the computer, but her fingers weren't typing.

"If I did something wrong, I'm sorry."

She took a deep breath, glanced up from the laptop screen. "I'm the one who did something wrong. Not you."

"What do you want me to bring for dinner tonight?"

Her gaze darkened. "I don't want you to bring dinner."

"You want to go out? Can Joyce stay with your mother?"

"Don't you get it?" Her annoyance thickened. "I don't want to see you after work tonight, Stone."

Stone's stomach twisted into a knot. "Why not?"

"I'm busy."

"Taking care of your mother?"

"Among other things."

"Let me help you."

"You can't help. I work a second job, Stone. Only, I've not been working it, because I've been spending too much time with you."

Carly worked a second job? On top of taking care of her mother and having a full-time position at the hospital?

"A second job I didn't do last night and I had an email this morning reprimanding me due to my significantly decreased production over the past two weeks. My boss wanted to know if I was ill." She pressed her fingertips into her temple, rubbing hard there, and lifted hollow eyes to him. "Please just go away and stay out of my life, before you ruin everything."

Her words pierced into Stone. They said history repeated itself. Apparently so. Stephanie thought he'd ruined her life, too.

He stood, pushed his chair beneath the table, and stared at the bristling woman sitting there.

She meant what she was saying. She didn't want his help. She wanted him out of her life.

"I won't bother you again."

Fighting back a dam full of emotion, Carly watched Stone leave for the second time that day. Only, as he walked out of the break room, there was no backward glance.

Good. She needed him to leave, needed to get her mind back onto managing her life and the insurance claims. She didn't usually bring her laptop to work, but had today so she could work during whatever break she got.

She'd made a little headway, too. Right up until Stone showed and got her brain jumping every which way. Her pulse, too.

She dropped her forehead to the tabletop and rolled her head back and forth. Ugh.

Pushing Stone away was the right thing. Being with him had made a mess of everything.

So why didn't she feel better?

Because she'd known better, but had dallied with him too long, and she was going to have to take her juggling act to new heights.

Even worse, she was going to have to bury her pride and ask Joyce if she could pay her two weeks late, something she'd never had to do before and something she'd make sure to never have to do again.

Stone didn't show at Carly's that night.

Carly hadn't expected him to, but thoughts that he might distracted her more than she liked. Her mother had had a decent day with Joyce and had settled in for the night, allowing Carly to get through a fair amount of claims, but not nearly enough to make up for lost time.

For the next week she spent every spare second she had working on claims, foregoing sleep in favor of processing as many as she could.

If she'd calculated correctly, she should have pulled off enough to be able to make up Joyce's pay. There wouldn't be any extra, but she would be able to pay her immediately pending expenses and Joyce's back-pay.

That was enough and she'd count her blessings.

She'd fallen into her old routine: wake, take care of her mother, work, come home to relieve Joyce, take care of her mother, insurance claims, sleep a few hours, repeat.

At the hospital, she saw Stone. How could she not when she took care of his patients? But he didn't smile or go out of his way to speak to her. If communication was necessary, they were both to the point with no pleasantries.

She lost weight. She had no appetite, could barely force food down her throat. Just as well as there had been no money for food beyond her mother's and she'd lived on leftovers and freebie packs of crackers.

"You don't look so good, girl."

Carly gave a small smile. Leave it to Rosalyn to bluntly tell her the truth.

"You and Dr. Parker aren't making googly eyes at each other and you look like you've lost your best friend. Something bad happen?"

Only of Carly's own doing.

It had needed to be done, but letting him go hurt.

She met her friend's eyes, gave a little shrug and fought to keep her tears in check.

"Oh, honey!" Rosalyn wrapped her into a bear hug. "Did he hurt you? I told him he'd better not hurt you."

Carly shook her head. "It wasn't his fault. It was mine."

"Yours?" Still holding onto her shoulders, Rosalyn pulled back and stared. "You did Dr. Parker wrong?"

Carly sighed. "From the moment I ever let him think something could be between us, I did him wrong."

Confusion contorted Rosalyn's face. "Why can't there be something between you? You were both walking on clouds just a couple of weeks ago."

Carly agreed. For a short little bit of time she had walked on clouds. Only clouds had no substance and she'd quickly crashed back to reality.

"I fooled myself into thinking that I could manage my life and have Stone in it, too," she admitted, surprised she was revealing so much. Then again, her co-worker had been right when she'd said Carly looked as if she'd lost her best friend. She had lost him. "I couldn't and we said goodbye."

Rosalyn frowned. "You okay?"

"Not really," Carly admitted, then shook her head to clear her mind. "I'm fine," she corrected, then went for broke. "It's my mother who isn't. She has end-stage Parkinson's complicated by dementia. I'm an only child, all she has." Her mother was all she had. "I don't have time to devote to a relationship and ended things before it got even more complicated." Was that even possible? How much more complicated could things have been than with her heart and body all tangled up in him?

"Stone deserves better," she added, knowing it was true. He deserved someone who could freely love him and give him all the things he deserved.

Rosalyn continued to look confused. "Don't you think that's something he should decide for himself? Maybe he didn't want better than what you can give him?"

Any sane man would want more than what she could give him.

"You make it sound simple but it isn't. I work. All the time. When I'm not here, I work for an insurance company processing claims. I get paid by the job. If I don't work, I don't get paid. If I don't get paid, I can't pay the bills. There isn't anyone else. I have to do it. I don't have time to have Stone in my life."

"That's a bad way to be in, girl. That man is a good one and they are few and far between. I got lucky with mine. Thought you'd gotten lucky with yours. Didn't know you didn't want him."

"I wanted him," Carly admitted, realizing how much she'd missed having someone to talk to, realizing that, despite the fact that she'd always held everyone at the hospital at arm's length, she'd developed a genuine caring for Rosalyn. "I do want him," she corrected. "I just can't have him and survive. Not financially or mentally or emotionally." She sucked in a deep breath. "I wanted to, but it didn't work. Stone and I both paid the price for my having deceived myself that I could spend time with him."

She gave her friend a wobbly smile. "Even when logic tells you the truth, it's amazing what you can convince yourself of when you want something badly enough."

"What if he was willing to wait for you?"

At the male voice, Carly spun. "Stone!"

Carly's gaze cut from the handsome doctor standing before her to the African American nurse, who just shrugged.

"I've got work to do and am not needed here," she said, then left the room, leaving Carly and Stone alone.

Heart pounding, Carly soaked in the man she'd been talking about. "I didn't know you were behind me."

"Obviously."

"You really need to stop eavesdropping."

"It seems we've come full circle." His gaze bore into hers. "You didn't answer my question."

"You mean wait until my mother dies?" Her question sounded crass, but wasn't that essentially what he was asking? "That's morbid. I couldn't do that."

"Obviously there's a lot of things you couldn't do. Like tell me the truth, for instance."

"I didn't lie to you."

"You didn't tell me about your second job, that I was interfering in your life."

"I did tell you," she corrected.

"Not until it was too late and you'd pushed me away."

"You wouldn't have listened. I told you repeatedly I didn't have time for a relationship, but you thought you knew better and wouldn't listen," she reminded him. "I... I got sucked into the magic of being with you and it almost cost me everything."

"By my letting you sleep when you were so exhausted you could barely hold your head up?"

"I shouldn't have slept." At his tightened expression, she clarified. "If I don't work the extra job, I can't afford Joyce. If I can't afford Joyce, my mother would have to stay at home alone or go into a nursing facility. Neither of those options appeal. I have to work. When I am with you, I don't work."

Finally seeming to grasp the stark reality of her situation, he raked his fingers through his hair. "You could have told me, Carly. Why didn't you?"

"Tell you I was in dire straits financially and worked two full-time jobs, plus took care of my invalid mother?" She shook her head. "What man would have stuck around for that?"

"Which seems a moot point since you didn't want me to stick around and told me to leave."

"My telling you to leave just sped up the natural progression of our relationship."

"The natural progression of our relationship was that I'd leave?"

"Are you saying you wouldn't have? We both know you deserve better than what I can give you, that you'd have tired of me soon enough."

Not looking away from her, he shrugged. "I guess we'll never know, will we?"

"I guess not." Unable to bear the intensity of his gaze, she glanced at her watch. "Sorry. My break is over. I have to go clock back in."

"Work waits."

His sarcasm wasn't lost on her. He didn't understand. No one could. Not really. She lifted her chin, held her head high, and told herself she was better off without him.

"It always does."

* * *

"Joyce, I'm home," Carly called when she got home that evening. She'd worked over an hour beyond her shift, but hadn't minded the extra work. She'd welcomed it. Just as she welcomed the insurance claims she worked on night after night until she fell asleep in exhaustion.

She needed exhaustion to keep her mind off Stone.

Off their conversation.

He wouldn't have waited for her. He hadn't even answered her question when she'd asked if he would have.

Of course, he wouldn't have. He'd have grown tired of coming second to her mother, to her having to work all the time and not being able to meet his needs, to go to normal social functions with him.

"Joyce?" she called again, stepping into her mother's room.

Her mother was asleep, as was the person sitting in the rocking chair.

He wasn't Joyce.

Stone sat in the chair.

What was he doing there?

Stone opened his eyes, saw Carly standing over him. He hadn't meant to go to sleep, but hadn't slept well much at all since Carly had pushed him out of her life.

"What are you doing here?"

"To answer your question."

"What question?"

"The one I didn't answer at the hospital today." He stood from the rocking chair, but didn't move towards her. "I wouldn't have left you, Carly. Not in a million lifetimes."

She closed her eyes. "Why are you saying this?"

"Because it's true. Because I miss you. Because I never really believed we were just friends. I wanted you for myself from the beginning, but when I learned about your mom, I realized you deserved a life without being tied down to someone."

"I don't consider taking care of my mother as being tied down," she defended, crossing her arms, and daring him with her expression to say otherwise.

"I didn't mean your mother," he clarified. "I meant me."

What he was saying seemed to sink in and her expression softened. "I'm not sure I understand."

"I'm sure you do."

She didn't deny his claim, just glanced toward her sleeping mother, then took on a resolved look.

"I was practically engaged in college," she told him. "His name was Tony and we were crazy about each other. We were going to graduate with our nursing degrees and sign on to be travel nurses and go around the world together."

She walked over to the foot of her mother's bed, straightened a wrinkle in the quilt that covered her.

"Everything was wonderful until Momma got so sick and quit working. She'd made a mess of her bills, taken out loans against the house, and was on the verge of losing everything. I moved home, took on extra hours waitressing at the restaurant where we went that first night, and somehow managed to keep going to school and keep my scholarship."

"I've said it before and I'll say it again—you are the strongest woman I know."

"I feel weak," she admitted. "I feel weak that I wanted you so much that I carried on with you at the hospital and pretended it meant nothing because I didn't want to stop. I feel weak that I didn't make you stay away, that I wasn't strong enough to stop this before it got started, before emotions got all tangled up." She paused, took a deep breath. "I feel weak that I'm not able to juggle all this so I can keep you in my life."

She stopped, closed her eyes. "I feel weak that I want you so much that I want to just forget everything else and be with you."

"Carly," he began, but she held up her hand.

"I'm not that person, Stone. I'm not somebody who can turn her back on someone she loves and I love my momma." Her face became pained. "The problem is, I love you, too."

Carly couldn't believe she'd said the words out loud. That she'd just told Stone that she was in love with him.

That he hadn't run out of the room. Or laughed in her face.

Instead, he stood next to her mother's hospital bed and just stared at her.

"I'm not sure what I'm supposed to say to that, Carly. Am I supposed to tell you that I'm sorry you love me?"

She swallowed the knot forming in her throat.

"Because I'm not," he continued. "Maybe I should be since it obviously stresses you, but I'm not," he repeated, his gaze searching hers as he walked to her, placed his hands on her shoulders and stared down into her eyes. "I want you to love me, Carly," he admitted. "Even when part of me doesn't want to complicate your life or add to your stress or to tie your future down, I want you to love me."

She trembled within his hold, then whatever walls were still in place crumbled and, tears running down her cheeks, she leaned against him. "I'm sorry, Stone," she mumbled against his chest. "I'm sorry I didn't tell you everything from the beginning, that I let things happen between us when we can't be together. Not now or ever because I can't bear the thought of asking you to wait."

Stone hugged Carly, breathed in her sweet scent, wanted to freeze time to this moment when she was safe in his arms.

Unfortunately, he couldn't.

And maybe he didn't really want to, because there were still things between him and Carly that needed to be removed.

"I need to tell you about that baggage I once mentioned." He took a deep breath. "I got married while in graduate school."

Carly jerked out of his arms, gawked up at him, her expression one full of betrayal. "You're married?"

"Divorced," he corrected. "We didn't make it a full year."

She was confused, her expression softening. "What happened?"

"I didn't love her, but…she was pregnant and marriage was the right thing. I wanted to help her, to make things better for her and our baby. It's what I planned to do. What I tried to do."

Mind obviously blown, she choked out, "You have a child?"

He shook his head. "No. She miscarried."

Carly winced and Stone had to take a deep, steadying breath to be able to continue.

"I wanted to help her, Carly. I really did. I could see she was struggling with her pregnancy and the changes to her life. But she kept pushing me away because she knew I didn't love her. She says I willed her to have a miscarriage because I didn't want a wife and child."

Carly's eyes were wide, her jaw slack, her expression one of shock. "Oh."

"Yeah, oh. She was already battling depression and the miscarriage compounded everything." He sucked in another deep breath. "She refused everything I tried to do. I could see how bad things were for her, but she blamed me for her problems and wouldn't let me in."

"Like what I did, even though it was my fault for not nipping our attraction in the bud," Carly mused, pacing across the room as she tried to work through the things he was telling her. "I really am sorry, Stone."

What had happened with Carly was nothing like what had happened with Stephanie. It had taken him a while and overhearing her conversation with Rosalyn to realize that. But he had realized it.

"When Stephanie divorced me…" He shrugged. "I felt I'd failed her, that I hadn't been able to help her and was guilty. I married her because I wanted to make her life better and I just ended up making everything worse. Just as I wanted to make things better for you, but ended up making things worse. I didn't plan to ever marry again, Carly, but you need me."

"Don't," she stopped him, shaking her head emphatically back and forth from where she stood across the room. "Don't offer to marry me to solve my problems. It's what you did with her, why your marriage fell apart, because it was for all the wrong reasons. Don't make the same mistake twice."

"That's not what I was going to do."

"Isn't it?" she challenged. "You're a good man. A man who has a big heart and wants to help those in need. It's what makes you such a great surgeon. But I don't need you playing the role of superhero in my life. I really can manage okay on my own."

"I know you can, Carly." She could do anything she set her mind to. She truly was the strongest woman he'd ever met. "But haven't you heard a thing I've said? I want it all. The good, the bad, I'll take it all if it means having you."

Carly's lower lip disappeared between her teeth at the same time as fresh tears streamed down her face. "I can't let you do that."

"Can't let me be with the person I want to be with?"

She began pacing again, still shaking her head. "You

have no idea what you're offering to take on, the cost, the emotional and physical burden."

"I'm a doctor, Carly. I have some idea." He crossed to where she stood, took her hand into his, and dropped to one knee. "Marry me, Carly. I've been lost without you. Say yes, quit the insurance job." He shrugged. "Quit both jobs and stay with your mother, and let me take care of both of you."

She didn't answer him, just cupped his face with her free hand and asked, "Why would you want to do that?"

"Why?" He laughed self-derisively. "Because I love you."

Carly's body lifted with joy at Stone's words. He loved her. How could that even be?

Yet even as excitement filled her she quelled it and closed her eyes.

"Saying yes would be taking advantage of how wonderful you are. How can I do that and not feel guilty?"

"Taking care of you would make me happier than you can imagine."

"You won't leave me?" she asked, not quite able to believe what was happening.

"Never."

She stared at him for long moments, saw the truth in his eyes. There were so many unknowns in life, so many things that could change in the blink of an eye. Anything worth having came with risks.

Love came with risks.

Looking into Stone's eyes, holding tightly onto his hand, trusting in him, didn't feel risky.

It felt right.

"I love you, Stone."

"That's why I'm here. Once I set my wounded pride aside, it didn't take much for me to realize you had strong feelings for me. Otherwise, you wouldn't have risked everything to be with me."

"I think I loved you from the moment we met."

"You going to answer my question?"

She smiled, caressed his face, and nodded. "Yes."

"A-about t-time."

Both Carly and Stone spun toward the bed.

"Momma! I didn't know you were awake."

"G-glad I w-woke up."

"Miss Evans, I'd like your permission to marry Carly."

"B-bit l-late t-to b-be asking th-that," her mother slurred. "B-but, y-yes."

Carly hugged her mother, so grateful to see the recognition in her eyes that she'd not seen in days. She wasn't sure how long it would last, but she'd enjoy every precious second.

Just as she'd enjoy every precious second with the man she'd been blessed to love and be loved by.

EPILOGUE

CARLY AND STONE married a month later in Carly's backyard. The weather was perfect, as was the day.

Carly's mother knew who she was, knew what was happening, that Carly was marrying her best friend.

Stone had arranged repairs to the outside of the house that had included a new roof and fresh paint. He'd had the landscaping redone with lots of vivid flowers that brightened its appearance, and had even surprised her with two white rocking chairs to put on the front porch with the ferns he'd hung.

Gone was the neglect and in its place was happiness and a new beginning. One where they would live in Carly's home to care for her mother, after which time they'd decide where they wanted to live, what they wanted to do.

Carly had kept her job at the hospital, but had quit the insurance claims job so she had time to spend with her mother, and with Stone.

Stone's family, Rosalyn, Joyce, and several of Stone's friends were in attendance at the small ceremony in Carly's backyard and celebrated there with them after the vow exchange.

Carly had never been hugged so much as she had that day by Stone's family, by his parents, his sisters, nephews and nieces, by his friends.

When he finally rescued her from them and pulled her into his arms, he grinned down at her.

"Hello, Mrs. Parker. Anyone told you how beautiful you are today?"

Heart full of love, Carly nodded. "Almost everyone here."

He smiled. "You are beautiful, Carly."

He made her feel beautiful. That day and every day after.

* * * * *

MILLS & BOON

Coming soon

BOUND TO THE SICILIAN'S BED
Sharon Kendrick

Rocco was going to kiss her and after everything she'd just said, Nicole knew she needed to stop him. But suddenly she found herself governed by a much deeper need than preserving her sanity, or her pride. A need and a hunger which swept over her with the speed of a bush fire. As Rocco's shadowed face lowered towards her she found past and present fusing, so that for a disconcerting moment she forgot everything except the urgent hunger in her body. Because hadn't her Sicilian husband always been able to do this—to captivate her with the lightest touch and to tantalise her with that smouldering look of promise? And hadn't there been many nights since they'd separated when she'd woken up, still half fuddled with sleep, and found herself yearning for the taste of his lips on hers just one more time? And now she had it.

One more time.

She opened her mouth—though afterwards she would try to convince herself she'd been intending to resist him—but Rocco used the opportunity to fasten his mouth over hers in the most perfects of fits. And Nicole felt instantly helpless—caught up in the powerful snare of a sexual mastery which wiped out everything else. She gave a gasp of pleasure because it had been so long since she had done this.

Since they'd been apart Nicole had felt like a living statue—as if she were made from marble—as if the flesh and blood part of her were some kind of half-forgotten dream. Slowly but surely she had withdrawn from the sensual side of her nature, until she'd convinced herself she was dead and unfeeling inside. But here came Rocco to wake her dormant sexuality with nothing more than a single kiss. It was like some stupid fairy story. It was scary and powerful. She didn't *want* to want him, and yet . . .

She wanted him.

Her lips opened wider as his tongue slid inside her mouth—eagerly granting him that intimacy as if preparing the way for another. She began to shiver as his hands started to explore her—rediscovering her body with an impatient hunger, as if it were the first time he'd ever touched her.

'Nicole,' he said unevenly and she'd never heard him say her name like that before.

Her arms were locked behind his neck as again he circled his hips in unmistakable invitation and, somewhere in the back of her mind, Nicole could hear the small voice of reason imploring her to take control of the situation. It was urging her to pull back from him and call a halt to what they were doing. But once again she ignored it. Against the powerful tide of passion, that little voice was drowned out and she allowed pleasure to shimmer over her skin.

Continue reading
BOUND TO THE SICILIAN'S BED
Sharon Kendrick

Available next month
www.millsandboon.co.uk

LET'S TALK
Romance

For exclusive extracts, competitions
and special offers, find us online:

f facebook.com/millsandboon

◎ @millsandboonuk

🐦 @millsandboon

Or get in touch on 0844 844 1351*

For all the latest titles coming soon, visit
millsandboon.co.uk/nextmonth